She was damned if she did, damned if she didn't. To go after him could tip her hand. It all had to do with appearances and intention, she convinced herself. People strolled the ferries constantly, checking out all the various decks and cabins. All she had to do was put one foot in front of the other and take her time. Stroll, don't walk, don't hurry. Use peripheral vision. Don't inspect the ship, enjoy it. She would *stroll* in the opposite direction from him – toward the stern. The crossing was thirty-five minutes. Ten of those had passed. It was a large, crowded ship, with hundreds of passengers, but a ship, a finite space, nonetheless. She would methodically work this deck stern to bow, then the next deck bow to stern. She would cover every inch of the ferry, top to bottom. Her police training kicked in: flush him out. Patience, she reminded herself, glancing at her watch.

She had about twenty minutes in which to find him.

BY RIDLEY PEARSON

*The First Victim**
*The Pied Piper**
*Beyond Recognition**
Chain of Evidence
No Witnesses
*The Angel Maker**
Hard Fall
Probable Cause
*Undercurrents**
Hidden Charges
Blood of the Albatross
Never Look Back
Middle of Nowhere

* features Lou Boldt

WRITING AS
WENDELL MCCALL

Dead Aim
Aim for the Heart
Concerto in Dead Flat

SHORT STORIES

'All Over but the Dying'
in *Diagnosis: Terminal*,
edited by F. Paul Wilson

COLLECTIONS

*The Putt at the End
of the World*,
a serial novel

RIDLEY PEARSON

MIDDLE OF
NOWHERE

ORION

An Orion paperback

First published in Great Britain in 2001
by Orion
This paperback edition published in 2001
by Orion Books Ltd,
Orion House, 5 Upper St Martin's Lane,
London WC2H 9EA

A CIP catalogue record for this book is available
from the British Library.

ISBN 0 75284 431 8

Typeset at The Spartan Press Ltd,
Lymington, Hants

Printed and bound in Great Britain by
Clays Ltd, St Ives plc

I'm honored to dedicate this book to my father, Robert G. Pearson, who not only brings to these pages an editorial pen, but enriches my life by demonstrating that a daily joy for living and a very real spiritual grounding can and does elevate one's experience. You are a trusted friend to your wife, and a mentor to all three of your children – and that makes us a very special family indeed.

ACKNOWLEDGMENTS

Thanks to Marsha Wilson of the Seattle Police Department; Lexis-Nexis; Louise Marsh, Nancy Litzinger, Mary Peterson, Courtney Samway and Debbie Cimino for office management; Paige, Storey and Marcelle; Gary Shelton; Matthew Snyder of CAA.

Thanks, too, to Dave and Michelle and Tater, Mitch and Janine, James and Stephanie, Amy and Lou, Little Stephen and Shift Tab.

Middle of Nowhere was edited by Leigh Haber. Thanks again, Leigh, for the patience and hard work.

I owe a special debt of gratitude to C. J. Snow and Michele Matrisciani.

Additional story line comments came from my agent, Al Zuckerman, and were much appreciated.

To the people of Seattle, my apologies for any liberties taken herein with your incredible city. They are either mistakes, or the necessity of fiction. Your tolerance is appreciated.

PROLOGUE

Behind her, the garage door groaned shut, a combination of hair-raising squeals – metal on metal – and the tight, quickened shudders of rollers travelling slightly off track. The garage opener's bulb was burned out, leaving only the yellow glare of car headlights, on a self-timer. Sharp shadows stretched across the tools and garden hoses that cluttered the walls. The room smelled of burning rubber, hot motor oil and lawn fertilizer – slightly sickening. A light rain struck the garage roof percussively.

Moving around the parked car, Maria Sanchez's body reflected the late hour – hunched shoulders, stiff legs. She wanted a bath, some Sleepytime tea and the Amy Tan novel that awaited her. She felt the weight of her sidearm in her purse as she adjusted its strap on her shoulder. When out on active duty she wore it holstered at her side, but the last four hours of her day had been paperwork, and she had transferred the gun to her bag. At least another four to go if she were to get even partly caught up. But no more on that night. She had clocked out. Amy Tan owned the rest of her waking hours.

She closed the side door to the garage, and stepped into darkness. The light alongside the back door hadn't come on, which surprised her since it worked off a sensor that should have automatically switched it on at sunset. It must have been burned out also. Just like the one in the garage. God, she wanted that bath.

Something moved behind her. A cop learned the difference between the elements and human beings. This was not wind, not the elements. It was human movement. Her right hand dropped and reached for a weapon she now remembered wasn't there – her terror mounted.

The crook of a man's elbow choked her windpipe. Next came a hard kidney punch. Sanchez's handbag slipped to the wet grass. She tried to respond as she'd been trained – as a police officer; to compartmentalize and set aside her terror. She drove back her elbow sharply and bent forward, driving her butt into the man behind her. The attempt did nothing to loosen the grip of that chokehold. Instead, the defensive move put more pressure on her own throat, increasing the pain, restricting the blood flow. She stomped down hard – hoping to connect with an instep, shatter it. She could smell beer and sour sweat and it was these smells that increased her fear.

Then another kidney punch. Sanchez felt herself sag, her resistance dwindle. She hadn't put up much of a fight, but now she knew she was going to lose it. She suddenly feared for her life.

Her reaction was swift and intense. She forced herself up, managing to head-butt a chin or a forehead. The viselike hold on her neck slackened. She felt the warmth of blood surge toward her brain. Briefly, relief. She tried once again to rock forward and this time break the grip for good.

But now the grip intensified. This guy meant business. He cursed and jerked his locked hold on her neck, first right and then sharply left. She heard her own bones go, like twigs snapping. And then cold. A brutal, unforgiving chill, racing through her body. In seconds, all sensation of her body was gone. She sank toward the mud and her face fell into the muck. Raspy breathing from above and behind her. And then even it disappeared, overwhelmed by a whining in her ears and that desperate cold that finally consumed her.

ONE

The night air, a grim mixture of wind and slanting rain, hit Boldt's face like needles. Seattle was a police beat where the weather could and did compromise a crime scene, often in a matter of minutes. On the advice of Bernie Lofgrin and his forensic team – the Scientific Identification Division, or SID – the department had issued foul weather directives for all first officers – the first patrol person to arrive on the scene. Regulations now required plastic tarps and oversized umbrellas as mandatory equipment for the trunk of every cruiser. But mistakes were still made, and that night seemed ripe for them.

As Boldt hurried up the home's short poured-cement driveway, he faced the garage, behind and to the left of the house. A basketball hoop and paint-chipped backboard faced the street. Boldt ignored the garage for the time being, his attention instead focused on the SID van parked there in the drive. Of all the divisions, SID should have understood the importance of protecting evidence, should have respected the department's attitude toward parking on private property. And yet there was the SID step van, inexplicably parked in the victim's driveway. One expected the occasional procedural error from the medical examiner's chuck wagon, even tolerated it when, as had happened earlier that night, an ambulance had been required to carry away a victim, and so had likely parked in the drive. But as the collectors and keepers of evidence, SID had no excuse for parking in a crime scene driveway for any reason. Some SID tech had wanted to avoid the rain, that was all, and that wasn't good enough. The infraction incited Boldt's temper, and in a rare display of emotion, he exploded at the first SID tech he encountered. He ordered the van relocated to the street.

Privately, Boldt blamed the 'Blue Flu,' SPD's first sickout by its officers in the history of the department. The Flu had so overwhelmed morale that it now apparently offered even civilian employees – like those who peopled SID – an excuse to turn in shoddy, rushed work. He wondered what chance law enforcement had if the five-day-old sickout continued. He also feared the consequences; shoddy work wasn't the only outcome of the Flu – officers, including Boldt, had been threatened by anonymous calls. Lines were being drawn. Violence bubbled beneath the surface.

A first-degree burglary indicated an assault, in this case a broken neck and the probable rape of Sanchez, a cop. Boldt felt the urgency of the situation – this case needed to clear before the press had a chance to run with it, before the press became fixated on the vulnerability of a police department weakened by the Flu.

Already on the job, Detective Bobbie Gaynes offered Boldt and the investigation a ray of hope. Because of the Flu, and a lottery-like case-assignment strategy that had the depleted ranks – lieutenants and above, mostly, accepting whatever cases Dispatch threw at them – this crime scene belonged to neither Boldt nor Gaynes, but to Lieutenant Daphne Matthews, whose official posting was that of staff psychologist. Boldt expected Matthews on the scene momentarily, even looked forward to it. They worked well together.

A woman in her early thirties who regularly altered

her looks for the fun of it, the diminutive Gaynes currently wore her hair cut short and colored a dark red. The heavy rimmed black 'Geek' glasses and light makeup created a style that was a cross between hip urban single woman and computer programmer, which actually went a fair distance to describing her personality as well. Gaynes lived for computer chat rooms these days.

Her prompt arrival on the scene came as no surprise. Boldt had personally brought Gaynes to Homicide following her stellar work on a serial killer case some years earlier. Before that, she had worked Special Assaults – Sex Crimes, as her fellow officers called it. With the Sanchez crime scene initially reported as a burglary/assault, rape couldn't be ruled out. Gaynes was a good detective to have on hand.

Boldt kept expecting the press. The lights. The questions. They would need answers immediately.

'You knew Maria Sanchez didn't you?' Gaynes asked.

'I *know* her personally,' Boldt corrected. 'Yes.'

'I only meant—'

Boldt interrupted. 'She sat the kids a few times.' He added, 'The kids loved her.'

Violent crimes against fellow police officers held special significance for anyone carrying a badge. All crimes were not investigated equally – a fact of life. Members of the immediate police family deserved and received special attention. Maria Sanchez would be no exception.

Daphne Matthews arrived and checked in with Boldt and Gaynes. As lead, Matthews handed out the assignments. Boldt deferred to her – a reversal of their usual roles.

Boldt thought of Daphne as a thoroughbred: dark, lean, fit and strikingly handsome. His system always ran

6

a little quicker when in her presence, in part out of necessity. She possessed both a facile mind and a trained eye. Technically it was her case, but they would all three work the crime scene together.

A civilian employee at first, a decade earlier, Matthews had undertaken the six-week academy training so that she now carried not just a title but a badge, rank, and weapon.

She assigned Boldt the second-floor crime scene, where the victim had been discovered, with Gaynes to assist. She would interview the first officer and speak to the SID team leader.

Even though Maria had been whisked away in an ambulance, the importance and power of the crime scene preoccupied Boldt as he approached the bedroom. Out on the street, the first of the press arrived. There would be more.

'How'd we find her?' Boldt asked Gaynes. He felt surrounded by women: Liz, Daphne, Gaynes, his own CAPers captain, Sheila Hill, even his little Sarah. He felt isolated but not alone, actually far more comfortable surrounded by these women than by a bunch of cartalking, sports-crazed men who commented on every chest that passed. He wondered why, of the seventeen detectives and two hundred uniformed patrol officers remaining on the job, some eighty percent were women. Why, when the going got tough, did the men quit and the women stay behind? Maybe it would be the topic of one of his guest lectures over at the U.

Boldt felt time getting away from him. He hoped for a clean crime scene and good evidence – something obvious that pointed to a suspect. He might as well be asking for a miracle, and he knew it.

Gaynes answered, 'House has a silent alarm installed. Security company telephoned the home when the alarm tripped, then responded in person, finding the place locked, then finally contacted us because they're not allowed to kick a door. All told, it took about forty minutes before our officers arrived.'

'Nice response time,' Boldt snapped sarcastically.

'First Officer was . . . Ling. Patrolman. He kept the security guys out, made the necessary calls and did a pretty fair job of protecting the integrity of the scene.'

Boldt said, 'Matthews and I will visit the hospital on our way home. See how she's doing. We not only want this one cleared, we need it cleared. A cop assaulted in the middle of the Blue Flu? Press will have a heyday.'

'Got it,' Gaynes confirmed.

The bedroom where Detective Maria Sanchez had been discovered naked and tied to the bed still smelled of sweat and fear. Sanchez's shoes, clothes and under-garments lay strewn across the pale carpet: gray blouse and dark pants heaped together to the left of the bed, underwear up on the foot of the bed, which remained made but rumpled. The woman's bra lay up by the pillow. An SID tech was working the adjoining bath-room for evidence and prints. Boldt studied the layout carefully, snapping on a pair of latex gloves almost unconsciously. He circled the bed carefully, like a photographer planning a shoot.

'No evidence of fluids,' he observed, 'other than the blood on the pillow. Not much of it.'

'The ligatures?' Gaynes inquired, pointing to the head of the bed.

Boldt noticed the two bootlaces tied to each side of the headboard. He glanced back down to the floor and the ankle-high, black-leather-soled shoes missing their laces. His stomach turned. The scene was confused. It didn't feel right to him.

'Ling cut the shoelaces himself, before the ambulance arrived,' Gaynes explained.

Both laces had been cut with a sharp knife, though remained knotted where they had been tied to the bed.

'Photos?'

The SID tech answered from the reverberating bathroom, 'We shot a good series on her.'

'Close-ups of the ligatures?' Boldt inquired loudly.

'Can't say for sure. You want it on the list?'

'Please,' Boldt answered, now at the head of the bed, studying one of the cut shoelaces himself. He'd had a case earlier in the week involving rape and a young girl bound by shoelaces. The similarities were obvious. He regretted that. A serial rapist was the last thing anyone needed – and most likely the first thing the press would suspect.

'Done,' the tech answered from the bathroom.

Boldt glanced around. 'Tied the wrists, but not the ankles?' His earlier rape had been tied by all limbs. The similarities suddenly lessened. A copy cat, Boldt wondered. The Leanne Carmichael rape had made the news.

Gaynes replied as if it were a test. They worked this way together – pupil and teacher. 'I caught that too, and I could almost buy it if the bed were more of a mess. But a woman left with her legs untied? The bed covers should be a mess.'

'Boyfriend? Lover? We want this wrapped and cleared,' Boldt reminded her. The department was grossly understaffed because of the Flu, and they each had too many cases to handle. A so-called black hole – an unsolved case – would incite the media and make trouble for everyone concerned – Maria Sanchez most of all. She deserved closure.

'You're looking a little sick, Lieutenant.'

'Feeling that way.'

9

Gaynes, standing on the opposite side of the bed from Boldt said, 'On Special Assaults I worked dozens of rapes, L.T.' Unlike Detective John LaMoia who out of habit addressed Boldt by his former rank of sergeant, Gaynes at least paid Boldt the respect of his current promotion, though called him not by name, but by his rank's initials. 'Maybe in one out of ten, the clothes are still in one piece. Usually torn to shit. No fluids? Listen, if the stains aren't in the middle of the bed where you expect them, then you find them on the pillow or the bedspread or the vic's underwear. But a clean scene? You ask me, this is date rape. Look at those clothes! Not a button missing! Spread out in a line, for Christ's sake.'

Boldt studied a large dust ring on the dresser. A television had been removed. A small, gray electronics device bearing a set of wireless headphones lay in a heap to the side of the same dresser. He picked the headphones up in his gloved hands.

Gaynes said, 'You use 'em so the spouse can sleep while you watch the tube.'

'She was single,' Boldt reminded.

'A visitor maybe,' Gaynes said. 'Date rape,' she repeated with more certainty. 'Guy ties her up and gets too aggressive. Accidentally snaps her spine and takes off.'

'The television?' he asked his former protégé.

'Stole it to cover up it was him. Make it look like someone broke in. The papers have been filled with stories about all the break-ins since the Flu hit.'

Studying the headphones, Boldt said, 'Maybe she just appreciated music or maybe she subscribed to the cable music channels.' He pointed to the stack of recent best sellers on Sanchez's bedside end table.

Boldt walked around the bed with a sick feeling in the

10

pit of his stomach. He and Gaynes traded places. Police ballet. Since the advent of the Flu, reports of robberies and burglaries were up exponentially. 'We'll want to check our sheets,' he suggested. 'See if this fits any patterns.'

'Got it,' she replied. She lifted the top book off the end table, an Amy Tan novel. 'Bookmarked with a receipt dated two days ago. And she's . . . a hundred and seventy pages into it—'

'And we're in the midst of a Flu,' Boldt pointed out. 'Not like she has a lot of fun time.'

'Maybe six, seven hours a night at home, max.'

'So she didn't watch much television,' Boldt concluded.

'Which means you're probably right about the cable music. A hundred and seventy pages in two nights? You think she's been entertaining a lover?' she asked rhetorically. 'Sounds more like insomnia.'

'Ask around the house about current boyfriends.'

'I'm telling you, a rapist wouldn't undress her like this, L.T. He tears her clothes off. It's rage, not courtship. And if he goes to the trouble to tie her up, he rapes her hard or fires juice all over the place. We're not seeing real good evidence here.' She hollered to the SID tech, 'What's that bathroom like?'

'It's light,' the tech fired back. 'My guess? The guy wasn't in here at all.'

Boldt migrated over to check the windows – all locked – so he didn't have to look at the bed while Gaynes talked so calmly about raping and beating and masturbating. Sex Crimes – Special Assaults – conditioned a detective in ways even a homicide investigator had a difficult time understanding. He looked out the window to where light from the house played on the small patch of backyard and the separate garage.

11

'Her underwear's clean,' Gaynes reported. 'So's the bra. This looks like someone she knew. And using shoe laces to tie her? A necktie maybe. A belt. Something handy and fast. What's the guy do: ask her to lie still while he unlaces her Hush Puppies and ties her wrists?'

'Maybe her neck was already broken,' Boldt suggested. 'Maybe she wasn't going anywhere.'

'Then why tie her up at all?' Gaynes asked, confusing the issue.

An uneasy silence settled between them. Not a black hole, he pleaded.

Gaynes continued cautiously, 'And that's another thing . . . The trauma supposedly occurred *after* she was tied to the bed? Is that the general consensus? Is that what we're thinking here? That's what's logical, right? He ties her up to keep her still. Goes for oral sex or something. Yanks her head a little too hard and snaps her neck in the process? Something like that? But he doesn't tie her ankles?' she said skeptically.

Boldt's only mental image was of the other case – little Leanne Carmichael, thirteen years old, the crotch of her pants cut away, her legs tied open. A dark basement. 'I worked a rape-kidnapping earlier in the week. He tied up the girl with shoelaces.'

'Carmichael,' she said. The case remained open; continued to make a lot of noise.

'We'll want the SID lab to make comparisons. The same knots? Anything connecting the two crimes?'

'The lab, sure,' she agreed, 'but not the media. So make the request that they do it quietly.'

He said, 'True enough.'

Someone must have finally been moving the SID van, for headlights spread across the wet backyard. Boldt didn't like what he saw there.

'I'm going outside to look around,' Boldt said.

'It's nasty out there,' the SID tech cautioned from the bathroom.

'Check her boots and meet me outside,' he told Gaynes. She cupped her hands to the window, peering into the backyard. She knew Boldt well.

'Now,' he reminded, his voice urgent.

'Got it,' she said.

'Nasty.' Gaynes tugged the GORE-TEX hood over her head. Boldt made a similar move with the collar of his green oilskin. He switched on a flashlight borrowed from a patrolman – one of the ones with six D-cell batteries inside – enough weight to club a skull to pulp, the flashlight's second function. Hunched over, he and Gaynes approached a disturbed area of mud in the backyard. They walked single file, electing to avoid the well-worn route leading from the separate garage to the house's back door.

'This is where he intercepted her?' Gaynes suggested, dropping to one knee.

'Looks like a possibility,' Boldt said. 'But there's no sign of dragging.'

'Her shoes show mud. The tech bagged them. Black leather jacket, presumably hers, had a partial shoe print on the chest. A set of keys and a garage clicker in the pockets.' She added, 'And *yes*, I'll have the shoe print typed, if possible,' anticipating the request.

Gaynes poked a raised rib of mud and grass with her gloved finger. 'It's recent enough.'

Boldt kneeled beside her, the flashlight illuminating the disturbance. The grass looked like a rug scrunched up on a hardwood floor. Boldt tore some grass loose and sealed it into an evidence bag for lab comparison. He lived for such work – his lifeblood. He heard more

13

chaos around in front of the house. More press. More pressure.

Gaynes said, 'I can see Sanchez stumbling upon him unexpectedly, surprising him, a struggle and she goes down.'

From behind them, Daphne spoke. 'At first it's a matter of survival for him: get her to shut up and get the hell out of here. But then there's a change. Something primitive takes over. Primal. It's about dominance now, about her struggling and him overpowering her. He finds he gets off on it. He wants more than to simply subdue her. He has to possess her.'

'You're buying the burglary?' Boldt asked, peering up at her into the rain, the flashlight following. Even in the rain, Daphne Matthews looked good.

'Help me out,' Daphne said.

'Shoelaces on both wrists. Same as Carmichael, my thirteen-year-old rape victim.'

'But not the ankles,' Gaynes said.

'Not the ankles,' Boldt agreed, meaning it for Daphne. This was a jigsaw, with three players picking at pieces.

'The burglary is intended to mislead us?' Daphne asked.

'We've got a crime scene with two MOs,' Boldt said. 'A burglar. A rapist. Neither fits perfectly. Why?'

Gaynes announced, 'We've either got ourselves a twisted burglar, or a greedy rapist.' She tugged on her hood. A trickle of water slid down her cheek and dripped off her chin. Knowing full well it would be his next request, she asked, 'You want SID to work this site?'

'It's a start,' Boldt agreed.

Daphne said, 'Leanne Carmichael was raped. There's no medical evidence yet that Sanchez was.'

14

'And if she wasn't, then you've got yourself a couple of contradictions,' Boldt suggested.

'I don't want contradictions. I want a suspect. I want to clear this before it gets out of control.' Daphne sounded unusually nervous. She wasn't used to leading a high-profile case. The Flu had caught up to her as well.

Boldt shined the light over toward the garage. 'She parked in the garage and headed for the back door. She either ran into this guy—'

'Or he was out here waiting,' Daphne interrupted.

'I want to assign a guard outside her hospital room,' he said.

'L.T.. . . You're right, but who we gonna get to do it?' a frustrated Gaynes asked. The Blue Flu had taken four out of every five officers off the force.

'Notify hospital security. Let's move her to a private room away from a stair entrance. We'll require check-in at the nurse's desk. Some guy realizes he hit a woman cop, and maybe he decides he doesn't want any witnesses. Or maybe it's a boyfriend, and the same thing goes. I want her under protection.'

'Got it.'

Boldt felt the pressure of the investigation then – a sixth sense for a black hole and a case that wouldn't clear. He knew from the look in her eye that Daphne sensed this as well. 'Contradictions,' he said.

'Yes,' she agreed. 'Not *this* case, okay?' she pleaded.

'We'll each have six more cases on our desks by the time we get back,' Boldt reminded.

Gaynes chimed in, 'And *then* our phones'll start ringing and Dispatch will dish out another couple each.'

'We need the sickout over with,' Boldt said.

'Dream on, L.T. They're firmly entrenched.'

Daphne saw her investigation headed for a black

hole. 'With Sanchez gone,' she said, 'we're down to sixteen investigators left – detective or higher.'

Boldt felt sick inside. A thirteen-year-old, raped. A policewoman paralyzed. A burglar on the loose. The public was certain to panic. The Emergency Communication Center's 911 lines would be crippled with hundreds of bogus reports and sightings. Seventeen detectives had become sixteen.

'The press is going to screw us on this one,' Gaynes whispered. 'This is fuel to their fire.'

'Yes,' agreed Boldt, 'that's just what we don't want.' He had come here hoping for evidence. Perhaps the contradictions were the place to start. They didn't offer him much.

Daphne remained angry about the Flu. 'It's a fellow officer! They've got to come back on the job now! It's time to circle the wagons.'

'I wouldn't count on it,' Boldt and Gaynes said nearly in unison.

TWO

'What exactly did Sanchez's doctor say?' Daphne Matthews moved fluidly, like a dancer. She set the pace, climbing the hospital fire stairs faster than Boldt might have liked. Sanchez's room was on the fourth floor.

Boldt was relieved to be able to tell her that the rape kit had come back negative. He had made the call to the hospital while Daphne was reporting back to headquarters, where a reduced, overworked staff attempted to cope with a growing number of reported crimes.

'Is there any eye movement? Limb movement? What exactly did the doc say?' she asked.

He didn't answer right away, preoccupied with thoughts of the threatening phone calls he'd received in the last few days and what to do about the risk they posed to his family. Liz, his wife, was not easily moved out of her home.

Daphne asked, 'What's this about your knowing Sanchez personally?'

'I know her,' Boldt confirmed. 'She lost her sister and her sister's two kids to a traffic fatality—'

'*That* Sanchez?' Daphne exclaimed, interrupting.

'The same.'

'I thought she transferred out when she graduated.'

'She did, but only for a few months, after which we met at a couple crime scenes. She met Liz and the kids at one of Phil's baseball games.' Phil Shoswitz had been Boldt's immediate superior for nearly a decade.

Currently he was captain of Crimes Against Property. 'Offered to sit the kids. I suggested off-duty uniform work paid considerably better, only to find my foot in my mouth. She wanted to be around the kids. It had nothing to do with money.'

'She baby-sat Sarah and Miles?' Daphne asked incredulously.

'I know,' Boldt said, understanding her concern over such financial fraternization. 'But it wasn't for any favors. It wasn't for promotion consideration. It was simply that Miles and Sarah were the same ages as her niece and nephew had been, and she wanted the contact. It didn't last all that long, but I've got to tell you: the kids loved her. Liz will be crushed when she hears.' Slightly winded from the climb, he added, 'This should never happen to any officer. But in particular this should have never, *ever* happened to Maria. She's a great person.'

'You're a great person,' Daphne said. She added reluctantly, 'You and Liz – for taking her in like that.'

Boldt stopped his ascent, as did she. It wasn't all sweet and innocent between them. They shared a past rarely discussed.

They hugged the steel rail as a flurry of white and green hospital uniforms blurred past. Their eyes met, and briefly an energy passed between them that they both felt. 'Liz and I,' he repeated, echoing her. But from his lips it sounded more like a statement.

'Right.' Color rose in Daphne's long, elegant neck.

Boldt took the lead. Daphne followed up the stairs and into the busy hall.

'Eye movement,' he whispered before opening the door to Sanchez's hospital room. This was the information she had originally sought from him, and he chose his

18

timing intentionally, for the woman in question now lay on the other side of this door. 'She apparently has some eye movement.'

Daphne nodded solemnly. Boldt swung open the door. 'It's your case,' he reminded. 'Your lead.'

As she passed him, she whispered, 'I know that.'

A fogged plastic tube, inserted through a surgical hole at the base of her throat, supplied Maria Sanchez's oxygen. Her torso was held fast by a white plastic brace that was itself connected to the bed frame, preventing movement of any kind. Too many tubes to count. A modern Medusa. Blinking lights and flashing green numbers in black boxes on rolling stands of stainless steel. A bag of intravenous fluids. Drip, drip, drip. A blue plastic clip over her index finger ticking out her pulse and measuring her blood oxygen. The glare of tube lighting. The hum of machinery and the disturbingly symmetrical rhythm of her computer-controlled breaths.

Boldt's throat constricted. His chest seized in a cramp. This wasn't just a woman lying there; she was also a police officer. A friend. Family. Liz had once lain in just such a bed. He knew the things they could do to a person in here. He had seen Liz's roommate being wheeled out, and she had never been wheeled back in. The thought of Liz returned him to his concern over the threatening phone calls. He didn't trust where this Flu was headed. He wanted out of that room.

Maria Sanchez's bloodshot eyes showed through small slits, and Boldt could detect slight movement in them as she tracked their entry into the room. Boldt recalled her on the couch with his two kids. Sitting up. Laughing. *Goodnight Moon* in her lap. He could envision her hugging his children with two arms that worked. But it was that laugh of hers he remembered.

Her time with his kids had helped in her recovery from grief – she had learned to laugh again in his house. To live. And now this.

'Officer Maria Sanchez,' Daphne said, seeing Boldt struggle, 'I'm Daphne Matthews, the department psychologist. You know Lieutenant Boldt – Homicide.'

'Matthews is lead on your assault,' Boldt managed to say. 'I'm playing Watson.' He had wanted to inject humor. He'd failed. Again he realized he had spent too many hours in hospital rooms of late. There should be quotas, he thought. He foresaw pain and hardship in that bed. Time. Waiting. For eighteen months of cancer treatment his family had suffered. Now still they waited, hoping Liz's remission held. The waiting hurt most of all. Sanchez would feel the full force of it.

His voice broke as he said, 'I'm sorry for your situation, Maria.'

Daphne offered, 'We don't pretend to know what you're going through, but we are going to put away whoever's responsible.' She added, 'We're told the doctors plan some experimental surgery and that the prognosis is good. Be strong, Maria. We're pulling for you.'

'The whole department,' Boldt said. Adding, 'What's left of it.'

The patient blinked once. At first it appeared to be a reflex, nothing more. But it drew their attention.

Boldt carefully chose his words. 'We've been over to the scene just now . . . your house, Maria. Looks a lot like you interrupted a burglary. Stereo gear and at least one TV appear to be missing.'

'We'll need for you to confirm as much of this as possible – as soon as you're able,' Daphne added.

'The report is sketchy at best,' Boldt said. 'When you're better, we'll work on this one together, okay?'

His attempt at positive thinking sounded hollow and fell flat. Boldt didn't know quite how to act, so he decided to just stick to business. 'We're pursuing this as a first-degree burglary. I guess we just wanted to say it goes without saying that we're not sitting on this one, that the Flu isn't going to delay this in any way. Matthews got the call – the lead – and that's a good thing. We're going to chase down this offender and lock him up. Guaranteed.'

'We *need* you, Maria,' Daphne encouraged her. 'You're going to pull out of this.'

Another blink. A tear slithered from her eye, down her pale cheek and cascaded to the pillowcase. When her eyelids opened again fully, Sanchez's dark pupils were lodged to the left of her eye sockets.

'Maria?' Boldt inquired, the eye movement obvious. He checked with Daphne.

'We're watching your eyes,' Daphne stated firmly to the woman. 'Are you trying to signal us, Maria?' she asked. For Boldt, the air in the room suddenly seemed absolutely still. The sounds of the machinery seemed louder. He felt cold, chilled to the bone.

Another blink. Reflex or intentional? Her pupils faced right.

'Oh my God,' he mumbled, letting it slip. He glanced toward the door and the freedom it offered.

'Right is "yes"; left is "no". Is that correct?' Daphne inquired.

The woman closed her fluttering lids with great difficulty. When her eyes reopened, her pupils remained locked to the right.

Daphne met eyes with Boldt, her excitement obvious.

'We're going to ask you some questions,' Daphne suggested tentatively. 'Okay?'

The eyelids sank shut. As they reopened a crack, the

pupils faced left, her answer a solid no. Her eyes fluttered shut and remained so. Boldt felt a wave of relief.

'She's too tired,' Boldt said, indicating to Daphne they should leave the room.

Daphne nodded, but wouldn't let it go. 'You go ahead and rest, Maria. We'll be back when you're up to it.' She followed Boldt into the hall. He assisted the room's oversized door to shut as quietly as possible.

'Medicated,' Daphne said. 'Fatigue plays into it too, but chances are it's as much her unwillingness to confront and relive the assault and the associated trauma as anything else.'

'She's terrified,' Boldt said, relieved to be out of the room. 'And she has every right to be.' He added, 'You see that, don't you?'

'You didn't have to be in such a hurry to leave.'

'Yes, I did,' he argued.

'She can answer questions, Lou. We can build a list of questions and she can answer them! We can interview the victim. You realize that?'

Boldt complained, 'You don't have to sound so excited about it, you know?'

'What's wrong with you?' Daphne asked. She crossed her arms indignantly against the artificial chill of the hallway.

'It's *all* wrong with me,' Boldt answered, feeling a chill himself that had nothing to do with thermostats. 'Her. This place.' Motioning back toward the room he said, 'A pair of eyes, Daffy. It's all that's left of her.'

THREE

'It's a difficult situation,' Boldt said.

'So talk me through it. Is it the strike, or this case?' his wife, Liz, asked.

'Both,' he answered. The Sanchez assault was nearly twenty-four hours old. No arrests. No suspects. He feared a black hole.

The Boldt kitchen confirmed the laws of chaos, a study in the science of randomly placed objects: dinner food, dishes, pots and pans, plastic toys scattered as an obstacle course, a high chair, a booster seat, stained dish rags. Something sticky had been spilled by the pantry door. A path of mud and pebbles led from the back porch, despite the door mat. Boldt stood at the sink, elbow deep in dishwater.

By nine o'clock they typically would have had the kitchen cleaned up – with or without each other's help – but their daughter Sarah's upset stomach had kept them busy these past several hours. With both kids finally asleep, husband and wife tackled the cleanup.

'Wish that dog would stop. Does it ever shut up?'

'Maybe they wouldn't have bought an attack dog if you guys hadn't gone on strike,' Liz teased.

Boldt groaned. She was trying to make light of it, but it struck a nerve. 'It's not a strike, it's a sickout,' he corrected her.

Liz policed the countertops and the kitchen table, which looked as if a food fight had taken place. Boldt watched her in the reflection of the window above the sink. In his opinion, she still needed about twenty pounds. The cancer had won that as well as her hair. Most of her hair had returned, but not the weight. And the hair looked wrong, because she had always worn it longer than that. Boldt wrestled with the carrots burned onto the bottom of the saucepan. That dog just wouldn't stop. If Boldt hadn't been a cop, he might have called one.

Liz brushed against him as she shook crumbs out of a rag. He enjoyed the contact, any contact at all, anything to remind him of her presence.

'So what's bugging you?' she asked, adding quickly, 'besides our neighbor's dog?'

'The Flu. I realize it's complicated.' A new sports stadium had gone over budget. The mayor instituted cost-saving measures. The new police chief cut overtime pay for detectives and, at the same time, restricted off-duty work for uniforms because one off-duty cop had embarrassed the department. 'But it has messed up everything,' he said.

'Listen, I hate to see you like this.' She offered, 'Maybe it's worth thinking about how much you, personally, can do about any of it.'

'But that's the point! It gets worse every day. Now Phil and the other captains are effecting a slowdown. Doing just enough work to get by, which isn't enough, of course. It's their way of supporting the sickout.'

'But if you're working as hard as always, what more can you ask of yourself?'

'Thanks,' he said sincerely.

'Is there *anything* positive to focus on?' Forever Liz. Spiritually determined.

He answered, 'Homicide's bathroom stays cleaner than I've ever seen it. The coffee lounge no longer stinks of burned grounds. Precious little.'

'All you can do is—'

'Pray?' he interrupted. He didn't need to hear this right now.

She grimaced. 'Not what I was going to say,' she said.

He apologized, but she walked away and went about the cleanup.

He didn't mention that the eerie emptiness of the fifth floor, the vacant halls and office cubicles, reminded him more of a school in the midst of a fire drill than a homicide squad. The hallways and offices of Crimes Against Persons required bodies to occupy them – like suits in a storefront window.

Boldt caught sight of himself in the window's glass, and was troubled by the growing exhaustion that hung beneath his eyes. The extra caseload brought on by the sickout meant fourteen-hour work days. Investigators in any department accepted whatever case was handed them. Vice, narcotics, burglary, it didn't matter.

He glanced up again. The window, fogged by steam, offered only a blurred image, but he could still see his face. He could still pass for late thirties. Mid-thirties in low light. In truth, forty had come and gone a few years ago.

These days he was making an effort. No more neckties bearing catsup stains, no more permanent wrinkles in his khakis. A single comment from Liz about how 'the run-down-professor look adds ten years' had cleaned up his act. Since then, he'd looked like a new man.

The burn came out of the bottom of the pan, but his elbow ached.

'You know I'll be supportive,' Liz said, now tossing the wet wash rag into the sink. 'But, Lou, please, try to see that it stays outside the family. I'm afraid for you, for us—' She didn't need to complete the sentence.

Those threatening phone calls of the past few nights were on both their minds.

As if on cue, the phone rang. Liz looked over at her husband. They had talked about just letting it ring, to allow the machine to pick up, but Liz instinctively lifted the receiver from its cradle and held it out to him.

Boldt dried his hands and accepted the phone. Liz pushed through the swinging door and into the family room.

'Hello?' Boldt said into the phone.

For a moment he believed whoever had called might have hung up. But life these days just wasn't ever that simple. 'Hello?' he repeated.

He heard music, not a voice. His stomach turned: another threat? Pop music – a woman's plaintive voice. 'Hello?' he repeated a third time. At first, he took it as wallpaper – background music – and waited for a voice. But then he listened more clearly. It was Shawn Colvin, a recording artist he admired, whose lyrics now gripped his chest. 'Get on out of this house,' the anguished voice cried out in song.

Boldt understood, though too late: it wasn't a threat, but a warning.

The best explanation for why he ripped the phone from the kitchen wall was that he'd forgotten to let go of the receiver as he ran into the family room to alert Liz, failed to let go until he heard the explosion of breaking glass from the other side of the swinging door. At that instant, both the cop and the husband and the father in him warred over his having locked up his handgun in a closet safe in the bedroom – family policy whenever he crossed the threshold into their home.

He burst through the swinging door, his wife's screams ringing in his ears. He heard a car racing away at high speed. Liz lay on the floor in a sea of broken glass. She wasn't moving.

'No!' he hollered, lunging across the room toward his fallen wife. He heard one of the kids wake up crying. Liz had a strange mixture of fear and confusion in her eyes. He would not soon forget that look . . . it seemed to contain an element of blame.

He reached out to her and rolled her onto her back. Her forearms bled. Her face was scratched, though not cut badly. She mumbled incoherently at first.

'Shhh,' he whispered back at her.

'I thought it was a bomb,' she mumbled.

Underneath her lay a brick. It had been painted policeman's blue.

FOUR

'Feeling a touch of the Flu coming on, I hope?' Mac Krishevski asked. Boldt shoved the man back into the living room, kicked the Krishevski front door closed and removed his gun from his own holster, setting the piece down by a bowling trophy alongside a faux-marble lamp made out of formed plastic. The gesture made it clear to Krishevski that no weapons were to be involved. Beyond that, there were no promises made.

'Lieutenant?' a cocky but concerned Krishevski queried.

Harold 'Mac' Krishevski reminded Boldt more of the man's Irish mother than his Polish father, though he'd never met either. The capillaries in his cheeks had exploded into a frenzied maze of red spider webs. His nose, with its sticky, moonlike surface, fixed to his face like a dried autumnal gourd. His rusty hair, awkwardly combed forward to hide the acreage of baldness, failed miserably in this purpose, so that in strong overhead light, the shadows that were cast down onto his scalp looked like cat scratches. His teeth belonged to a heavy smoker, his plentiful chins to an overeater or beer drinker. A man in his early fifties, he wore his Permanent Press shirt unbuttoned at the collar, a threadbare undershirt attempting to contain escaping chest hair.

'You want an appointment,' Krishevski suggested, attempting to sound in control but clearly under the effect of Boldt's fixed stare, 'you gotta call ahead.'

'My wife dove onto this, thinking it was a bomb.' Boldt tossed the blue brick into the center of the room. 'She cut her arms on the broken glass. We just got back from having her sewn up.'

Boldt believed that, as president of the Police Officers Guild, Krishevski bore the responsibility not only for the walkout but also for the blue brick.

'Teenage vandalism,' Krishevski said. 'It's amazing how the kids go wild when there are fewer officers on the beat.'

Boldt took issue with Krishevski's confident grin and steely-eyed glint. The man looked like a trained watchdog. The room smelled of stale tobacco, garlic, and booze, and the combination turned Boldt's stomach. Krishevski had taken unwarranted pot shots at Boldt and his department's handling of evidence in the run-up to guild elections two years earlier, all in a blatant attempt to portray Homicide as an ivory-tower department in need of an overhaul, an attempt to keep Boldt from receiving the lateral transfer back to his old squad. Krishevski's complaints had fallen short of outright accusation, but had crossed acceptable lines. In point of fact, their troubled history went back twenty years, to a time when Boldt had been selected for advancement and Krishevski had not. The sores from those wounds remained. Boldt had little doubt that the blue brick had been ordered by this man, little doubt that his own selection as target had been as much personal vendetta as union strategy.

The Police Officers Guild had been organized in the late fifties to represent officers in contract negotiation, and to provide legal representation for any officer who required it. The guild represented all personnel below the rank of lieutenant, accounting for the majority of SPD's twelve hundred officers. The administrative ranks of lieutenant, captain, and above – less than one hundred in number – were represented by a separate management team, effectively separating uniforms from the white-collar jobs. Membership in the guild was theoretically voluntary, but nearly every uniformed officer belonged, as well as most of the detectives. Its elected officials came out of its own ranks of active officers.

As the elected president of the guild, Mac Krishevski, senior sergeant in SPD's Property room, was guild spokesman – its public voice and point man. Boldt, among others, not only blamed Krishevski for allowing, if not encouraging, the first illegal strike in the department's history – despite the man's claims otherwise – but also for permanently tarnishing the badge and the public's view of law enforcement.

'You being president of the Chapter,' Boldt said, 'I'm holding you responsible for what happened to my wife tonight.'

'Now wait a second!' Krishevski complained.

Boldt boiled. 'If you don't control your fellow striking officers, if you don't bring those responsible forward for discipline – to set a proper example – then in effect you're condoning what happened tonight. If that's the case, then I'd prepare myself for certain consequences.'

'Are you threatening me, Lieutenant?'

Boldt calmed outwardly, though internally he continued to churn. He said clinically, 'I'm asking for your assistance in querying guild members for any knowledge of my wife's assault. I'm asking you to make this right, no matter what the history between us.'

'I'm not responsible for this . . . absenteeism, Lieutenant. I'm simply a dog on a runner: back and forth between the blue and the brass.'

'Right,' Boldt said sarcastically. He'd heard it all before.

'The move to restrict overtime and prohibit off-duty employment opportunities for our officers was viewed by certain individuals within the department as intrusive and destructive and is apparently the driving force behind this current situation.'

'This absenteeism,' Boldt said, 'that the papers and courts are calling a strike.'

'I'm in constant contact with both the chief's and the mayor's office, as I'm sure you're aware. As Chapter president, I'm forced to put my own personal feelings aside and to represent the majority opinion of my constituency. I do not condone tossing a brick through a window, and I'm sorry for your wife's injuries and any upset this may have caused you and your family. But the brick could just as easily have been from an angry neighbor. Am I right? Someone pissed off over the Flu – improperly associating you with the sickout. The public understands *so little* of our inner workings.'

It was true, though Boldt was loath to admit it. His neighbor's acquisition of an attack dog was proof enough of the public's current perception of safety. 'All I'm saying is – if you start a war, you had better be prepared to fight it.'

Krishevski's eyes hardened. 'I seriously doubt that the current absenteeism had anything to do with your wife's incident.'

'A blue brick? The reports of slashed tires? Coincidence?' Boldt asked.

'An angry public,' Krishevski repeated.

Boldt did not appreciate the man's slight grin. 'You brought my family into this. For that, you'll be sorry.'

'Another threat!'

'You know what I think, Krishevski? I think you

enjoy all the attention, the cameras, the headlines. Seeing your name in print. But the sad truth is you're misusing the trust of your fellow officers – this entire city – for your own personal gain.' Boldt picked up the brick off the carpet and placed it on a small end table. He retrieved his gun and returned it to its holster. 'Sticks and stones, Mr Krishevski.' He intentionally left out the man's rank. 'Be careful what you ask for.'

Krishevski's tension and anger surfaced in his now menacing voice. 'Dangerous ground, Lieutenant.'

'A threat?' Boldt fired back, mimicking the man. 'Control the troops, Krishevski. Bring in whoever was responsible. Or you and anyone else connected to this will be facing charges.'

'I'm trembling all over.'

Boldt pulled the front door shut with a bang that carried throughout the peaceful neighborhood. He hurried toward the car, anxious to return home and be with his family. Krishevski was a wild card. Boldt knew there was no telling if the threats would stop with blue bricks.

FIVE

Cathy Kawamoto ignored the deep, low rumble that had become such a commonplace sound, it could be anything from a passing truck to the garage door opening or closing. She wasn't alarmed. Kawamoto's basement home office felt unusually warm, and she was uncomfortable. She'd heard the phone ring just a minute earlier, but as was her habit, she allowed the machine upstairs to pick up rather than interrupt her work. Her thin fingers danced across the computer keyboard, the translation coming effortlessly now. When the screen briefly went dark she saw herself reflected in its 'nonreflective' glass: jet black hair, almond eyes with tight folds of skin that instantly labeled her Japanese. Then another page of text appeared and Cathy Kawamoto returned to her work. Sometimes the translations were of textbooks or technical documents, but her favorites were the American and Canadian romance novels that within a few months would populate the Tokyo subways, read intently by commuting women. At times the torrid love stories became so compelling that she found herself carried away.

The low rumble stopped and then started again. Cathy paused in her work this time. The sound seemed suddenly close. Perhaps it wasn't simply that the basement was warm, perhaps it was nerves. But then again the rental house was always full of strange noises, especially when her sister was home.

A flight attendant for Alaska Air, Kira came and went at all hours, for days at a time on an unpredictable schedule that Cathy could neither understand nor attempt to track.

Footsteps overhead . . .

At first Cathy simply glanced up toward the floor joists wondering what Kira had forgotten this time – she had left the house only a few minutes earlier, rushing off somewhere, yelling down into the basement that she was borrowing the car if that was all right. She hadn't waited for an answer. Late again.

Cathy translated another sentence – *Her unbridled passion sought escape* – before another squeak in the overhead floorboards once again attracted her attention.

This time it didn't sound like her sister. Her sister didn't move that slowly. Not ever, especially not when she was late, and she was *always* late.

A third careful step overhead. A mixture of curiosity and fear unsettled her. The telephone's in-use light indicated the phone was busy. Cathy felt relief wash over her. It was her sister, after all. Clearly, she had returned home to make a phone call. Cathy sat back down at the computer. But she couldn't concentrate. Something just didn't feel right.

She felt restless with it, a fire smoldering inside her.

Her fingers hesitated above the keys, her eyes drifting over to the telephone's in-use light. It continued to flash. When the footsteps started up again, left to right, directly overhead, the pit in her stomach became a stone. The kitchen phone was a wall phone, not a wireless walk-around. How could it be in use at the same time someone was walking around?

The stairs signaled both the direction of movement and the fact that the person up there was heavier than either she or her sister. They normally didn't make noise.

She thought about calling out, just shouting, 'Who's up there?' but she was afraid of giving herself away, letting the intruder know she was at home. She was now allowing herself to think there could be an intruder. The previous night's late news report began to cloud her thoughts. A policewoman had been attacked in her own home. *A policewoman!*

She lifted the phone's receiver to eavesdrop. She heard no one – only the hissing silence of an open line, ominous and frightful. 'Hello?' she tested in a whisper. No one answered. Cathy Kawamoto fought back panic. She quietly climbed the basement stairs. She could hear her unannounced visitor ascend the stairs directly overhead. The footfalls were strangely tentative, cautious, and she could only conclude that someone was trying hard not to be heard.

She climbed and reached the kitchen, first looking to the phone to see if by some chance it was off the hook. It was in place, and her alarm heightened. She could see now that her sister's purse was not hanging by its strap over the ladder-back kitchen chair, in its usual place. Kira was not at home.

She felt a tightness in her chest. She desperately wanted to announce herself, but this was tempered by her recollection of the policewoman news: She wasn't going to *volunteer* herself. On the other hand, she had trouble thinking of herself as a victim. *Other people* ended up on the evening news, not her. *Other people's* lives went to hell in a handbasket. This couldn't be happening to her.

'Hello?' she finally called out softly, unable to bear it any longer. 'Kira?' With her inquiry, the noises upstairs stopped. Cathy moved involuntarily toward the staircase, a decision she would find so difficult to explain later on.

She reached the top of the stairs, adrenaline surging through her system. She glanced down the hall. Back down the stairs. She felt cornered and yet exposed. The stairs suddenly seemed *so incredibly long*.

No sounds whatsoever. Panic seeped in and took hold. She attempted to run, but instead she froze with fear. The assault on the news had been of a single woman living in a relatively affluent community. What if this was a pattern?

Her mouth fell open to scream. No sound came out. Her chest was now fully paralyzed by fright.

Where the intruder came from, she wasn't sure. He seemed to materialize in front of her – a blur of dark color and tremendous speed. She felt an aching blow in the center of her chest, right where that knot had been. She flew through the air, limbs flailing, down to the open stairs. Landing on her back, she slid and tumbled head over heels, her skull catching the wooden treads and feeling like someone was clubbing her. Pain owned her. A thick haze consumed her and drew her down toward unconsciousness. She hit hard on the landing. That same dark shape flew over her. He grazed the wall. Her crotch ran warm with pee.

The shooting pain would not release her. Her fear was unforgiving. A cold, impenetrable darkness, devoid of light and sound.

Please, God, no! was Cathy Kawamoto's last conscious thought.

SIX

'Who's this?' said the sorry-looking, trash-talking white kid with the shaved head and a dragon tattoo under his left ear.

Boldt wasn't used to anyone else's interrogation rooms. The North Precinct had a brick-and-mortar quality that reminded Boldt of a converted ice house, when in fact it had formerly been an elementary school. Daphne had joined him not only because she was vital to any interrogation, but because some of the answers, if forthcoming, pertained directly to her case: Maria Sanchez.

Boldt stared at the kid's handcuffs, knowing these were just the first domino in a long chain of lost freedoms. He saw no need to explain himself to the suspect, to dignify the questions of a confessed rapist. But Daphne's assessment was clearly different, for she answered the kid immediately.

'This is the detective who discovered Leanne Carmichael in the basement where you left her. Alone. Malnourished. A hole cut into the crotch of her pants through which you repeatedly raped her. The man who untied the shoelaces from her wrists and ankles. The man who dealt with the urine and defecation before the ambulance arrived. Who dealt with the frozen-eyed terror of a little girl who went out to pick up the barbecued chicken, and never came home.'

'Ruby slippers went out a long time ago, honey,' the

kid said, eyes and lips shiny wet. He wore a small silver ring pierced through his left eyebrow. Daphne wondered if Leanne Carmichael might recall that ring.

Boldt edged closer to the table where the kid sat, an ominous aura about him – his rage barely concealed. The kid wanted to pretend he wasn't bothered by the man, but his glassy eyes flicked in Boldt's direction repeatedly, like a nervous driver checking the rearview mirror.

Daphne continued, 'This is the man who would like you alone for a few minutes. The handcuffs off. One on one. We discussed it on the way over. He won't get that chance, of course. But he takes solace in the fact that he's been on the force long enough to know everybody and anybody, long enough to know which of the arrests in lockup enjoy the . . . services . . . of other men. Solace in the fact that you'll be raped night after night, anally, orally – raped until you bleed, raped until you can't swallow even a sip of water. You'll be sent to the infirmary, where the male nurses will know what you did to little Leanne – and they'll make sure you get proper treatment. At which point, of course, you'll be sent back into the jail's population for another trip down honeymoon lane. And this is all before you get to the big house, where you will spend the remainder of your natural life – not likely to be too long, given that child rapists tend to have a short life span – behind bars.'

The suspect said nothing. Daphne had a way of reaching out to her clients. She'd knocked the wind out of him. Knocked the glib comments out as well.

Boldt leaned his arms against the table, so that he craned over the suspect, face to face. He dropped two five-by-seven glossies in front of the kid. Both showed a woman's wrists bound with knotted shoelaces. He said, 'Last Tuesday night.' He waited. 'We have a pretty good idea where you were, but we'd like some confirmation.'

The suspect tried to pretend he didn't care about Boldt, but the attempt failed. He finally broke off eye contact and glanced down at the photos. 'These that girl?'

'These are Tuesday night,' Boldt answered.

The kid squinted. 'Tuesday?' He shuffled the photos back and forth. 'You found her Saturday. I watched from across the street. Did you know that?' Boldt reared back and raised his hand.

'Lou!' Daphne stopped him. Perhaps with that one blow, Boldt might have killed the kid. Whatever the case, she saved him a review with her reprimand.

Boldt repeated, 'Tuesday night. You want to identify the location for us?'

'What is this shit about Tuesday?' he said, having difficulty with the pictures, given the handcuffs.

Boldt asked, 'Where were you last Tuesday night?'

'Tuesday night?' the kid repeated, some light sparking across his freakish eyes. 'Mariners' night game. Pre-season. It went extra innings. Junior pounded one down the third-base foul line in the twelfth and drove in the winning run.'

'You have the ticket stub?' Boldt asked quickly. 'Were you with anyone? Can you put a time on it?'

'Time?'

'I need a time and a place for you on Tuesday night,' Boldt said. 'I need you to write it all down.'

'Not happening.'

Boldt slapped the table so loudly that even Matthews jumped. The kid looked good and frightened. Boldt placed four more photos on the table. 'Take a good look.' Boldt pointed out what the lab had showed him only a few hours earlier. 'Shoelaces. Knots. Tuesday night knots.' He pointed out the other two photos – not giving him Sanchez's name. 'You going to deny it?'

Studying the photos closely, the kid said, 'So you already know it wasn't me who done these. Is that right?'

'I don't know anything about these until and unless you tell me. Educated guesses – I've got a few of those. Expert opinions – never a shortage there, not in government work. But witnesses? I think I'm looking at him.'

'The hell you are.'

'You've got to write it down. And try starting with the truth. Little Leanne Carmichael, then Tuesday night—'

'I was at the ball game,' the kid interrupted. Pointing to the photos he said, 'You can see right here this wasn't me. These are granny knots. They can pull out. I use square knots. Made it to first class in the Scouts. You were at Carmichael!' he reminded Boldt, who wanted nothing to do with that horrific image. 'Tied with square knots. Check it out, you'll see I'm right.' He repeated, 'Tuesday night was the ballgame.'

Boldt glanced over at Daphne.

She said to the kid, 'Write it down.'

'Why should I?' the kid protested. 'You're only gonna screw me. You say I did something Tuesday night? What? Another girl? Sure, I did it. There! You happy now?'

She explained calmly, 'You care because on Tuesday he made mistakes. Because this one will go into your column and it's a loose job, a lousy job. A middle-aged woman. A cop. Which shoves it hook, line and sinker into maximum security's F wing. Twenty-three-hour lockup. No chance of early parole. You want to grow old there?'

'Old?' the kid asked sarcastically. 'Like your age or

something?' He eyed her and looked repulsed. 'Not interested.'

Boldt slammed his weight against the table, smacking the kid in the chest, and tipping him back in his chair so that his head struck the concrete block wall with pronounced contact. Boldt said, 'Slipped. Sorry about that.' He came around the table – the kid shied – and he violently stood that chair back up, driving the kid's chest into the edge of the table for a second time. 'There,' Boldt said. 'That's better.'

'Write it down,' Daphne told the suspect, as she took Boldt by the elbow and pulled him to her side. They didn't need the arrest going south because of abuse. She needed to get him out of there.

The kid picked up the pen and aimed it and the pad of paper at Daphne. 'You write down that you'll go lightly on me if I help you with that girl, because that other one, it wasn't mine, wasn't me. This bitch cop. No way. Granny knots? Fucking things never hold.'

She turned the pad around yet again. 'Last chance. If we step away from this, who do you think will give you another one?'

The kid hunched forward and started to write.

Standing by Boldt's Chevy, Daphne kept to her thoughts.

'You're mad,' Boldt offered. 'My pushing him around.'

'Surprised. More like something John would do.'

'He shouldn't have spoken to you that way.'

'We've heard worse,' she reminded.

'I'm losing the edge,' he suggested. 'Is that what you're saying?'

'He didn't do Sanchez,' she stated. 'That's all that matters.'

'You believe that?' he said, a little surprised.

'Yes.'

'So do I,' he added. Almost a whisper. A shudder passing through him. 'Oh, God,' he mumbled.

'Yes. I know what you mean.' She headed down the line of parked cars to her Honda.

His pager sounded. Another first-degree burglary. Just his luck.

SEVEN

'Minor injuries, L.T. Nothing to worry about,' Gaynes informed Boldt. The same could be said about Liz's injuries, but Boldt wasn't buying. It all came down to perspective. Worry, he did. Behind Gaynes, EMTs closed up the back of a private ambulance. 'Vic's name is Cathy Kawamoto. Single. Lives alone. Sound familiar?'

Boldt didn't want this. Didn't need it. Not another. They were attending their second burglary / assault in as many days. Gaynes had drawn lead on the case, courtesy of the Blue Flu and Dispatch's current lottery system of assigning the first available detective who answered his or her phone. He told her about the interrogation, about losing the connection between Carmichael and Sanchez.

'So we clear one,' she said, 'and the other heads for a black hole.'

'Do *not* say that,' Boldt scolded. Gaynes suggested he head inside while she caught back up to the ambulance driver for a final word. Boldt seized the chance to see the crime scene for himself.

A burglary assault committed in the middle of the day. Technically a violent crime, minor injuries or not. The Blue Flu was lending the criminal element courage. *While the cat's away, the mice do play.* Bright sunshine broke loose from behind quickly moving dark clouds, the wind steady and warm. Summer struggled to be rid of spring. Boldt struggled to be rid of the Sanchez crime scene; he didn't want one influencing the other, but it proved almost inescapable. What he wanted was some good, solid evidence. Something valuable. Something to kick this thing in the butt and help get someone behind bars. Before another. Before the press descended like locusts. Before the looming black hole of Sanchez's unsolved case widened.

'What do we have?' he asked sharply of the first officer, a young woman who, judging by her crisp uniform and pronounced nervousness, was more than likely one of the police academy trainees temporarily promoted to patrol. Her quick-footed effort to keep pace with him, and a strained voice that cracked when attempting a reply, belied the stiff shoulders and confident chin. This stop-gap action taken by the chief to maintain a patrol-level presence on the streets had been written up in the press and condemned in the Public Safety coffee lounges. If a minimum number of uniforms could not be mobilized, the governor had threatened, or promised (depending which side of the argument one took), National Guard troops and curfews – political disaster for the mayor. But so-called 'freshies' had no place behind the wheel of a cruiser, or as first officer at any crime scene, much less on an assault. For all his experience and wisdom, this new chief was out of his mind.

'Single female.'

'I've got that,' he said. Impatience nibbled at the center of his chest. He needed some basic information, but he longed to be left alone with the crime scene.

'Living with a sister who stays here every couple weeks.'

'Didn't have that,' Boldt admitted. 'The scene?'

'Exterior doors all found locked.'

He interrupted, 'You're sure?' This information registered in Boldt, for the back door of the Sanchez home had been left unlocked.

'She placed the 911 call, so maybe she locked up.'

'Security system?'

'The home has one. Yes. But apparently the answering machine was engaged, keeping the line open – she remembers the indicator light on the downstairs phone. The guy must have had a tape recorder on it: sending out a single beep every five seconds, so the machine kept recording and didn't hang up. Tricky stuff, Lieutenant. Smarter than just snipping the line, which instantly sounds the alarm. With the primary line engaged, the security system couldn't dial out. Gives him time to get inside and bust up the alarm's speaker.'

'So it never did dial out,' Boldt said.

'Not that we're aware of, no.'

Boldt noted yet another contradiction to the Sanchez scene. Sanchez's home security system had dialed the provider – not that it had done her any good; Kawamoto's had been prevented from doing so.

'What else do we know?' Boldt questioned her.

'Personal property reported missing. Vic's name is Cathy Kawamoto. Banged up a little but—'

'I've got that already. How 'bout a description?' He felt like an instructor now, slipping out of his primary role. Freshies needed so damn much help. Chief was out of his mind.

'Female. Japanese/Brit. Early thirties. Book translator.' The woman skipped along, rushing her thoughts, like a kid trying to avoid the cracks in the sidewalk. 'Working out of a home office in the basement. Thought she heard something upstairs. Investigates. Takes a blow to the chest at the top of the stairs. Goes down hard.'

'Evidence of anything sexual?' he asked, still trying to keep Sanchez out of his head.

'No, sir.'

'Not to your knowledge,' he corrected.

'Not to my knowledge,' she agreed.

'No clothes torn off, anything like that?'

'Nothing like that, Lieutenant.'

'Ligatures? Tied up in any way?' he inquired.

'Negative.'

'Which stairs?' he asked, returning to her earlier statement.

She told him.

'What's the extent of the personal property loss?'

'Looks like he may have been after a PC, a cable box and a thirty-seven inch. But that's just the bedroom. Who knows what else he had in mind?'

'He didn't lift any of it?' At the Sanchez scene, despite the assault, the burglary had gone through. Perhaps that pointed to timing. Perhaps it pointed to yet another inconsistency. He wanted evidence: a shoe print to compare to the one lifted off Sanchez's coat; a knot to compare to the shoelaces found bound to her wrists. Something. Anything.

'No, sir. The suspect apparently fled immediately following the assault.'

'Good work,' Boldt offered. He felt distracted by his concern for Liz and the kids, suddenly wondering if they were safe at the Jamersons, where they were staying temporarily until Liz and he could figure out how much danger they were actually in. What if the Blue Fluers *meant* for the families to suffer? he wondered.

'How's your wife, sir?' the recruit inquired in a moment of uncanny timing. 'If you don't mind my asking?' This one was looking for immediate promotion. To answer truthfully, his wife was upset, angry, though not necessarily at him. The relocation to the friend's home on Mercer Island was a temporary fix at best. To keep trouble from following them, Boldt would sleep at the family house, only visiting the Jamerson home for the occasional meal. A workable but undesirable arrangement that obviously challenged a husband and wife who relished being together, who needed each other. In truth, he was deeply worried about his family, worried to the point that he hadn't eaten in at least ten hours. The blue brick had shattered more than the window – it shattered certain limits too. With it, Boldt's work had come home in a way he'd vowed would never happen again. Previously, they had endured threats of arson, the kidnapping of their daughter: each time the family had rebounded, though not without scars. The brick had reopened those wounds. He saw no immediate fix. He and Liz would talk. There wouldn't be any simple, fast answers, but they would find them. Liz's blood was on the living-room rug. No matter how small the stain, the damage was immense and permanent.

He counted on Krishevski to identify those responsible – not just a scapegoat. But he wasn't holding his breath.

'She's better,' Boldt finally answered. His private life was nobody's business. 'Did Ms Kawamoto get a decent look at him?'

'No, sir. The offender was apparently moving pretty fast. Shoved her down the stairs and took off. That's about it for the blow-by-blow.'

'Breaks and bruises for the most part,' he repeated, attempting to reassure himself. He stopped so that he could ask this before they entered the home, before he might be overheard by anyone. 'SID?' he asked.

'Has been notified. Yes.'

'How many have been inside?' Boldt inquired.

'Me and my partner,' she said, pointing through the open door to another recruit who stood at the bottom of the interior stairs. The uniformed officer reminded Boldt of a Boy Scout. What was a roll-call sergeant doing teaming two freshies in the same radio car? Was the department that hard up? He'd heard that another twenty to thirty uniforms – patrol officers – had failed to show up for work this morning. But this pairing of two freshies indicated the situation was far worse than he imagined.

'The two EMTs,' she continued. 'Other than that, we've got a good scene.'

'Well done, Officer,' Boldt said, wondering if he might have been the first to address her in this manner, for her face lit up.

'Thank you, sir!'

He felt like a den mother. 'The victim was fully conscious after the fall?'

'Not as far as I know, sir. I think maybe she passed out briefly.'

'She saw him leave? Heard him leave?'

'Not to my knowledge. I believe she only heard him upstairs and went to take a look. A sister lives with her part time. He surprises her and shoves her down the stairs. I think the situation got the better of her. Maybe she fainted – passed out for a minute or two. It scared her pretty bad.'

'He left the premises how?' Boldt asked, still thinking about the timing of the crime. Daylight. A day after Sanchez. No shoelaces around the wrists. He didn't want so many differences between the two crimes.

'No idea. Front and back doors were locked tight when we arrived.' She touched her breast pocket. 'Made note of that specifically.'

'Locked,' he confirmed.

'Correct.'

Boldt opened the front door and inspected the mechanism. 'No night latch,' he said. 'Keyed dead bolt and keyed knob.'

'If I may, sir?' the young woman officer inquired.

'Go ahead.'

'Upon being admitted through the back, my partner and me found this particular door's dead bolt in place. That is, a keyed dead bolt as you've pointed out. Subsequent inspection of the back door – the door through which we had entered the premises – indicated the same basic arrangement. The victim, Ms Kawamoto, could not recall if she had thrown that particular dead bolt or not. So my assumption was he both entered and departed the premises via that back door.' She took a breath and dared to submit speculation. 'I'm thinking that subsequent to the offender's departure our vic locked the door – whether or not she's currently aware of that fact.'

'It's a kitchen door?'

'No, sir, the kitchen door accesses the garage. This would be off the living area, sir.'

So the doer watched the house, Boldt thought. Knew which door to hit – a back door typically left unlocked. And it had to be from a vantage point that provided a view of that back door. 'I'll keep your partner assigned to the front door,' Boldt said loudly enough for the other officer to hear him too. 'You will canvass the neighbors with an eye toward anything. The offender, his vehicle, anyone seen parked around here in the last couple days.'

'Yes, sir.' The recruit seemed thrilled. Boldt had little choice: he didn't have much of a pool from which to draw.

She left through the front door, passing Gaynes, who

was on her way in. As the Boy Scout opened his mouth to speak, Boldt lifted a finger and said, 'Not now, okay, unless it's a top priority. I need quiet. Your job is to keep everyone and anyone out until either Detective Gaynes or I give you the nod. Okay? First one through that door is to be SID, but only on our say-so. No matter what, you remain outside along with everyone else.' Reading the nameplate pinned to the uniform, he said, 'You okay with that, Helman?'

The kid had the wherewithal to nod sharply rather than open his mouth again.

'Good,' Boldt said.

Gaynes said, 'I'll take the basement and the ground floor, L.T. You'll take upstairs.' Ordering around her lieutenant was an uncomfortable act at best. 'If that's good with you?'

'Fine.'

'The assault happened up there on the stairs. She came to rest on the landing.'

'I'll tread lightly,' Boldt offered.

Despite the dozen cases back on his desk, and the dozen more that would be assigned in the coming days, the Sanchez assault and the Kawamoto break-in were what interested him. Any investigator liked a clean case that cleared quickly. But Boldt had worked dozens, perhaps hundreds of such cases; he lived now for the challenge – not the black holes that would never be solved, but the cases that both meant something and offered contradictions. Sanchez and Kawamoto appeared vaguely related – burglaries gone bad, women assaulted. They presented an urgency, both for the sake of the public, and the media.

There was no apology to be made, no words that would return Cathy Kawamoto's sense of safety. She would never fully trust this city again, would never feel safe, even behind the locked doors of her own home. This weighed heavily upon him. Boldt felt that as a peace officer, his role was to preserve a sense of safety, and yet Cathy Kawamoto would have none now, he knew.

Boldt felt the case closing in on him – it just wasn't coming together. He carefully climbed the stairs, on the one hand wanting a few minutes alone to immerse himself in the crime scene, on the other wanting the differences sorted out and the offender in lockup by evening, well before the news dumped it on the dinner plates.

A crime scene, alone, in silence. Lou Boldt felt alert and alive.

As an investigator, Boldt experienced no prescient sense from the perspective of the offender. He could not transport himself into this role as some investigators suggested was possible. He saw the crime scene from the role of the victim – often viscerally, but exclusively from this side of the crime.

Boldt headed upstairs in the footsteps of Cathy Kawamoto, a woman about to disturb a thief. He assumed the thief was a planner – not some junkie kicking in doors and stealing a purse or string of pearls. And here comes Cathy Kawamoto up the stairs, chasing noises. He stopped briefly to study the landing because the freshie had told him the victim had recovered consciousness on the stairs. This was supported by the drying bloodstain he saw there, the result of a bloodied nose.

If the offender had shoved her downstairs and yet fled the premises, he had jumped right over her. This thought coincided with Boldt's observation of a long, black rubber smudge on the wall that seemed to fit with a person in a hurry jumping over a body on the landing. He made a note to have the SID techs sample the rubber smudge, and to analyze it. 'No stone unturned,' he mumbled to himself, well aware that the press and the public would attempt to connect this to Sanchez – and perhaps even Carmichael – and that on top of the Flu, public concern would figure politically in both investigations, demanding immediate arrests.

He found the offender's apparent target in the bedroom: A corner hutch that faced the victim's bed. A television, VCR and one of those all-in-one music centers with CD player, double tape system and stereo receiver. The offender had not had time to steal the electronics – Kawamoto had headed upstairs at an inopportune time. But the man had moved the hutch from the corner in an effort to free wires. Boldt peered behind. The television had been unplugged, its wire neatly coiled and fastened. What kind of person took the time to neatly coil wires before heisting a television?

More than the coil of wire, it was sight of the white plastic loop secured around the coil that intrigued Boldt. A sophisticated version of a garbage bag tie. Had any such ties been inventoried at Sanchez's, he wondered. Another contradiction? The other wires were snarled in a tangle and covered with dust. Who was this guy? What kind of burglar showed such confidence? Daphne would have a heyday evaluating such a personality.

Then a second thought occurred to him: if the thief had possessed plastic ties at the Sanchez break-in, why not use them to bind her wrists, instead of shoelaces?

Why shoelaces and not the plastic ties?

He took notes, albeit unnecessarily – he wasn't about to forget any of this. Perhaps the Burglary unit had files on record that mentioned white plastic ties being used. He had in hand the physical evidence he'd hoped for.

Now, he had to connect it to a suspect.

EIGHT

'I need help, Phil. I need the names of who did this to Liz, and I also need your Burglary files for the past month. I thought you might be able to speed things up for me on both counts,' Boldt said. 'Unless you're "too busy",' he added. He needed to connect the white plastic ties to earlier burglaries, to establish a pattern crime, to widen the scope of evidence and increase the number of leads to follow. Captain Phil Shoswitz seemed the means to that end.

'Are you suggesting I'm intentionally slowing things down around here?' Shoswitz questioned defensively. In point of fact, some of the lower brass had effected a slowdown, and Shoswitz was probably part of it. The man paced his cluttered office. A baseball fanatic, the captain of Crimes Against Property (which included Burglary) had bookshelves overflowing with intramural trophies and major league souvenirs. A bat autographed by Junior. A hardball scrawled upon by the entire Mariners team. A photo of himself taken outside Safeco Field on opening day, his ticket proudly displayed. He rubbed his throwing elbow – a nervous tic that indicated both deep thought and irritation. 'I detest what happened to Liz. You know I'm with you on that – everyone's with you.'

'Are they?' Boldt had come up through the ranks with Phil Shoswitz, had spent nearly a dozen years serving under the man in Homicide, over eight of those years as sergeant to Shoswitz's lieutenant. Now that Shoswitz carried a captain's badge in Crimes Against Property, and Boldt a lieutenant's shield in Crimes Against Persons – CAProp and CAPers respectively – Boldt suspected the man had a touch of envy despite the higher rank. Homicide remained the golden egg, the most prestigious posting on the department. Shoswitz had sacrificed that posting for his captain's badge promotion and higher pay.

'Maybe not everyone,' Shoswitz admitted, 'but you've only yourself to blame for that. You mouthed off to the press about the absenteeism; you pointed fingers at people.'

It was true. Boldt had been interviewed by a reporter, and the story had hit the national wires, painting a pretty ugly picture of the detectives who had joined the sickout in sympathy. If Shoswitz was telling him that the blue brick had been thrown through his window in response to that interview, then for Liz's sake, his family's sake, Boldt regretted giving that interview, even if what he said had to be said, which was how he felt about it. The politicians, in an effort to keep nego-tiations open, failed to express any feelings – rage, disappointment, anger – over the events of the past week, and Boldt felt such attitudes did more damage than good, for they subtly condoned the walkout while taking a 'hard-line stance' against it. He loved police work and was proud of the department; the Flu had damaged its reputation, perhaps forever.

'I need access to your files, Phil,' Boldt repeated. He took Shoswitz's concern for Liz as lip service. After nearly two decades of friendship, he saw his former lieutenant in a whole new light. If the man cared, he'd have already been on the telephone to his buddy Mac Krishevski, and would have demanded the names of those responsible for that brick. But he was mad at Boldt for talking to the press, mad at Boldt for continuing to carry the caseload dumped on him. Mad at life. Anger had consumed him, and if he didn't watch out it would consume Boldt as well.

Boldt asked, 'What's so complicated about your helping me get those files?'

Shoswitz's eyes flashed darkly and his nostrils flared. He stopped his pacing and stared at his former sergeant in an all-too-familiar angry glare. 'Without the investigating officer or officers present, it would hardly be appropriate—'

'They're out *sick*,' Boldt pointed out.

'My point, exactly!'

'Their decision, not mine. Not yours! What are you suggesting, we delay all active investigations? We delay an investigation into the assault of a fellow officer in order to appease the Blue Fluers?'

'Don't use that term in this office.'

'It's a sickout, Phil. What's the—'

'It's more complicated than that,' Shoswitz complained, interrupting.

'Not to me it isn't,' Boldt argued. 'I need someone to stand up for what happened to Liz and I need a look at your files. Explain how any of that's complicated.'

Shoswitz glared and returned to his aimless pacing, reminding Boldt of a pit bull in a cage.

He pushed away his personal concerns over Liz and the blue brick – Shoswitz wasn't going to help him there – and tried to stay focused on gaining access to the paperwork he deemed crucial to the Sanchez investigation. A burglary was handled by the uniform who responded to the call. Typically, he or she conducted a short interview, inspected the scene, and filled out a report, leaving the victim to deal with the insurance underwriter. Detectives in the Burglary unit shuffled these reports, looking for possible pattern crimes or anything of substance that might connect up with information from snitches or fences they'd squeezed. They did far less field work than their counterparts in Homicide, Special Assaults, or Organized Crime, because a single, unconnected burglary was not worth a detective's time – the likelihood of recovering and returning the stolen property was infinitesimal. Boldt needed Shoswitz to access his unit's case files. He would also need the man's outright cooperation if he were to round up all the recent burglary reports from the three other precincts. Shoswitz could pull this off with a couple calls to the other houses. But his entire team had walked out with the Fluers, and he seemed bound and determined to protect them. It didn't come as a complete surprise to Boldt – Shoswitz was a guild player through and through, even though his rank of captain and the existing management contract prevented him from following the guild's lead.

'Is this for you or Matthews?' Shoswitz asked sarcastically.

Any detective was practiced in the art of changing subjects, but Shoswitz had not been in the field in years. His attempt to derail Boldt succeeded only because it stabbed for the heart.

Boldt knew not to get sucked into this, but his mouth betrayed him. 'What the hell does that mean?' he fired off indignantly.

'She's lead on Sanchez, not you, right?'

'So?'

'So who's here asking for favors?' Shoswitz asked rhetorically. 'It means what it means.'

'Which is?' Boldt asked.

'Lou, do I have to spell it out?'

'You have to spell it out,' Boldt assured him. His face burned. His mouth had gone dry. Phil Shoswitz had been a friend for years – and here he was questioning Boldt's loyalty to his wife and family.

Shoswitz continued working that sore elbow. 'You two . . . you work well together,' he said, drawing out the statement and meeting eyes with Boldt, who felt a hollow sinking feeling in the pit of his stomach. 'She dumped that rich guy for good, I hear.'

'There's nothing there, Phil. Leave it alone.'

'Of course not.'

'You're pissing me off here, Phil.'

'How do you think I feel – we *all* feel – about your current enthusiasm for the job?'

Politics. It hit him like cold water down the back. He had not expected Shoswitz to be so blatant in his support for Krishevski. Boldt felt stunned. Another ally down, and this one still wearing the badge, still working in the office. A friend. How many others on the job felt similarly, he wondered. How much internal sabotage was taking place in support of the Flu? 'You were guild secretary for five years. I understand that, Phil.' He tried to remind the man, 'But you and I – we're not only bound by a different contact, we're bound by friendship. We're not guild members. Not anymore. Are we still friends?'

Shoswitz huffed. Half a laugh. Half a groan. 'This new chief shouldn't be playing games with people's wallets. Big mistake. Look at us,' he said, indicating himself and Boldt. 'Would we be here arguing like this if it wasn't for him?'

'He's new.'

'He's a jerk. What does someone from Philadelphia know about this town?'

'He's one of the best in the country. We both know that.'

'Strange way of showing it,' Shoswitz said. 'Pulling overtime. Cutting out off-duty work. It's asinine!'

'A stadium went over budget. You want asinine? You look at Liz's left forearm!' Boldt fired off. 'They brought this into *my house*, Phil. They crossed a line.'

'Agreed,' Shoswitz said quickly. 'You have no argument from me there.'

'Don't I?'

'Meaning?'

Boldt said, 'Tell Krishevski to bring forward whoever's responsible.'

'I'm forbidden from contacting Krishevski or anyone involved in the . . . absenteeism,' Shoswitz reminded him. 'Another wonderful decision from our new chief.'

'Krishevski will start a war, he keeps this up. Blue against Blue. What's that about? That has no place on this job!'

'No one wants that.'

'Tell that to Liz. Or Sanchez. She's got her head screwed down so she can't move, Phil. She's a pair of eyeballs at the moment. Have you been to visit her? Has anyone? Where the hell is everyone? What if it was me or you who'd taken that fall? What does it take to get people back on the job?'

'Promises,' Shoswitz said. 'That's where Mac Krishevski comes in. He's playing both sides of the fence, Lou. He has to.'

'Yeah? Well he should keep the bricks on his side of the fence.'

A hard silence settled between them along with the looks of betrayal from both men.

'These files,' Shoswitz cautioned. 'Tread lightly. No one on this squad is going to want to hear that you're nosing around in their files. It doesn't look right, a Homicide Lieu stepping in and taking over a CAProp case.'

'I can't be worried about that.'

'You need to be.'

'No, I don't. What I need is those files. You have the authority to round them up for me.' Boldt pressed, 'I need you to do that. I need to see if the Sanchez assault fits into any kind of pattern your boys may have on the books.'

'Why do you think we file in triplicate?' Shoswitz asked.

The Public Safety Building housed administration for all of SPD. Boldt understood the message. 'They're here? Copies of all those reports are already here, regardless of precinct?'

Shoswitz said, 'Where else?'

'You'll request them for me?'

'They'll be on your desk in an hour,' Shoswitz said. 'But this conversation never took place. You thought of this on your own. You pulled a favor from someone in the boneyard. You play this however you want, but my name doesn't come up.'

'Priorities,' Boldt said. 'How long do you support a guy like Krishevski?'

'To each their own,' added Phil Shoswitz.

'Yeah, sure,' Boldt said in disgust. 'Who are *your* own, Phil? These guys who walked off their beats? Or Sanchez over there in the hospital doing staring contests with the ceiling tiles?'

'Be careful, Lou. You say that kind of thing in the wrong company and you won't be making any friends.'

'Are you the wrong company, Phil?'

'Get out of here before I change my mind about those files.'

'I'm gone,' Boldt said. He didn't add that he'd gotten what he came for, though he felt tempted to do so. He wanted the last word, but didn't take it. He left Shoswitz with the illusion of control. He accepted the promise of the files, savoring an undeclared victory.

The last three weeks of reported burglaries arrived on Boldt's desk ninety minutes later, most of them nothing more than the requisite property loss report – one hundred and fourteen in all. Boldt switched on his desk lamp, a cup of Earl Grey at the ready. If there had been a night shift it would have been just arriving, but the Flu had killed such shifts. Civilians still manned their desks, but with the detectives out 'sick,' the place was a graveyard. He rubbed his eyes, cleaned his reading glasses with a long, slow breath and a piece of tissue, and examined the reports.

Each report detailed a burglary represented by a numbered code. This was followed by name, address, time of day. First officer. Investigating detective, if any. List of stolen goods. A concise summary of events: *returned home, broken window, missing stereo; awoke to a noise, entered the living room, suspect seen fleeing.* Eye-numbing repetition. Uniformed patrol officers going through the routine of making the ripped-off public think someone cared. No one did but the insurance companies. They wanted a report filed and signed off on. Boldt studied those reports, fighting off drowsiness.

He looked first to the list of stolen goods, separating out those that inventoried large-screen TVs, home computers, cell phones – all items believed stolen from Sanchez. A single TV didn't count. A single computer didn't interest him. With the exception of a cell phone, the items stolen from Sanchez each had retail values in excess of a grand. Picky. Exact. Kawamoto's 37-inch TV had clearly been targeted; the VCR's wire had not been coiled. Had it been too inexpensive to worry about? Or had Kawamoto's interruption come before the burglar had enough time to examine it? TVs and stereos would normally be considered the domain of a junkie looking for his next fix, but junkies didn't put white plastic ties around the electrical cords. Junkies didn't trick home security systems by tying up the phone line.

Boldt suspected that this particular rip-off artist sought out high-end electronics in enough quantity to justify the risk. A computer, a couple TVs and a cell phone to be cloned later might net him fifteen hundred from the right fence – not bad for a day's work. Better than cop pay.

Based on the list of stolen goods, Boldt narrowed his pile to twenty-three reports. Some of the forms had the small box checked off that indicated home security systems, but not all. On two of these reports he noted that the officers made mention of the security systems being compromised. Boldt smelled a possible insurance fraud – homeowners arranging for the 'theft' of their own electronics; they would then collect the insurance money, have the electronics returned, and pay out a percentage of the take to he who committed the 'burglary.' The Stepford Thieves. Wouldn't be the first white-collar crime investigated by SPD.

Boldt flipped through the stack of pink, archived triplicate copies, wanting some other identifier. He read each of the twenty-three reports in more detail, taking the time to study the notes, wanting something to narrow these to a more manageable number. Twenty-three phone calls would take days, if not weeks, under the current caseload. Even shared with Daphne, he thought the job could take a week or more. Two or three weeks was not out of the question if they reached a bunch of answering machines. Shoswitz's comments about his relationship with Daphne troubled him, stayed with him. He wanted to see it as exaggeration. Lies. He wanted to feel it in his heart as school-house rumor, but it triggered fear instead – as if he'd been caught at something, and that bothered him most of all.

His blunt concentration passed the time quickly. The tea went cold. His butt hurt. All the little pleasantries of police work. City traffic had slacked off outside. He heard a distant whine of tires, but not the up-close-and-personal street traffic with which he hummed along by day. The place smelled of janitor's disinfectant, a chemical lime smell that had a hint of melting rubber to it. The janitor had passed through unnoticed.

He glanced up at the clock – it was late; he owed Liz an apology. But before he picked up the phone to call her, he checked the clock a second time, recalling that Kawamoto had been hit in the daytime – extremely unusual. Sanchez had not, but for the moment he managed to separate the two cases and keep them that way. Back through his pile of reports he went. From the stack of twenty-three, he began pulling out reports, his heart racing as the new pile grew to six burglaries – the shared element: broad daylight.

He went through all hundred-and-something files again. This time, a total of nine reports made up his pile. Nine burglaries. Nine violations of private property in broad daylight, all with thousands of dollars of high-end electronics stolen. Big hits. Tricky hits. Some with home security devices apparently compromised. Well-orchestrated crimes. Practiced. Judging by Post-it notes and stapled attachments, Shoswitz's detectives had apparently spotted some of these same similarities – these overlapping loose connections – had probably been developing leads when the Flu came along and sent them home to watch reruns. Now Boldt had them, and he suddenly felt like a runner being passed a baton.

There was no mention of white plastic ties. No assaults. Just nine pink sheets on missing electronics and some attached notes from bone-weary detectives. Police work.

The smell of burned coffee drifted down the hall. The janitor had forgotten to turn off the pot. Boldt did so, stretching his legs, appreciating the moment away from the eyestrain and the tight back. He yawned. He washed out the coffeepot and shut the door to the lounge to keep the smell contained. All the while, he kept a weary eye over one shoulder. He kept thinking of that blue brick lying on his living-room floor, his wife in a sea of glass and her strained voice choking out, 'I thought it was a bomb.' He thought of his kids, his responsibility, his promises. He recalled Shoswitz's warning that his intrusion into Burglary's turf and open cases would not be appreciated. But Sanchez's eyes came back to haunt him.

He would want to speak with all nine burglary victims; visit them in person, if possible. Daphne should accompany him, to read their answers. What they didn't say, and how they didn't say it, was often more important than what they put down for the record. He felt high, his spirits lifted by the discovery. Taken together, the reported crimes had been committed in broad daylight, in houses where the occupant had vacated the premises, in houses left locked, often with the home security system armed – with *not one* of the security systems announcing an intruder. Sanchez's assault remained the anomaly – committed at night, with the security system engaged, but the same high-end

64

electronics stolen. Location was another possible tie – some of the burglaries had occurred in the North Precinct; others in the East or South, but always in white, upper-middle-class neighborhoods.

Boldt's excitement grew as he sat back down. The cases looked damned good strung out in a line. Stacked in a pile. They made sense as a package. It was dark outside and nine o'clock. He had missed the family dinner at John and Kristin's, had missed putting his kids to bed. Had worked through a date with his wife and family and friends. At 9:30 he called Liz and apologized. She sounded a little upset but said she missed him, which he reciprocated. He didn't mention his partial victory on the case because it didn't seem appropriate at the moment. Missing dinner was one thing in their family; missing the kids' bedtimes another. He hated to disappoint Liz, even for a good cause.

He and Liz had formed their courtship around jazz, films of every kind, and late-night dinners filled with stories and laughter. He had thought her too pretty for him; she'd feared even early on that he was too much of a workaholic. They had married young and for years had kept the marriage that way as well. Careers and the pressure to consider a family had briefly driven Liz to an affair, which in turn had encouraged Boldt to give in to temptation with Daphne Matthews for a single night. But that original connection between husband and wife had never been severed – it remained strong, if strained. They rarely made it to movies as a couple any longer – it was all Disney videos and the occasional Ice Capades musical. Boldt sometimes played Happy Hour jazz piano as a distraction, but Liz stayed home with the kids. The connection remained. Sometimes it took the form of a late-night movie or a rented video, a shared bath, or lovemaking on the couch with the kids asleep.

Sometimes, nothing more than a look or a tone of voice. A long talk. They practiced mutual tolerance, mutual support; they limped through the challenges thrown up by daily life, sometimes overcoming, sometimes only surviving. But on this night he could feel Liz attempting to be tolerant and not entirely succeeding.

'Call me in the morning,' she suggested, a little too quietly, but still gently.

'Sure will.'

'Maybe you can come over for eggs.'

'Maybe so,' he replied.

'You'll keep working tonight,' she said.

'Yes.'

'Okay.' She didn't sound overjoyed about that.

They said their good-byes and hung up.

With a monthly calendar laid out on the desk before him, Boldt charted the nine burglaries that seemed to have led up to Maria Sanchez's tragedy. Sanchez – if part of that string – was number ten. Kawamoto, eleven. There was no particular day of the week to tie the events together, no exact hour, though all but the Sanchez crime had occurred during daylight; nor had there been a particular neighborhood. At first blush, a detective's nightmare – circumstantial connections linking the crimes but lacking the hard evidence necessary to provide a trail to follow. Nonetheless, for Boldt the similarities remained substantial enough to impress him. He believed all eleven were connected, even if it wouldn't be easy to prove it. He had yet to discover how the burglar selected or targeted the homes – and this was, of course, of primary importance to the possible identification of a suspect. Certainly the residences had not been chosen at random – not since they were loaded with high-end electronics. The connection between these targets – an insurance provider? a security company? – eluded him, but remained a top priority.

Or so he thought. Those priorities began to shift when he noticed a circled pair of initials on the top of one of the nine files. The initials crowded the box reserved for the investigating detective, for in this particular box two detectives had left their initials. The home belonged to a couple listed as Brooks-Gilman, living over in Queen Anne, a mitt-shaped neighborhood immediately north and west of downtown. The Brooks-Gilman case had been passed to a second detective, probably as a result of the Blue Flu. The circled initials were elegant and easily read:

MS

Maria Sanchez? he wondered, as he then noted the date on which the detective in question had accepted responsibility for the case. That date was just two days before the Sanchez assault. That exceeded the boundaries of acceptable coincidence. MS. Maria Sanchez. Had to be.

NINE

'I don't see what we're after,' Daphne said, hurrying to keep up with Boldt as he ascended the hospital stairs.

'Her connection to the Brooks-Gilman burglary investigation,' he answered.

'I understand that much,' she said, a little miffed that he wouldn't give her at least some credit. 'I read the memo!' Boldt had circulated an interdepartmental E-mail requesting any information on all cases Sanchez had been working prior to her assault. 'But how does that get us any closer to the thief? So she took over some cases after the walkout happened. We all did. So what?'

Boldt didn't answer her. Not one person had responded to his E-mail, again reminding him that the Flu had sympathizers still on the job. He felt disheartened, even defeated.

Daphne matched strides with him in the long hallway. 'Lou, she's my case. It's only right you tell me what you're thinking.'

'Shoswitz said his boys would not appreciate any of us doing their work for them. The implication being pretty obvious.'

'We're considered scabs,' she gasped, 'just because we accept some assignment passed to us by Dispatch?'

'Maybe Sanchez was. Maybe they got pissed off at her for crossing over into their department. The only way a strike is effective is when the work doesn't get done. Maybe I got that brick through my window because I'm supposed to stay in Homicide, not take cases from other departments.'

She mumbled, 'So to make the strike effective, they intimidate us.'

'Or worse,' he said.

'Break her neck, strip her naked and tie her up?' she questioned. 'Does that sound like cop against cop? I don't buy that.'

'Hey,' Boldt defended, 'I'm not selling. I'm just investigating is all. Leaving open all possibilities.'

'There's a big difference between a brick through a window and what happened to Maria Sanchez.'

'I don't disagree with you,' Boldt said. 'I'm just investigating is all.'

They reached the door to Sanchez's room and showed their badges to the hospital security guard posted outside. He carefully checked the IDs, then permitted them to go in.

Sanchez's condition had deteriorated since their first visit. The decline had manifested itself in her skin tone and in the proliferation of ICU equipment that was now attached to her. Daphne acknowledged her read of the situation with a grim look that told Boldt to proceed with caution.

Daphne stepped closer to the tangle of tubes and wires and said the patient's name softly. Maria's eyelids strained open, followed a moment later by recognition.

Boldt's overwhelming sense of concern momentarily prevented him from speaking. He felt painfully reminded that homicide cops rarely deal with the living.

'We promise to come right to the point,' Boldt informed the patient, stepping closer, so he could meet her now haunted brown eyes.

'Something has come up,' Daphne jumped in, 'that requires clarification.'

Sanchez's eyes never left Boldt. He felt they somehow held him responsible, though he wasn't sure for what. He knew that Sanchez somehow understood their visit was at his initiation, that the questions would come from him. And so she waited. She has no choice, he thought.

'Are you okay to answer some questions?' Boldt asked.

The eyelids closed and reopened, eyes looking right. How, he wondered, could something as simple as blinking one's eyes become so labored and difficult?

Boldt leaned closer. He could smell medication and hear the rhythmic efforts of the respirator. 'Among your cases prior to your assault was the burglary of the Brooks-Gilman residence in Queen Anne.'

'Yes,' she answered with an eyes-right.

Boldt felt a slight flutter in his chest. The initials MS: Maria Sanchez.

He asked, 'Had you identified a suspect?'

'No,' came her reply, though clearly with great difficulty.

'Lou,' Daphne said, correcting herself to, 'Lieutenant. I think she's too tired for this right now.'

Boldt ignored Daphne, remaining focused on Sanchez. 'Do you believe your assault had anything whatsoever to do with your investigation?'

Maria clearly struggled. With her condition, or with the question? Boldt wondered. An exasperating thirty seconds passed before her eyes fell shut and then reopened. 'Yes,' came the answer. But this was followed by a 'no,' as well, and Boldt took to this to mean she didn't know, couldn't be sure.

Boldt gasped.

'Lou!' Daphne whispered sharply.

'Had you made some progress on the case?' Boldt asked.

Again Daphne attempted to stop him.

The eyes blinked open: yes.

'But not a suspect,' he repeated for his own benefit, his mind racing, his connection with this woman nearly visceral. 'Evidence?'

'Yes.'

'Did others know about this possible evidence?' he queried.

She paled another shade or two, if that were possible. Whatever the monitors were saying, Daphne didn't like it.

'You're going to have a nurse in here in a minute,' Matthews warned. 'I'm asking you to stop.'

Boldt couldn't stop. Not when he was so close. He asked, 'Had you told anyone about this new evidence?'

Sanchez stared at the ceiling. No eyelid movement. No answer. He heard footsteps, voices, and then the door swung open.

But Boldt still didn't give up. He leaned into Sanchez, getting as close to her as he could and asked, 'Did you tell anyone who was out on strike that you were working a burglary case?' He added, 'It's extremely important to the investigation that I know this.'

'That's it!' Daphne announced, coming around the bed and taking Boldt by the arm. 'Come on! We're out of here before they throw us out.'

'One more minute.'

'Oh, my God,' he heard Daphne gasp.

Boldt turned around to greet the nurse or doctor, unprepared for who had entered the room. The normally cool and collected Sergeant John LaMoia stood straight and rigid, as surprised as they were. 'What are you doing here?' Boldt asked.

TEN

'She's Hispanic, Sarge,' a macho LaMoia said coolly as if this explained something.

Boldt had bullied them into a nurse's lounge for the sake of privacy. The room smelled of Danish and was lit like a supermarket. Two Dave Barry columns were taped to the wall by the microwave. Someone had scratched out a NO SMOKING sign and changed it to NO CHOKING.

'It was a little overheated, in and out of bed.'

'How long has it been going on?' Boldt asked.

LaMoia shrugged.

Boldt fumed. LaMoia manipulated the world around him in a way Boldt couldn't, even if he wanted to. LaMoia got away with this kind of thing all the time.

What you saw of LaMoia was what you got: pressed blue jeans, carefully coifed, brown curly hair that nearly reached to his shoulders, deerskin jacket, silver rodeo belt buckle, porcelain white smile, oversized mustache. And Attitude. He carried it in his walk, his posture, his dark eyes. His confidence surfaced behind a soft-spokenness. He was a hell of a cop. Somewhere between a fraternity brother and a war buddy for Boldt. A former protégé who took what he wanted from life, he'd made himself the stuff of legend around Public Safety, both for his sexual prowess and his abilities as a detective. He'd disappointed Boldt greatly when he'd called in sick at the start of the Flu.

Women found the package appealing, something Boldt would never fully understand. The Attitude accounted for some of it, but not as much as people believed. Boldt thought it was more the man's soft brown eyes and the vulnerability they often expressed – puppy eyes, pure and simple. Maria Sanchez had fallen. She wouldn't be the last.

'I heard Bobbie Socks was asking around about her squeeze,' LaMoia offered. He meant Gaynes. 'I think you can take the squeeze off your list of suspects, Sarge. You're looking at him.'

He continued to refer to Boldt by the man's former rank, the same rank LaMoia now wore. Like a coach and a player, these two had a history that promotions couldn't ruffle and others couldn't explain.

'If you felt anything for her *at all*, you'd have come back on the job,' Boldt complained. 'What's that about?'

'I came up through the front seat of a radio car, Sarge. I still drink beer with the guys wearing unis. Hit balls at batting practice with them. My name's on the guild roster. The chief is wrong about this. I gotta stand up for that. You can see that, can't you?'

'You and Sanchez. How long?' Boldt repeated, knowing they could argue the Blue Flu all night long.

'We've been seeing each other about a month now.'

Although the department didn't expressly forbid relationships between officers, it discouraged them. No 'involved' officers could work the same division and were more often exiled to separate precincts, sometimes having their careers destroyed in the process. The credo 'Personal lives do not mix with police lives' hung on the lips of every superior.

'And how long were you going to sit on this relationship?'

'I'm here, and I'm talking. Right?'

Daphne snorted. 'We *caught* you!' She said, 'A lot of good you're doing Maria on the sidelines.'

'Maybe I'm doing more than you think,' LaMoia said.

'Working the cop bars for information, I suppose,' she offered derisively.

'Anybody angry at her about her dating a *gringo*?' Boldt asked.

'I knew you were going to ask that! God damn it, Sarge!'

'Family? Fellow officers?' In a city with a large population of Asians, Hispanics seemingly suffered under extreme prejudice. Tensions flared on the force between uniforms from time to time. Boldt didn't want to face the possibility that Sanchez's assault might have been racially or relationship motivated – a hate crime – and therefore disconnected from his current line of investigation.

'Nothing like that,' LaMoia promised. 'Besides, we kept it quiet. Neither of us wanted a transfer across town.'

'You're sure?'

'This is me, Sarge.'

'That's why I'm asking,' Boldt said. LaMoia made trouble for himself. From captains to meter maids, he'd made the rounds, suffering suspensions and reprimands. Miraculously, he had not only kept his badge, but had managed to advance to squad sergeant in the face of rumor, innuendo, and outright scandal. Boldt had managed to keep LaMoia's affair with Captain Sheila Hill quiet, or LaMoia would have been forced off Boldt's CAPers squad. Both Hill and LaMoia owed him for that. Boldt rarely collected on such debts, though right now he felt tempted to pressure LaMoia back onto the force.

Boldt said, 'So let me ask you this: You know anything about this burglary investigation she was working?' LaMoia twitched, belying his outward calm. Boldt knew he had scored. 'John?' Boldt inquired.

LaMoia maintained eye contact with Boldt. Something begged to be spoken but did not reach the sergeant's lips. Standing from his chair, LaMoia said, 'You two take care of yourselves,' and hurried from the room. Boldt called after him, but his voice fell upon deaf ears.

'What was *that*?' Daphne asked, a tinge of fear in her voice.

'He knows something about Sanchez but is afraid to tell us,' Boldt whispered, wondering once again if Liz and the kids were safe, even tucked away miles from home. John LaMoia wasn't afraid of anything or anyone, so why the sudden change in attitude?

ELEVEN

Anthony Brumewell struggled through another dinner alone. When the phone rang, the balding man was in the middle of eating some seashell pasta and broccoli in a pool of yogurt and butter covered with packaged parmesan – plastic cheese, he called it – and drinking from a can of Lite beer. Reading the *Seattle Times'* sports page, he cursed in the general direction of the phone as it rang. Annoyed, he nonetheless stood up and answered: He didn't get all that many calls, after all.

'Hello?'

'Mr Anthony Brumewell?'

'Speaking. Who is this?' He tentatively identified the call as a phone solicitation, a spike of indignation welling up and working toward boil. Didn't call me Tony, he thought. Other voices in the background. Keyboards clicking.

The words of the man on the other end were rushed though clearly, carefully rehearsed. 'I'm calling on behalf of Consolidated Mutual Insurance, Mr Brume-well. *Before* you hang up, you should know that, without obligation, we're offering you *two free tickets* to the movie of your choice—'

Anthony Brumewell considered himself a film buff, even if he mostly saw these films by himself. Did two free tickets mean two different films, or two tickets to the same film? This meant a world of difference to him, and he assumed the latter, which accounted for the receiver heading back for the cradle, the salesman's voice barely audible through the tiny earphone. He stopped himself from hanging up . . . *Two free tickets to the movie of your choice.*

'Two tickets to one film,' he asked, 'or one ticket to two films? And you should know there's a big difference to me.'

'However you would like to use the tickets,' the salesman answered.

The man had won another minute of his time. 'Go ahead, I'm listening,' he said. In fact, he was holding the receiver an inch away from his ear, as if this represented less commitment on his part.

'At the end of this phone call Consolidated Mutual will *guarantee* a fifteen percent reduction when compared to your current homeowner's policy. *Absolutely guaranteed!*'

'The tickets. And I got to warn you, I'm this close to hanging up on you.'

'Two free tickets at any Pantheon theater, arranged electronically for pickup at the theater's new automated ticket teller for the movie – or movie*s* – of your choice, at the time of your choice, on the day of your choice.'

'Two free tickets. Two different films.' Brumewell made it a statement.

'Yes. Absolutely, yes!'

'Any Pantheon theater?'

'One second here . . .' Brumewell heard the sound of a keyboard even louder – his salesman was typing. 'Seattle . . . Wallingford . . . I'm showing eleven Pantheon theaters in three different locations within ten miles of your residence.'

'I'm aware of the Pantheon theater chain,' Brumewell said knowingly, wanting the idiot on the other end to get to the point. He eyed his cooling seashells and briefly thought about the fact that these phone solicitation people knew too much about you and used it against you at every turn. 'Could I use the tickets as early as tonight?'

'Tonight would work, certainly. Once we've completed the agreement. Any night you choose.'

'The "agreement"? Okay, what's the catch?'

'Consolidated Mutual would like you to complete a very brief survey, which I can go over with you now, if you wish. After the satisfactory completion of that survey, the tickets – and the guaranteed savings on your homeowner's policy – are yours. Or, if you prefer, we can arrange for the tickets at a later time. The offer is good for three months.'

'A survey? A phone survey? That's it?'

'That's all. No obligation whatsoever, and a *guarantee*—'

Brumewell chimed in, 'I got that, okay? Now we gonna get down to this survey or what? How much time are we talking about anyway? My dinner is getting cold here! How come you people always call at dinnertime?'

'We can do the survey now, certainly, sir. That would be fine. Or, I could call back, if you would prefer.'

'Nah . . . My dinner's probably already cold anyway. Go ahead. How long did you say?'

'Seven to ten minutes, sir. Some questions about your coverage is all. You may find it worthwhile to have a copy of your current homeowner's policy in front of you, though that is not required by any means.'

'I'll pass on the policy.'

'We'll have it done in no time.'

'Okay . . . Okay . . . Let's get on with it.' Brumewell eyed the microwave. Dinner could wait.

TWELVE

As he stepped out of his battered, department-issue Chevy, Boldt immediately sensed that something was out of place. A moment later the same sensation registered as relief – the neighbor's dog was not directly on the other side of the rotten fence greeting Boldt after a long day of work. Instead, he was barking furiously at the far corner of their shared property – thankfully a decent enough distance away to reduce the ear damage.

The Boldt driveway led past the left of the house to a detached garage. Liz's spanking-new Ford Expedition typically won the inside parking while the Cavalier was relegated to the elements, where it rightfully belonged. But with Liz and the kids at the Jamerson home, Boldt nosed the front bumper to within a foot of the garage door and parked with the engine running. He didn't carry a clicker. He would have to trip the automatic door from inside the garage. His watch read 11:00. Suddenly it hardly seemed worth parking the thing in the garage for a few brief hours while he attempted sleep. He killed the engine and pocketed the keys.

Though he'd been preoccupied with the Sanchez case and now Brooks-Gilman, he had nonetheless put in some time on other cases, including a teen shooting at a drugstore. Just as he was leaving the precinct, he sent off a second department-wide E-mail requesting information on any of Sanchez's activities or known cases prior to her assault. But he wasn't holding his breath.

Neither was that damn dog. The thing was suddenly berserk with the barking – wild to where Boldt shouted, 'Shut up!' loudly enough to hope his neighbors would hear. If his own kids had been home, they would have been sleeping. That seemed reason enough for the reprimand. *Eleven o'clock*, he thought. *Gimme a break!*

The back door to his house, just ten to fifteen yards away, suddenly felt much farther. His neighbor's fence was to his left; the garage, directly in front of his car, blocked his way to the back porch, forcing him to come around the rear bumper. Three sides of the box were closed to him – his only egress to the street. He wasn't sure why any of this mattered; perhaps it had something to do with the blood-curdling yelps of that annoying dog and its steady approach up the fence toward Boldt. The air felt electric. Adrenaline charged his system. *What the hell?* he wondered.

Someone jumped him from behind. Someone big. Someone strong who'd probably come up along the narrow space between garage and fence, because that barking dog was now immediately on the other side of that fence. Boldt's brain kicked in: muggings were up a hundred and fifty percent since the walkout.

The chokehold was decisive: Boldt's neck in the crook of an elbow, enough pressure to slow the blood to his brain and air to his lungs. A stinging rabbit punch below and behind his right ribs. He heard his gun thump to the driveway.

Another person to his right. Big, and broad-shouldered. Too dark to see faces. Or maybe masks – he wasn't sure. They meant business. Another rabbit punch. More pressure on his windpipe.

A hand found his wallet. It registered in him again that he, a cop, was being mugged. But his body felt hard and frozen. He was in no shape to put up much resistance. Another devastating blow found his side. Caught a rib. Maybe broke it. A hand slipped down his pants side pocket and pulled out some bills and change. He took another charge of voltage to his gut and weakened. One or two more like that and he'd be throwing up blood.

A third man appeared to his left – or had the second simply moved? Boldt caught sight of a black balaclava covering this one's face. The next abdominal blow buckled him forward, further choking him and thrusting him toward unconsciousness. Down there by his own shoes he saw a pair of gray and brown Nike running shoes, one of the curved logos partly torn off.

He raised his head. It *was* a third guy, and this one carried a baseball bat, its polished aluminum winking in the ambient street light. Boldt thought that a hospital bed might be wishful thinking. This guy seemed intent on a home run to the head.

The neighbor's crazed dog sounded ready to climb the fence.

The dog! What little strength Boldt still had lay in his legs. He rocked back into the chokehold and simultaneously pushed off his car, driving the man behind him into the fence. The chokehold faltered. Boldt broke the hold and spun around. Either the baseball bat or more fists found his upper back – his chest and lungs felt stunned, his right arm numb. He was going down.

The man who'd lost the chokehold around Boldt's neck wanted it back, and now danced around Boldt in an ungainly step, using the fence to pin him in. Boldt took advantage of this human shield, protecting his abdomen by leaning over. At the same time, he kicked the rotten fence like one of the kids in the park practicing penalty kicks. The bat hit a single to first base, using his shoulder as the ball. The old plank fence had seen endless winters of relentless rain, had stood witness to days, weeks, even months of it without a single ray of sunshine to dry it out. Boldt's second kick split it open. The black shiny nose of the angry creature with the gleaming white teeth poked through, quicksilver saliva raining from its gums.

The chokehold reinstated itself with authority, and Boldt gagged and choked. He felt a glove against his ear and pressure began to twist his neck to the right. He kicked the fence again as the man behind him attempted to drag him away from that wall. Extremely strong, Boldt thought. No junkies, these three.

He kicked a larger hole through the rotting wood, this time big enough for the thing's entire bearlike head to poke through. That limited success provoked further enthusiasm from the dog. He took over for Boldt. The hole widened even more.

'K-9,' a voice warned from behind. The baseball bat found the dog, bouncing off as if it had hit a stone statue. The dog clearly took umbrage at the use of an aluminum bat on its head. It shrugged and wiggled forward, enlarging the hole and making progress through it. The dog's entire head popped through, ears and all, followed by the shoulders. Splinters of rotten wood rained out onto the Boldt driveway. He was some kind of hybrid – bred for teeth and head and muscle. An oak body, but flexible. And fast.

Perhaps Rin Tin Tin had been trained to identify the victim versus the assailant – perhaps it was a matter of posture, but the four-legged trained killer went straight for the calf of the man holding Boldt, who was released in a nanosecond and purposefully fell to the ground, both to distinguish himself from the others and in hopes of retrieving his weapon.

The man cried out as those jaws tore into him and ripped flesh.

Boldt felt blindly around the blacktop for his gun, the fervent growling like a wind in his ears. A dull thump of that baseball bat won a whimpering whine and a momentary relapse as the dog considered the time zone. Footsteps fleeing. Car doors thumping shut. At least one engine starting. Ferocious barking as the dog regained his bearings and ran down the drive in pursuit. Tires screeching. Boldt tried to roll over, hoping to catch a car profile or even the license plate, but his body belonged to Pain, and Pain alone. He gasped for air. A huge, wet tongue found his face. 'Good boy,' Boldt said, more than a little afraid of the animal. 'Good boy.'

His right ear rang like an alarm clock sounding in a distant room – he'd been struck in the head with the bat and was bleeding buckets, the way only head cuts can bleed.

'Good God,' a man's voice said.

His neighbor, the owner of the dog.

'Police,' Boldt groaned, finally able to straighten up. He fished for his ID wallet, but his attackers had apparently taken this along with his wallet and money. 'I live here,' he managed to cough out. 'Neighbors.'

'Don't move! I'll call!' The man took off at a run. The dog followed, probably expecting a Tasty Chew.

'No!' Boldt stopped him. He lay there in the dark, the smell of the rotting fence and his own blood over-whelming him. He didn't want a 911 call. He didn't want the press getting hold of a cop getting mugged. An inquiry. Reports. Paperwork. Invasion of privacy. He didn't want to worry Liz, didn't want her arguing for him to take sick leave – thinking that maybe that had been the intention of his muggers, and not wanting to face that right at that moment. 'I could use a little help here,' he said. He needed to patch himself up and think this through.

Daphne, he thought, as his neighbor attempted to help him to his feet, and he felt the effort like a bone-raw punishment.

THIRTEEN

Daphne wore tight blue jeans and a caramel sweater that complemented her dark eyes. With the sleeves of the sweater pulled up, she looked like a woman who meant business. The twisted silver bracelet signaled she wasn't at work. Boldt figured that she had plenty of other such leftover trinkets from her courtship with Owen Adler – the man would have bought her the Space Needle if it might have guaranteed her love for him.

She switched on Boldt's bedside lamp and leaned in close and studied him. It seemed strange to see a woman other than Liz in this bedroom. It even inspired guilt in him, despite the pain.

'Take your shirt off,' Daphne ordered him.

'I don't think so. The last time I had my shirt off with you—'

'Take it off and sit up on the bed or I'm getting in my car and going home.'

'Maybe that's best.'

She asked, 'Are you sure there isn't something broken?' His ribs and chest carried crimson blotches and eerie blue bruises. She gently touched one or two and Boldt winced with the contact.

'Not exactly positive,' he said. The ear had been patched up with a Band-Aid used as a butterfly.

'Turn around,' she instructed.

'I just love it when you boss me around,' he teased.

'Now!'

He obeyed. 'I'm amazed you can breathe. And this one, this one's right on the kidney. Have you peed yet?'

'What?!'

'Are you peeing blood, Lou?'

'No.'

'You need to see a doctor.'

'At which point I'll have to report a mugging. At which point I'll have twenty reporters camped on my front lawn and ringing my phone off the hook. No, thanks.'

'You really need to see a doctor,' she repeated.

'No.'

'What about Dixie?'

'His patients are all dead,' Boldt replied. Dr Ronald Dixon, chief medical examiner for King County, was one of Boldt's closest friends.

'Lie back,' she advised. 'I'm going to pour you a hot bath, feed you some aspirin, make some tea and call Dixie. When you're out of the bath, I'm driving you down to the ME's and he's going to look you over. They have X-ray there, access to the hospital. Fair enough?'

'It's not fair at all.'

'Or I walk out now and leave you to patch yourself up.'

'Sounds fair to me.' He lay back, every bone, every muscle complaining. He wasn't sure he could sit up again without some help. 'That's extortion, you know?'

'Do you want bubbles?' she asked, heading into the bathroom.

'Ha, ha!' he replied.

'Is that a yes or no?'

'Yes, please,' he confessed. 'The eucalyptus.'

'That's just so the bubbles hide you when I deliver the tea. Mr Modest.'

'Damn right. That is, unless you're going to get in the bath with me and scrub my wounds?'

Mocking him, she said, 'In your dreams!' She started the water running. He could only hear it out his left ear.

Boldt was thinking: sometimes you are, yes.

The Medical Examiner's office, in the basement of the Harborview Medical Center, was eerily quiet when empty of Doc Dixon's staff.

Dixie pronounced Boldt 'reasonably intact and still alive.' He added editorially, 'If you had come in as a cadaver, I'd have guessed you had jumped from a moving train, or fallen from a very high ladder.'

'That's my story and I'm sticking to it,' Boldt said softly, finding it too painful to speak. The pain grew inside him, like roots of a tree trying to find water.

'I could write you a couple of prescriptions. Pain. Sleep.'

'No, thanks.'

Daphne said, 'Maybe just write them anyway.'

It hurt too much to object. 'Listen to the little lady,' Dixie said.

'How's Liz anyway?' Dixie asked, his back to them as he wrote out the prescriptions. Was there innuendo in that question? Boldt wondered.

'Healing rapidly. She doesn't like to discuss it.'

'When do you tell her about this?'

'Not yet,' Boldt answered.

Daphne mocked, 'He doesn't want to go through the paperwork.'

'Uh-huh,' Dixie said.

'Who needs another case to investigate?' Boldt reasoned.

'That was a baseball bat,' Daphne said, as Dixon once again studied the ear.

Boldt mumbled, 'K-9.'

'What's that?' Dixon asked, still probing the damaged ear.

'Since when does a mugger call a dog a K-9?'

'Uh-oh,' Daphne said. 'I smell a conspiracy theory coming.'

Boldt asked, 'Okay, so it's a mugging. So why not take off once they had my stuff? Why stay to punish me with the baseball bat?'

'I thought that since the Flu, assaults like this are up,' Dixie said.

'Dozens,' Daphne answered.

'True enough,' Boldt agreed.

'Blood in the urine?'

'No.' Boldt felt Daphne's stare.

'You want to watch for that as well as dark stool.'

'So noted.'

'And I want to hear about it immediately.'

'Affirmative.'

'You got lucky here.'

Boldt winced. 'Yeah, I'm feeling like a real winner.'

'No cop would ever do such a thing to another cop, Lou. Sickout or not, I just don't see it,' Dixie said. 'That brick? Sure. Some name calling? Some harassment? You bet. But this? Just to keep you off the job?'

'I guess you're right,' Boldt admitted. 'Though it certainly crossed my mind.'

'Muggings are up,' Dixie repeated.

'I caught that the first time,' Boldt said.

'Can you have him stay with you?' Dixon asked Matthews. To Boldt he said, 'I understand your not wanting to alarm Liz before you know what's going on. I *know* you. But you can't stay alone at your house tonight. You just can't. Doctor's order. You need someone there. So, you either head over to the Jamersons—'

Boldt shook his head interrupting him.

To Daphne Dixie said, 'So you play nurse. Take his temperature every four hours, feed him more aspirin, if necessary. Call me if there are any rapid changes in his condition.'

'I need to call Liz,' he said from the passenger seat of Daphne's Honda.

'Now you're coming to your senses.'

'But I don't want to wake her up, and I don't want to frighten her.'

'That's out of my territory.'

'I'll wake everyone up and turn this into a huge deal and make promises to her that by the morning I'll break, because I'm not going to take time off – and that's what she'll want.'

'Lou—'

'If I take sick leave, what the hell's it going to look like?' He answered his own question. 'Flu. And I'm not going to give Krishevski a chance to play that card. No way.'

'And this has to do with calling Liz?' she questioned.

'It's complicated,' he said.

'It must be.'

'It can wait until morning,' he convinced himself. 'No need to wake anyone tonight,' he justified. 'Sleep it off and see how I'm doing.' He tested, 'Right?'

'This is your decision, Lou. Am I heading to Mercer Island – to the Jamersons?'

'No,' he answered. He leaned his head back. A moment later he was asleep and lightly snoring.

Daphne drove Boldt to her houseboat and made up the futon couch in the downstairs living area. Just north of the NOAH docks on Lake Union, the floating community of houseboats had taken on a mythical

90

reputation, raising property values fivefold in just eight years. Two thousand square feet of living space dressed in redwood shingle and asphalt roof, her houseboat had a red enamel wood stove and a sea kayak tied up to the deck outside her living-room window. There were ten other such homes on her pier, five to a side, a half dozen piers running up the lake's shoreline, little hen-houses of mailboxes out on the road where the mail-man knew each resident by name. Community still meant something here. The hippie feel of the past twenty years was giving way to Microsoft geeks who looked stupid smoking their cigars while sucking down microbrewery beer on warm summer nights, with the city's killer skyline forming a stage set in the near distance. An animosity existed surrounding the influx of the chip set, despite the lift it had given the economy. But the quaintness of her houseboat remained: small spaces, carefully decorated so as not to clutter, a faint trace of cinnamon incense, the sound of lake water lapping at the sides. If she ever sold, she'd be able to retire.

'Listen, I appreciate the gesture,' he said, 'but we can't do this.'

'Sure we can,' she replied, retrieving a pillow from her loft bedroom. Boldt lacked the strength to fight. He wanted sleep.

'I need sleep,' he complained.

'You need a bath and some tea. The sleep will come of its own accord.'

'I'm sure you're right.'

'I'm always right,' she said. 'You just don't always choose to listen.'

He awoke to the smell of tea and bagels, Daphne at work in the houseboat's small galley. She wore Lycra that fit her like plastic wrap. It was better than a sunrise, which he'd missed by an hour or more.

He didn't want to dress himself in the soiled and bloodied clothing from his beating. Anticipating this, she had left him an Owen Adler navy blue polo shirt, complete with the alligator, a pair of underwear and a pair of athletic socks. He didn't ask any questions. Their engagement had failed twice – enough said.

He showered, barely moving beneath the hot, hot water. There seemed to be pieces of him missing, others that shouted at full volume. He only heard things from half his head.

When he reached the galley, feeling refreshed but bludgeoned, he found a buttered bagel next to a jar of raspberry jam and a note that showed a stick figure running.

He ate outside, alone with a view of the morning activity on the lake – a seaplane landing in a gray-green knife stroke on the water's still surface; ducks flying in unison and veering north over Gasworks Park with its eerie skyline of pipes, reminding him of a refinery. He felt incredibly grateful to be alive. Odd that he had that dog to thank, that dog he had hated so much.

He took a bite of the bagel. It hurt his ear to chew. He searched the fridge for applesauce or yogurt – something that didn't require any chewing. He found something with 'live culture.' The thought disturbed him.

The city ran wild with crime while his coworkers willingly stayed home awaiting policy change. He couldn't see the sense in that, just as he couldn't under-stand why a trio of muggers would start working on him with a baseball bat. Unless they had found his badge and suddenly panicked or filled with hate over his being a cop. Hate corrupted even the best-intentioned mugger.

Hate corrupted everything in its path. And he felt filled with it all of a sudden, and not a verifiable target in sight.

FOURTEEN

'Where's Maria Sanchez gone?' Boldt asked, displaying his badge to the attending nurse at the nurses' station. He'd arrived to find her room unguarded and empty. He felt as if the floor had fallen out from under him.

The nurse checked the computer, and it troubled him that she wouldn't know this off the top of her head. 'She was transferred out of ICU to the third floor. Room 317.'

'Then she's better?' Boldt said hopefully, recalling that on his last visit she had definitely slipped backward.

'The move would indicate she's stable,' the nurse corrected.

'Any movement . . . other than the eyes?'

'You'll have to discuss that with her physician,' she advised.

Boldt rode the elevator, as he had coming in. For a man who normally took the stairs, this felt wrong, even privately humiliating. He shuffled down the hospital corridor, painfully aware that he probably looked too much like an old man. His father had raised him to believe there was no way around pain, only through it. Right now he was even aspirin free. He pushed his limbs to move, his ribs to tolerate breathing, his head to survive the throbbing.

He'd told Liz that he'd been mugged, his money and badge wallet stolen, that the ugly dog next door had probably saved his life. He'd been roughed up before in service to the city; thankfully Liz didn't berate him for electing to keep working. She wanted to see him. He promised to make that happen.

She didn't know that the muggers had used the term 'K-9' and that one of the three had intended to do a Mark McGwire on his head. No one knew – not even Daphne, exactly – that a part of him suspected the attack was a Krishevski telegram, like those strippers that knock on your front door and flash you on your fiftieth birthday. A Krishevski invitation to get a bad case of the flu. He needed a second opinion.

He checked in with the new security man outside the door and confirmed Sanchez's guest list, discovering that LaMoia visited at least once a day, usually well past the posted visiting hours, typically for long stints. He could imagine the man in the dark of the room, alone in a chair as Sanchez slept. Others would find this image of LaMoia inconceivable, but Boldt knew the man as few others did. The blinds were pulled, casting the overly sterile room in a haze. The room's television was tuned to a public access channel that ran ads while nasal-sounding classical music played from a small speaker strapped to her bed. He recalled the headphones in her bedroom, and thought he should bring her something better: Hamilton, Peterson, Monk or Gatemouth Brown.

'Stable,' he recalled the nurse explaining. Of course she was stable, he thought – they had her head bolted inside a contraption that looked like it was part of a medieval torture chamber. She couldn't move. Just to look at her brought a queasiness to his stomach.

He recalled a slightly younger Maria Sanchez standing at his front door, there to baby-sit the kids for the first time – alive, bright-eyed, but cautious and uncomfortable at the same time. Not wanting to mix the personal with the professional, but unable to resist the idea of being with kids. He suspected that was why she hadn't hung around for too long – their shields had gotten in the way. It certainly hadn't been out of any lack of rapport with the kids – they had loved her from the start. And that won any parent's heart, including his. Boldt had liked her right away. Had talked her up around the shop from that night forward. Had tried to open some doors for her, the way he once had for Gaynes. Maybe he'd had something to do with her moving quickly to plainclothes, maybe not. It no longer mattered. He felt anger over her present condition. He seethed.

Those eyes flashed out of the darkness. Open. Awake.

'Hey,' Boldt said, caught a little off guard to be in the room alone with her.

She blinked.

'More questions. You up to it?' He half hoped she might refuse him. He felt at odds with himself over using this woman as a witness.

Eyes-right.

'Maybe tough questions,' he cautioned.

She shut her eyes and reopened them. Eyes-right. 'Okay.'

Boldt approached the overhead television and turned down its volume. Sanchez locked her eyes in a stare that reached past him. Not eyes-right, a 'yes,' nor eyes-left, a 'no.' Not a look that penetrated through him – thankfully. Her stare finally turned him around to face a chair. He pulled the chair up to the bed, now nearly eye-to-eye with her. She was tired of being looked down upon.

'Better?' he inquired.

Eyes-right. 'Yes.'

But it struck him as more than an answer, for her eyes

were soft and caring, filled with emotion he'd not seen since the first of their visits together. He remembered those same eyes from when they had first fallen upon his own children – they seemed to hold something very different now.

'Any better? Are you feeling any better?' No answer. She just stared. He wondered if she could feel any physical sensations at all. He agonized, right along with her.

'If I don't look right, if I don't sound myself, it's because I'm not. I was mugged last night.'

Her eyes seemed to focus and harden, but her face didn't change – it couldn't. That struck Boldt as the worst prison of all. 'And what I'm thinking, Maria – Officer Sanchez,' he corrected, 'is not something a peace officer wants to think. Not ever. So my apologies up front, but I need to ask you this, because we share these assaults now, you and I. Mine was headed badly – very badly indeed – until a neighbor's dog broke it off. So I'm counting myself on the lucky side.' Boldt continued, 'There are two possibilities. One is that I was mugged, although I've got to tell you: we haven't seen a mugging in my neighborhood in seventeen years. The recent muggings we've been seeing in the other parts of the city – and we've seen a lot of them in the past week – have been downtown in parking lots and garages, at sports events, movie theaters, convenience stores – out in public. They haven't been in people's backyards. We had a burglary where a woman was knocked down-stairs, but that hardly qualifies.'

'The other possibility,' Boldt continued, 'is what you might call involuntary Flu. Certain people might have thought that I was acting a little too healthy and disrupting the current efforts of some of our brothers in blue. They sent me a brick through my window as a warning and I ignored it. I stayed on the job and got assaulted in my own yard. And now I can't hear very well out of my right ear and it hurts to breathe. So what I'm wondering . . . Before your assault, had you received a brick or any kind of warning, anything at all, suggesting you cool it for a while?'

'No,' she replied, with her eyes.

Boldt couldn't think of another way to put it. He just had to ask. 'Maria, did you know the person who did this to you?'

'No,' she signaled.

'If you were afraid at first, afraid because you suspected a fellow officer, afraid of Matthews and me because we carry badges and you didn't know who to trust, I'm hoping now – now that you know what happened to me – that now you can trust me. So my first question is whether you believe you were attacked by someone who came to rob you, by a burglar.'

She stared over at Boldt for a long time, her head gripped mechanically. Her eyelids fluttered shut and opened. 'Yes,' came her answer. But her eyelids closed again and reopened with eyes-left. 'No.'

'You're unsure. Is that right?'

'Yes.' Her efforts were labored.

He scribbled a question mark in his notebook alongside the question.

'You were working a burglary before the assault. Brooks-Gilman over in Queen Anne. It was assigned after the sickout. Do you remember the case?'

'Yes.'

'Do you think your assault had anything to do with that burglary investigation?'

'Yes. No.' *Maybe*.

'So let me ask you: Do you think your assault had anything to do with your work?'

She closed her eyes and held them shut.

'Maria?' Boldt's heart beat faster. He repeated her name. He said, 'Is it possible that your assault had something – anything – to do with, or was a result of, your police work?'

'Yes.' Then, 'No.' *Maybe*.

'You're doing well, Maria,' Boldt said. 'Can we keep going?'

'Yes.'

'Okay then.' He glanced through the pages of his notebook and moved a question forward onto his list. A part of him didn't want to keep going. A part of him just wanted to leave this poor woman alone, to deal with, what for her, were more urgent problems. Why, he wondered, did he feel so pressed to squeeze something out of her right now?

'Is it safe to say that you believe your assault *may* have been at the hands of a fellow officer?'

Her eyelids fluttered shut. When they reopened, her eyes were locked onto Boldt's, and he began to feel all watery and weak inside. She wasn't going to commit to that, not yet. She was still as terrified of the idea as he was. Cop on cop. Strike or not, it seemed inconceivable.

She wasn't looking directly at him anymore. Now her eyes were fixed below the horizon of his gaze. Something else. Lower. He looked around the room for what held her attention. Seeing nothing that made sense, he wondered about her stare. Did she just want him to stop? Had he and his questions pushed her further toward frustration? Was he just giving her another problem to handle?

'Listen,' he began. 'I probably shouldn't be pressing you so hard.' He continued to try to figure out what it was – if it was anything – that had caught and held her attention, but he could see that her eyes had become more frantic, jumping to make contact with him and then dropping back down, locked onto whatever it was. *She's telling me something*, he realized, feeling a tension in the air, still searching. The floor . . . the wall behind him . . . his own right hand . . . his keys . . .

Liz had pointed out that he had a nervous habit of constantly fiddling with his keys. He barely even realized he was doing it. It was just something to do. Motion. Like a smoker rolling the ash of a burning cigarette.

He drew the keys out of the pocket and Maria's eyelids fluttered shut and opened, eyes right. 'Yes!' those eyes shouted, now focused onto him with a burning intensity.

'What about the keys?' he asked with growing excitement.

She didn't answer, her gaze still fixed on the keys and key chain.

'My keys?' he asked.

'No.'

Now her eyes seared him. His own eyes stung.

'Your keys?'

'Yes.'

The mechanical efforts of the respirator moved in time with her chest as it rose and fell with ungainly symmetry, its exhale a long, peaceful, artificial sigh.

'What about your keys?' he wondered aloud, trying to make sense of it. He held his up, until they rang like tiny chimes and sparkled in the glare of the tube lights. Again, her eyes lit up with anticipation and even fright. She didn't need to tell him anything more – keys were somehow significant in what she was trying to communicate.

He asked her directly, 'Are the keys important?'

'Yes.'

'You left your garage. You were headed to the back door, and you had your keys.'

She closed her eyes – he thought in frustration – and held them shut. When she reopened them, they bore into him.

'I'm off track,' he whispered.

'Yes,' she answered, the effort draining her. He sensed her fatigue, which she was fighting desperately. They both knew he was losing her. She closed her eyes to rest, this time for longer.

'Your keys,' he repeated, feeling he was working her too hard.

She struggled to open her eyes. 'Yes.'

'The robberies? The burglar made copies of the keys? Something like that?' And then he thought he knew where she was headed. 'Whoever did this was *inside* your house. He'd gotten your keys somehow – and he was *inside* waiting for you?'

'No.' Her frustration seethed from her eyes.

'I'm sorry,' he mumbled. The great detective can't string three useful questions together. He felt impotent. 'Damn it all!' he muttered.

Her eyes fluttered, sagged shut, and failed to reopen.

'Maria? Maria?' he gently tested. It took him a moment to realize the interview was over. Maria had fallen asleep.

FIFTEEN

'I'm not sure I see the point of this,' Daphne said, hurrying down the hallway toward Property. Boldt had rousted her out of her office.

'The point is,' Boldt said, pain ringing through him, 'her keys are important. How, I'm not sure. You're lead on her case, which means I don't get her keys out of Property without your signature.'

She held a door for him. He said, 'I'm beginning to believe my assault and hers are linked: that's what led me back to her hospital room. Now this – these keys, I've got to face facts: People don't get mugged in my neighborhood, Daffy.'

'I know that. So if they weren't muggers, who were they?'

'Maybe we don't want to find out.'

'The cop in me doesn't want to believe any cop would do this to another cop. Not ever.'

'You think I like it?' Boldt asked.

'The psychologist – she's a different story,' she went on. 'There's resentment here. Frustration on the part of the Fluers. Venting those pent-up emotions is a natural progression, a natural expression.'

'But the sickout is working.'

She agreed. 'To us it is, because we're worn out by it. But to those cops now on the outside?' she questioned. 'To them – and to the public too – we're wounded, we're down on one knee, but we're not on the mat.

We're not raising white flags. That could be the source of a lot of anger.'

'Violence?' he asked her.

She shrugged and reluctantly nodded. 'I'd rate it as a possibility,' she confirmed. 'But for the record: I'd put Maria's assault down as a burglary gone bad; your little skirmish, I'm not so sure.'

'So we listen to the victim and we chase the evidence,' he reminded her. Boldt's law of investigation. In the Sanchez case, chasing the evidence now meant a certain set of keys.

As its senior sergeant, Krishevski ran the evidence storage facility's daily operations, claiming the day shift for himself and his three-man squad. As guild president, Krishevski had caught a bad case of the Blue Flu, as had his squad, leaving what remained of the night duty and graveyard shifts to handle things.

Ron Chapman, a uniformed sergeant with two years less seniority than Krishevski, looked haggard. Barrel-chested, potbellied and pale, he looked as much like an Irish potato farmer as a cop in pressed blues. Boldt knew Chapman casually though not socially, having spent years passing the man in the hallways and seeing him working behind the Property room's wire-mesh screens in the process of cataloging case evidence. Any field detective worth his salt knew any and all of the officers who manned Property – the repository of all physical evidence from active and uncleared investigations and arraignments that had yet to reach trial.

As lead on the case, Daphne signed off for the Sanchez evidence at the cage, and Chapman retrieved it for her. A few minutes later, Chapman delivered the items in a sealed cardboard box that in turn contained a large plastic garbage bag kept shut by a wire twist that carried a tag bearing the case particulars. That tag had to be torn in order to open the twist and get to the contents. Daphne did so in front of Chapman, who held a computerized inventory of the bag's contents. She removed the woman's black leather jacket, now stained with chemicals used by the lab in an attempt to develop fingerprints. She held it up for both to see.

'I'm removing the jacket,' she noted.

Chapman said to Boldt, 'I got your E-mails about Sanchez.'

That won Boldt's interest.

'Thing about E-mail,' Chapman said, 'is they can trace it back to its source, you know?'

'You have something for me, Ron? You know anything about the Brooks-Gilman burglary?'

'Didn't say that, did I?'

'Was there any evidence collected in the Brooks-Gilman burglary?'

'Not that I know of.'

'May I see the log for the past two weeks?'

'Don't see why not,' Chapman said, typing for a moment before spinning the computer terminal to face Boldt and Daphne. Boldt checked his notepad for the date Sanchez had taken over the investigation for Shoswitz's flu-ridden burglary unit.

Boldt noticed that three days before her assault, Sanchez had visited Property both in the morning and the early evening. He counted four visits in all. But there was no case number listed, nor any victim name, which struck him as unorthodox at best. Ron Chapman's initials listed him as OD – the officer on duty for Sanchez's evening visit.

'What's with the lack of reference, Ron? No number. No name.'

'No kidding,' Chapman said, staring at Boldt in

nearly the same manner as Sanchez had stared. As if something were expected of him. As if he were supposed to pull this all together out of thin air.

'They're required,' Boldt reminded.

'Not always they aren't,' the man returned.

The statement confused Boldt. Since when wasn't a case number required for a Property visit? 'An officer can't just pay a visit and do his or her shopping,' Boldt said.

Chapman leaned toward the screen, like an inmate entertaining a visitor. He said faintly, 'Not all visits are recorded the same way.' He hesitated. 'These are tumultuous times,' he said, shooting Boldt another knowing look, clearly begging him to connect the dots.

Daphne announced formally, 'I'm searching the pockets of the leather coat.'

'That stuff's in here,' Chapman said, indicating a sealed manila envelope. He read from the label. 'Set of keys and a garage door opener.'

Boldt scrolled back through the listings. He didn't want to lose Chapman and the man's uncertain willingness to cooperate. 'How about a little help here, Ron?'

Daphne signed the manila folder and then opened it, dumping a set of keys and a clicker into her waiting hand. The keys and clicker had been dusted and fumed for latent prints, giving them a pale purple cast. Chapman swiveled the monitor back around and made notes in the computer log. Everything in its place.

But no case numbers alongside Sanchez's name. *Why?* Boldt had in his possession what he'd come for, but he was leaving with more questions than answers.

'Let me ask you this,' Boldt said to Daphne from behind the steering wheel of the Chevy. 'Since when does a uniform like Ron Chapman not walk in concert with Krishevski?'

'Bothers me too. Yes,' Daphne agreed.

'You're the psychologist.'

'Peer desertion?' she asked, looking for a cubbyhole. 'It would typically indicate a selfish motivation. Something personal, maybe. Retirement? Illness in the family? Some situation where the paycheck is deemed more important than the cause.'

'Then why cooperate with me at all?'

'It's troubling, I have to admit.'

'Then you thought that was strange back there,' Boldt said encouragingly.

'Unusual,' she said, choosing her own word. 'Unexpected.'

'He wanted to tell me something.'

'No,' she corrected. 'He wanted you to discover it.'

'Sanchez wanted that too,' he informed her. 'These keys. She was practically killing herself to help me figure this out, and I never did.'

'At least not yet,' she said, displaying the keys and letting them dangle.

He pulled the car to a stop, blocking Sanchez's driveway. 'I still can't forgive SID for parking in the driveway that night. Who knows what we might have missed?'

'Such as?'

'If it's burglary, robbery, whatever, this guy has to park somewhere. He's yarding in TVs, don't forget. Maybe he parked in the driveway. Maybe we might have lifted a tire pattern or something. Who knows?'

'*If?*' she questioned. 'Don't you hate this not knowing?'

'We know they got my wallet, and yet they stayed to finish me off. One of them used the term "K-9".'

'We also know there have been a dozen serious assaults since the Flu,' she reminded him.

'Right now, only these keys interest us.'

She quoted, 'Maintain focus and objectivity.' Boldt 101.

'Amen,' Boldt said, snagging the keys from her grasp and limping as he led the way to the Sanchez house.

'Okay,' he said, once inside. 'Let's review the inconsistencies.'

'I thought this was about the keys,' she complained. 'Can't we just try all the keys first?'

'It's your case,' he said, a little miffed. He passed her the keys. Attached to the ring was a black plastic bobble with a black button.

She sighed and gave in, saying, 'Most security systems were blocked. Hers was not. She was stripped and tied to a bed. The only other known assault was Kawamoto, and she was left alone.'

He added, 'Time of day was off. All the others were committed in broad daylight.'

'But all the burglaries involved high-end electronics, *including* Sanchez. Similar neighborhoods, similar MO: jewelry, silver, and other items left in plain view go untouched. How often does that happen?' Daphne walked them through the house, trying the keys on exterior doors. One key worked all the exterior doors. Three keys to go. She said, 'Are you going to explain how this guy bypassed the security systems?'

'He didn't. Not exactly,' Boldt answered.

'Are you going to make me beg?'

'I love it when you beg,' he said.

'You be careful what you ask for,' she said, trying a key out on a locked closet. She found one that fit. The closet was empty.

'Probably for renters,' Boldt said.

'So?'

Boldt said, 'The guy does this for a living, right? He knows damn well that home security systems dial out over the phone line. He scouts the place. He knows it's empty. So he calls the house just as he's going to hit it. The message machine picks up, engaging the line, which means it's now *busy*. The security system can't dial out. He's got a minute or more – however long the answering machine gives him – to break in. When he does, he busts up the system's siren and gets the phone physically off the hook.'

'Sweet. Except that siren is blasting from the minute he's through the door until he KOs it.'

'Those things false alarm all the time. As bad as car alarms. You think a neighbor's going to pay any attention if the thing stops within twenty or thirty seconds? No way.'

'Two keys unaccounted for,' she said. They'd been through the whole house.

'Garage?'

'Should be one of them,' she agreed.

They walked out back. The disturbed area in the grass was marked off and protected by yellow crime-scene tape. They reached the garage's side door, and the key fit. They opened it up and stepped inside.

Boldt said, 'All keys accounted for.'

'One left,' she said, indicating the smallest on the ring.

'You'll find it fits that dirt bike,' he said, pointing.

She slipped past the car into the far corner and tried the key just the same. When it fit, she said, 'You *do* impress the ladies, you know?'

'Do I?'

'Yes. Absolutely.'

'But I failed in my mission,' he pointed out. 'Why the keys?'

'Maybe you misread her?'

'Maybe.'

'If you'd asked me along,' she prodded, upset that he had not. She added sarcastically, 'But then again, it's only my case.'

She took the keys back. They'd been exchanging them back and forth like this, as if playing some kind of parlor game. Daphne took them, stepped toward the parked car and pushed the button on the key ring's bobble.

With both of them facing the car – a badly weathered Toyota – the garage door opened behind them. They spun around in unison.

She said, 'I figured it for the car.'

'Yes,' Boldt agreed, snatching the keys back and stopping the door mid-ascent. He pushed the button again, and the door started down.

Daphne was already digging in her purse by the time Boldt looked over at her. Her hand came out holding the clicker found in the pocket of Sanchez's leather jacket. She pointed it toward the door and squeezed. Nothing.

Boldt grabbed it from her. He aimed the clicker at the overhead garage door mechanism and depressed its button. Twice. Nothing. Again, he tried the small black clicker attached to the set of keys. Again, the door reversed direction.

Boldt and Daphne met eyes. She said, 'So it wasn't the keys after all.'

'No.'

'And you're thinking?'

'The obvious,' he answered.

'Who's it belong to?' she said, indicating the free-standing clicker.

'Exactly.'

'A boyfriend? Her parent's house? A sister? Someone she was house-sitting for?'

'One of the cases she was working?' Boldt suggested.

'I knew you were going there.' She sounded disappointed. She knew the time involved in going door to door to nine different homes.

'She wanted us to find this,' he reminded her, holding the clicker. Cherishing it.

'And now we have,' she said.

SIXTEEN

Boldt didn't like the look of the city streets. He could see the difference since the sickout: fewer pedestrians, anarchy at traffic lights, a pervasive restlessness. People walked faster and more determined, taking less time on street corners. There were few, if any, beat cops out here. No patrol cars. Attendance at Mariners games was off forty percent over the prior week, despite the new stadium. Benaroya Hall had hired a private security firm to patrol the area so that symphony patrons could reach their cars safely following a concert. The citizens of Seattle were scared, and for good reason – street crime was up double-digits in six days. The city was backsliding into the very urban problems it had previously managed to keep at arm's length. He followed the traffic out to Queen Anne, anticipation clouding his thoughts. Sanchez hadn't been trying to direct him to some boyfriend – he felt certain of this. The keys had led to the clicker; the clicker belonged to Brooks-Gilman, the burglary case she had signed off on. Or so his reasoning went. He felt certain of it. Or almost, anyway. Enough to talk Daphne into a drive to Queen Anne.

The Brooks-Gilman house had views of both Puget Sound and the downtown skyline. Before Boldt led the way up the walkway to the front door, he stood out on the street and tried the garage door clicker.

The door lifted open.

Daphne let out a small cheer. 'Sometimes,' she said, 'I actually get off on this stuff.'

Boldt said, 'We were stupid.'

'Were we?' she asked.

'In every case, the doors to the burglarized homes were reported locked. Even our own first officers put it down this way.'

She continued his thought. 'We wrote that off to doors being jimmied and owners panicking and locking up once they realized they'd been hit. But it wasn't that. It was that so few of us lock the door that leads into the house from the garage.'

Nodding, he pushed the clicker and stopped the garage door. 'Sanchez understood that. She saw the one point of vulnerability and pursued it.'

'But one still needs the clicker,' Daphne said. 'What? This guy steals them from the car's visor in car washes and parking lots?'

The garage door opened again, but this time Boldt had not triggered the device. He looked first toward his hand and then toward the house, and pointed to the silhouette of the woman standing at the mouth of the garage. 'She may be able to answer that,' he said.

Helen Brooks-Gilman. A hyphenate. A dot-com mom. Whole neighborhood was probably hyphenates, he thought. He attempted to return the clicker to the woman as he explained that detective Sanchez had been hospitalized and that he and Daphne had taken over the burglaries. She accepted the clicker, cautious until Daphne produced her ID wallet and Boldt unfolded a photocopy of his lieutenant's identification.

'You don't have a badge?' she inquired.

'My ID wallet was . . . stolen. It's a long story,' Boldt

answered, tempted to lift his shirt and show her his bruises.

Holding up the device, Daphne asked, 'Is this clicker yours?'

The woman invited them inside. 'It's a long story,' she answered, purposely matching Boldt's tone.

The interior was pastels and hardwoods. Programmers and internet CFOs took these 1930s clapboards and sunk a small fortune into flooring, moldings and windows. Boldt knew firsthand: he and Liz had done much the same to their place fifteen years earlier for a third the price, and a second mortgage they were still paying off.

'The first officer's report said there was no sign of forced entry,' Boldt said in a voice that bordered on impatient. He had a theory on that now; he needed it proved out.

Helen Brooks-Gilman wore a combination of REI and Nordstrom's. Tipped hair cut cleanly above her shoulders. A small Rolex, but a Rolex nonetheless. Leather deck shoes, though he doubted she sailed. 'Cup of coffee?'

Boldt declined the offer. Coffee went through him like acid. 'Were there, by any chance, any doors left unlocked?'

'No. It's funny. That's what the insurance people asked as well. All the doors have night latches, and we leave them that way all the time – with the buttons in. It can be inconvenient. For example, you take the trash out, and the kitchen door shuts behind you, and you need a key to get back in.'

Boldt asked, 'How about the door leading in from the garage?'

Helen Brooks-Gilman looked perplexed. 'Well, no. That's never locked. But the garage door is—' She caught herself, catching up to his reasoning. 'That's why the other detective wanted our spare remote.'

Boldt nodded. 'I think so, yes.'

'You loaned officer Sanchez the garage door opener?' Daphne asked.

Brooks-Gilman confirmed this with a nod. 'Our spare. She requested it.'

Boldt asked to see the garage and she showed them into the kitchen. Sub-Zero refrigerator and Viking range. He opened the door into a garage cluttered with gardening tools and sports equipment surrounding a gray minivan – the luxury model with leather and electric windows. He and Liz had looked at the same car, but couldn't go the four grand for all the bells and whistles.

'Your sheet lists a television and camcorder taken from your bedroom. A computer, wasn't there?'

'Our son's iMac.'

Boldt pulled out the white plastic tie from his pocket and asked, 'Any of these found since the theft?'

She looked a little stunned. 'Yes. In our bedroom. That's why I called back to you people in the first place.'

'And you got Detective Sanchez,' Daphne suggested.

'An operator took down my name and Detective Sanchez was the one who called me back.'

'And subsequently paid you a visit,' Boldt said.

Helen Brooks-Gilman explained, 'The strike had started. She explained to me she didn't typically work robberies.'

'Burglaries,' he corrected. 'And it's not a strike, it's a sickout.'

Daphne chided him with a single disapproving expression. She intervened. 'We need you to answer a couple more questions, Helen. We'd like you to sit down and get comfortable.' Brooks-Gilman led them to the kitchen table. This time she offered them decaf. They declined. Boldt and Daphne sat across the table from her so that they could measure her physical reactions as well as her facial expressions. Daphne continued, 'Detective Sanchez took your call, and then what?'

'She came over, as I mentioned. I gave her the thingy I'd found.'

'That would be the white plastic tie,' Daphne said.

'Yes, that's correct.'

Boldt said, 'And she looked around?'

'Top to bottom. She was very thorough. I liked that about her. She took it seriously. The other officer – the one who came after my 911 – he just wanted the forms filled out.'

'The garage?' he asked.

'Yes, she looked at the garage.'

'And then?' Daphne asked.

'She asked to borrow the clicker. She didn't say why and I confess, I didn't ask. She was doing her job. That was good enough for me.'

Boldt's turn. 'She asked you some other questions as well. Like who, if anyone, had serviced your home appliances recently. Pizza deliveries. That sort of thing.'

Daphne added, 'Any phone calls you'd received, especially any where the person on the other end hung up on you when you answered.'

'I've hung up on a few of them,' she told them. 'Dinnertime phone solicitations! My husband will talk to them – don't ask me why! – but I absolutely will not. I find the whole idea offensive.'

Boldt pushed her a bit more. 'As to the repairs . . . Washing machine . . . fridge . . . any deliveries?'

'She and I went over this, yes,' the woman answered. 'All I can tell you is what I told her: I have no idea how this guy picked us to rob, but it wasn't any of those ways. No deliveries. No strange phone calls – other than the usual phone solicitations.'

'You loaned her the clicker,' Daphne suggested. 'She said she'd return it?'

'Said she'd return it in a day or two. Yes.'

'Tech Services,' Boldt suggested to Daphne, who nodded. He suspected that would have been Sanchez's next stop. It would have been his.

Daphne apologized to the woman. 'I'm afraid we're going to have to borrow it again.'

SEVENTEEN

Boldt guessed right – Sanchez had in fact paid a visit to SPD's Tech Services and had asked a lab rat named Tina Ming a variety of questions about cloning garage door openers. Ming confirmed that duplicating the radio frequencies used by such a device was scientifically quite simple. They had not ended up providing Sanchez with a clone however, because their work had been delayed by the Flu. Ming suggested Boldt consult the FBI.

Flu or not, the FBI was never the fastest agency to respond. Boldt would seek solutions elsewhere. He thought he now understood where Sanchez had been headed: a black-market source for a cloned garage door opener. Nine of them, to be precise – over the course of the last several weeks. A way into homes otherwise believed locked up. If he could find that supplier and squeeze out a name of a buyer, he might have the repeat burglar – and quite possibly Sanchez's offender – behind bars by the end of the day. He felt pulled between two theories – cop on cop or burglary gone bad – but the solution to the Sanchez assault seemed paramount to both.

The apartment occupied the floor above the Joke's On You, Bear Berenson's comedy/jazz club that enjoyed an odd combination of a Happy Hour police crowd and a prime-time college clientele. Boldt pulled the Chevy down the back alley and parked, making sure to put the laminated blue POLICE–OFFICIAL BUSINESS card that would keep the tow trucks away. He hoped to only spend a few minutes with Bear, but the pot-smoking, angst-ridden, longtime friend could make a scenic drive out of the shortest errand. He practiced patience, preparing himself for an extended stay.

Required to address a white plastic box housing a badly scratched TALK button and a speaker grid that had inherited some chewing gum, Boldt gained admittance through a buzzing door jamb with Bear's distorted voice welcoming him. He climbed the long, dark stairwell, the smell of stale beer and cigarettes familiar to a man who occasionally worked the Happy Hour piano on the other side of the communicating wall. Where others might gag, Lou Boldt felt comfort. He had spent a lot of good hours at this bar, and its predecessor, the Big Joke. A few million notes had passed through his fingers here.

The steep stairs presented a challenge. His battered and painful body was still unwilling to climb. But he managed. Nearing the top landing, he smelled the weed. Knowing Bear, he had opened a window trying to air out the apartment, but his attempt had backfired and instead was blowing the smoke toward the stairwell. Boldt forgave him the habit, but asked that he not smoke in front of him, for obvious reasons.

'Sherlock!' Berenson had a smoker's rasp, a neatly trimmed black beard with gray streaks coming down like fangs, and something of a beer gut, maintained by the contents of the long-neck bottle gripped casually in his right hand.

'Live, and in person,' Boldt said.

'Tea?'

'You think I'd risk contamination?'

'You look a little *off*,' Bear said.

'And you a little sideways,' Boldt observed. He won a smile for that comment.

'I'm always sideways.'

'Sore is all,' Boldt explained. 'I've been dodging baseball bats lately.'

'Sit down before you fall down,' Berenson advised.

Bear loved an audience; he paced from side to side, as if working a stage.

Boldt said, 'I'd love to say it's a social call.'

'Did I forget to pay you or something?'

Boldt explained, 'It's more of a research visit.'

'Weed? Women? Retail sales?'

'Frankie,' Boldt said.

'Frankie?' Bear asked, wounded.

'I wouldn't ask if it wasn't important.'

'Frankie?' Bear repeated. He sucked down some beer and wiped his mouth.

'I'm not after him – even if he's involved. I promise him a free ride. A name is all I'm after. One name.'

'Are you paying?' Berenson asked.

'You're his agent now?'

'Just asking,' Bear replied.

'I'm paying,' Boldt answered.

Bear had a tendency to put himself in the middle of things, and no one wanted to get between Frankie and anything, including Boldt.

'Frankie isn't going to want *anything* to do with you – for obvious reasons. It had better be a shitload of money. Know what I mean?'

'A shitload of money,' Boldt agreed, 'and maybe I get the current charges reduced.'

'I've known the man a long time,' Bear said. 'It doesn't mean I know his current status with the PA. And I don't want to.'

'There's a woman officer in bad shape,' Boldt explained. 'Maybe Frankie can help with that.'

'I read the newspapers, you know?'

'So *Hooked on Phonics* actually works.'

'You're going to bite the hand that feeds you?' Bear added, 'You want a name. Is that all? Maybe I can get you the name myself.'

Boldt usually tended not to see the degree of Bear's intoxication. After years of friendship, he took him as he was. But now he saw that he was a little more stoned than usual, and decided to connect the dots for him. 'I'm interested in garage door openers.'

Berenson spit out some beer as he laughed.

'I've got to do this in person, Bear.' He offered, 'I'll give you a Happy Hour for free.'

Bear straightened up, took another pull off the beer, and said, 'No need to be rude. Since when do you and I buy favors off each other?'

Boldt suggested, 'Two hundred bucks and reduced charges. Run it by him, would you?'

'Garage doors.' A faint grin. Bear read the back of the beer bottle for useful information. He picked at the label. Boldt waited him out, knowing that stoned head of his was debating saying something or not. 'You be careful with Frankie,' he said. 'He'll have a blanket 'cross his lap. Never know what's under that blanket 'til it's too late.'

'Got it,' Boldt said. The expression reminded him of Bobbie Gaynes; she used it so often, she owned it. The only detective on his squad not to walk. He appreciated the loyalty in ways he would never be able to express. Berenson brought him back to the room with one long draw on the beer bottle and a thundering burp that apparently satisfied him.

'You want me to try to set it up now or later? Your call.'

'Sooner the better. Mind if I drift downstairs and play a couple numbers while you make the call?' Boldt asked. 'It's been a while.'

'Have I ever minded?'

'You know where to find me.'

'Yes, I do,' Bear said. 'At my piano, in my club, waiting for my phone call to my contact.' He added, 'You don't have a fence that needs whitewashing, do you?'

Frankie Maglioni filled the electric wheelchair from the waist up. A blanket covered his waist and withered legs, sucked dry from atrophy. Nine years earlier he had jumped from the third floor balcony of a Spanish-influenced estate as the security firm had breached the bedroom door. He'd landed on a steel air-conditioning unit, the impact snapping his spine like a twig and ending a successful career in cat burglary. Though never confirmed, he was believed to be the Dinner Bandit, a name gained for striking the wealthy elderly as they dined in their own house, a floor or two below. He was only convicted of the one crime, his sentence reduced because of the injury, but insurance claims accounted for seven hundred thousand dollars in missing jewelry over a three-year period, all of it attributed to the Dinner Bandit. He was now believed to be a fence.

He lived in a single-floor loft apartment that occupied the entire third floor of a former paste jewelry factory and was accessed by a freight elevator. Boldt slid open the elevator's wooden slats and introduced himself.

'We ain't never officially met,' the man said.

'No,' said Boldt.

'I guess because you're Homicide I'm told.'

'Most of the time.'

'But right now, no. You're standing in for Jorgenson and them.'

'I've got a Burglary case, yes,' Boldt informed him. 'And in case Bear didn't make it clear, I'm not after you. He broke a woman's neck, Frankie.'

'Yeah, Bear said so. I kinda got me a weakness in terms of that kind of thing. Someone does that to someone else – does *this*,' he said, indicating his legs, 'a person like me – in my particular situation – kind of thinks twice about letting that slide. You know?'

'I can imagine that's right.'

'Which is on account of why you're standing here. Plenty of businessmen such as myself you could have talked to.'

'I needed the best.'

'That's bullshit.'

'I need to know about garage door openers.'

Frankie Maglioni shot Boldt a look of surprise, respect and reluctance. 'In regards to?'

'It's his way inside, I think.' Boldt added, 'It's a new one on us. I need a little education.'

Maglioni backed up the chair behind an electronic hum and the whine of tight gears. The chair turned and wheeled forward to a low table. 'No, thanks.'

'And if I can get your probation tossed?'

'That's a PA I'd be hearing from.'

'And maybe you will.'

'And maybe you and I have a chat right about that time. Know what I'm saying?'

'We can chat right now.'

'A cop can't get probation tossed,' Frankie said.

'This cop can,' Boldt fired back. 'I'll get the probation tossed *and* the arrest taken off your sheet.' Boldt waited for that to sink in. 'You want me to make the call?'

'To some dick on your floor who knows the game and makes like a PA? Don't think so.'

'So you make the call,' Boldt suggested. 'An APA, name of Williamson.'

'Maybe I will.'

'You go ahead,' Boldt said. 'I know the number.' He recited it.

'Don't want no number from you.' Maglioni's distrustful eyes reviewed Boldt from his tie to hairline and back down again. He wheeled back to a drawer and a phone book. 'Only reason I'm doing this is because that jail ain't no place for a man in a chair.'

'The only reason you're doing this, Frankie, is that with probation lifted you can plea your next arrest. Otherwise it's hard time. This gets you back to work.'

'You see? Every po-lees-man assumes the rest of us got nothing better to do than to break the law!'

'It's under government – the listing,' Boldt instructed.

Maglioni reversed the pages and ran a stubby finger down the page. A moment later, after a brief discussion with Williamson, he motored back over to the table. 'So you think ahead,' he said. 'So what?'

'I didn't say anything.'

'You making fun of me?'

'Not at all.' Boldt said, 'Garage doors.'

'Pretty damn simple, Mr Smart. You bat a car window, lift the registration and the clicker. If you hurry, you're home before daddy. Registration gives you the address, clicker gets you inside.'

'And if we're not talking about busting out a car window?'

The man nodded faintly at Boldt. 'Yeah, okay. Different deal, you understand. Not that I done it myself.'

'Heavens, no.'

123

'Them guys clone cell phones? You know, they got this little box lifts the valid codes?'

'I know about cloned phones,' Boldt answered. 'I'm interested in garage door openers.'

'A white boy was asking around on who could build him a custom scanner – not for no cell phones, you understand.'

'When?'

'A couple months back.'

'Who?'

'Them clickers work off radio crystals. You got yourself the right kind of machinery, and you're laying by close enough to pick it up, you can lift that frequency.'

The thrill of discovery keeps any detective in the game. But outwardly, Boldt sat deadpan, as if dissatisfied with Frankie's explanation. He said, 'I know about cloning clickers. What I need is the guy who built the scanner for this white boy you're telling me about.'

'That wasn't our deal,' Frankie complained, his nostrils flaring again.

'Our deal was: you make me happy, your probation goes away.'

'That's bullshit.'

'I need a name.'

'I don't have no name!' he complained. 'You think this is the Radio Shack or something?'

Boldt repeated, 'I need the name of the guy who can build these things, or the name of the guy who bought one.' He added, 'You get me either name – and it proves good – and your probation goes away. If I get the buyer your arrest record disappears.'

Frankie negotiated, 'The probation goes away now, as agreed. I locate this technician, the arrest is erased.'

Smiling, Boldt removed a business card from his

pocket and placed it on the table. 'My rules, Frankie, not yours. And it's got to be within the next twenty-four hours, or I forget I ever saw you.'

Boldt walked toward the freight elevator, his back to the man in the wheelchair.

He pulled the elevator gate shut behind himself and pushed the button.

EIGHTEEN

The voice on the other end of Boldt's cellular sounded artificial or forced – disguised in some way – and as a result immediately troubled him. 'You shouldn't miss this call. It's important to you.' The line went dead.

He looked up to meet eyes, first with Liz and then with Kristin Jamerson, both of whom sat across the dinner table, awaiting his response to the call. This, their first dinner without kids, the adults forestalling their own meal until after eight when the last of them, Natalie, the Jamerson's eldest, went to sleep. The cell phone call was clearly an intrusion.

No one said anything, but John Jamerson stopped chewing and also glanced over at Boldt. Liz and the kids had been guests at their home for over a week now – a six-bedroom home overlooking Lake Washington; a Gary Nisbet collage centered on the largest wall; a Deborah Butterfield horse in the living room. Nice digs.

Liz had cooked a lamb dinner as a thank-you for the two-bedroom guest cottage above the pool house. With Boldt's mugging, it looked like they would be here a bit longer.

The meal was less than ten minutes old. He still held the cell phone. It remained the focus of everyone's attention.

Boldt addressed his audience, 'If I told you it was a mysterious call that implied I was missing something of great importance?'

Liz's fork went back to work on her plate. 'Intriguing,' she said. 'Worth a follow-up.'

Kristin's eyes implored Boldt to forget the call. But how could he dismiss it so easily? To what 'call' had the mysterious message referred, he wondered. A phone call? A radio call indicating a crime-scene investigation? This latter thought held the most weight. Should he have to beg forgiveness to do his job correctly?

What *kind* of investigation? he wondered. Who had called with the warning? A person who knew or had access to his cell number. A person who knew his innate curiosity.

Liz suggested he take care of it. 'Follow up on the call, Love. Why do you think the microwave was invented?'

He felt he owed it to Kristin to finish dinner. But what did he owe Sanchez? What about the importance of a fresh crime scene? 'I'll just quickly call downtown and find out what's up.'

'Lamb's good cold,' Liz said, without resentment. Her 'healing,' her 'new faith,' seemed to carry her through these situations.

Husband to wife: 'If I possibly can, I'll stay.'

'We know that,' Liz answered. 'Do what you have to.'

There had been a time in their marriage when such a situation would have condemned them to impossibly long hours of cold stares and failed communication – sometimes a day or more of it. He credited Liz with the turnaround, not himself. Her struggle with her health had been turned into something positive. He knew in his heart of hearts, had known forever, that music was a gift from God. Knew this unquestionably. It was only since the birth of his children and his wife's medically unexplained recovery from cancer that he saw himself on a slow road to the discovery that all of life was, equally, a God-given gift, and that it might do to credit the source from time to time.

She said, 'I'll keep a plate warm for you,' knowing he was going to leave if he made that call.

'Don't lock your bedroom door,' he said.

With that, Liz blushed and smiled, and for Lou Boldt the whole room grew brighter.

With his left cheekbone virtually missing, Lieutenant Rudy Schock looked only remotely human. He looked more like some sort of flesh balloon, with what appeared to be a giant blood blister where his ear and neck should have been. Schock's left arm and hand had borne the brunt of his attempts at self-defense. His elbow was no longer capable of a right angle, and his wrist hung limp and useless. His breathing was long and slow.

Lieutenant Mickey Phillipp had been the first struck – with a single blow to the base of the skull – unconscious, so that he lay in a pool of his own blood, but otherwise didn't look as brutalized as his colleague.

The sight of the two injured officers turned Boldt's stomach. He knew them both, though not as close friends; however, tonight they felt like brothers. Boldt could feel his own rage building, percolating dangerously near the surface. No matter who had struck the blows, Boldt directly blamed Mac Krishevski and the sickout that had caused such dissension in the ranks. This was no mugging, that much seemed clear.

An EMT said to Boldt, 'A little harder and this one was either dead or never walking again.'

'Blunt object?'

'You got it.'

'Both lieutenants,' Mark Heiman whispered softly from behind Boldt. Heiman was himself a lieutenant –

who until a week earlier had been with Narcotics. Such labels were gone now. Rank held little purpose anymore.

The alley was a block and a half from the Cock & Bull – an Irish bar in the Norwegian neighborhood of Ballard. Seattle demographics. The wet, narrow lane between brick buildings owned a pair of Dumpsters, a teetering stack of discarded wooden pallets, a Dunkin' Donuts bag and a flattened McDonald's fries carton oozing a sickly green mold that had once been potatoes. The alley smelled sour with urine and faintly metallic from the spilled blood. There was a lot of blood everywhere. 'Somebody saw this,' Boldt suggested hopefully to Heiman, who was lead on the case.

'Other than the guy who did it?' returned Heiman. 'If true, he hasn't come forward.'

'How do you see it?' Boldt asked, wondering how Heiman's report would read.

'How I see it,' the other said, 'is one thing. A couple of lieus fifty yards from a major watering hole for the North Precinct? Does the name Krishevski mean anything to you?' He paused. 'How I write it up? Robbery. Assault. Deadly force, with intent to kill.'

'A mugging,' Boldt stated dejectedly. There was no other way to put it on paper, but he suddenly wished he had reported his own attack so he might have established a pattern: first Sanchez, then him, now these two. Krishevski indeed.

'Without witnesses or further evidence—' Heiman sounded apologetic. 'How would you write it up?' A little defensive.

'Same way, Mark. I hear you. But we're thinking along the same lines, if I'm reading you right. And maybe it might help you to know that someone took an aluminum Louisville Slugger to my shoulder and back two nights ago, and that I passed on reporting it because I didn't want the paperwork.'

Heiman considered this pensively. 'Then why don't you look like the back of Phillipp's head?'

'Rin Tin Tin. A K-9 on the other side of a neighbor's fence. Hated the thing 'til it saved my life.'

Heiman fumed. 'These guys are going to get a war if they don't watch out.'

Boldt nodded. 'I said the same thing to Shoswitz. Told him to pass it along to Krishevski.' Looking down at the paramedics trying to stabilize the fallen lieutenant, he said, 'But I'm thinking maybe the message didn't get through.'

'Yeah? Well, it better, or I'll deliver it myself.'

'You'd have company there.'

'Just say the word,' Heiman suggested.

'Steady as she goes: it's what Krishevski wants. If he can't get us to join them, he'll get us suspended for conduct unbecoming, and he wins either way.'

'Is that what this is about? He lights the fuse, and watches as we self-implode?'

'Keep me up to speed, will you?' Boldt requested, handing him a card with his cell phone number. Heiman returned the gesture. 'While you're putting this to bed,' Boldt said, viewing the bloody landscape, 'I think I'll have a beer over at the Cock and Bull.'

Heiman understood the implications: Boldt was known on the force as a teetotaler.

NINETEEN

The Cock & Bull had been fashioned after an Irish pub, with low ceilings, exposed beams, low lighting. It served up fifteen micro-brewed and specialty beers on tap, another sixty in the bottle, fish and chips, burgers and sixteen-ounce T-bone steaks with Idaho baked potatoes. The place smelled of cigarettes, hops and campfire charcoal. Irish music played a little loudly, forcing patrons to shout, lending the crowded pub a sense of celebration and revelry. There was no explanation for the bars cops picked or the short-order grills they frequented. Sometimes the connection seemed obvious – an officer's brother owned or managed the establishment, or the proximity to a precinct house made it an obvious choice. In the case of the Cock and Bull, a favorite haunt of the North Precinct, Boldt thought it was probably the name of the place and the emphasis on beer.

A few heads turned as he entered. Then elbows nudged. No one noticed that it was Lou Boldt; they noticed a lieutenant from the West Precinct. Two young waitresses ushered trays through the throng of lustful eyes and rude comments, used to it. A cop bar was part junior-high locker room, part mortuary, an uncomfortable blend of the morbid and the adolescent.

A pair of elevated color TVs at either end of the bar showed a stock-car race. Boldt attempted to contain his anger and rage at those in the room, all Blue Fluers. He

131

wanted to drag one of them by the hair over to the alley and rub his face in the spilled blood. To show all of them the eerie electronic silence of Sanchez's hospital room. He knew damn well there wasn't going to be much sympathy in this room for two assaulted officers, and he had to wonder at how one week of absenteeism could change people so dramatically. How some over-time pay could wipe out all signs of loyalty. How could they go on drinking and telling jokes as if nothing had happened?

Would a thorough search reveal a baseball bat in the trunk of one of the cars parked out back? Had it come to that? So quickly? Could the trust built via years of working side by side be cancelled out by the edict that there would be no more off-duty work and the denial of overtime pay?

He found himself drawn to one particularly raucous group, a dozen or more men crowded around a table like gamblers at a cock fight. Boldt edged up to the outside perimeter of this knot and caught the balding reddish tinge of a scalp he knew to be Mac Krishevski. The guild president held court at the center, explaining in a loud, drunken voice the difference between the fuzz on a peach and a sixteen-year-old girl and winning peals of laughter with the punch line: 'licking the pit.' He and Boldt met eyes – Krishevski's glassy and excited, Boldt's narrow and fierce.

'Dudley Do-Right rides again,' Krishevski said, not averting his gaze.

'We've got two lieutenants with their heads beaten in,' Boldt announced. He added disgustedly, 'You guys aren't celebrating that, are you?'

'We're aware of the situation, Lieutenant,' Krishevski replied, suddenly sober, 'and there's not a man in this bar who isn't pulling for Schock and Phillipp, so don't go suggesting otherwise. If you've got business here, state it. Otherwise, find your own corner and let a fellow officer enjoy the camaraderie he's entitled to.'

'My business is to gather information useful to the investigation.'

'Yes. Well, I'm sure you'll want to start at one end or the other and work the room. Certainly not in the middle.' He indicated their location – dead center in the bar.

'If you have time between the tasteless jokes,' Boldt said, 'you might discuss amongst yourselves what you know about the incident tonight.'

One of the drunker men said, 'I know that by morning my head's gonna feel worse than theirs do now.'

A couple of the others laughed, but not Krishevski, who once again met eyes with Boldt. There was a flicker of recognition there, a moment of understanding. Krishevski stood, addressing the drunken man, 'You want to joke about a fellow officer's injuries, you drink without me.' He moved to a different table, where he was greeted like a general returning from the front.

Boldt received a half dozen evil eyes from the men that Krishevski deserted. He turned and glanced around the room. He hadn't taken a step before he felt himself the attention of someone's stare. He thought nothing of it, realizing he was odd man out: a working lieutenant in a den of strikers; an officer based in the Public Safety Building, a world away from the North Precinct.

But that burning sensation persisted, and he looked to his right, intent on staring down whoever was responsible: John LaMoia stared back at him from a corner booth.

Boldt felt a chill. Had the phone call that had

interrupted his dinner come from LaMoia? His former protégé? Friend, even.

LaMoia stood and headed down a hallway toward the men's room. Boldt wanted to follow, but resisted. His sergeant had made no indication or signal whatsoever; he thought it best to wait him out.

LaMoia fit in at the Cock & Bull the way the suspender set fit in at McCormicks and Schmidts. He was a man who moved seamlessly between the uniforms and the brass, the meter maids and the Sex Crimes detectives, the entrepreneurial friend-to-all, who always had an investment worth your making or a bet worth placing. He navigated a thin line between snitches and interrogation rooms, right and wrong, never quite crossing into criminal behavior, but always carrying a cloud of uncertainty in the wake of his swagger.

Boldt's cell phone rang. He moved to the front of the bar and stepped back outside to answer it where he could hear. LaMoia's voice spoke into Boldt's ear.

'It would be natural for you to say hello to me,' LaMoia said. 'And when you do, I'm going to be rude. Just so you know.'

'And now I know.'

'The marina out at Palisades. One hour.'

'I'll be there,' Boldt confirmed.

Boldt put some effort into questioning unwilling and uncooperative officers, reeling from their unwillingness to help him out. But his heart wasn't really in it, following that call from LaMoia. He wanted the hour over quickly, and it wouldn't cooperate. It dragged on like a sack of cement left out in the rain. When he finally checked in with Heiman, reporting he'd gained nothing from his interviews, it felt as if the entire night had passed him by.

He was back in his car when his cell phone rang.

'Lou?' It was Phil Shoswitz. 'Got a minute?'

'You heard about Schock and Phillipp?' Boldt asked.

'I heard,' Shoswitz confirmed, 'but I'm delivering another message.'

Boldt attempted to clear his head, knowing this had to be something of major importance. On the occasion of their last meeting, Shoswitz had been questioning the very nature of their friendship. 'I'm listening.'

'The chief is going for a stolen base. He's facing the possibility of National Guardsmen taking over his turf, so he's gonna smoke a couple fastballs over the plate and hope to clean out the top of the lineup.' Mention of the chief got Boldt's heart racing. 'Cleaning out the lineup' didn't help matters. What the hell? He knew Shoswitz's opinion of the newcomer, and feared the worst. But it was worse than even that. 'What I'm telling you is, you're not going to sleep tonight – you're gonna be on the phone to every goddamned officer of yours, because those officers were mine not long ago, and to a man they're the best we've got and I'd hate to see you lose them.'

'Lose them?'

'He's sending out something like a hundred health care personnel in the morning, door to door, to verify every officer's claims of illness. Those that aren't ill will be held in violation of the guild contract and will be terminated without pay and will forfeit all benefits, including four-oh-one Ks.'

The static sat heavily on the open line. The implications were enormous: the chief would break the guild and restructure SPD in a matter of hours. Boldt could foresee a string of lawsuits stretching out over years, and a younger more vital police department for its newly installed chief. With the guild broken, he could negotiate new levels of pay and recruit from across the country, possibly cutting a deal with King County Police in the process and bringing the two departments under one roof. 'Oh, my God,' Boldt muttered into the phone.

'Your people have to report for tomorrow's day tour, Lou, or they're thrown out of the game.'

'If he fires that many people, it's going to be Molotov cocktails instead of blue bricks.'

'Just don't let it be your people. Use the emergency calling tree. We've got to drop all the animosities and get as many people back by tomorrow morning as possible.'

'Amen.'

'And, Lou? I'm calling from a pay phone, because when the chief finds out this thing leaked, he'll be looking for a scapegoat, for sure. He won't appreciate some people being tipped off and others left to eat it. But that's how it's going to be, no matter how hard we try. There's no way we'll reach everyone by morning. Just so you know. I wouldn't be making calls from my home or my cell.' He added, 'The airport might work – they've got those business centers on A concourse.'

'I follow.' He sensed the man about to hang up. 'And thanks, Phil.'

'What are friends for?' The line went dead.

Palisades, a marina and upscale restaurant, hung off the south shore of the Queen Anne peninsula, supported by pilings and enough docks to house several hundred pleasure craft, all neat and shipshape and sparkling white under the lights. Teak and aluminum and enough fiberglass to wrap the city in a dome.

Boldt appreciated the view of the skyline, and La-Moia's choice of location. The prices at the restaurant guaranteed they wouldn't run into fellow officers.

Palisades was more for the professional set and gold card tourists. Boldt walked the docks, drinking in the cool night air and charting the determined progress of the slowly moving cavalcade of lights from the state ferries. He made out the man's distinctive silhouette from a distance. Bold. Confident. Even aggressive. You wouldn't walk up to LaMoia at night without knowing him.

Boldt approached him in silence, distant city lights reflecting in the silver black water a mirror image that looked like a giant, glowing key, or the mouth of a shark. Boldt felt an urgency to get this meeting over with and head to the pay phone. If Schock and Phillipp hadn't had their blood shed, he would have postponed the meet.

'Sorry about the cloak and dagger,' LaMoia said.

Boldt answered, 'I appreciate the call. We need to talk.' The two of them worked in concert to watch for anyone watching them, an unspoken system that had one looking toward the restaurant, the other searching the neighboring docks, then switching assignments in a dance born of years of working the field together.

LaMoia supplied: 'Many hands make light the work.'

'Yeah?' Boldt complained. 'Well, I'm a little short-handed, thanks to you and the squad.'

'Don't go forming stereotypes, Sarge. You think I'm home watching *CHiPs* reruns or something? I'm working Maria's case.'

Boldt's surprise registered on his shadowed face as confusion.

'Damn right. Figured a slouch like you could use a little help.' LaMoia added, 'I'm working *all sorts of shit* you don't wanna know about.'

That much was probably true. LaMoia's investigative approach was anything but conventional. 'You have to come back on the job,' Boldt informed him. Not only were LaMoia and his wealth of contacts invaluable, but Shoswitz's news threatened the man's future with Homicide.

'Don't look a gift horse—'

'I'm serious, John. The chief—'

LaMoia interrupted. 'Schock and Phillipp had Ron Chapman under surveillance. I'd lay odds on it.'

'Chapman?' Boldt questioned, his thoughts jarred. Chapman swinging a baseball bat on a fellow officer? Not likely. 'Krishevski is Property. Chapman is Property. But I don't see Ron Chapman doing Big Mac's dirty work. Chapman hasn't even joined the Flu! That doesn't make sense.'

'I'm just telling you what I saw. Those boys were eyeing him.'

'That's a crowded bar, John.'

'Chapman doesn't hang at the Bull. I *do*, Sarge. As much as I hang at the Joke when you're on the ivories. And Chapman's out of place. He stuck out tonight because everyone knows he's still on the job. You could say he got a lukewarm reception – same as you.'

'Go on.' Boldt continued to scan their surroundings, ensuring they weren't being watched. It was no longer safe for one cop to talk to another. He hated the way things were.

'Chapman came in looking for someone. No doubt about it. Completely obvious. Schock and Phillipp weren't far behind – a staggered entrance, one through the front, one through the back. Textbook shit. Phillipp's a couple minutes behind his partner. About as long as it takes to double park in an alley down the street, if you hear what I'm saying. I'm putting 'em on Chapman, on account that's the way I read it. Chapman wanders around craning his head this way and that, gives it up and takes off. 'Bout as subtle as a whore at a tea party. Maybe he signaled someone. Maybe not. I'm thinking Schock hangs to maintain appearances. Phillipp's out the back door a couple beats behind the mark . . . I'm telling you, Sarge. Couple minutes later, Schock follows. Maybe he gets a call. I didn't see that. Can't say. But they don't make it far, right? And if that's a mugging, then your bruises came from falling down stairs.'

LaMoia apparently had heard Boldt's in-house explanation for his pains and aches. Not much sneaked past him.

'The chief is sending health services door to door.' Boldt explained what Shoswitz had passed along to him.

'It's a bluff, Sarge. Shoswitz was supposed to leak it.'

'If I'm the chief, uniforms are promoted to detective. Academy recruits who're past the three-week mark head straight to patrol. I keep the National Guard out of my house.'

LaMoia looked a little more convinced.

'You and your squad need to be back on the floor tomorrow before this hits the fan.'

'It's the perfect bluff, I'm telling you. A couple lieus leak this and they get thirty, forty percent of us back with nothing more than a phone call.'

'Phil Shoswitz was guild secretary. Whose side do you think he's on?' Boldt said, 'Don't double guess this, John. The information is good. We need to work the call tree, and we need to do it tonight. Phil thinks we should avoid our home lines.'

'Oh, this is precious.' LaMoia snorted and shook his head and looked Boldt over, trying to read him. He asked tentatively, 'You buy this?'

Boldt knew to leave it alone. It was the only way to convince his obstinate sergeant. As much as he wanted to argue his case, he returned to LaMoia's reason for the meeting. 'Schock and Phillipp are Vice. Why are they sitting on a guy like Chapman?'

'Are they?' LaMoia asked. 'Vice? You're Homicide, Sarge, but are you at the moment?'

'One cop watching another? What, they got handed an I.I.?' Internal Investigations had been wiped out by the Flu same as Burglary. It wasn't out of the question, no matter how unlikely. I.I. was a closed unit – a dreaded assignment. But it only made sense that these investigations would have to continue in spite of the Flu. He considered this possibility. 'We need to know who Chapman was looking for.'

Saddled with obvious reservations, LaMoia informed Boldt, 'Maria got hooked up to something first day of the Flu, Sarge. She wouldn't talk about it – and we talked about *everything*. I got pissed off, partly 'cause she wouldn't talk, partly because she wouldn't join us in the sickout. Basically, Sarge, she threw me out. Next time I see her she's got her head screwed down to that bed.'

'I.I.?' Boldt asked.

'It might explain why she wouldn't discuss whatever it was,' LaMoia suggested. The unit operated under strict secrecy acts. The explanation satisfied Boldt. LaMoia added, 'Let me sniff out Chapman. You chat up Maria about that case. With me involved, it would only get her pissed off again. Hispanics and temper, Sarge! I'm telling you!'

'The call tree.'

'I'll think about it.'

'Thanks again for the call,' Boldt repeated. 'I would have missed that crime scene.'

'What are you talking about, Sarge?'

'The call. Putting me on to the assault.'

'The only call I made was from the bar,' LaMoia said.

'Earlier?' Boldt asked.

LaMoia shook his head. 'Wasn't me.'

Boldt's gut twisted. Who had wanted him to see two badly beaten officers? And much more important: Why? So he could help out with the investigation, or as a warning of how close he had come to incurring the same fate?

TWENTY

Boldt placed the call from his cell phone, disturbing Phil Shoswitz at home. Boldt's former boss had the kind of contacts within the department that John LaMoia had in the private sector. LaMoia could come up with any and all information on a suspect or witness, be it financial, tax-related, insurance or medical. He had 'Deep Throats' – sources within institutions and industries – that would have made government agents blush. Shoswitz had formed similar relationships within SPD – ironically, in large part, due to his many years of guild service – and had ways of turning gossip into hard fact. He knew the scuttlebutt in the department's vehicle garage as well as the chief's social calendar. Exactly as Boldt needed.

Recognizing Boldt's voice immediately, Shoswitz said, 'You're supposed to be working that phone tree.'

'Already in motion. What about Schock and Phillipp's condition?' Boldt asked.

'Word is both are going to pull through, although Schock may lose the eye. Phillipp won't be completing any full sentences for a week or so, but he'll be back on the job.' Shoswitz already had the full medical reports on the two and understood Boldt wanted this information first.

Boldt said cautiously, 'I need to know if they had drawn I.I. duty as a result of the Flu. I hear they may have followed a fellow officer into that bar.'

'I can ask around, but I won't get confirmation, Lou. Not if it's I.I.'

'And that lack of confirmation will tell us what we need to know.'

'Not necessarily.'

'I read this wrong, Phil. Blue on blue. I was thinking we were getting roughed up in order to cut our numbers, strengthen the effect of the Flu. And sure, maybe a brick through a window. Some rookie pissed off his paycheck isn't coming in and drinking too much. But assaults? Sanchez? Schock and Phillipp?' He left himself out of it. 'Would we do that kind of damage to each other over guild politics?'

'Don't underestimate what a desperate man will do,' Shoswitz cautioned.

'Six months into a strike, maybe. But one week? Does that make sense? And so carefully executed to look like muggings. The things are textbook, Phil.'

'Your point?'

'I could use a little help here,' Boldt prodded. 'I've got two Vice cops poking around a bar and apparently following a Property sergeant. What's that about?'

'I'll ask around,' Shoswitz confirmed. 'But if they were I.I., about the best we'll get is a denial. We'll be working hunches is all.'

'I have another source I can work,' Boldt told him. 'Sanchez may be able to fill in some of this.'

'I thought she's comatose.'

'So does everyone,' Boldt said. 'Right now, that's the one advantage I've got.'

It was too late to visit Sanchez at the hospital. She'd be medicated and fast asleep. But it wasn't too late to grab onto a few limbs and start shaking the tree. Whoever had committed the assaults would have fresh blood to hide, might even have defensive wounds to show for their efforts.

Boldt called Gaynes and Matthews and caught them up on the assaults, as well as Shoswitz's alert about the surprise health inspections. He put them onto the task of firing up the departmental phone tree and to start making calls. Gaynes rallied without complaint, a soldier in the trenches.

Daphne, as ever, ferreted out Boldt's true intentions: to question Ron Chapman at his home. She refused to allow him to go at it alone, and informed him she was bringing a stun stick along as backup. He knew better than to argue with her, or to admit that he'd welcome her company. He picked her up at her houseboat, and they drove to Chapman's together, using the drive time to prepare.

'The two of you at this hour, it's not social,' Chapman said, shutting the door behind them. He had made no effort to keep them out. Perhaps, Boldt thought, he didn't want to eat alone.

'Little late for dinner, isn't it, Ron?'

Chapman lived in a studio apartment with a partial view of Pill Hill. He had the TV going and a Stouffer's microwave meal on a folding table in front of the room's only chair – a La-Z-Boy recliner. He'd been widowed several years earlier, and the dust bugs and dirty windows confirmed a life of a man turned within. To Boldt, the room felt sad and depressed, crowded with too many snapshots of the late wife. Some people couldn't let go. Chapman suddenly struck him that way, and Boldt found it odd that his attitude about a man he'd known for years could change with a single look inside that man's home. If there had ever been joy here, it now rested in the urn that held his wife's ashes.

Chapman didn't offer them seats, in part because the only two chairs were at a small table that framed the galley kitchen's doorway, and there didn't seem to be any more room for them elsewhere.

'Little late for a house call, isn't it, Lieutenant? Strange times, these.'

'You hear about Schock and Phillipp?'

'Rudy Schock?'

Daphne said calmly, 'They were assaulted tonight.'

'Not far from the Cock and Bull,' Boldt supplied.

Ron Chapman carried an extra thirty or forty pounds on his Irish bulldog looks. It wasn't easy for such soft flesh to remain so absolutely still. Then, at once, he returned to his dinner like a dog to its bone.

'You were at the Cock and Bull tonight, Ronnie. What's that about?'

'A guy can't buy himself a drink?' Chapman complained, working on the dinner in the small plastic tray. 'Since when?'

'What do Schock and Phillipp mean to you?'

The man glanced up, as hot as his prepared dinner. 'Who says they mean anything?'

'Why play games?' Boldt asked. 'Are you into something here? Tell me I'm wrong.'

'You're wrong.'

'Convince me,' Boldt said.

'I've got my dinner to eat.'

Daphne asked, 'Are you afraid of them?'

Chapman stiffened.

She clarified, 'I'm not talking about Schock and Phillipp. I'm talking about whoever did that to them. Are you afraid of *those* people?'

He wouldn't look up from his food. 'Way I heard it, they were mugged. A street assault. Why should I be afraid of that? Their bad luck is all.'

She said, 'You don't have to swing the baseball bat to be guilty of assault. There's conspiracy. There's intent. You want to think about that.'

Boldt said, 'Next to Narcotics, Property is probably easily the most tempting duty of all of 'em. You guys are carefully hand-picked. Doesn't mean temptation doesn't win out now and then. There's a heck of a lot of goods on those shelves.'

'There's cash on those shelves,' Chapman said. 'Jewels. Weapons. And as far as I know it's all still there, Lieutenant. Go ahead and check.'

'You came to that bar looking for someone. Two officers right behind you were assaulted. What if I told you they were following up on a case that was being worked by Sanchez just before her assault?'

Daphne turned her attention to Boldt, angry at not having been included in on this.

Chapman wouldn't take his head out of his dinner.

Boldt said, 'Maybe I've got it wrong. Maybe you were doing a favor for Schock, or Phillipp. Wearing a wire? Making a contact?'

'It wasn't like that!' the man objected heatedly, fork in mid-air.

Daphne picked up on Boldt's lead. 'The rumor mill is brutal,' she said.

'You can't do something like that to me! Label me a squirrel for I.I.?' He thought this over and flushed. 'It's not funny, Lieutenant. Especially not the way things are going right now.'

'Let's take you out of the equation, Ron. That's what I'm suggesting. Let's put Schock and Phillipp working the Cock and Bull – it isn't their usual bar, or yours either, Ron.' He let this sink in. 'They're looking to work someone. That leaves me asking who. Who in your opinion, might they have been looking for up there?'

'I know what you're asking,' Chapman said. 'And you got this all tangled up.'

'So help me untangle it.'

'I was in for a drink is all.'

'And Schock and Phillipp? A drink as well?'

'I didn't talk to them. Wouldn't know.'

'Sergeant,' Daphne said calmly, 'you've stayed on through the Blue Flu. Precious few others have been so . . . bold as to do so. If you hadn't stayed on, others who've never worked Property would have been assigned to that duty. But you stayed. One could almost imagine you're protecting Property from outside eyes. And now these assaults . . . Sanchez, Schock, and Phillipp. Someone even showed up in Lieutenant Boldt's backyard uninvited. You want to talk about mistakes? *That* was a mistake. You know the lieutenant's reputation as an investigator. Do you think he's going to let this go . . . four brutal assaults?'

'You two do what you have to. You come to whatever it is by yourselves,' Chapman suggested. 'Leave me out of this.'

Boldt craned forward. 'But then there *is* something, right, Ron? Something to leave you out of?'

'You're tangling this all up.'

Boldt repeated slowly. 'So . . . help . . . me . . . untangle . . . it.'

'Dinner's getting cold.'

Daphne said, 'We *can* be convinced otherwise. Tell us it was Schock and Phillipp doing the dirty work. Tell us they pursued you into that bar. What do they have on you? What do you have on them?'

'I'd like it if you left now,' the man said.

Daphne stepped closer to Chapman. Boldt admired her technique. 'He's Property, Lou. There have to be people who owe him favors.' To the subject she said, 'Is covering for someone the right way to play this?'

'It's not like that!' Chapman shouted. 'Now leave!'

Twenty minutes later Boldt pulled the Chevy to a stop at the end of the dock that led to Daphne's Lake Union houseboat. He escorted Daphne to her front door. He wasn't going to add her to the list of assaults.

'So we know Chapman's caught up in something,' the psychologist said.

'Yes, we do.'

'But not what, nor to what degree.'

'No.'

'So what's next?'

'I go back to John for an update. You start working the phone tree. We save as many people as we can before the axe falls.'

'And if John has something, you'll call?'

'Your line'll be busy,' he said, 'from all that calling you'll be doing.'

'Lou . . .'

For a moment, the connection between them was everything, and he had to remind himself of Icarus's perilous journey too close to the sun, or that even the most loyal husband remained subject to the laws of gravity. They paused at the front door to her houseboat, and for one awkward moment it felt to him as if they might kiss; then he turned and left.

John LaMoia lived on the third floor of a waterfront loft that thirteen years earlier had been a drug lab in the heart of a gang-controlled neighborhood. The lab had been busted by police, including a wet-behind-the-ears patrolman who, when the raid was concluded, noted the spectacular view on the other side of the painted-over windows. LaMoia had never forgotten that view, nor the neighborhood, because of the repeated radio calls taking him there: disruptions, street wars, stabbings. He bought low, well ahead of the gentrification that followed, restored the interior, installed security, and scraped the paint off the windows, so that now he commanded views of the waterfront – the piers and tourist restaurants on Alaskan Way – as well as Elliott Bay's sublime gray-green waters and the white-capped peaks of the Olympics beyond.

It wasn't often that a blue-collar policeman like LaMoia celebrated a capital gains cut, but when Congress voted a lowering of the surcharge to twenty percent, John LaMoia threw a beer bash for fifty of his closest friends – mostly women.

Boldt stepped inside, and LaMoia threw a lock behind him. It clicked into place with authority.

He caught him up on the Chapman visit. 'I wanted to go back over what you saw at the bar before you went to bed and lost the immediacy of the moment.'

'Worried my memory will slip? That sounds like something Matthews would say,' LaMoia countered.

'Does it?' Boldt questioned, distracted – even disturbed – by the comment. 'The Flu,' Boldt said apologetically, 'has thrown us together round the clock. You know how it is.'

LaMoia said, 'Hey . . . I was just teasing, Sarge.'

'Let's go back over who was there tonight at the Cock and Bull,' Boldt said.

'Sarge, it's a pub. Probably a hundred of us in there. All unemployed cops. You expect me to recite the roll call?'

Boldt interrupted. 'Anyone from Property at the bar?'

'Property?'

'Chapman clammed up, but he grew all nervous when

149

I pointed out he didn't belong in that pub. Daphne and I are thinking we've got this one wrong. What if Schock and Phillipp were into something Ron Chapman found out about?'

'Something inside Property,' LaMoia said, connecting the dots. He nodded, 'I suppose it could fall that way, couldn't it? What about Maria and the possible I.I. connection?'

'Tomorrow morning,' Boldt said. 'Tonight we deal with the assaults while the blood's still fresh.'

LaMoia squinted his eyes shut. When Boldt had first started working with him, LaMoia had been a smooth-faced young loudmouth, smart but a little too sure of himself. Now the face showed ten years of rough road, and though the mouth still broadcast his unparalleled self-confidence, the eyes revealed a more practical, seasoned man. 'What I remember,' he said, squinting ever more tightly, 'in terms of Property, is that Pende-grass and some of them guys were whooping it up over the race – a NASCAR qualifying heat – on account I was trying to hear about this unscheduled pit stop, and I couldn't hear nothing because of their racket. And I'm trying to think now, but I gotta put Chapman's arrival right about then. Maybe I looked up and caught sight of him or something, you know? Maybe I had this little brain fart on account Chapman's still active and I'm thinking it was gonna be *him* getting the shit beat out of him, and how I'm not gonna let something like that happen, and what a pain in the ass it was going to be for all concerned. And then I'm thinking how stupid it is for Chapman to show his face at the Bull. You know? And then I'm wondering if maybe he took a brick the way you did, because there's been more of that, you know, and so maybe he's showing up pissed off and ready to settle the score or something, and that kinda leans me

150

away from wanting to help him out too much. I mean, if a guy is stupid enough to walk into a room like that, maybe it's Darwin's law that he get the living shit beat out of him. But the point is, the pit stop was something to do with communications. Radio problems between the crew and the driver, and they didn't want to get into the final third of the race without communication—'

'John . . .'

'Which means I heard the explanation, Sarge. Get it? I heard the guy explaining the pit stop. Which means that Chuck Pendegrass and his riot squad had either shut up, cut out, or all gone to take a piss at the same time, which is technically impossible on account the men's room is only one urinal and a crapper, and there must have been three or four of them over there hooting it up.' He repeated, 'I got a hunch Pendegrass split the minute Chapman walked through that door. And let me just say that he and his buddies did not impress me as being ready to leave a few minutes before that.'

'When Chapman arrived, or Schock and Phillipp?' Boldt pressed.

'You got me there. Maybe it was a minute later.'

'But Chapman didn't speak to Pendegrass?'

'I can't say one way or another. Maybe Pendegrass shut up when he saw Chapman, same way Chapman caught my eye.' He added, 'Chapman caught a lot of people by surprise, Sarge.'

'So Pendegrass left when?'

'No clue.'

'They could have talked,' Boldt theorized. 'For that matter, they could have simply made eye contact. Some kind of visual.'

'We don't even know that Chapman came looking for Pendegrass,' LaMoia reminded him.

'No,' Boldt agreed. 'But we could ask him.'

'Yes, we could at that,' LaMoia replied, collecting his coat off the back of a chair.

'Doesn't Chuck Pendegrass have a boy about ten?'

'Tanner,' LaMoia answered knowingly. 'But what's that about?'

'Nothing,' Boldt said, but inside he was thinking that ten was a good age for Little League and aluminum baseball bats.

Before LaMoia knocked on the front door of the gray house, he said to Boldt, 'I hate this shit. Cop on cop. I don't even want to *think* it, much less confirm it.'

'We don't know that that's what we've got,' Boldt said. 'Sanchez could have been a burglary gone wrong. She could have nothing to do with Schock and Phillipp. Probably totally unrelated.'

'Then what the hell are we doing here, Sarge?'

'I'll tell you what . . . Boredom does weird things to people.'

LaMoia tugged at the sleeve of his deerskin jacket. 'This rain's a bitch.'

'That's the wrong coat for Seattle. I've been telling you that for a couple years now.'

'They make chamois out of deerskin, Sarge. Doesn't hurt the jacket.'

'Jacket doesn't stop the rain,' Boldt said.

'Can't have everything.'

Pendegrass met the front door himself, his face enmeshed in a three-day beard, already in a snarl. His hair was wet, his eyes rheumy. 'Don't want any.' He stepped back, intending to shut the door on them.

LaMoia slipped the toe of his cowboy boot up onto the jamb. 'I've seen this done in movies,' he said, giving Pendegrass his best Pepsodent smile.

'A pair of detectives got hurt tonight,' Boldt said.

'Is that right?'

'Thought you might tell us what you know,' LaMoia added. 'Maybe out of the rain.'

'Pass.' Pendegrass eyed the detective. 'Since when are you back on the job?'

'Since Schock and Phillipp took an ambulance ride,' LaMoia answered. 'You ever heard of loyalty to the badge?'

'We could use some help,' Boldt said, suspecting the man had an alibi in place.

'You saying I'm a suspect in this assault?'

'A suspect?' LaMoia glanced at Boldt as if this was the furthest thing from his mind. 'We were thinking *witness*.' LaMoia explained, 'You and I were both down to the Cock and Bull earlier tonight.'

Boldt chimed in, 'And LaMoia didn't catch a whole hell of a lot of what was going down. But he remembered you were there.'

'I bet he did,' Pendegrass said, cautiously eyeing the detective. 'And by the way, get your foot outta my door.'

'Maybe you saw something . . . someone,' Boldt said, 'and don't even realize its importance.'

'There were a whole lot of someones at the Bull tonight, Lieutenant.'

'Ron Chapman showed up,' Boldt said.

'Is that right?'

LaMoia ventured, 'That would be about when you left.'

'We're thinking baseball bat or pipe,' Boldt added, catching the man's eye.

'Nightstick, maybe,' LaMoia said, reminding Pendegrass of a possible police connection.

'You mind if we come in and talk about it?' Boldt asked, a rivulet of rainwater running down his neck.

'I'm home sick, Lieutenant. In case your forgot. Not a real good time for me.'

'Your name will never get mentioned.'

'Even so . . . I'll pass.'

LaMoia complained, 'All we need is five minutes on what you maybe did or did not see in that bar. Right? You know the drill.'

'That's right, I do.' He added, 'I can crush your foot in the door, if you'd prefer.'

LaMoia left his boot there.

Pendegrass looked pretty drunk. The longer he stood there, the more apparent it was. He was known as a mean drunk. Boldt didn't want this degenerating into a rumble. Drunk cops like Pendegrass loved a chance to fight, and LaMoia always seemed to find his way into the middle of such things.

'You weren't too sick to visit the Cock and Bull,' Boldt reminded him.

'A medicinal visit.'

'Chuck?' a woman's voice called out from inside the house, distracting the man. 'Who is it, honey?'

'You were there,' LaMoia said, 'during the time in question. You left around the time Chapman arrived, which was only minutes before Schock and Phillipp. You're jamming us up here, Chuck. You see that? You see the way it's gonna look? You not wanting to talk. In the right place and the right time? So you didn't see nothing. You heard something, maybe? Like a head getting cracked open or someone in some kind of pain.'

Boldt wanted to take advantage of the man's apparent drunken vulnerability, not give him the chance to sober up and rethink his answers. 'We'd like to do this tonight. Now,' he said strongly. 'You know how it is when a witness avoids you or delays you. These are fellow officers who got hurt, Chuck. We want to clear this one.'

'Before the morning news, I'll bet. Before John Q. Public pressures city hall to cave in on this sickout.'

'Politics?' Boldt gasped. 'You think we're playing politics?'

'Do whatever it is you boys gotta do. But this here ain't happening. No way.'

'We've got two *brothers* down, you know,' LaMoia repeated, 'and your not talking ain't right, no matter how you slice it. Don't matter what you think of Phillipp and Schock. It ain't right.'

'Chuck?' the woman called out again. She rounded the corner and approached the door wearing a per-plexed expression. She was small and mousy, her hair a mess. 'Chuck, it's raining. These men are standing in the rain. John LaMoia, isn't it?' she said to the sergeant. Every woman associated with the department knew LaMoia's face.

'And Lieutenant Boldt,' LaMoia said, extending his hand.

'Chuck?' she said, her concern obvious. 'They're standing out in the rain.'

'No, they're leaving,' Pendegrass said, meeting eyes with Boldt.

Boldt took his best shot at the woman. The back-ground sound had taken him a minute to identify. 'Funny time of night to be doing a load of laundry.'

She clearly didn't appreciate the tone of his com-ment. 'Chuck brings back that cigarette smell, and it's straight into the machine for the clothes and into the shower for him. One of the few laws around here that *I* made up.'

Boldt caught sight of the studio shot of the two kids hanging on the wall as the woman pulled the door open further. He said, 'Does your son own a baseball bat, Mrs Pendegrass?'

'Whose doesn't?' Pendegrass asked. He shifted his weight, preparing to shut the front door, boot toe or no boot toe. As he did, he offered Boldt a glimpse of the stairway climbing to the home's second floor and, sitting on one of the steps, a pair of ankle-high hiking boots bearing the Nike logo. He wondered if there might be a slight tear in the nylon above the side logo. Boldt had seen a similar Nike logo at point-blank range while lying face down in his driveway.

Pendegrass elbowed his wife out of the way, kicked LaMoia's boot clear, and slammed the front door shut.

On the way back to the car Boldt said, 'I'm starting to think if we searched his closets or his locker downtown, or the trunk of his car, that maybe we'd find a baseball bat or a balaclava,' Boldt said. 'And that might begin to make sense of things.'

'Eggplant? What's with that?' LaMoia asked naively. 'Or is balaclava one of those Greek desserts?'

Boldt dismissed the man's ignorance. 'He's on Krishevski's squad. Right?'

'Right as rain.'

'So maybe that's all we need to know.'

They ducked through the downpour and ran for the parked car, LaMoia calling out loudly and complaining about how much he loved his deerskin jacket.

TWENTY ONE

'You're being awfully quiet,' Daphne said, stung by the irony of the prominently displayed sign that reminded hospital visitors to keep silent.

The morning routines kept the corridors busier than on their previous visits. Doctors were doing their rounds, med students in tow. Nurses and orderlies seemed harried and overworked.

'Thinking,' Boldt replied.

'About last night's assaults,' she completed for him.

'Pendegrass is a loyalist. He'll do whatever Krishevski asks. You're the staff psychologist. You know there's a thin line between cop and criminal.'

'From what you told me, his wife's explanations made sense. Tell me how that connects to Krishevski.'

'You didn't see his eyes. His attitude. Pendegrass, Riorden – Krishevski's boys down in Property – they all ride in the back of the bus.'

'It doesn't mean they cracked open a couple of heads.'

'But they *could* have,' he said. He needed answers. He still believed Sanchez the best source for those answers.

The rent-a-cop security guard on Sanchez's hospital room recognized Matthews and Boldt. Daphne led the way through the door. It warned of oxygen in use, but Boldt thought they might post other cautions as well. This woman's assault seemed to be tearing at the fabric of SPD's integrity, implicating misplaced loyalties to labor unions and dissolving the bonds between fellow officers. He came to find out if Sanchez had worked an Internal Investigation prior to her being found tied to her bed with her neck cracked. He came hoping that her assault was nothing but a burglary gone bad. Without confirmation otherwise, this was how the case had to be investigated. It was rare for him to enter an interrogation desiring his hunches and instincts to be proved wrong, but that was exactly what he felt as he stepped into the room and looked over at the paralyzed woman lying in the bed.

Sanchez's haunting eyes had come to plague Boldt. Pleading. Silent. Saddened. A young, vital woman had been sacrificed. Maria Sanchez was trapped – her spirit was confined to a body that would not release her. Within the next few days or weeks, surgeons would apparently know if her surgery would reconnect this woman to the life she had previously known.

'We know this is difficult for you, Officer,' Daphne began after greeting her. The reference to the patient's rank was intentional. They needed the participation of a policewoman. They needed honest, difficult answers.

'We've had several important developments in the case,' Boldt informed her. Her eyelids shut with some difficulty, and as they opened her dark brown irises focused intently on Boldt, whose voice caught as he said, 'Some questions we'd like to ask you.'

Her eyes shut and then reopened again, her pupils fixed to the right. 'Yes,' came the woman's answer. She seemed worse today than the last time he'd seen her. He reeled.

'There have been two more assaults,' Daphne said, stepping closer to Boldt at the foot of the bed to make it easier on the patient. 'Both officers. Both badly off.'

The eyelids shut.

Boldt said, 'There seems to be the possibility of a

158

connection that we would prefer not to face, but face it we must. Our primary interest remains this burglar – especially in your case, where your possessions went missing. We're pursuing all relevant leads. But unfortunately, another possibility has raised its ugly head – that these assaults on officers, my own included, have to do with an I.I. investigation. That this investigation, whatever it is, or was, is the common thread we've been missing.'

'And that's why we're here,' Daphne said.

Boldt said cautiously, 'Sometimes the system itself can stand in an officer's way. We need answers, and we're not getting them from upstairs.'

'We need your help.'

When her eyes opened this time, they aimed to the right. 'Yes.'

'Prior to your assault,' Boldt began, 'were you involved in an Internal Investigation?' Her eyes fluttered shut and remained so.

'Please, Maria,' Daphne pleaded.

'Yes,' came the answer.

Boldt experienced a combination of relief and anxiety. Sanchez had been working an I.I. prior to her burglary assault. A dozen questions danced on the tip of his tongue.

'Did the investigation involve Property?' he asked.

She stared at the ceiling. Unable, or unwilling to answer? Boldt wondered. 'Krishevski?' Boldt asked quickly, for his suspicions remained with the Property sergeant.

The ceiling. But he thought she struggled not to answer.

'Pendegrass?'

The ceiling. Perhaps she was overmedicated, he thought.

'Chapman?'

Her eyelids fluttered, she squeezed them shut tightly. When they reopened, she stared at the ceiling.

'Maria . . .' a frustrated Boldt pleaded. 'Please. You're the only one who can answer these questions.' He allowed this to sink in. 'Do you believe someone – anyone – from Property was involved in your assault?' He asked this with as little emotion as he could summon, and yet his own convictions surfaced.

'No,' replied the injured woman.

Daphne glanced at Boldt – Sanchez's first definite answer took Property out of the assault. A part of him felt satisfied. He could focus on the burglary and let others turn over the rocks – if those rocks even existed. But Chapman's anxiety the night before remained in the forefront of his thoughts, and cautioned against accepting Sanchez's answers.

'Do you believe your assault was related in any way to your I.I. case?' Daphne inquired.

Again, she stared at the ceiling. Boldt's frustration built.

'Maria, we have two more officers in this hospital this morning. We have suspicious movements from officers in Property. We have far more questions than answers, and you're apparently one of the few people who knows what's going on. I know it's asking a lot – too much even – but please, help us out here!'

Her eyes shone. A tear escaped down her cheek.

'We've upset you,' Daphne apologized to the woman. 'Are you avoiding answers, Maria, because we are not I.I., not directly your superiors on this case?'

'Yes!' Somehow those eyes shouted.

Again Maria stared at the ceiling, tears running.

'But we want to *help*!' an exasperated Boldt pleaded.

Daphne repeated softly, 'Do you think your assault might be connected to your I.I. case?'

Her eyes shut and reopened. 'Yes,' she replied, now staring directly at Boldt.

Daphne looked across to a relieved Boldt and said, 'We need this burglar in custody. If he can give us an alibi for the night of her assault, then—'

'Maybe that would be enough to take a good long look at whatever case she was working,' Boldt interrupted. The secrecy surrounding I.I. cases was notoriously impossible to crack. He said, 'You're right about the order of things – this burglar just might become our star witness.'

TWENTY TWO

Anthony Brumewell caught a glimpse of himself in the driver's side mirror as the garage door flipped shut electronically and he stepped out into his garage. Working nights was not his thing; he felt exhausted. He entered the home's small kitchen, dumped his briefcase onto a kitchen chair, and headed straight for the refrigerator and a Coors Lite. He yanked down a jar of dry-roasted peanuts, popped off the yellow plastic lid and spilled out a handful. He blindly reached over for the TV's remote and came up empty. When he turned toward the TV itself he realized there was no remote control because there was no TV. And that was when the first pang of dread overcame him.

What the hell, he wondered, his mind fishing for a recollection that might explain its absence. He dropped the beer can on the counter. The peanuts spilled like pebbles onto the floor, and his heart raced furiously. The television had been stolen, he realized now. Was someone still *inside* the house? He panicked.

He picked up the wall phone. No dial tone. 'Hello?' It was off the hook somewhere else. There were two other phones: one in the living room, one in the bedroom. He scrambled to get out of the house. Only then did he notice his home security box had been smashed up.

Terrified now, Brumewell hurried back out to the garage and into the safety of his car. He locked the car doors, tripped the garage door to open, turned the key and shoved the car into reverse, knocking a mirror off in the process. He reached for the car phone, already stabbing the three numbers he had never before dialed: 911.

TWENTY THREE

Another break-in. Boldt contacted the Brumewell crime scene by cell phone and uncharacteristically drove over the speed limit to get there. Phil Shoswitz had caught him while he was on his way to the Jamersons' for breakfast. Shoswitz's burglary unit had drawn the investigation on a chaotic morning when nearly nine hundred officers – out of the eleven hundred who had walked out – had returned to work 'unexpectedly.' The media was camped in the lobby of Public Safety, making a zoo out of the place. The victim – the owner of the house – was waiting for their arrival. The radio led with 'breaking news' that the strike had been broken by a tough stance from the new chief. Rumors and stories abounded.

Without asking if the victim's home had a garage, Boldt requested that the garage's clicker be waiting for him.

SID had not yet arrived. The sunrise had brought rain, then sunshine, now rain again – like Boldt, it couldn't make up its mind. There had been no assault and therefore no detective initially assigned. It was only through the diligent eye of a dispatcher that Shoswitz had been notified at all. With Flu-time burglaries at an all-time high, and low on SPD's priority list, Anthony Brumewell might have been missed by the radar entirely.

Boldt intentionally blocked the short driveway with

the Cavalier. Sunshine again. He hoped it might hold. He didn't want SID pulling their van in there as they had at the Sanchez crime scene. Cleanliness *was* next to godliness at a crime scene.

The patrolman said, 'I've got the owner in the front seat of the cruiser, if you want to—'

'Later,' Boldt said, accepting the clicker from the man. 'Take down his statement, Officer . . . Mallory. No editorials. Just let him talk. You've got five to ten minutes.'

'Yes, sir.'

'If the press shows up, you keep them away from him. You got that?'

'Got it.'

'SID waits outside as well. Anyone entering while the captain and I are inside will be chalking tires. That includes you, Officer Mallory. You want me, you page me. Dispatch has the number.'

The officer nodded but looked a shade or two paler than a moment earlier. He took off as Shoswitz caught up. Boldt pressed the clicker and the garage door opened out and up, reminding Boldt of a mouth of a tomb. He handed Shoswitz a pair of latex gloves. 'You ready, Captain?'

Shoswitz rubbed his elbow violently. Boldt took that as a 'yes.'

Brumewell's garage was crowded, though not cluttered, with collapsible lawn furniture and rusted garden tools hanging from nails on the wall. Boldt and Shoswitz steered their way clear, and then Boldt tripped the clicker he held in his hand, the garage door slowly closing.

'What's with your interest in the garage?' Shoswitz asked.

'Point of entry,' Boldt answered. 'Dead-bolted homes,

Phil. It took us a while to see the common denominator. Our boy clones the garage door clickers, probably by hanging around nearby and picking up frequencies. I had someone looking for a name for us, but I haven't heard from him, so I suspect we've drawn a blank.'

'My guys didn't have this garage thing?' Shoswitz queried, a little troubled.

'Neither did I, Phil. Sanchez gets the credit on this one.' They entered the kitchen. Boldt speculated, 'My guess is that the burglar takes only one big risk: He backs his van into the victim's garage in broad daylight and then shuts the door. If he pulls that off cleanly, he's home free. Probably carries a police-band scanner with him. If it's me, I put the scanner in a pocket and an earpiece in one ear. If I hear this address called in, I'm gone. Otherwise, once he's inside, he's inside.'

Shoswitz followed Boldt out of the kitchen and into a living area, where several vacant spaces on shelves marked some of the stolen electronics. A cable TV box sat on a table's empty surface. A VCR, untouched. 'My guys didn't get this?' a frustrated captain repeated.

'Not important,' Boldt said.

'It is to me.'

'You made inquiries about an I.I. connection?'

'First thing. But the chances I'll hear back—'

'I know,' Boldt interrupted.

Boldt had greeted LaMoia's return to the fifth floor by dumping a copy of all eleven burglaries on his desk and ordering him to use his contacts in the private sector to look for possible insurance fraud.

Standing in Brumewell's living room, he made notes about the missing electronics.

'Clean job,' Shoswitz said. 'It's no junkie, that's for sure.'

The comment triggered a thought, and Boldt dropped

166

to his knees, searching the area behind the cabinet that had held the TV.

Shoswitz followed obediently, also dropping to the carpet. A moment later, he asked sheepishly, 'What exactly are we looking for, Lou?'

Boldt stretched, squeezing his arm between the cabinet and wall. As he touched the object, his mind leaped ahead wondering where Pendegrass and Chapman fit in, and if he'd ever prove a connection between these men and the assaults.

'This!' he said, suddenly jubilant. Pinched between his latex-gloved fingers he held a white plastic wire-tie.

TWENTY FOUR

The noon news carried a plea from Krishevski to the mayor to drop the 'hardball tactics' and allow police officers to 'once again take their place, protecting and serving the city of Seattle.' But it proved too little, too late. The mayor had played his card – health services had invalidated dozens of sick leaves and officers were being fired from the force.

Krishevski attempted to turn Schock and Phillipp into martyrs, claiming that inexperienced officers promoted prematurely by the chief, with the mayor's blessing, had failed to support the detectives and that the chief should be held directly responsible for their injuries. The pressure failed. In a press release, the mayor announced that the two hundred and twelve firings were not under reconsideration, that health services had determined that these officers claiming sick leave had been perfectly capable of serving their city and had lost the public's trust, causing permanent damage to the reputation of all city employees and services. Krishevski, it was announced, was himself fired, and the mayor announced he would no longer be considered president of the guild, as this position, according to charter, had to be held by an active police officer.

Viewed as nothing more than a negotiating position, the nature of Krishevski's status remained in question. A compromise seemed inevitable. The cost to both sides – politically and economically – had not yet been calculated.

'You look awful,' LaMoia told Boldt upon entering the man's office. 'But this . . .' he said, indicating the busy fifth floor, 'this, is beautiful.'

The floor teemed with activity.

'Partially trained cadets promoted to uniform; uniforms to plainclothes,' Boldt complained. 'It's a circus. No one knows what the hell they're doing. And they're all acting like they won the lottery, for Christ's sake.'

'Beggars can't be choosers,' LaMoia said. 'You wanted it over, Sarge. Krishevski will be gone by the end of the day. Everyone wanted this thing over. Once you've seen all the *Seinfelds* twice—'

'I feel more like a schoolteacher than a lieutenant.'

LaMoia grinned and said, 'We got more members of our unit back than any other division. That's what I hear.'

'Thirteen shields out of seventeen.' Disappointed. He had wanted them all back.

'Yeah, well, those other four? Poor, poor pitiful *them*,' he said, intentionally misquoting a Warren Zevon song. LaMoia was Zevon's biggest fan.

Boldt recognized that cocky grin of LaMoia's. With no less than a dozen active cases on the desks of every returning detective, including his sergeant's, this wasn't a social call. 'So give it up,' Boldt suggested.

'I made some calls,' the man confirmed proudly. 'It isn't insurance fraud,' LaMoia said, knowingly disappointing his boss. 'And I tried everything I could think of, in terms of trying to connect the vics to each other . . . in terms of trying to determine how our boy is picking them as targets. Their finances came up blank. No overlaps I could see. Mind you, it's a quick pass, and not all my calls have been returned. There may still be something there. A gas station they all used.

169

A department store. Some one place they all shared in common.'

'Then why that look?' Boldt asked.

'What look?' LaMoia asked, offering the look again.

'Are you going to chortle over there all day, or you going to tell me what you have?'

'Who says I have anything?'

'John—'

'It's not exactly convincing evidence, Sarge. It's a connection, is all.' He added confidently, teasing the man, 'Sure, maybe even *the* connection we're looking for, but not something you can take to Shoswitz or Hill.'

Boldt elected not to speak, not to engage the man. LaMoia would drag this out as long as he could, would make Boldt beg, if possible.

'The silent treatment?'

Boldt said nothing. He offered only a lazy-eyed stare.

'Okay . . . Okay. You wanted me to work the insurance angle. So I did like you asked. A decent idea worth pursuing. But it came back blank, as I said. Zip. Zero. And then I catch the unexpected, and I'm thinking, "Well, maybe not exactly zero." ' He waited for Boldt to react, but the man remained as patient as a fisherman.

At that point it became a contest, and Boldt finally gave in. 'Caught what?'

'Lucky as hell I did catch it, because it wasn't anything I was looking for. You know? You know how that is, Sarge? You're looking so damned hard for that missing red shoe that you overlook something way more important. Something right there in front of you. A knife . . . a gun . . . I don't know . . .'

'John—'

'A name is all,' LaMoia said. 'Of the nine burglary vics, three of them had switched their household policies

170

in the weeks prior to the break-ins. All three to the same company, Consolidated Mutual.'

Boldt sat forward. 'Three of the nine had switched insurance carriers.'

'That's what I'm saying. Yes.'

'New policies.'

'Yes.'

'Bigger policies?'

'No. Not one of them. It's not that,' LaMoia said. 'It's not fraud – it's just that switch.'

'A salesman. Maybe door to door,' Boldt speculated. 'He gets a look inside. He picks his targets.'

'More what I was thinking. Yes.' LaMoia said, 'Maybe he's in as partners, maybe just sells the info to our burglar and lets him take it from there. But it's a connection, something that ties one to the other, and either way, we've got to chat up this company.'

'Consolidated Mutual,' Boldt repeated.

'Not actually,' LaMoia corrected. 'Something called Newmann Communications. They're out of Denver.'

Boldt scribbled down the name. He knew that look: LaMoia had rolled over a large rock.

'Our problem is that it never showed up on any of the burglary reports,' LaMoia stated obliquely. Again Boldt waited him out rather than feed the flames. LaMoia asked, 'You spoke to this Helen Brooks-Gilman, Sarge. And to Kawamoto. Did either happen to mention a pair of free movie tickets?'

Boldt asked sarcastically, 'Are you on some kind of medication?'

'How about phone solicitations?'

Brooks-Gilman had in fact mentioned phone solicitations, though it had been nothing more than a denigrating comment about the intrusion upon their privacy. She'd said something about how those were the people who should be arrested. He thought he also recalled Kawamoto saying something similar to him. 'Phone solicitations?' Boldt queried.

'You check the phone logs at Newmann Communications, my guess is you'll find out that that's what all the burglary victims shared in common: they all received phone solicitations from Newmann. Several chose to up their insurance coverage; others cashed in on free movie tickets. It's the linkage, Sarge. It's how they were targeted. So tell me what you're really thinking,' La-Moia said, crossing his arms and leaning back. 'Tell me how fucking great it is to have me back on the job.'

TWENTY FIVE

Squeezed by Seattle's prosecuting attorney, Newmann Communications found itself facing the possibility of a federal investigation into interstate fraud if it failed to cooperate with Seattle PD.

With the Sanchez case still belonging to Matthews, she and Boldt were dispatched to Denver to confirm the role of a phone solicitation campaign in the string of burglaries and, if possible, identify the particular employee responsible for tipping off the burglar back in Seattle on which homes to hit.

Hoping they might accomplish the task in a single day, both Boldt and Matthews nonetheless packed overnight bags and booked hotel rooms, believing two, or even three days more likely. Police work rarely went off like clockwork.

Newmann Communications occupied a four-office suite in a mud-colored cement block building that housed KSPK, a conservative talk radio station, and Irving's Red Hots, a diner featuring hot dogs. The sausage odors fouled the building.

The employment flyers in the firm's reception lobby – a room that reminded Boldt of a department store changing room – gave away its game – Earn Money While Staying At Home! Internet Opportunities, Retail Management, Adult Entertainment. Printed on green construction paper, the small flyers fit well in the human palm – perfect as handouts on downtown sidewalks and college campuses.

Phillip Rathborne listed President/CEO on his office door. The oily scalp, bad complexion, and knock-off Armani suit suggested a man in his forties or early fifties, but the degree on the wall from North Florida Junior College put his graduation just six years earlier, meaning he had not yet crossed thirty. The office tried too hard to imply money but reminded Boldt instead of a room found in a truck stop motel with a heart-shaped bath. The clock, phone and desk lamp had been bought through the Sharper Image catalog, but the desk was granite veneer, chipped at the edges, and the jungle plant in the corner needed a serious vacuuming. The computer looked authentic – its monitor screen was large enough to be a window, something the office lacked; the screen saver played images of fairways at Pebble Beach and Augusta.

Boldt was all business. 'You received a call from the Colorado Department of Justice,' he began. Boldt had called the office and had been informed that the count had increased: seven of the nine burglary victims recalled the phone solicitation offering free movie tickets and had accepted the offer. Lawsuits seemed certain to follow. Newmann Communications could anticipate leniency in return for cooperation. Boldt expected nothing less.

'I did,' Rathborne confirmed. The man seemed pre-occupied with Daphne's silence and her intense beauty, a common enough occurrence. Useful to interrogations, her looks could be used as a means of distraction. She wore a scarf to hide the neck scar where a knife had cut her a few years before, and a blouse buttoned to the top. The less skin the better – unless she needed something from someone. Her job this time around was to play the silent, powerful type. When she finally chose to speak, she would be the more difficult of the two, leaving Rathborne surprised that ice could flow from such heat.

'And they suggested you cooperate.'

'They did.' The man had the annoying habit of wincing or grinning after every comment, expressions that somehow did not belong on his face, like those obscene reproductions of the Mona Lisa that change the smile.

'You run pay-per-call numbers out of here,' Boldt said, indicating the flyer in his hand. 'Area code nine hundred numbers.' He wanted the man on his heels, wanted him thinking in the wrong direction. 'Stroke lines?'

'Adult entertainment. All perfectly legal.'

'I don't see any phone banks.'

'The beauty of technology, Lieutenant. Our sales representatives operate out of their own homes for the most part. Through a computerized switching terminal we receive and re-route all calls.'

'College coeds?' Boldt asked.

'Housewives, mostly.' He waited for Boldt's shock to register. 'The woman moaning on the other end of the phone is doing her ironing in front of the television half the time. Cooking dinner. Playing solitaire on the computer. It's all about role playing, Lieutenant. The men call to be turned on, and to hear what they don't hear at home.'

'At eight dollars a minute,' Boldt pointed out.

'Supply and demand.'

'And the Internet site?' a repulsed Boldt inquired.

'Some soft porn shots,' he said, directing this at Daphne, 'to get the juices going. Our nine hundred numbers are promoted there. Someone wants to hear a human voice. For a credit card number, the photos go video and get a hell of a lot hotter. We grossed sixty thousand last fiscal quarter off the site alone. Wave of the future.'

'The Pantheon theater group?' Daphne asked.

'We handle a wide range of telemarketing needs for our corporate customers. Special promotions, like the Consolidated/Pantheon campaign; travel reservations; catalog sales. Our rate sheet is typically about forty percent less than our competitors, and our service just as good if not better. Keeps business brisk.'

'Lower labor costs?' she asked.

'Look around. Low overhead translates to customer savings.'

'Housewives again?'

Rathborne affected that same grimace. 'Telemarketing campaigns are much more difficult to facilitate because of the need for networked computers and a shared database. If we used isolated individuals for the telemarketing, the technology requirements would kill us. No, we subcontract. In the case of Consolidated, they're working strictly off demographics. The computers target households based on income and real estate value. The sales rep sees a name, phone number and address on his or her screen. It's slick. Consolidated Insurance owns the Pantheon theater chain. They've installed these new electronic ticket kiosks nationally and wanted to use this campaign as a synergistic way to introduce their targeted insurance sales customers to their theater chain simultaneously. It was my idea, actually, and we've hit a home run, I'm happy to say.'

'Subcontract?' Daphne pressed. 'To whom?'

'The justice department didn't tell you?' Rathborne asked Boldt. 'I assumed that was why you were here. You're Washington State, right? I thought you were looking to model our system out there in Washington . . . something like that. The state benefits as much as we do.'

Daphne said, 'Nothing like that. We're Crimes Against Persons. We're working an assault investigation—'

'Now wait a minute here!' the man objected, slipping out of his corporate image. 'No one said anything about this. I was told you'd have some questions for me about the Consolidated Mutual campaign,' the man said. 'I assumed—'

'We have no intention of charging you,' Boldt said quickly, 'nor anyone else at Newmann Communications. It's more than likely one or two of your employees – these subcontracted sales reps – that we're interested in.'

Daphne suggested, 'You may have a bad apple.'

Another waft of frankfurter-and-mustard invaded the space. Boldt felt sick to his stomach. He clarified, 'We would like to speak to this subcontractor. You put us in touch with him and we're out of here.'

Daphne repeated, 'We have no intention of involving your company in any of this, as long as you cooperate.'

'It's all about labor costs – this business. All about putting people on one end of a telephone. The automated programs suck. And Denver? In this boom? You try finding people willing to work on commission.'

Daphne inquired, 'What are you trying to tell us? All we need is the name of the subcontractor on the Consolidated Insurance campaign.'

'I don't understand why they didn't tell you when you talked to them,' an irritated Rathborne said. 'We've used them for three years now. Never once had a problem.'

'When we talked to whom?' Daphne pressed. 'Consolidated passed us on to *you*.'

'No! Not Consolidated. The justice department should have told your guys. We use correctional facilities, state prisons, inmates.' Rathborne explained, 'Our subcontractor for all our telemarketing campaigns is the Colorado Correctional Services.'

'Inmates,' Boldt mumbled, stunned by the announcement.

Daphne clarified, 'You have inmates making your phone solicitations.'

Rathborne replied, not without some pride: 'Technically, it's part of their rehabilitation.'

TWENTY SIX

A sunset flaring red beyond the Continental Divide, Boldt drove the rental through the third guarded entrance to the privately owned prison, coils of razor wire sitting atop the twenty-five-foot chain-link fence. The facility's outer wall rose thirty feet high, its masonry block connecting the four heavily armed guard towers. The middle fence, which was nearly invisible, carried High Voltage warnings on large red and yellow signs. The facility's physical plant – owned and operated by the Etheredge Corporation – housed both maximum and medium detention units, with separate visitor entrances. One of a dozen such compounds nationally, all built and managed by private companies, the correctional services contracted back to the state and were paid for by tax dollars. Etheredge Corporation traded on the NASDAQ. 'Prisoners for Profit,' Daphne read from a photocopy of a two-year-old article found in the downtown Denver library.

'Keep reading,' Boldt said. He had timed their visit to the facility purposefully, knowing that the telemarketing would likely be under way in the evening when the callers could catch families at dinner or watching TV.

She read on. The public had been outraged, the politicians impressed by the prospect of reducing corrections costs. 'Unsubstantiated charges' accused 'unnamed' state representatives of taking bribes for pushing the private corrections concept through the state legislature. With three such private facilities operating in Colorado and two more under construction, the point seemed moot. Nevada had four, Idaho two. The federal government was getting into the act. Corrections had gone private. Boldt and Matthews intended to play on the fact that Washington State had a similar proposal on a referendum that was scheduled for the fall election.

Boldt found a parking space reserved for visitors. A sign reminded them to lock the car and take the keys.

Corrections, in private hands, had gone high tech. Electronically keyed gates requiring both a guard's handprint and the swipe of a credit-card-size magnetic key permitted access to various areas of the medium-security facility. The floor plan was an octagonal layout that placed the only guard station in a center hub allowing unobstructed views of every cell. Video surveillance, infrared sensors, and electronic 'LoJacks' secured around the ankle of every prisoner rounded out the cutting-edge security technology. Evidently Colorado could not afford to build such an elaborate facility, and yet could pay the forty thousand dollars per year to house each prisoner.

Boldt had not approached Etheredge Corporation on his own, knowing full well that no privately held company would appreciate law enforcement discovering a fault with their business plan. Instead, he had used a friend in Washington State Corrections to make the introductory call for them, alleging that a pair of detectives on a fact-finding mission to Colorado were interested in touring Etheredge's Jefferson County Corrections Facility and citing in particular the medium security's so-called private commerce program. Etheredge executives, aware of the impending referendum in Washington State, saw a potential client.

Boldt and Daphne were greeted by the facility's

'managing director' – its warden – forty-five, with close-cropped hair and a steely glint to his eye. Two administrative assistants, both men in their mid-thirties, reminded Boldt of Army or Marines. Corporations knew where to recruit.

'Impressive,' Boldt said, indicating the security through which he and Daphne had just passed. The warden, a talker, a salesman, went against the stereotype. Boldt had difficulty fitting him in with the other wardens he'd known over the years.

The private tour lasted forty minutes, all show-and-tell of the facility's high-tech security. The infrared gear was sensitive enough to detect 'any mammal with a body temperature above a rat.'

'Who else have you toured?' the warden inquired, competition in his blood. He led them down a long, plain corridor.

Daphne pulled out a name from the article she'd been reading aloud only minutes earlier.

The warden nodded. 'They came in behind us. Still trying to catch up,' he suggested immodestly. 'We turned a profit after just four years of operation, don't forget. Nationally, I'm talking about. We maintain ninety-seven percent occupancy. Best bed-to-inmate ratio in the business. Zero escapes in four years of operation. Zero,' he repeated. 'Nationally!' he said again.

'The private commerce program,' Boldt said, assuming this was where he was leading them. He asked, 'Does the state share in any of that revenue?'

'Absolutely!' The warden beamed. 'I believe the state's take is twenty percent.' He turned to one of the two sycophants and said, 'We can verify that.' The young commando took off down the hall to a white wall phone.

Boldt stabbed. 'So Etheredge takes eighty percent of the private commerce profit for itself.'

'Seventy computer workstations, wide-bandwidth data lines, over five dozen phone lines – we have expenses, Lieutenant.'

'Telemarketing in a prison,' Daphne said. 'Who would have thought?'

'We didn't invent it,' the warden reminded them defensively. 'It has been around for years. Catalog sales, surveys, even airline reservations. And yet those early programs failed to take advantage of what they had. We use the computers in our alternative education program as well. It's the multi-use concept. What you really come to appreciate about Etheredge is our designers. Best in the business, swear to God.' Still defensive, he added, 'Seven states currently use telemarketing as a revenue enhancer in corrections facilities.' He was back to his salesman attitude. 'It's an effective way to partially subsidize costs while simultaneously training for employment opportunity on the outside. Over sixty percent of inmates participating in our private commerce program will be offered similar work upon release. Recidivism in this portion of our population drops noticeably.'

Boldt said, 'It's a fascinating use of prison labor.'

The comment intrigued the warden, who stopped at a secure door and placed his palm into a reader. He swiped his card next, and the door unlocked. 'You're in luck,' he informed Boldt. 'Appears we're in session.'

Except for the jumpsuits with their wide, navy blue, horizontal stripes, one might have mistaken the seventy inmates and the enormous room for a university computer lab – gray office cubicles with soundproof baffling and bright ceiling lights. In many ways it reminded Boldt of Homicide's fifth-floor offices but on an even grander scale, the irony not lost on him: the inmates had it better than the cops. The room hummed with sales pitches, computer fans, and keyboards clicking furiously.

Daphne and Boldt exchanged knowing glances. Somewhere in this room a connection to the assaults and burglaries existed: he wore a headset and manned a keyboard.

'The Consolidated program?' Boldt asked, revealing information he shouldn't have. 'Newmann Communications?'

The warden's contempt rose in a cardinal display, inflaming his neck and ears. 'What's going on here?' he inquired.

'Is it all Newmann in this room?' Boldt repeated. 'All the Consolidated campaign?'

One of the man's assistants spoke up too quickly for the warden's tastes. 'Half Newmann, half Air Express electronic ticketing.'

'How do you know about Newmann?' the concerned warden asked.

Boldt replied, 'Lieutenant Matthews and I need to see the phone logs, sorted by workstation. We have Newmann Communications' cooperation in this.'

'You lied to us!' the warden gasped. 'You're not part of any search committee.'

'We're searching all right,' Boldt confirmed, 'but not for a new prison.'

Always one to appeal to human nature, Daphne added, 'Our state *is* in the market for a private correctional facility. If we take home a favorable impression—'

'You're wrong about this,' the warden told Boldt, realizing the trouble it might mean for him personally as well as the corporation.

'The prosecuting attorney's office has already contacted Colorado Corrections. Privately run or not, it's still their show. This can end up a real mess for everyone,' Boldt suggested. 'It's all how we handle it.'

'I'll need to make some phone calls,' the warden suggested.

'Understood,' Boldt said.

'What exactly do you need?'

'Access,' Boldt answered.

'Perhaps we start with a place to talk,' Daphne suggested.

The warden was clearly disgusted. 'The home office is not going to like this,' he said.

Boldt replied, 'Neither does one of our police officers, who can't feel her legs.'

TWENTY SEVEN

Daphne used frequent flyer miles to upgrade her hotel room, which meant a few more square feet, a deep bathtub with jets, and a view of the Rockies. In his own, slightly smaller room, Boldt ordered a pot of Earl Grey tea from room service, drew himself an incredibly hot bath upon its delivery, and spent twenty wonderful minutes soaking away the stiffness still present from the assault. When the kids had been infants, Boldt had taken baths with them – glorious memories of splashing, laughing and soap in the eyes. He missed his family terribly. He wanted this case solved, the Flu over, and his family back intact.

Daphne called to say she had made dinner reservations downstairs; coat and tie required. She sounded excited – *the case*, he thought. Boldt ironed a shirt that had suffered in the shoulder bag. Dinner. The two of them alone in a hotel a thousand miles from home. Maybe Sheila Hill should have assigned LaMoia to the trip, he was thinking.

Feeling homesick, he called Liz. She had reinvented herself following her illness. She lived cleanly, spiritually minded, more centered, more collected than ever. An anchor. Her brush with death had invigorated her pursuit of life. She made few demands upon him, other than as the father of their children, and did her best to support him in a job she did not particularly care for him to have. Her work at the bank brought in a good salary, and she occasionally nudged Boldt to consider corporate security work for one of the giant multinationals in the area. But she didn't push. He had nearly interviewed for Boeing once. Their conversation was good – she was thrilled to be home again with the kids. Boldt made absolutely no mention of his impending dinner with Daphne, despite a couple of perfect openings for him to do so. And when he hung up, he wondered why he hadn't told her.

He pulled his necktie tight, choking himself. A forty-page fax was delivered to his room. Etheredge's attorneys had made the right decision – he was in possession of a portion of the Consolidated Mutual phone solicitation log for area code 206.

Daphne wore a cream-colored silk blouse with a Mao neck buttoned to hide her scar. A single strand of pearls swept gracefully across the ghost of a delicate lace bra, rising and falling behind her every word. She smelled earthy, a hint of sweet.

One look at her and he experienced a systemic warmth, like after a stiff drink.

She worked slowly on a glass of Pinot Noir; Boldt nursed a cranberry juice.

She said, 'Newmann and Consolidated give those inmates – convicted felons – access on their computer terminals to property tax assessments, full credit histories, number of dependents, number and value of registered motor vehicles . . . What did they expect would happen?'

Boldt had given her half the fax. Together, they combed the list for the phone numbers of any of the nine burglary victims. He wanted to tell her that she looked great. He kept his mouth shut and his eyes aimed at the fax.

'And that survey! Did you get time to look that over? Estimated income. Value of residence. Personal property in the residence. Number of computers owned by the family. Number of CD players; number of VCRs. All these little demographic triggers that satiate an insurance company's appetite for data, but in the wrong hands . . .' She lifted her head. He felt it as a warm wind. 'Are you listening?'

'Appetite for data,' Boldt repeated. He had other appetites going. He tried to quiet them.

'And the guys on the other side of the room are booking travel plans. You can't hit the homes while they're out of town – it'll lead us right back to you – but you could scout them, make your plans. Hit one or two, maybe, but far enough apart we don't connect the dots.'

'I've got one!' he announced a little too loudly, drawing the attention of the diners at the next table. 'Brooks-Gilman is down as having been called by an inmate identified as number forty-two,' he informed her.

'Number forty-two,' she repeated, running her finger down the column that indicated which inmate in the private commerce program had placed the phone solicitation. 'Brumewell!' she exclaimed excitedly, matching a phone number. 'Number forty-two did Brumewell too.' She was radiant when excited like this, one of those people who generated an electricity, a palpable, physical, sensuous energy that sparked across the table and infected Boldt. He felt that energy run wildly through him – though he didn't like where it landed, where he felt it the most. He shifted in his chair, relieved at the approach of the waiter. They both put the faxed pages aside.

They ate their salads slowly and in silence. He felt like skipping the main course. He wanted to get back to the faxed pages.

Boldt caught Daphne's eye, read her mind. 'It's all right that we enjoy ourselves,' he suggested, trying to sound convincing. 'No harm in that.'

'No harm whatsoever,' she echoed, though clearly not convinced.

Another minute passed before he spoke. 'The thing about us—'

'Yes?'

'The silence isn't uncomfortable.'

'No.'

'It's fine. It feels good, even.'

The salads were withdrawn, replaced by pewter-domed entrées. As the lids were whisked off in unison, rosemary and garlic stirred the air.

'It's comfortable is all,' he said, once they had been left alone.

'That's not all, and you know it,' she replied.

'No, maybe not,' he conceded.

'We've been there, Lou. And we've had plenty of opportunities since then to revisit, and we don't, which is good, I think.'

'You think or you know?'

'Her illness . . . The cancer – it pulled you two even closer together.'

'Yes, it did,' he agreed.

'It's making the most out of a bad situation. You two did that. It's admirable.'

'Thank you,' he said sincerely. 'It doesn't mean I care for you any less.'

She reached out across the table and took his hand in hers. 'I know that. And it goes both ways, you know.'

Their eyes met, smiling. He lifted his water glass. 'To private commerce caller number forty-two. I'd say we've got a suspect.'

'I'd say we'd better get through the rest of that list

tonight. If we can connect Mr Forty-two to more of the victims, our case is only that much stronger.'

'Agreed.'

'My room? Or yours?'

'Yours, it's bigger,' Boldt answered.

She pushed back her chair and excused herself without looking at him, and hurried across the dining room in that graceful movement of hers.

When she returned, he felt her urgency to leave the table.

'How about one dance before dessert?' she asked.

A jazz trio in the hotel bar. Boldt had tried to block out the music because it could so overpower him and demand his full attention. So could a dance. He was thinking it was a bad idea.

She added that she'd taken care of the tab, charging it to her room, making it impossible for him to stall.

'Why not?' he said, his mouth working against his better judgment.

A mistake. Boldt knew it the moment he put his arm loosely around her and felt the warm indent of her back in the palm of his wide hand. Secrets were lost in such moments. Kingdoms fell. With Daphne in heels, they stood nearly the same height. She pulled herself closer and their chests made contact. 'Okay?' she asked, her breath warm on his neck.

'You know what I think?' she asked, this time in a hoarse whisper that sent chills down him. Their hearts beat contrapuntally.

'Extraordinary,' he said, marveling at the sensation.

She placed her head gently on his shoulder, and answered herself. 'I think this is dangerous.'

'Feels that way to me,' he admitted, not letting her go.

'Song's over.'

So it was. He hadn't noticed. Only the one song, or had they stayed out there longer? He took her by the hand and led her off the dance floor.

They walked together down the long corridor of rooms. She used her electronic key to open the room door and Boldt found himself reminded of the prison's security. She leaned a shoulder against the door and it opened. 'This is all right? Right?'

'Right,' he answered, not taking his chance to back out. The faxed pages bulged in his coat pocket.

She reached up, lightly stroked his cheek, then playfully took him by the necktie and said, 'Into my room, big boy.'

But her words were lost to the kiss that Boldt delivered more out of reflex than conscious decision. He kissed her on the lips, not the cheek. Right there in the hallway; she, holding his tie. Brief, but delivered like he meant it.

The kiss stunned her, but she didn't falter. She pulled him through the door by the tie, turned once inside and returned that kiss with all her enormous powers. They kissed hard and hungrily, a kiss that had fermented for years.

His fingers worked the tiny buttons to her blouse, the silk melting away and exposing her chest as she unknotted his tie. A car backfired, and they both froze intuitively, and then, looking at each other in the early stages of undress, one of them started to laugh and the other followed until the laughter grew, by which point her blouse was buttoned and her face red behind a girlish blush.

'Maybe we go through the fax tomorrow morning,' she suggested nervously.

Boldt felt awkward. Devastated. 'I—'

'Don't say anything,' she pleaded, placing a warm

finger to his lips and holding it there too long. Her blouse was buttoned incorrectly. His shirt was partially open, his tie hanging from his button-down collar.

TWENTY EIGHT

The Jefferson County Corrections Facility appeared somehow otherwordly as they approached, the sprawling sand-colored facility surrounded by silver waves of razor wire, all of it pushed out into the scrub of high desert. The ride had been unusually quiet.

Daphne rolled a Starbucks cup between her palms, as if warming them. It was eighty degrees outside the air-conditioned car, the sky a blue found only in the mountains.

Boldt felt a little blue himself. He found it difficult to focus on the investigation, which was, after all, the purpose of the trip. This, despite the fact that before going to sleep he had connected inmate 42 with another four of the burglary victims' phone numbers. He and Daphne were on their way now to have a little chat with number 42.

Boldt turned left onto a long gravel road that led toward the shimmering facility. Dust rose behind the rental in a growing plume that colored the sun. He said, 'Listen, Daffy. I've thought about that kiss for a long time. Now that it's behind us, maybe we can make it another five or six years.'

'No harm, no foul?' she questioned.

'I don't want you mad at me.'

'Is that what you think?' she asked. 'You know, for being such a good detective, sometimes you don't have a clue.'

'True story,' he said.

He mugged a smile for her, squinting eyes giving him away. He pulled the car up to the first of three guard booths, and slipped his ID wallet out of his blue blazer. Daphne did the same, and the conversation ended.

Boldt and Matthews sat across a speckled vinyl tabletop in an employees' cafeteria. Boldt read from the folder in front of him. 'Inmate number forty-two, as listed on the phone solicitation sheets. David Ansel Flek – no 'c.' Serving a three-year sentence – get this – for grand larceny. He's been part of the private commerce tele-marketing program for the past eight weeks.'

'Right about when our robberies started,' Daphne said.

They had half the connection: Flek had been the telemarketer who had spoken to each of the burglary victims. Before interrogating Flek, they needed the other half: contact with the outside. They awaited the warden.

When the man arrived, Boldt noticed that some of his military composure had worn off. He understood the implications of all this for his facility. Nothing less than his job was at stake. Yet he was on orders from Etheredge to cooperate – a private facility refusing to cooperate with law enforcement would sound a death knell for state prison contracts.

'Our pay phones here are owned and operated by an Etheredge subsidiary,' he began.

'Never leave a dime unturned,' Daphne said.

'The home office is still working with the database of calls placed from those pay phones. The attorneys will eventually have to sort out the first amendment issues. Many, if not most, of the calls made from our pay phones are placed using calling cards owned by relatives or friends on the outside. We can get these numbers from the various carriers, I'm told, but it will take some time. In the meantime, I have this.' He handed Boldt a stack of twenty faxed sheets. 'They are not sorted by area code,' he apologized.

'We'll live,' Boldt said.

'But I did have my secretary highlight any direct-dial calls made to the 206 area code.' He added somewhat proudly, 'And she put a check by four of the calls that could have been made by inmate number forty-two.'

'Determined how?' Daphne inquired, pulling her chair next to Boldt's and looking over his shoulder.

Boldt pointed to the top sheet. 'By time.'

'Schedule,' the warden said. 'It's not open access. Pay telephone time is closely controlled.'

Boldt said, 'So how many others had access to the phones at the same time Flek did?'

'There are five pay phones,' the warden explained. 'We give each inmate fifteen minutes a day.'

'So four other guys,' Boldt suggested. It was a nice, narrow field, something he could work with. He recognized the prefix of the highlighted 206 number as a cellular prefix. He would call LaMoia and have the owner of the cell phone identified. He would make sure David Flek made no more calls. If they got lucky, they'd have their burglar. He wasn't holding his breath; it was rarely that easy.

Daphne tested him. 'So our chances are one out of five that Flek called Seattle and passed along the names and addresses of possible burglary targets?'

'He doesn't know that,' Boldt answered. To the warden he said, 'I think it's time we meet Mr Flek.'

'We can arrange that. But first, you mind explaining how all this works? My people are going to ask me, and

I'm going to look a hell of a lot smarter if I know what I'm talking about.'

Boldt thought it sounded fair enough. 'Flek is supplying names to someone on the outside. Through the phone solicitation, this survey conducted by Consolidated through Newmann, he identifies homes that have a couple computers, a high-end stereo or a couple TVs. A nice bottom line.'

Daphne had returned her attention to the original fax of phone numbers called by the phone solicitation team.

Boldt continued, 'He calls out on the pay phones – probably to this cell phone number – and supplies the names and addresses of potential high-end targets. At that point it's in our part of the world. We get a burglary call.'

Daphne, her nose still in the fax, said, 'Lou! Granted, three of the burglary victims are not anywhere on this list from last night. Maybe they were placed a week earlier than the records we've been provided. Maria's not on the list either.'

In his excitement over the connection to inmate forty-two, Boldt had neglected to search out Sanchez's number in the database. It was such a simple oversight, but suddenly the absence of her number from the phone solicitation's master call sheet loomed largely over their efforts.

'She could have been called earlier as well,' he suggested.

The closer they came to the interrogation of a possible suspect – even an accessory to the fact like David Ansel Flek – the more Boldt dreaded the possibility of discovering that Maria Sanchez had never been one of the burglary targets. The implication would then be that Maria's assault had been cop on cop, the same way he feared his own assault had been. Now that he approached whatever truth existed, he did so cautiously, well aware that on rare occasions, some truths were better left undisturbed.

'No,' she said, shaking her head. 'In every case the burglaries come within ten days of the initial phone solicitation. That being the case, she'd be on here.'

'Erased?' Boldt inquired of a confused warden. He and Daphne exchanged glances, and he could see her concern as well.

'To my knowledge,' the man said, 'the system does not allow it. You can't erase any information from the private commerce database. That's one of the stipulations. Just in case something like this ever happened.'

To Daphne, Boldt stressed, 'We need Flek to implicate whoever was doing these burglaries. If that guy was not at Sanchez's . . . if he never hit Sanchez's place . . . if we can confirm it . . . *prove* it . . . then maybe we have the ammo we need to go knocking on I.I.'s door and get a look at whatever they know.'

She nodded, though her concern, like his, was palpable.

To the warden, Boldt said, 'We need to speak to Flek right now!'

The prison's interrogation room still smelled of the glue used to fasten down the vinyl flooring. It ranked as the cleanest interrogation room Boldt had ever seen. Better than even the FBI or BATF. A video camera looked down on the occupants. Built into the wall was a twin cassette tape recorder that kept track of every spoken word, every sound. The twin cassette concept, borrowed from the Brits, ensured that no one could later edit the content of the interrogation to fit his needs; one tape went with the officer in charge, the other was filed in a vault accessed only by the warden – a failsafe against corruption.

David Ansel Flek wore the demeaning zebra suit, his number EJC-42 on a patch sewn onto the right breast pocket and on another that ran shoulder to shoulder across his back. 'Forty-two,' the guards called him, never using names, never personalizing or humanizing the process. A team of privately contracted criminal psychiatrists had advised Etheredge Corporation on how to treat the prisoners in order to maintain discipline and keep peace, so it came as something of a shock to the man in the jumpsuit when Boldt and Matthews addressed him by his Christian name. It also served to mark the two as outsiders – exactly as Matthews had advised Boldt.

'Who are you?' the man inquired. Flek's boyish face and blond surfer-dude hairstyle, his blue eyes and white teeth reminded Boldt of one of the Beach Boys, or Tab Hunter in a Fort Lauderdale movie. His smallish frame had been beefed up in the gym. Boldt knew the ordeal such looks suffered in any prison. They called them babes, wives, soapies – the young men forced to lie on their stomachs for the rulers of the pen. But to his surprise, Boldt did not see the steely-eyed resentment he associated with the abused. The more he studied Flek, the more he believed the man had somehow escaped the role of girlfriend, either a credit to Etheredge's management of the facility, or testimony to the ruthlessnes of Flek himself.

'We're your only hope,' Daphne said.

Boldt clarified, 'Your only hope, unless you like it here.'

'Unless you're thinking of turning fifty in here,' Daphne said. Dates or age had a way of shaking up any inmate – the passage of time was the only god in such places, the only redeemer. According to his file, the man was twenty-nine years old, and Boldt's comment seemed to hit home.

'What's it about?' he asked.

'The harder you make us work for it,' Boldt informed him, 'the fewer years we trim off what's going to be added to your sentence. You want to get out of here by forty? Thirty-five? Then don't play dumb.'

His ice blue eyes searched them both. They favored Daphne, and for a little too long.

Boldt cautioned, 'There are no second chances, Flek. We leave, and we take twenty years of your life out the door with us.'

'I requested my public defender,' the man reminded.

'And she's on her way, as I understand it,' Boldt said. 'You know how busy they are.'

'So we wait,' Flek said confidently.

Boldt and Matthews exchanged glances. Daphne spoke to the inmate. 'I'm not advising you one way or the other, David—'

'Ansel,' he corrected a little too quickly.

'You're somewhat new to the system,' she said. He winced; he didn't want to be told that. 'We've seen your file. First offense, light sentence. They were lenient with you. You're lucky in that regard, as I'm sure you found out once you took up residence here.'

'You have a little over a year left to go,' Boldt reminded him. 'So why add ten to twenty to that?'

'Our point is,' Daphne continued, 'that going the attorney route is your legal right, and even if we could help you out here, we can't do anything to stop you from exercising that right. And, in fact, you've already invoked that right, which is perfectly acceptable to us, though in my opinion not in your best interest.'

In a calm voice, he answered Daphne. 'But you are in my best interest? A couple of cops? I don't think so.'

'Ten to twenty,' Boldt informed the man.

Daphne echoed, 'You need to be thinking about turning fifty here at Etheredge.'

Boldt reached across the table and forced the man's hands up in plain view.

Flek said, 'I was scratching, is all,' still not breaking his eye contact with Daphne.

Daphne allowed the facility's forced air system to account for the only sound in the room. It swallowed the three of them. She asked, 'Maybe you want to put the idea of an attorney aside for a moment and at least listen to our offer.'

'What can it hurt to listen?' Boldt asked.

'So talk,' Flek said.

Boldt felt a minor victory. He knew from the man's file that Flek had graduated from junior college, and decided to approach him in a businesslike manner. Boldt informed him, 'We'd like to start with the phone solicitations you made and then continue onto the subsequent pay phone calls made to the cell phone based in Washington.'

Daphne added, 'The more details you provide . . . the more they prove out for us . . . the stronger voice we'll have in your sentence recommendation, which for you translates to fewer years the judge tacks onto your time here.'

'No matter what, you hold out on us and you're looking at more time,' Boldt explained, 'including the possibility of accessory charges to a felony assault. So the smart money says cooperate before the attorney arrives and screws it all up.'

'Wasting your time,' Flek told him, his words spitting

across the table. He motioned toward Daphne, 'I enjoy the scenery. But all the small talk I could do without. I don't have a clue what you're talking about.' What she knew about his background didn't jibe with the man in that chair, making her psychologist side immediately suspicious. He was hiding behind his inmate persona. Why?

'We have the phone logs,' Boldt countered. 'The phone solicitations are all tracked on computer. The pay phone calls to the cellular number – we've got those too. Are you dumber than you look, or what?'

'I'm represented by a public defender,' he said. 'All inquiries should go through her.'

'What happens in places like this,' Daphne said, meeting eyes with him, 'is you get tunnel vision. You get so you can only think like everyone else thinks. And the everyone else I'm talking about are not exactly the cream of the crop, you know? They're losers. You start to think like a loser. Don't be a loser, Ansel,' she said, switching names. 'We're talking about adding twenty years to your time in here. You'll be forty-nine years old before you're eligible for parole.'

The man's nostrils flared and his eyes shone wetly. He repeated, 'All inquiries should go through my public defender.'

'You don't win anything,' she pleaded, 'by playing tough.'

Flek shook his head.

Boldt asked the man, 'Why would you willingly add twenty years to your time here? You answer a half dozen questions and maybe we just walk out of here as if none of this ever happened? You can't be that stupid.'

'We wait for my attorney.'

Boldt stood from his chair. Daphne followed his lead. 'Wrong answer,' Boldt said.

The events of the next few hours unfolded in a way that he never would have expected.

TWENTY NINE

Boldt's official complaint, which he filed with the Colorado Department of Corrections, clearly touched off a nerve. It took the spotlight in news reports – politicians quickly attempting to distance themselves from state-sanctioned phone solicitation programs involving inmates. At first it seemed nothing more than election-year candidates seizing an opportunity to grandstand. How else could Boldt's one-page report have mushroomed into a media feeding frenzy? No doubt some clerk had leaked the complaint within minutes of its filing. That leak had spread through media, and the media's subsequent outrage had caught fire when combined with the ulterior motives of politicians seeking reelection.

By the time Boldt and Daphne returned to the hotel at mid-day, a half dozen press and radio reporters were already waiting for them in the lobby.

Boldt and Daphne issued, 'No comment,' pushing toward the elevators.

When they returned to the lobby thirty minutes later to check out, the reporters had been joined by two television crews, three state representatives, the staff of a United States senator, and two mayoral aides. The hotel had requested and received crowd control from the Denver police – two of whom pressed through the reporters to help Boldt and Daphne reach the registration desk.

The shouting from the reporters was nearly all the same: 'Is it true that inmates at Etheredge's Jefferson County facility were engaged in a phone sales campaign?' 'Do you know who authorized such a campaign?' 'Has the governor had any comment, to your knowledge?' 'Is it true that inmates conducted crimes from within the privately operated prison?'

It amused Boldt that neither he nor Daphne answered these questions, but instead the various politicians and their assistants. Facts surrounding the private commerce program at Etheredge unfolded. According to a congressman's aide, the program had been approved by a handful of politicians and had been kept quiet these many months under the pretense of it being a test program. As such, a statement had been made to the voting public that Etheredge Corporation was paying both the county and the state substantial fees on a commission basis – no mention that certain influential state politicians had been generously entertained, and their campaign coffers padded, prior to the subcommittee's closed-door vote that had authorized the program in the first place.

Boldt's letter of complaint to the state's Department of Justice lit a fuse that would burn for many months to come, finally destroying more than a few in the hotel lobby.

'Is it true this program was initiated under the guise of prison reform?' a reporter shouted.

'What was David Ansel Flek's role in your investigation?' a well-informed woman called out from the crowd. Boldt and Daphne met eyes. How had that leaked? 'And what does your trip here, to Denver, have to do with your ongoing investigation of the tragic assault of Seattle police officer Maria Sanchez?'

Daphne grabbed him by the arm, stopping him. 'We

need to deal with this. We need to head it off. If the Flek investigation leaks home, we lose our jump on his possible accomplice.'

'Agreed!' Boldt said. He assumed this reporter had searched the *Times'* Internet archives for one or both of their names and had uncovered their participation in the Sanchez investigation. A guard or someone in the warden's office had Flek's name.

Daphne spoke up loudly, and as she did, the crowd quieted down for the first time. 'Ladies and gentlemen! Please! Thank you! Lieutenant Boldt and I are with the Seattle Police Department, investigating *a string of burglaries.*' She looked this woman reporter in the eye to drive home her point. 'We came to Denver to follow up on possible leads that may or *may not* be connected to the Etheredge facility in Jefferson County. We spoke to a *variety* of individuals at the facility, including inmates and administrative personnel, *none* of whom has been charged with any crimes. I want to stress that point: to date, no one in Colorado has been charged with any crime associated with our investigation. This was, and is, a fact-finding mission and nothing more. The lieutenant and I are returning to Seattle now to follow up on what we've learned here. Any forthcoming charges or connections to our investigation will be released to the press in a timely fashion. We are working in cooperation with the Colorado Department of Corrections, and the justice department. That *is all* we have for you at this time. Thank you.'

Boldt and Daphne exited the room, following a pair of patrol officers. A reporter pulled at Boldt's overnight bag, and the lieutenant elbowed the man away. Camera flashes blinded him as they staggered out into the daylight, expecting their rental but instead finding themselves shoved into a waiting stretch limousine bearing the hotel logo. Moments later, they were on their way to the airport.

When the two weren't calling out on their cellular phones, the devices were ringing. ABC radio broke the story nationally ten minutes into the ride, ensuring that even more press would be awaiting the two at the Denver airport. Two cars and a television van dogged the limousine, pulling alongside, reporters leaning out of the cars and shouting for one of them to put the window down and answer questions. The limousine's cellular phone rang; it was the television van following right behind them. The driver hung up.

Boldt's cellular rang. 'Lieutenant Boldt?' a man's voice asked.

'Speaking,' Boldt answered into his cellular.

'John Ragman, Colorado Department of Corrections. We spoke this afternoon.'

'Yes.'

'There's something here I wanted to share with you. It concerns . . . the inmate you interviewed out at Etheredge.'

'I'm listening.'

'You run the man's surname through our system and you get more than one hit. You follow me?'

'Yes, I think I do.'

'You're on a cellular – I can hear it. Digital?'

'No.'

'So maybe I shouldn't say much more. The reporters – often scan the analog frequencies.'

'Yes, I understand. The person you want to talk to is a Sergeant John LaMoia.' Boldt gave him the direct number. 'I'll call LaMoia from a land line out at the airport to be caught up, or I'll call you directly if I can't reach him . . . if you two haven't spoken.'

'Got it.' Ragman added, 'You're gonna like what I've

got. Or maybe not, I guess. But either way, you need it, Lieutenant.'

Boldt disconnected the cell, waited for Daphne to get off her own phone, and told her, 'There's another Flek in the Colorado system, maybe a relative.'

'Maybe currently living in Seattle?' she deduced.

'One has to wonder,' Boldt agreed.

'Hence Flek's reluctance to cooperate with us,' she said. 'Protecting a brother, a cousin?' She had felt something odd about his demeanor. Now, maybe she had an explanation for it.

'Worth pursuing,' Boldt said.

'That call I just hung up from?' she said. 'The number called from the pay phone at Etheredge? It looks like maybe it's a cloned cellular phone. That bill has dozens of calls being disclaimed by the customer.'

'A cloned number offers anonymity. It makes sense,' Boldt agreed.

'Which means we'd have to catch this guy in the act to connect him to Flek – relative or not. And we'll lose that chance, because he'll be warned off by all this media attention.'

'*Beat the Clock*,' Boldt said. He remembered the quiz show from his youth.

'You think we made a mistake, Lou? Interrogating him? Tipping our hand? Maybe we'd have been better to sit on him. Intercept the activity.'

Boldt believed she was probably right, but also knew there was no looking back during an investigation. He didn't answer directly. Instead he said, 'We work this relative of Flek's and we work this cell phone that was called. We work it fast before too much of this makes it onto the evening news. Maybe we get lucky.'

'Since when?' Daphne asked.

THIRTY

Upon returning to his job, LaMoia thought the excessive workload facing him must have seen some kind of cruel joke, perhaps cooked up by Boldt to prove how hard things had been for him during LaMoia's absence. There were nine active investigations on LaMoia's desk. He had responded to two of the crime scenes and taken reports from the other seven. At the same time, he was wearing the hats of Burglary detective, Special Assaults detective, and Homicide sergeant. And he'd only been on the job for two days.

When some guy identifying himself as Ragman called from Colorado Corrections and mentioned Boldt by name, LaMoia focused his attention on the message being relayed – the name of a possible accomplice.

He scribbled the name *Bryce Abbott Flek* into his notebook.

Ragman said, 'Brother Flek owns a pink sheet the length of your arm. A juvie gone bad. His more recent history here puts him in double jeopardy. One more felony conviction and the guy does fifteen without parole.'

'Flek,' LaMoia repeated, reading from his notes. Having spoken to Boldt earlier, he knew about the failed interrogation out at Etheredge. He had asked a friend at InterCel to identify the cellular phone number called from the prison, and then had spoken with Matthews ten minutes earlier to deliver the bad news: the number had indeed been cloned.

Ragman warned, 'His jacket is littered with references to what one officer called "the volatile nature of his personality." There's also a reference to a psych evaluation in here, although I don't have my hands on it. Way it looks to me: this is a dog that bites. Little brother is tame by comparison. This one took out two uniforms trying to arrest him back in ninety-three – both hospitalized, one with a broken neck.'

'Broken neck?' LaMoia repeated, yanking his feet off his desk and sitting upright in the chair. 'You have aliases for this mope?'

'You got a sharp pencil? It's a long list. Better yet, what if I fax you as much of this as I can?'

'Is he on WestCrime?' LaMoia inquired.

'NCD,' Ragman said. The National Criminal Database. 'You guys lined out with that yet?'

'You bet. We've got access to WestCrime, NCD, and all the federal databases.'

'Then you're set on the aliases,' Ragman said. 'I'll still fax you the liner notes, in case that stuff didn't get posted to the database. The way it shakes out: he's a thief with a fondness for anything electronic, a violent son of a bitch when he wants to be, and I guess that's most of the time. Just so you and your boys know to wear vests.'

'Got it,' LaMoia said, drawing a thickening ring around the name *Bryce Abbott Flek* to where it dominated the page.

He called Boldt, who said, 'Can't talk on the cellular. I'll call you back from the airport.' The line went dead.

He accessed the NCD database and downloaded both Flek brothers' criminal records. Bryce Abbott Flek operated under six aliases, all ending in 'ek,' or 'eck.' LaMoia typed in the various names, all separated by commas. He tried SPD records, King County records and state records. No arrests. He tried the man's Colorado motor vehicle registration – a 1991 blue Dodge van. A subsequent request with the licensing bureau kicked five unpaid in-state parking tickets, all within a three-block area of Ballard. The first of these parking tickets was dated a year earlier, the same month as David Ansel Flek's conviction. The pieces started falling into place. LaMoia grew increasingly excited.

Fingers drumming, he considered various means to pinpoint the address and locate Bryce Abbott Flek. One option was to drive around the three-block area looking for that blue van with Colorado plates and put it under surveillance when they found it. He would then wait for Flek to show up and hope to follow him back to an apartment, put that under surveillance. The time and manpower requirements seemed enormous.

He tried a friend at US West. No go: not one of Flek's aliases kicked for a current listing. No great surprise – if the man was using a cloned cellular, why bother with a Ma Bell installation?

If Flek was renting a room or an apartment, LaMoia had no way of finding out where. There were no tax records and no utility bills, at least not that he could locate. He racked his brain for some other way to find the guy, and to find him fast, before the news leaks Boldt had warned of reached Flek, and he heard of his little brother's contact with Seattle police. If and when that happened, Flek was certain to go underground, perhaps not surfacing again. He debated whether to put out the word on the street – he had Flek's mug shot, courtesy of the NCD database. He thought of liquor stores and Domino's Pizza, delivery boys. He called a friend at a credit bureau – no credit cards, no loans, no bank accounts under any of the aliases.

In the end, using the patrol force to search Ballard for

any blue vans appeared the best choice. He put the word out over the Mobile Data Terminals network – notifying nearly two hundred patrol cars simultaneously.

An hour before Boldt and Daphne's plane touched down at SEATAC, LaMoia was notified by an SPD radio car that a blue van with Colorado plates was currently fueling at a gas station in Ballard, not five blocks from LaMoia's current location. LaMoia had issued the Be On Lookout for the van with little hope. To his surprise, he had been notified of four blue vans in the past thirty minutes. This radio call represented the first mention of Colorado plates. Within minutes, LaMoia confirmed the registration: Bryce Abbott Flek.

About that same time he double-parked his fire-engine red 1968 Camaro with a view across the street. The gas pump's black hose hung from the van's tank like an elephant's trunk, the driver nowhere to be seen. He spotted the cruiser patrolling a block away, hailed them over the radio and ordered them to park out of sight. He then radioed dispatch and ordered all SPD patrol cars kept out of a ten-block area surrounding the gas station. He didn't want anything, anyone, alerting Flek to their presence. When he requested additional unmarked cars, the dispatcher had the audacity to laugh at him. 'Request is noted,' the uncharacteristically amused dispatcher announced. LaMoia understood the subtext: in terms of winning unmarked cars and plain-clothes detectives as backup, he was in this alone.

The Quik Stop gas station teemed with activity. Some customers pulled up to the pumps; others parked, shopping for a soda, a bag of chips, or a quart of milk. But by his count, every customer arrived and left by automobile. He observed no bicycles, no pedestrians.

This latter realization prompted a second study of the back of a big man already a half block behind the Quik Stop and moving away. The man wore a thigh-length leather jacket, blue jeans and high-top running shoes. The telltale sign that got LaMoia's adrenaline pumping had nothing to do with clothes but instead, the lack of anything carried. No paper or plastic bag. No soda. It seemed conceivable the man had purchased a pack of cigarettes or something small enough to be pocketed – it was no crime to leave a Quik Stop on foot – but his recollection of the case file suggested otherwise: the burglar was believed to monitor police radio bands, probably on a portable scanner, and LaMoia had impetuously cleared the area around the Quik Stop *by radio*, naming the gas station's location. Foremost on LaMoia's mind: where had this guy come from? He had not seen anyone *arrive* on foot in the last few minutes.

More to the point, according to his criminal records, Bryce Abbott Flek stood six foot one, and weighed in at two hundred pounds. That fit well with the man now nearly a block away.

LaMoia needed someone to watch the blue van while he pursued its apparent owner on foot, but he didn't want the car's police radio to communicate about it. The real Flek, whether or not he was the man on foot, might be listening in, wandering the aisles of the Quik Stop, wondering how to play his situation.

Realizing he had to take a chance, LaMoia grabbed the radio's handset and informed the dispatcher he was switching to one of the four 'secure frequencies' used by SPD. Illegally modified scanners could not intercept these digitally secure frequencies. He requested the dispatcher to assign a patrolman from the nearby cruiser to take up a position with a view of the blue van and to report any activity. Naming the cross street behind the

211

Quik Stop – the intersection where the blue-jeaned pedestrian was headed – LaMoia requested that two cruisers position themselves as backup, bookending the street. This done, he took off on foot.

He did not run, but instead walked with a brisk, long-legged stride, calculated to quickly close the distance between himself and his mark. He had not thought to bring along a portable radio from the squad room, and so he was on his own – 'cloaked,' 'in the dark.' Only his cellular phone connected him to the world outside of Bryce Abbott Flek – if that was in fact whom he was following.

By the time his suspect reached the intersection and turned right, LaMoia had closed the gap to half a block. Following several weeks of inactivity, LaMoia felt awash, invigorated by the pursuit, hungry for confrontation. He loved his job. There was nothing quite like slamming a mope up against the wall and slapping a pair of bracelets around his wrists, taking another piece of infectious waste off the streets, out of the game. Duty called. He felt positively electric with anticipation.

The first blow came from behind – a devastating show of force, unexpected and overpowering. An open-palm smack to the back of his skull, delivered with such ferocity that his chin bruised his chest, and a whole series of muscles at the nape of his neck ripped loose. He heard his gun clink to the sidewalk, the dull sound of metal on cement, useless where it lay. That blow to the head stunned the muscles of his upper back and numbed his spine to where his arms suddenly weighed upon him like sandbags. He attempted to turn around to fight back, but his arms hung at his side, swinging like gorilla limbs, and the man behind him directed him otherwise, smashing his face into the brick wall twice and then working a volley of rabbit punches from just above his hip points into the center of his back ribs. The man hit, intending to do harm, intending to quickly eliminate LaMoia from the field of play, swinging through the punches at the brick wall, with only LaMoia's flesh and bone in between. The man's knee bruised LaMoia's coccyx, and the heel of his foot found LaMoia's instep to where, as he let go, the sergeant sank to the sidewalk, bloody and broken, a mass of misfiring nerve endings, his lungs burning, his legs unable to support him.

He never even saw the man's face.

THIRTY ONE

Shying from the obnoxiously bright light, Boldt rushed through the emergency room's automatic doors, met there by the on-call physician who had tended LaMoia's injuries. Daphne spoke to a nurse. Upon being informed of the assault, they had made the drive from SEATAC in just over ten minutes – roughly half the usual time, even in good traffic.

The doctor spoke breathlessly, also trying to keep up with the lieutenant. 'Fluid in the right lung, bruised kidneys, contusions, partial concussion, fractured ribs, bruised coccyx. If I hadn't gotten the report from the officers who delivered him, I would have said he'd been hit by a vehicle from behind.'

They stepped into the oversized elevator and the doctor hit a floor button. Boldt felt ready to explode. 'So nothing permanent,' he said. 'Nothing disabling.'

'A good deal of pain, a long convalescence, and he's back to normal,' the doctor said. 'The guy's got a hell of an attitude, Lieutenant. He's making jokes as we're wiring his jaw shut.'

'His jaw?' Daphne said.

'Didn't I mention that?' the doctor asked as the elevator toned its arrival. 'Broken mandible.'

'Jesus,' Boldt hissed.

Daphne reached out and squeezed his forearm in support. He turned to face her. 'I'm the one who put him there,' he wanted to say. He charged out of the elevator, and hurried toward room 511.

A powder blue blanket hid most of him. Lying flat on his back, without a pillow. A variety of monitors. A dozen bright yellow numbers, some flashing.

At first Boldt thought they had the wrong room because he didn't recognize the man lying there. Then he realized they had shaved LaMoia's mustache to deal with the cuts and abrasions, and to stitch up a spot where a tooth had come through his cheek. Boldt had to look away, he was so overcome with emotion.

Boldt didn't always deal well with his anger, and he was very angry now. A rational thinker, he tried to avoid anger altogether by compartmentalizing explanations and analyzing situations, though he frequently failed. LaMoia was too close a friend for Boldt to see him solely as a wounded sergeant. Boldt had connected Ragman to LaMoia – and from the sketchy details he had, Boldt believed himself responsible for the injuries.

'How long like this?' Daphne whispered to the doctor, but so that Boldt could overhear. She wanted to bookend this for Boldt, to show him it wasn't forever, to make it finite.

'The lung will keep him here for a day or two. We'll get him pretty healed up by then. He'll be home with just a couple bumps and bruises in no time. Six to eight weeks, it never happened.'

'Try telling him that,' Boldt said.

'Medically speaking,' the doctor replied.

The body in the bed grunted, its bloodshot eyes open now and fixed on Boldt, who slowly made his way to the injured man's bedside. Boldt saw a familiar morbid humor in those eyes, and for some reason this made his anger all the more palpable. How dare LaMoia make

215

light of this! How dare he try to forgive him – Boldt knew what that attempted humor was about.

'Flek?' Boldt asked.

The man's lips moved, but Boldt couldn't hear.

The doctor warned, 'He shouldn't attempt to speak. Please. In the morning, maybe.'

But LaMoia grunted, drawing Boldt's ear closer to his lips.

'Good drugs,' the man whispered.

Boldt felt tears spring from his eyes. 'Jesus, John, I'm sorry.' He dragged his arm across his face, trying to hide his reaction.

LaMoia just grunted in response. The doctor pulled Boldt away and checked the monitors.

'It's rest for you,' he said to LaMoia, addressing an I.V. pump and increasing the rate of flow. 'And stop flirting with the nurses,' he added.

'Never,' LaMoia whispered, meeting eyes with Daphne, and trying to smile.

'Healthy as ever,' Daphne said.

THIRTY TWO

'The Flek brothers,' Daphne said. 'You want to hear this?'

Boldt sat at his office desk, still preoccupied by his hospital visit to LaMoia. He nodded yes, all the while thinking about LaMoia's empty office cubicle just around the corner.

'We have a pretty classic Svengali here. Bryce Abbott Flek, the older brother, has been in and out of trouble – *in* mostly – since he could ride a bike. The bully in school. Truant. Petty theft – bicycles, cigarettes from the candy store. A couple juvie arson arrests. Possession of a switchblade. Grand larceny auto at the ripe age of fourteen. Liquor store robbery, fifteen.'

'Model citizen.'

'One troubled kid. Trailer park life in the Colorado oil fields. Statutory rape charges when he was eighteen – turned out it was consensual, charges dropped. He beat up a lot of people. One hell of a volatile personality. It's endless.'

'You don't need to sound so excited,' he said. Daphne's professional curiosity about the criminal mind exceeded one's reasonable expectations. She was always looking for ways to interview suspects *ahead* of their arrest – while they still showed their true colors.

She cast him a disapproving look and continued, saying, 'In and out of youth detention facilities, corrections. Six months for this, eighteen for that – minimum or medium facilities, never the big house. Fast forward: he's thirty-three years old, he has two recent felonies on his dismal sheet, one aggravated assault, one grand larceny.'

'File that for a moment,' she said, motioning for Boldt to set Bryce Abbott aside. 'Rewind. David Ansel Flek. Little brother. Same trailer park, same parents, same schools. But no truancy. No arrests until he's seventeen, and that one's for loitering and curfew violation following a winter flood that takes out the family trailer and Mom along with it. It's sketchy at best, but a *Denver Post* article I pulled from the Net mentions her by name – Adrian Abbott Flek – electrocuted when the flood hit. Got to be the mother. Father blew off the sons and headed to the Alaska fields. David drifts south, although he never leaves Colorado – his brother's influence can hardly be said to be positive. David enlists in the Army, makes it two years, goes AWOL. Is arrested on one of his brother's robberies. Turned back over to the Army. Serves a couple months in the brig, serves out his stint and is dishonorably discharged at twenty-three. State tax records show him employed briefly with a computer software firm. Mail room or programmer, we have no idea, but he's basically on the straight-and-narrow. It's during this period that brother Bryce is making his mark with the local blues, one arrest after another, increasingly violent. Make note of this: David's next job is with a discount electronics retailer, a Best Buy type. He moves up to manager in a two-year period – he's twenty-five, twenty-six now. There's a break-in at David's store right after a major delivery – two dozen TVs, VCRs, twice that many computers. David is busted and eventually confesses. His first felony, he goes down for two to seven.'

'In Etheredge,' Boldt said.

'Correct.'

'He's out in two with good behavior,' Boldt said.

'Correct. Which means we have all sorts of leverage. If we convince younger brother David that with both the Sanchez and LaMoia assaults, Bryce faces bullets from the first uniform to make him, maybe he gives us a lead. Or maybe we simply hold the threat of an added ten years over him, although that sure didn't work the first time.'

'I like playing him for the brother's safety. The only thing is, we don't have either brother for Sanchez – no phone solicitation records, remember? – and we don't have Bryce for LaMoia. He never saw his attacker's face. So we're looking at burglary at best, unless Kawamoto can make him.'

'Someone walked away from that blue van and never came back. How difficult is it for a judge or jury to see that?'

'It's circumstantial. When and if we catch up with Bryce, he'll tell us the van was stolen an hour before. We can't disprove that.'

'What about the convenience store's security camera? Did it pick up his face?'

'The system's VCR was lifted a month ago and never replaced by management. There is no tape. We can't put Bryce Flek at that gas station.'

She said, 'What exactly are you saying?'

'David is our way to find Bryce. We find Bryce, maybe we wrap this thing up.'

'Maybe,' she said. 'But Bryce would have to confess to Sanchez to get any decent charges to stick.'

Boldt answered, 'Maybe not.' He hoisted a black-and-white mug shot of Bryce Abbott Flek and turned it to face Daphne. 'What if Sanchez can ID him?'

Boldt's private line rang, and he took the call. Hanging up a moment later, a satisfied grin playing across his lips, he informed her, 'We found the apartment where Flek has been staying.'

THIRTY THREE

Bryce Abbott Flek's photo was recognized by a guitar maker. The rented room, one of five that occupied the two floors above Fletcher Brock's custom instrument shop, consumed three SID field technicians who combed it floor to ceiling. LaMoia's assault could be felt here too – normally Boldt would have been lucky to get even one tech to a potential suspect's abode in under an hour.

'What have we got?' Boldt asked a SID tech from just inside the doorway. He wore latex gloves and a snarl. The place was a pig sty.

'Stroke mags, beer drinker, junk food, dirty laundry. Three cellular phones, all apparently working. Could be a college dorm room, if I didn't know better.'

'The phones? Clones?' Boldt said.

'Three of 'em? Probably.'

'Weapons?'

'Negative.'

'Prints?'

'A lot of lifts – mostly the same guy. Maybe a woman, by the size of the others. Box of Tampax on the floor by the toilet. Blond pubic hairs mixed in with the more abundant darker ones, collected from the sheets, toilet rim, and shower drain – platinum blond.'

'Shoes?'

'Pair of high-top sneakers, is all.'

'Nike?' Boldt asked, recalling the shoe at his own assault. Had that been brother Flek?

221

'Converse. We've already bagged and tagged the clothes. We'll go over them for hairs and fibers. If there's anything that links this place to Sanchez or your other sites, you'll hear about it.'

'Drugs? Alcohol?'

'Valium and amphetamines in the bath. Street grade. No prescription bottles. The beer. Some Cuervo Gold. That's about it. Purely recreational stuff.'

'Not in combination,' Daphne said softly into Boldt's left ear. 'Two bennies, one Valium, and a shot of Gold. That's a street cocktail they call a glow plug. A couple glow plugs and a guy'll think he's bulletproof.'

'As in beating up a cop from behind?' Boldt suggested to her.

'That would certainly fit.'

He turned to the tech and asked, 'Electronics? Parts? Computers? Anything in that category?'

'Just the three cell phones.'

'Any of these?' he said, pulling from his pocket one of the plastic ties he'd recovered from the Kawamoto crime scene.

'Not here, but in the van,' the man answered.

'You did the van?'

'The blue van. Colorado plates? All three of us,' the tech replied, indicating the woman and man still busy behind him. He stepped forward and picked the white plastic tie from between Boldt's fingers. 'Must be a couple hundred of these lying around loose in that van.'

Boldt looked over his shoulder at Daphne and said, 'That's a start.'

Revisiting the hospital wasn't easy for Boldt. This time he was there to see Officer Maria Sanchez.

He perked up the moment he and Daphne entered the room, as the woman lying there was able to somewhat jokingly wave hello to them with her toes. Movement had returned to the digits of both feet, and with a great deal of concentration, her left ankle could be flexed. Though she remained paralyzed from the knees up, the woman's hopefulness and enthusiasm now filled the room like warm sunlight, replacing the fear and terror that had so recently been in evidence.

'We have a suspect,' Daphne announced.

The woman looked right, signaling 'yes.'

'Not yet in custody,' Boldt added. 'We would like to show you a photo array. You know the drill, Officer.'

Another 'yes.'

Daphne explained, 'There are six faces in the array, all numbered. If you recognize one of the individuals as your assailant, we would like you to blink the number to us. Number two – two blinks, et cetera. Is that okay with you?'

'Are you up to this?' Boldt asked.

'Yes,' came the indicated reply.

'If you have doubts,' Boldt continued, 'we'll get to that. For the moment, we simply need to know if any of these faces looks familiar to you.'

The woman looked right with her dark eyes. 'Yes.'

'Good,' Daphne said, checking with Boldt who nodded to go ahead. Daphne pulled the array from her shoulder case. Sandwiched layers of heavy stock, the six head shots sat behind equally sized cutout windows, a number below each. Four were black-and-white, two color. She held it an arm's length from Sanchez's pillowed head, and knew within seconds that the victim did not recognize any of the men in the photos. Then she reminded herself that Sanchez was incapable of facial expression, and because of this, she held out hope.

Sanchez closed her eyes.

Boldt held his breath in anticipation, ready to count

the number of blinks. He wanted desperately for the number to be four: Flek's position in the array – though doubted she could identify the man who had done this to her. If she identified Bryce Abbott Flek then they had linkage between all the robberies. Either way, they still needed Flek in custody if Boldt hoped to pry the lid off the I.I. investigation.

When she opened her eyes, Sanchez looked left.

'No?' Boldt questioned.

'You don't recognize any of them?' Daphne clarified.

'No,' came the woman's answer.

'You're sure?' Daphne asked.

'She's sure,' Boldt answered. An assault at night. Boldt had been through that. He knew. 'The victim doesn't recognize any of the faces in our array,' Boldt pointed out. 'We take it from there.'

'We take it where?' Daphne asked. 'Without Flek in custody—'

'So we get him in custody,' Boldt fired back. 'And when we do we'll sit him down, and we'll question him. And then maybe we get some answers.' He added in a hoarse whisper, 'If we're really lucky, then whoever brings him in has a hard time of it, and makes him pay for what he did to LaMoia.' His eyes sparkled. 'Which is why I hope I'm the one to bring him in.'

THIRTY FOUR

Meeting in the fifth-floor conference room with a deputy prosecuting attorney named Lacey Delgato, a woman with whom he'd worked a dozen other cases, some successfully, some not, Boldt struggled to find a way to bring David Ansel Flek to the table as a witness. The Prosecuting Attorney's office was crucial to his effort.

Delgato's unflattering nickname, 'The Beak,' was a result of her oversized nose. With a low center of gravity, and a voice that could etch glass, Lacey Delgato surprised anyone who made the mistake of judging her by her appearance. To Boldt, she represented the best and the brightest of the up-and-coming trial attorneys in the PA's office. Her loud mouth, and the fact that she wasn't afraid to jump in with locker room vocabulary, turned off some people, but not Boldt; for anyone who worked with LaMoia and Gaynes, all else was tame.

Into their second hour of discussion of the brothers Flek, Delgato and Boldt had yet to solidify a legal strategy that might force the incarcerated David Ansel Flek to open up and provide leads to help police locate his older brother. With this the most obvious and direct way to end the case, Boldt pressed on relentlessly.

'Maybe we should be looking at the girlfriend,' Delgato suggested.

'We've got some pubic hairs and a box of Tampax,' Boldt reminded. 'That's a pretty wide-open field.'

'And some lifts,' Delgato reminded, indicating SID's

record of the fingerprints developed inside Flek's boarding room.

Boldt explained, 'Lofgrin ran them through ALPS' – the state's automated latent print system used to analyze and identify latent fingerprints – 'and struck out. We've posted them on the Bureau's database.'

'And if he brought her from Colorado with him?' Delgato asked.

The missed opportunity stabbed Boldt in the center of his chest. Such a simple idea, and he had overlooked it for the better part of the last eighteen hours. 'Damn,' he mumbled.

'Just an idea,' Delgato said in a doubtful tone of voice that implied he had screwed up.

Boldt placed a call down to the lab. The unidentified fingerprints lifted from Flek's apartment would be posted over the Internet to Colorado's Bureau of Criminal Identification – CBCI – in the next few minutes.

'That's why they pay me the big bucks,' Delgato said once Boldt was off the phone.

'You might be the better cop of the two of us,' a somewhat defeated Boldt suggested.

'A woman looks at the relationship between the principals. A guy looks at the evidence. That's the only difference. It's what makes you and Matthews such a good team. You're lucky to have her.' Boldt didn't touch that. He thought of her too often. That kiss had still not left his lips, and he knew that wasn't right.

Delgato continued, 'The whole time we're sitting here, I'm looking over this SID report – the pubic hair the lab ID'd as being bleached blond – and I'm thinking, what kind of babe dyes her privates? You know? And I'm thinking stripper. Sure it could be an older woman who's trying to dye a few years off the truth by taking the gray out of *anywhere* it shows. But someone hanging with a burglar? More likely young and obedient – black leather pants and a halter top. A real gum chewer. Flek says, "I want you a blond all over," and little Miss Junior Mint is off to the pharmacy for some Nice 'n Easy. Which just about describes her perfectly. And if she is who I think she is, then she's not so different from Flek. Some drug charges, some soliciting. Maybe some fraud. Maybe even armed robbery, who knows? Maybe she drives for him. A lookout? Maybe she's giving him a hum job before the hit for good luck. Maybe she knows nothing about his game. But I like her for a juvie sheet. She has that feel about her. She's the kind that smiles for the mug shots. You know the type.'

'All that from dyed pubic hair? I'm glad you're on our side,' Boldt said. 'If you were a PD, I'd retire.'

'You'll never retire,' she fired back. 'And I'll never be a public defender. We both hate the bad guys too much, you know?'

'Yeah, I know,' Boldt agreed.

A sharp knock on the door drew their attention. A woman civilian from the secretary pool whom Boldt had only met that same morning. 'Lieutenant,' she said, 'call for you, line one. They said it's urgent, or I wouldn't have—'

Boldt interrupted, thanking her, and scooted his rolling chair over to a phone. 'Boldt,' he announced, into the receiver. As he listened to the man's voice on the other end of the call, his shoulders slumped, his head fell forward and his right hand clenched so tightly into a fist that his fingers turned white and ghostly. He hung up the phone.

'Lieutenant?' a concerned Delgato asked in her strident voice.

Boldt's voice caught. He cleared his throat and tried

again. 'We're going to need another game plan,' he warned her. 'Another angle. Something—' He finally looked up at her, stealing her breath away.

'Lieutenant?' she repeated, a little more desperately.

'Seems the inmates didn't like having the private commerce program shut down. Probably enjoyed the extra income, not to mention the access to information. Can you imagine how many games were being run out of that facility?'

'Lieutenant, what the hell's going on?' she demanded.

'The call was from Jefferson County Corrections. David Flek was found beaten to death in the showers. They would have called us sooner, but it took them a while to identify the body.'

Delgato frowned. 'Luck of the draw.'

'We're screwed,' Boldt said.

THIRTY FIVE

The woman believed to be connected to Bryce Abbott Flek was identified through her fingerprints by Colorado's BCI as Courtney Samway. The mug shot came back as a cream-skinned sixteen-year-old with a pretty face and a home haircut that made her into a tomboy vixen with a curiously rebellious expression.

Samway's Colorado parole officer had required her to register in Seattle upon her fulfilment of obligations and her departure from the Colorado corrections system. Samway had, in fact, contacted the Washington State Parole Board upon her arrival, as required, meaning that a tiny, insignificant computer file in the vastness of the endless mainframes that constituted law enforcement's efforts to track thousands of offending juvenile felons provided an address of residence for the recently released teen.

'She kicked from Colorado two months ago,' Boldt told Bobbie Gaynes, who rode shotgun in Boldt's brand-new Crown Vic. Nearing midnight, the city still teemed with activity. Ten years earlier it would have been dead this late at night. The car replaced his Chevy Cavalier. He'd earned the Crown Vic apparently for his loyalty throughout the Flu. The Chief was handing out perks. Boldt wasn't complaining. The Crown Vic was twice the car and even came with a remote device that locked and unlocked the door or popped the trunk from thirty yards. 'Mug shot is two years old.'

Gaynes said, 'She's a punk slut. You can see it in her eyes. Age doesn't matter.'

Boldt said, 'She registered with a parole officer here, claiming the move was to support a job offer.'

'She turned eighteen last month,' Gaynes said, reading from the woman's jacket – her record having been forwarded by Colorado's BCI. 'The alleged job is with a fish processor – probably someone Flek bought off to write her a letter of employment. The address is not the same one her P.O. provided. Not that it matters. I'm betting this address is smoke. You want five on that?'

'Have I ever taken one of your bets?' Boldt asked, checking the rearview mirror to ensure that the radio car was following as planned. 'The address is good,' he guessed. 'She registered with the parole board. That tells me she didn't like serving time – she doesn't want to go back there. She played by the rules laid out for her in Colorado. The address will be good. Maybe I should take that five,' he contemplated.

'Yeah, right.' Gaynes laughed. 'The day you take a bet, L.T., I'm having your head examined.'

The brick structure had been built fifty years earlier at a time when this south part of the city had prospered from timber and fishing. Time had not been kind to it. The street was paved in wet, matted trash. The carcasses of vehicles resting on rusted rims lay alongside broken glass and spent syringes littering the alleys like discarded cigarette butts. It was not somewhere to take a stroll.

They had waited impatiently to conduct a midnight raid. A daytime operation in this neighborhood was worthless: rats only returned to the nest at night. Boldt used only secure frequencies – believing Flek might be monitoring the normal channels. If this was in fact

Samway's apartment, with Flek's roost already raided, it seemed possible, even likely, he might be inside.

On command, the cruiser behind him turned up the side alley. He would allow his team a minute or two to take positions. According to city fire records for the once commercial building, three possible exits offered egress. At each of the three, a uniform would be waiting for anyone beating a hasty retreat – anyone who managed to get past Boldt and Gaynes. With Gaynes at his side, Boldt knew not many would slip past.

Once inside the wet and cold building, loud rock and roll from a downstairs apartment obscured Boldt's hearing. He relied on his sensitive ears the way a bloodhound depended on its nose, and he found the overpowering music frustrating and troublesome.

Gaynes gestured through a series of hand signals indicating that she would take lead on the climb up the stairs. Boldt's chest knotted and his skin prickled with sweat. A month earlier he would have had Special Ops as his advance team, but the Flu had taken its toll. In the company of one other detective – albeit a bulldog in the form of a poodle – he prepared to take on some animal who had cracked one officer's neck and rabbit-punched another into the hospital.

Weapons drawn, he and Gaynes worked up the staircase as if an adversary had already spotted them, Gaynes in the lead, Boldt trying to cover her both top and bottom, nerves rattled.

A sudden movement behind and below. Boldt swivelled silently to see a rail-thin junkie cross the hall in a T-shirt and bare feet, moving between neighboring rooms. Boldt signaled Gaynes to continue.

The staircase smelled strongly of cats. Crushed candy wrappers, spent Lotto tickets, and cigarette butts littered the edges of each step. They reached the first landing. It smelled of pizza. The thumping of the down-stairs music faded behind them. Boldt heard at least two televisions and a considerable amount of muted talking.

They turned right at the top of the stairs, Bobbie Gaynes looking stressed and tension ridden, her movements sharp and angular. They passed three closed doors before Gaynes raised her hand to stop them. She pointed across the hall to their target. Boldt signaled back an acknowledgment, and moved Gaynes to the side, her back to the wall immediately alongside the door.

His gun aimed to the side and down to the floor, Boldt tried the doorknob and found the door locked. He rapped his knuckles loudly against the wood, stepped back and waited. When nothing happened, Gaynes reached around and pounded on the door.

'Police!' she announced. 'Open this door!'

Shock waves reverberated down the hall: police! Through the closed doors behind them, they heard much shuffling, but the door before them remained quiet.

Boldt reared back onto one leg and hammered on the door, kicking it hard, most of his weight behind the blow. His second attempt broke the door loose from the jamb. The door crashed loudly into the wall as it swung open.

'Police!' he repeated, eyes darting to Gaynes, who confirmed she was ready. Boldt stepped inside and snugged his back against the near wall. Gaynes flowed in behind him, moving to the center of the small room. Boldt took the galley kitchen to her right.

'Clear!' he announced.

Gaynes rushed the tiny bedroom to the left. 'Clear,' she echoed.

They lowered their guns, though kept them at the

ready. Boldt shut the door as best as possible. 'Need a pair?' he asked, indicating the latex gloves in his hand.

'All set.' She retrieved a pair from her pocket.

They moved through the small area fluidly, two investigators accustomed to their work. The warrant called for a plain-sight search for any materials relating to the thefts, but Gaynes conveniently found drawers and cabinets surprisingly left open to where she could search them. Boldt made sure his back was turned.

'Milk is dated next week,' he announced. 'So she's been living here recently.' He wondered if kicking the apartment had been the right thing to do. They could have placed it under long-term surveillance, but Boldt's guess was that if Samway was hooked up to the Flek brothers, then she'd already been advised to avoid her own digs.

'Couple of roaches left in the ashtray,' Gaynes announced. 'We could get her on that if we had to. She's on a year's probation following her parole.'

'We want her,' Boldt reminded. He would worry about the technicalities later.

'Here we go,' Gaynes announced from the bedroom.

Boldt approached her voice, but with his back to it, his attention mostly on the apartment's broken door. He glanced to his right – an unmade bed; cigarette butts piled high in an ashtray. Facing the bed was a 37-inch Trinitron with a cable box on top. He said, 'We should have checked the cable company. Maybe we'd have found her or Flek's name there.'

'Not that. This,' Gaynes said, swinging the bathroom door open further. Bathing suit thongs and bikini tops the size of corn chips.

'I guess she likes the pool?' Boldt said, the image not fitting with his vision of Courtney Samway.

'This here is her work uniform,' Gaynes corrected.

'She's stripping, L.T. We're looking for matchbooks, coasters—'

'Check stubs, T-shirts—' he interrupted. 'Something with the name of the club on it,' he said.

Boldt walked through the small bedroom, carefully studying the place. He reached the side of the bed and a mound of cigarette butts in a plastic ashtray. He dumped the butts onto the floor without a second thought. His gloved fingers wiped away the ash and tobacco smudges, cleaning the bottom of the ashtray. He held it up then for Gaynes to read from across the small room.

'Mike's Pleasure Palace,' he said.

'Table for two,' Gaynes replied. 'I shouldn't admit it, but I love strip joints.'

'I like the female body,' Gaynes told him from the Crown Vic's shotgun seat. 'You guys fantasize about jumping their bones, but I fantasize about looking like that. They're gorgeous, these girls. On top of it they can really move. And they choose to be there, so don't give me that shit about it being exploitive. They rock their hips and some asshole stuffs a twenty into their G-string, thinking he's some kind of big shot, when she's gonna take that thing off regardless. He's gonna pay her *another* twenty. And then she goes backstage and drinks for free and awaits her next performance.'

'And the lap dancing?' Boldt asked.

'Hey, most of that is voluntary. Extra credit work. Sometimes not, sure. Sometimes management demands it. But it's a power trip for the girls – it's gotta be. Drag your crotch down some guy's thigh and cream him in his pants. Fifty bucks for five minutes' work? There's no kissing, no fluids exchanged. No harm, no foul.'

'I'm hearing this from a woman.'

'A woman who likes to watch other women,' she reminded him. 'Not *touch*, despite what they say about me. Not woman on woman – nothing like that. But I appreciate the SI swimsuit edition as much as any of you. The boys can't understand a woman appreciating the female body – but they can watch one guy pound another guy on the scrimmage line every Sunday – so that's their problem, not mine. I'd never been to strip joints until the guys from our squad dragged me in one time. And them thinking they would gross me out. You should have seen them! Have I ever gone down on a woman? No. Do I want to? No. Disgusting! Do I like marble nudes? You bet. Nude dancers? Why not?'

'I think I have more information than I need,' Boldt said.

'If I had a body like that, I might show it off for a few bucks. I'm built like a truck. So what can I do about it?'

'You are not!' Boldt objected. 'You're a good-looking woman.'

'That's horse shit, L.T.'

'Lacey Delgato is one thing.' He hesitated. 'I'm not having this conversation,' he said vehemently.

After a long silence, Gaynes said under her breath, 'Thank you for saying that, L.T. You're a peach.'

'So I'll make you a deal,' he said.

'Shoot.'

'I'll handle the bouncer and the bartender if you'll do the talking with the ladies.' He checked to make sure a cruiser was following, as ordered. 'If she's here, it's straight into the radio car for a ride downtown. I want her scared.'

'They're girls, L.T.' Correcting him. 'Bodies as hard as that; they just don't last all that long.'

Upon entering Mike's Pleasure Palace, Boldt shouted to be heard above Don Henley's grinding rock and roll.

'These girls don't often use their real names, even with the help,' Gaynes said, pulling him down to hear. 'Use the mug shot from BCI.'

'Unnecessary,' Boldt said, pointing to the stage where pulsing blue light welcomed the next dancer to the platform. Wearing a translucent wet T-shirt and an equally showy, wet white cotton thong, the relatively small-chested Courtney Samway strutted out onto stage, her platinum blond hair showing slightly from beneath a black wig. There was no mistaking her. She didn't have the meaty frame of a stripper, and the crowd of men seemed to be assessing her until she began to move to the music, at which point all eyes took to the stage.

Boldt scanned the crowd for Flek. 'You see him?'

'No,' Gaynes replied. 'But I'm thinking we might want to hang for a while in case he shows. We approach her too soon we could scare him off.'

'I'm not hanging around, if that's what you're suggesting,' Boldt said. 'I want her downtown. I want some answers.'

She slithered like a snake, wrapping herself around her own frame suggestively. The T-shirt came off somewhere in the process, followed a moment later by the thong. Boldt told himself he wouldn't have watched if he hadn't been required to, but in truth there wasn't a male not watching. She didn't have a centerfold body, but she was shapely enough.

'Hair coloring's a match,' Boldt said, still looking.

'Thing looks like a sheepskin rug,' Gaynes said. ''Bout as natural-looking as one of those car seat covers.'

'You take the dressing room,' Boldt advised Gaynes. 'I'll stay out here.' He reminded her: 'Radio car's out front.' Probably hadn't been helping win Mike any customers.

Gaynes never met Samway face to face that night. Following her dance, the woman slipped into a robe and stepped off out front, summoned for a lap dance. Boldt cut the private performance short. Two minutes later Samway was escorted to the backseat of the police cruiser and was headed downtown to Public Safety.

Samway occupied the chair inside the interrogation room in her satin robe. Chewing gum kept her jaw pumping. Deputy Prosecuting Attorney Delgato could see this all for herself, since Boldt had summoned her to the 1 A.M. interrogation. The witness had requested a public defender despite the fact she was only in for questioning. Where a public defender appeared, prosecuting attorneys followed; hence Delgato. Daphne too had been rousted. Gaynes watched from the other side of the room's one-way glass with Delgato. Boldt's A-Team. All but LaMoia. It hurt Boldt to think about him laid up in the hospital.

'You talk to us now before your court-appointed attorney arrives,' Daphne told the young woman, 'and the lieutenant here forgets about the probation violation of associating with known felons and we forego the urine test to see if you've been smoking pot.'

'I'm sure,' she said.

'You want to hear it from a deputy prosecuting attorney?' Daphne asked. 'I give the signal and she's in here laying it out for you.'

'Trust me,' Boldt intervened from the chair next to Daphne. 'All we want is a little frank discussion about your roommate.'

'He saw *you* on the news at that Denver hotel,' she said ominously while staring at Boldt.

'Meaning?' Daphne asked.

Samway said, 'Listen, who's talking to you? I've never seen you before. But *him*?' She eyed Boldt.

Boldt wanted Courtney Samway the focus of the discussion, not the other way around. He tried to signal Daphne, but failed.

Speaking directly to Boldt, Samway said venomously, 'You're the one shut down the program. The one got Davie killed. Abby said you're a dead man. I heard him say it. I don't need to talk to you – I'm talking to a dead man.'

Daphne grew several inches as her spine stiffened. Boldt reached out and gently touched her forearm.

He said, 'Let's start there, then. Abby was . . . You and Abby were watching the news on television. You saw me. Here in Seattle?'

She shied, smelling the trap he laid for her. 'I'm not saying nothing.'

'You see the problem?' Boldt asked her, trying to keep her mind engaged and slightly off her game. 'If it isn't us who catches up to Abby to speak with him . . . let's say it's Denver, or Reno or Portland, for that matter. All that the police there see is the sheet, the warrant, the Be On Lookout, the All Points – a guy wanted for questioning in regard to the assault of police officers. You see how that looks to a cop? Like trouble. Big trouble. Serious trouble. The kind of trouble where you shoot first and ask questions later, because this guy is on the sheet for doing cops. Forget about me. Do I look dead to you? It's Abby – Bryce Abbott Flek – you need to be concerned with here. He's the one in danger. And honestly? You're his only hope right now.'

'Bullshit.'

'It's not either. It's the God-given truth. Matthews and I want him alive. We need him alive because we're not so convinced what his role is in any of this. We know David called him from Etheredge. So what? Where's the crime? We need to *talk* to him, no matter what he believes my role was in his brother's murder. I wasn't the one who beat David to death, Courtney. I'm not going to be the next guy lying on a slab. You and Abby watched the news,' he said, 'so you know we have a hell of a lot of young officers on the job. Maybe not the best trained at the moment. One of those guys sees Abby out on the street. What do you think's going to happen? And how are you going to feel when you look back and see you could have prevented it?'

'Bullshit,' she said, a little more tentatively this time.

'Where's he gone, Courtney?' Boldt asked.

Daphne said, 'You want to be the one who could have helped him, but didn't?'

The witness glanced back and forth between her two interrogators, both of whom saw opportunity. Courtney Samway would talk, if pressured correctly.

Boldt said, 'We've confiscated his van, so what's he driving?'

Daphne added, 'We've seen the apartment. Did you know that? Not *your* apartment – we got it too – I'm talking the rented room in Ballard. So where does Abby have left to go? And how does he get there? He had better go somewhere, because if he's out on the streets . . . the buses . . . the ferries . . . well, these young officers are out on the street as well. You see where that leaves him, Courtney?'

Boldt took a wild stab. 'Where's it leave *you*, Courtney? Where's it leave you once he knows you've been brought in for questioning? No matter what you tell him, the first time he stumbles upon a cop, Abby's going to think you set him up. You tell me: where does it leave you?'

Daphne flashed a look at Boldt that suggested he

might be stepping on her psychologist toes. She didn't need him playing psychologist any more than he needed her playing detective.

'I want a lawyer,' Courtney said now, her lips wet and trembling.

'One has been appointed,' Boldt said, 'and is on the way over here. Count on it.'

'I want my lawyer now!' Courtney repeated, this time with more of an edge.

'You don't have to talk to us, if you don't want to,' Daphne reminded, 'but it might be in your best interest. Either way, we can't leave you alone right now, so you're stuck with us.'

'You don't know him,' she mumbled, the cracks widening.

'Why don't you tell us,' Daphne suggested.

'There's like a switch in him, you know? I've never seen anything like it. When Davie died—'

Just then, her young attorney burst into the interrogation room, a blur of briefcase and words. 'Violation of rights! Protecting my client!'

Boldt had heard it all too many times before. 'We'll give you five minutes,' he announced.

Courtney Samway looked over at Daphne, and with a frightened-sounding voice she whispered, 'Snookers, the bar. He hangs there.'

THIRTY SIX

Snookers was a biker's bar, a beer and pool hall with two voluptuous waitresses who wore plastic cowboy hats and tight jeans. The bartender was the size of Sasquatch. When Boldt and Gaynes entered, all but a handful of the twenty or so men in the bar noticed the pair immediately. A half dozen slipped quietly toward the back exit. There, these seven men encountered four patrol officers that Boldt had assigned to watch the back door. Two of the seven escaped. The remaining five were pushed up against a brick wall and searched.

Boldt and Gaynes walked past the back pool tables and let the screen door slam shut on their way out.

A patrolman informed Boldt, 'We lost two of them, Lieutenant. Of what's left, we got two handguns, a blade, some pot and what looks like cocaine. Only one guy is clean out of all of them.'

'We'll take the clean one first,' Boldt informed the man, after studying each face for Flek and not finding him. Addressing the group as a whole, Boldt announced loudly, 'We're Seattle PD. We have a few questions.'

Gaynes spoke deliberately and slowly to the group. 'Bryce . . . Abbott . . . Flek. Abby. Information or whereabouts buys you an instant out. David Ansel Flek. Davie. Abby's brother. Recently deceased. Information buys you an out.'

Boldt dragged the 'clean' suspect away from the others, out of earshot, Gaynes at his side. The officers kept the other suspects engaged to the wall. He said, 'You get the first shot at a hall pass.'

'You can't hold me,' the young man complained. 'On what charges?' He had some Latino blood in him, maybe some Asian as well. He was short but solid. He wore leather, jeans, and Air Jordans.

Gaynes fished out the man's wallet. 'We can run your name though BCI and see if you've been a good boy or not. If you're on parole and any of these others guys turns out to have a record, well, then, that's a violation, isn't it?'

'Do whatever you have to do. But you can't hold me. And I don't have shit to say to you.'

Gaynes stepped up like she was ready to hit him. Boldt signaled her to back off.

Boldt said, 'Who are we interested in over there?' indicating the lineup against the wall.

'Third guy. Black hair. Name of Robert. Knows the one you're looking at.'

Gaynes returned to the wallet. 'We know who you are. We know where to find you. If you're blowing smoke at us—'

'No way! He mentioned this guy Abby, okay?' the kid admitted. 'Heard him saying something about him.'

'Take off,' Boldt said, releasing the kid.

The third one from the left, a tall, lanky kid, had junkie's jaundice and the smell of a boozer. As one of the two caught carrying a piece, Boldt had a noose to hang him. He led the man away from the others and launched into a discussion about unregistered handguns and mandatory prison time. It won the man's attention.

'Abby Flek,' Boldt said, adding no editorial.

'Guy has flipped out.'

'What was your business with him?'

'Me? No business, man.'

Gaynes encouraged a closer intimacy with the brick wall. 'Think harder,' she said.

'No business with him.'

Gaynes leaned her knee between the man's legs, and then lifted her leg sharply. 'That gun you were carrying is going to cost you a year. The lieutenant here has run out of patience, and so have I. You want the year, you keep telling us you had no business with him, because we're too busy to give you a second chance. Got it?'

'Hardware,' the man said.

'Weapons,' Boldt said.

'Let's just say I'm connected, okay?'

'Let's just say you're a collector,' Gaynes corrected. 'Sound good? Nothing illegal about collecting a few weapons.'

'Whatever. Abby has lost it, okay? The guy will start a fight over anything. He comes to me, I'm not about to say no.'

'Of course not,' Gaynes said.

'But I couldn't say yes either, because . . . my connections,' he said, straining to meet eyes with Gaynes, 'my collection . . .', he corrected, 'I didn't have what the man was looking to score.'

'Which was?' Boldt asked.

'Semi-auto long rod. Russian-built was okay, but he wanted a particular German scope.'

'A sniper's rifle?' she asked incredulously.

'Way out of my league,' the guy said.

'And then some,' Boldt said, wondering if he was the intended target. He added, 'When was this?'

'Three, maybe four o'clock.'

'Today?' Boldt gasped. They were only eight hours behind the man.

'And you referred him to a fellow collector,' Gaynes said, leading him on.

'What would you have done?'

'And the name of this individual, this fellow collector?' she said.

'Macallister,' the guy whispered so quietly that Boldt wasn't sure it had come from his lips.

'I know Macallister,' Gaynes told her lieutenant. She slammed the suspect's groin again and warned, 'This blows up in our hands and we're coming after you. Understood?'

'Yeah, I got it.'

''Cause if Macallister hasn't heard of this guy, right or wrong, it's your ass we're coming after. And there will be *no* second chances. So take a moment to contemplate your existence, my friend – to ruminate – because you gotta be good with this, and I'm smelling that this is some bad shit you're peddling.'

'Manny Wong,' the man corrected. 'Not Macallister, Manny Wong. Down in the District. Most of his stuff is Chinese, but Abby said Chinese was okay as long as he got that German scope.'

'Don't know him,' Gaynes warned Boldt. 'Never heard of him.'

'That's all right,' Boldt answered. 'I know someone who knows everyone down there.'

THIRTY SEVEN

The woman reminded Boldt of Orson Welles in a muumuu. She wore a piece of black embroidered silk big enough to wrap a small car. On her shoulders pink hummingbirds flew toward vivid red blossoms. Tiger faces with sequined eyes roared from her ribs. Ivory bone buttons speared through silk loops and strained at her enormous girth. He felt grateful she wore her teeth, for in the past he had found it hard to understand her pidgin English without them. Her eyes appeared as black half moons beneath the arcing Chinese curve of her painted eyebrows, her face in a permanent blush behind the applied rouge, puffy cheeks reminiscent of Dizzy Gillespie.

Mama Lu sat enthroned in a huge rattan chair, a gigantic rising sun woven into the chair back above her, looking like a second head. Two black enameled chests flanked her, their surfaces as lustrous as mirrors. The second-story room where she met them was rather dingy, accessed by a narrow stairway from the butcher shop of the Korean grocery store below, but the room's contents belonged in a museum collection, as did this woman.

'Mr Both,' she said. She had never pronounced it correctly.

'Great Lady,' he said, 'allow me to introduce one of my detectives, Roberta Gaynes.'

'Mama Lu,' Gaynes said, using the woman's street name.

'Roberta,' Mama Lu returned. To Boldt she said, 'I heard of Ya-Moia. Sent small gift to hospital.'

Boldt imagined something grandiose despite her surface modesty.

Placing a pudgy, swollen pale hand on her enormous bosom she said, 'Heart made sad by this.'

'It's why I've come,' Boldt explained.

'Sit,' she instructed.

'We won't be staying,' Boldt said, 'but thank you.'

'You must eat,' she said, looking him up and down. 'You are not eating. Why? A woman, or work?'

Boldt felt his face flush and wished that Gaynes was not there to witness it. He said quickly, 'We're after the person who did this to LaMoia.'

'And Mama Lu can help?' the woman inquired hopefully.

'A gun dealer named Manny Wong. We think he's had contact with the individual responsible for LaMoia.'

Gaynes added, 'We mean no trouble for Mr Wong.'

When Mama Lu squinted at a person, it felt as if all the lights in the room were dark, and a hot spotlight switched on in their places. Gaynes took a small step backward.

'Police always trouble,' Mama Lu informed her. To Boldt she said, 'Present company excepted. What is offer?'

'She's right,' Boldt said, indicating Gaynes. 'No tricks. All we want to do is talk to Manny Wong. Far as I'm concerned, when he walks out of that interview room I forget his name and ever having heard it.'

'Me too,' Gaynes said, though Mama Lu didn't want to be hearing from her.

'Just questions,' the Great Lady repeated, testing them.

'That's all,' Boldt confirmed. 'Answers to those questions.'

She had to physically turn her wrist with her other hand. The watch face hid in a massive gob of silver and pieces of turquoise the size of quarters. 'You will be at Public Safety in one hour?' she checked with him.

'That'll work,' Boldt agreed.

'He comes in voluntarily,' she reminded. 'If he's helpful, you return favor next time he may need it.'

'I can do that,' Boldt assured her. The trade-offs bothered him and always would – they kept him awake at night, this long list of favors owed, but he never let them affect his negotiations. You couldn't work the streets based solely on principle; it just wasn't possible. Deals begot deals.

Mama Lu sucked at her front teeth. Boldt feared they might be about to fall out, and he wanted to spare himself the sight, as well as her the embarrassment. She said, 'I do this for Ya-Moia and Peggy Wan.' Addressing Gaynes, she explained, 'My niece. She like Ya-Moia very much.'

Gaynes nodded. Boldt noticed the beads of sweat on her upper lip. Not much could make Gaynes break out.

'Soup?' She tried again.

'Rain check?' Boldt asked, but then thought she wasn't familiar with the expression. 'Another time,' he said.

She pouted and nodded. 'You wait too long to visit poor old woman,' said one of the richest women in the city. 'Soup always hot,' she offered.

Boldt looked at his own watch for the sake of reminding himself. 'One hour?' he asked.

'No worry, Mr Both. Mama Lu not forget.' She smiled, the dentures pearly white. 'Not forget *anything*.'

*

Manny Wong carried his large head on bent, subservient shoulders, and peered out of the tops of his eyes, straining to catch some of the glass in his smudged bifocals. His forehead shone. His ears, too large for his body, looked like small wings. Boldt sensed a wolf in sheep's clothing. The man had thin, moist lips and bad teeth that whistled with some words.

'A sniper rifle,' Gaynes said. The news that Flek had possibly acquired such a rifle had been included in the Be On Lookout as a matter of safety. Rumors were already circulating that Boldt was the intended target. 'Chinese manufacture.' She looked remarkably fresh; if she felt fatigue, she didn't show it. 'This is the man who purchased it.' She slid a mug shot of Bryce Abbot Flek across the table and in front of Wong. She held it in place with outstretched fingers. Wong wouldn't touch it – hadn't touched anything since he'd removed the driving gloves. He wasn't going to give police any prints they didn't have. And they didn't have his. Never would, as far as he was concerned.

Boldt and Wong had run the rules of engagement for the better part of the last half hour, Wong careful not to get a foot snagged in an unseen trap. For his part, Boldt had not mentioned the kid interviewed behind Snookers by name.

'German scope,' Wong said. 'Scope very important. Maybe he had used such scope before. Maybe he only read about it. Maybe just trying to sound like he knew what he was talking about. Get better price.'

'The range of the weapon and accuracy?' Boldt asked.

'With that scope . . . sighted correct . . . if weapon handled by expert? 300, 400 yards. Amateur, if he rests on a mount, 200 yards, no problem. On shoulder, 100, 150 yards he can still hit target.'

'Semi-automatic,' Boldt stated.

'Magazine holds thirty-two. One in the chamber, thirty-three.' A child could empty the magazine in a few seconds, Boldt realized. Wong never lifted his head, his eyes floating in magnification and the rosy fatigue of red webbing. Meeting eyes with Boldt, he mumbled, 'Cops and guns! I *never* understand police.'

'You're sure it's him,' Boldt said, indicating the photo. Boldt felt those thirty-two shots in the back of his head.

'Fifteen hundred dollar sure.'

'You see what he was driving?' Gaynes asked.

'No.'

'His clothes?' Boldt questioned.

'Jeans. Leather jacket, I think.'

'Boots?' Boldt asked. 'Sneakers?'

'Not remember. Not see man's feet.'

'Ever sold to him before?'

'No.'

'How about this man?' Boldt asked, producing a photo of David Ansel Flek, the younger brother.

'Never seen him.'

'He's in possession of the weapon, then?' Gaynes asked.

'He owns weapon, yes.'

'She asked about possession,' Boldt reminded him.

The man fixed his attention on Boldt, but said nothing.

'The scope?' Boldt inquired.

Those eyes roamed around behind the smudged glass again.

'I'll take that as a negative,' Boldt said.

'That's correct.'

'He still has to pick up the scope,' Boldt stated, glancing hotly at Gaynes as he sensed an opening.

'That would be correct,' the man repeated.

'When?'

'Use new Internet site called i-ship. Delivery guaranteed, tomorrow ten o'clock.'

'Ten o'clock. You told him that?' Boldt said.

'After lunch,' he corrected. 'Need time check merchandise.'

'To sight the scope for him,' Gaynes suggested.

Both men looked over at her – Wong with an urgent appraisal that came too late, Boldt with respect.

The gun dealer said nothing.

Gaynes said, 'If you've handled the weapon before it's used to kill somebody, you could be accused as an accomplice. Especially if we lift a print.'

The man smirked at this impossibility.

'Even without your prints on it,' Boldt said. 'So be glad none of this is on the record.'

Gaynes asked, 'What distance did he want you to calibrate it for?'

'Cops and guns,' the man repeated, shaking his head.

'Answer the question,' Boldt said.

'A hundred and fifty to two hundred yards,' the man replied.

'So he's planning on firing from the shoulder,' Boldt said.

'A hundred fifty yards. That is request. That is what I deliver.'

'No,' Gaynes told him firmly. 'You'll sight it for fifty to seventy-five yards. The first shots'll fly low.'

The man shook his head. 'Not possible. My reputation.'

'Seventy-five yards,' Gaynes repeated.

'He maybe test weapon,' the man complained.

'With your reputation?' she mocked. 'I doubt it. Maybe he'll sight it, maybe not. If not, then maybe we spare his first intended target a bullet.' She ended this sentence with her eyes on Boldt, who felt chills run down his spine.

Boldt said, 'We'll collar him before he ever gets the chance to fire that weapon.'

'Maybe we will,' Gaynes said.

Turning to Wong, Boldt informed the man, 'We're going to need you to put one of our people behind your counter with you.' Wong shook his head vehemently, those haunting eyes rolling like dice. Boldt had to amend the deal he'd made with Mama Lu, and it bothered him to do so. 'And if you won't agree,' Boldt continued, 'we'll detain you indefinitely and put our guy in your place.'

THIRTY EIGHT

Seattle's reputation as a rain forest was largely unde-served. It was true that during the rinse cycle, November through March, northern Pacific storms tracked through regularly, leaving the city without so much as a glimpse of the sun, sometimes for weeks at a time. True that spring and fall saw their fair share of 'partly sunny' days that were actually 'partly rainy,' as a thick and dreary mist fell, broken by moments of spectacular sunshine, the warm power of which could almost evaporate the moisture before the next wave of clouds passed over. But for all those stereotyped storms and images of umbrellas and slickers presented by the Weather Channel, the glory days of clear skies, a light breeze and sixty degrees were just as common. The moisture brought lush vegetation, wonderful gardening, and clean streets, the air fresher and purer than perhaps any other city in the country.

Boldt and Gaynes orchestrated their plan to capture Flek as he arrived to pick up his rifle scope. The International District lay under a rich summer sky, the air crisp and clean. Seagulls flew down the city streets, their cries echoing off buildings. The towering snow-capped peak of Mount Rainier loomed impossibly close, as if part of a Hollywood backdrop. It was a day when Liz would tell Boldt to 'pinch yourself.' That good.

'You with me, L.T?' Gaynes asked from the shotgun seat.

'What's that?'

With their unmarked van parked a block from the street entrance to Manny Wong's electronic repairs shop, Boldt and Gaynes had an unrestricted view of the surveillance target. Asians peopled the sidewalks and occupied the vehicles in proportions that made Caucasians stand out. For this reason, Boldt and Gaynes stayed put behind the van's tinted windows. And although the department's demographics prior to the Flu had included dozens of Asian patrol officers and detectives, the suspensions and firings imposed by the chief had drastically reduced their numbers to where Boldt's field team consisted of Detective Tom 'Dooley' Kwan – currently inside the shop – and three relatively green patrol recruits out on the street in plainclothes: a twenty-something African American, Danny Lincoln, playing the role of a bike messenger who, on one knee, was busy with what looked like a blown bike chain; a middle-aged Vietnamese woman, Jilly Hu, outside the shop looking left and right as she acted out anxiously awaiting a ride, her hands occupied with the ubiquitous cellular phone; and a third man, Russ Lee, a Chinese American, in a wheelchair with a blanket over his lap concealing a loaded assault rifle, keeping speed with the first rule of engagement: Never be outgunned. Hu and Lee were partnered; Lincoln and Dooley were solo – on their own.

Four patrol cars, two uniforms each, maintained a three-block perimeter, in case backup was needed.

Gaynes explained, 'I was saying that it's kind of eerie without all the normal radio chatter.'

Boldt reminded her that the bicyclist, Danny Lincoln, was wearing a radio headset – as so many messengers did. It happened that Lincoln's headset connected to SPD dispatch. They had Jilly Hu on the cell phone.

Dooley wore a wire – a concealed transmitter and receiver. They weren't exactly in the dark.

The police coverage of the rifle sight pick-up had been hastily thrown together. As the impending moment drew nearer, Boldt feared that if it went wrong they might not only lose a suspect, but someone might get hurt. He had LaMoia to remind him of that.

'What's your take?' Boldt asked Gaynes. She had a nose for such things.

'Not great.'

'Same here.'

'Our people look good. It's not that,' she said. 'And I think it's smart that we have Dooley working in the back of the store, not out front at the counter. That's way more natural than if Dooley is just loitering out front and making Flek nervous. And maybe it's just all the goddamned Asians milling around these streets, but something feels wrong about it, you know? Like it's going to go south.'

'Yes, I know,' Boldt conceded.

'Doesn't mean it has to.'

'No, it doesn't,' he agreed.

'Maybe it's just everyone warning us what a crazy son of a bitch Flek is – the hair-trigger temper, the violent nature. I hate that shit. Maybe it's thinking about Sanchez and John, and how this guy doesn't seem to give a shit about us wearing badges. You know? What's that about?'

'Downright disrespectful, I'd say,' Boldt said.

She grinned into her slight reflection off the glass. 'Downright right you are.'

'I think you can take Sanchez off his list, though we won't know until we collar him. He did LaMoia. He'll pay for that.' He told her about Sanchez's inability to ID Flek, and of her earlier uncertainty concerning who was responsible.

A large Ben and Jerry's truck momentarily blocked their view of the gun dealer's storefront. After the truck passed, Boldt saw that Lee, Hu and Lincoln had all adjusted their locations, signaling a development.

The cell phone in Hu's hand carried an open line to Gaynes's right ear. Gaynes wore a small headset attached to her cell phone to keep her hands free. She mumbled into the headset and then informed Boldt, 'A Caucasian, female, just entered the store.'

Boldt turned up the volume on the dash-mounted police radio receiver. Being in the back room, Dooley Kwan and his RF microphone provided no insight into the goings-on in the front of the store. Boldt desperately wanted to know what was going on.

The slightest movement on Kwan's part resulted in a scratching through the receiver's small speaker.

'You turn that up any louder,' Gaynes commented, 'and we're going to hear him sweating.'

'Description?' Boldt requested.

Gaynes repeated the request into her headset. Poking the earpiece firmly into her ear to hear Kwan's reply she reported, 'Female. Late teens, early twenties. Caucasian. Five-six, five-seven. Platinum—'

'Courtney Samway,' Boldt said. 'Flek sent her to pick up the scope for him.' He had an undercover team in place following Samway – later that day he would have heard about this visit in the team's daily report, albeit too late. He used the radio to notify her surveillance team to leave the area. He didn't need any additional confusion.

They transmitted Samway's identity to 'Dooley' Kwan and informed the others to follow the suspect if and when she left. Jilly Hu on foot. Danny Lincoln by bike.

The radio picked up Dooley as he responded to

Wong. Boldt and Gaynes listened intently. The exchange was brisk. Dooley delivered Flek's scope to the front of the store, at which point his concealed microphone picked up the conversation in the room.

Wong told Samway, 'Tell your friend all sales are final. The modifications he requested have been made, and that next time I don't deal with a go-between. It's not how I do business.'

'Whatever,' the woman said. 'He just asked me to pick the thing up for him. I don't know what he wants with some microphone anyway.'

'It's her,' Boldt said to Gaynes, recognizing the voice. 'It must be in a microphone box.'

Gaynes nodded. 'Yup. The girlfriend. I overheard her in the Box,' Gaynes said. 'You think it's conceivable she doesn't know what it is?'

'I think he does her thinking for her, if that's what you're asking.'

Over the radio, Wong said, 'A hundred and fifty for the modifications.'

'He only gave me a hun,' Courtney Samway complained. She was fifty dollars short.

Boldt checked that the cassette hubs were spinning. He said, 'That connects her pick-up to a man, and we already have her connected to Flek. That'll help Delgato in terms of arrest warrants.'

She complained, 'Does us no good without the collar.'

'Notify the street team the mark is good,' Boldt ordered. 'And remind them that Flek may have simply dropped her off. He could be in the area.'

Boldt then radioed SPD dispatch and dictated instructions for the uniforms in the patrol cars. For security's sake, the messages to the patrol cars would be sent over the vehicle's onboard mobile data terminal

– MDT. These digitized text messages were impossible to intercept.

He wanted his team alert. If Flek was in the area, he probably had the assault rifle in his possession. Scope or no scope, it represented lethal firepower.

Wong and Samway argued money over the radio worn by Dooley.

Samway's voice said faintly, 'Hang on. Let me make sure he only gave me the hun.'

Boldt didn't want Wrong to refuse her the scope. He needed that scope to lead him to Flek.

'What do you know?' Samway said. 'I had it all along.'

'Next time no go-betweens,' Wong complained, heard over the radio. 'I no do business with go-betweens.'

'Yeah, yeah,' the young woman scoffed. A doorbell rang softly, signaling her departure.

Courtney Samway appeared on the sidewalk in front of Wong's store.

'Doesn't look like a stripper from here,' Gaynes said.

Boldt watched and listened as his crew kicked into gear. Jilly Hu followed on foot.

Danny Lincoln fixed the chain, mounted the bike and pedaled out into traffic. Samway walked west. Boldt's team followed. He and Gaynes carefully monitored the radio.

Lincoln informed dispatch that Samway had boarded a bus.

Gaynes asked, 'Eastbound or westbound?'

'Damn!' Boldt shouted, traffic blocked by a double-parked bread truck.

'Wonder Bread,' Gaynes said, reading the back of the delivery truck. 'Wouldn't you just know it?'

*

As the eastbound bus pulled away from the curb, Samway aboard, Boldt's team scrambled to follow – although to look at them, one would not detect the slightest bit of anxiety; this, in case Flek was himself watching.

Boldt drove the van with Gaynes as shotgun; Lee drove a Ford with Hu as his passenger; Danny Lincoln pedaled furiously on the bike.

Predictably, in tortoise-versus-the-hare fashion, the bike outpaced the slower vehicular traffic and kept up with the bus, Lincoln reporting its location block by block.

Dispatch reported that Phil Shoswitz had arrived to act as the surveillance team's coordinator. Shoswitz knew his way around mobile surveillance.

The bicyclist kept up with the eastbound city bus without much trouble due to the vehicle's frequent stops. Shoswitz deployed the Ford, the van and four cruisers around an extended perimeter as a safety net. The chess match had begun. Boldt's team had to prepare for Samway's departure at any bus stop; at the same time they had to be prepared to follow a moving bus.

The strategy paid off. Courtney Samway disembarked the 7 line and gathered with others awaiting the 60, unaware that just fifteen feet away, a plainclothes policeman monitored her every movement. Samway placed a quick call from a corner pay phone, a call that was not monitored, but would be the cause of much legal wrangling immediately following. Deputy prosecuting attorney Lacey Delgato would battle with the courts to be given access to the pay telephone's call sheet, a situation that had legal precedent on her side, but a liberal court's policy toward expectation of privacy working against her. Boldt believed absolutely that the call had been placed to Flek, in all probability to

258

a cell phone – across the street, across town, across country, he couldn't be sure until that call sheet was made available.

'What does it matter?' Gaynes asked. 'It's bound to be a cloned phone. It's not like we'll lift a physical address.'

'Triangulation,' Boldt answered. 'It's got to be a cell phone. That works in our favor.' Cellular service providers possessed software to locate an individual cellular phone using radio triangulation methodology developed for the military in World War II. Currently the technology was used to locate 911 emergency calls placed from cellular phones. Law enforcement had been quick to take advantage of the existing technology, tracking down drug dealers and gang members. The technology was currently slow however, and Boldt was caught unprepared to deploy it.

'What do you want to bet,' Gaynes replied, 'she'll lead us to him anyway?' Then she added, 'Oh, yeah. I forgot. You don't bet.'

Boldt said, 'I think he'll park her for a while – an hour, an afternoon, a day. Keep an eye on her himself. Maybe just let her stew. The guy knows us. Knows the way we think. He's been in and out of the system his whole life. His brother's dead. He's wanted and on the run.'

'Pissed off.'

'That too. Depending on that temper of his, he could exercise some patience at this point. There's no real rush, other than staying away from us.'

'You overestimate him,' she disagreed. 'He's an impatient, wild man. And if we believe Samway, his one purpose at the moment is to take you out for getting his brother killed. That's urgent. That's pressing. Ask Daphne – he's irrational, unpredictable and impatient. That call she just made? He called her in. We've got this skel.'

Samway rode the Broadway bus north for eleven blocks – a cop sitting a few rows behind her – and then disembarked in front of a Seattle's Best Coffee, where she drained the next hour off the clock. Jilly Hu entered the same establishment, wearing a scarf over her head, and read the paper and sipped tea for this same hour, one eye on the suspect, another ready with her cellular phone.

By the time Samway departed the coffee shop, Shoswitz had unmarked cars in place – ready to continue the game of chess. Boldt and Shoswitz remained in constant contact. The radio hummed with activity. Boldt lived for these moments.

When an hour had expired, Samway reboarded the 60 – the northbound Broadway bus. Jilly Hu remained behind in the coffee shop.

'You're biting your nails, L.T.,' Gaynes said. 'You don't normally do that.'

Boldt glared. Her timing was off. He envisioned the movement of the various cars as Shoswitz re-deployed them, fully aware that Flek could be on any street corner, or waiting in a car nearby.

'You're thinking he's a planner,' Gaynes said, reading well his steadied concentration.

'I am.'

'That he's waiting out there, watching for us.'

'Tracking her,' Boldt said, 'like a stalker.'

'And if he spots us—'

'He'll never make contact with her again. It'll be the last we ever see of him.' He sensed something from Gaynes. 'What?'

'I have a hunch you're gonna hear from him, L.T. The rest of us, maybe not. But you? He's not through with you.'

'Thanks,' Boldt said. 'That's reassuring.'

'I call 'em as I see 'em. Which is on account of why I'd like to see us catch him first.'

'Well, at least we're in agreement there.'

Broadway teemed with college kids: restaurants, record stores, grocery stores, moviehouses. On foot it would prove far more difficult to follow her, given the environment. Thankfully, Samway remained onboard the bus at the busiest stops. When she did disembark, it was to transfer from the 60 to the 43 – a move that left Shoswitz hustling through bus route schedules. But Gaynes knew the 43, putting their van a jump ahead of the rest of the surveillance teams.

'It goes through Montlake to the U-District.'

Boldt speculated. 'He wants her in areas where there are a lot of kids her age. First Broadway, now the U.'

'We can beat the bus there, L.T. And get me into the field – onto the street. If she tries to use the crowds to lose us . . . I'm already on the ground and running.'

Boldt felt somewhat obliged to let Shoswitz orchestrate the manpower, but Gaynes was right: they had a window of opportunity, and though a gamble, it seemed worth taking.

Reading his thoughts, Gaynes said bluntly, 'This woman is *not* getting off in Montlake, L.T. He wants her in the U.'

Boldt turned away from his assigned route without reporting in, while the radio spit static as Shoswitz hurried to comprehend bus route 43. Gaynes reached for the radio's microphone.

'We gotta call it in, L.T.'

'Wait,' Boldt instructed. He continued north on 10th Avenue, making for University Bridge.

As Shoswitz began to bark orders, Boldt keyed Gaynes to report that they were already under way to the University bus stop.

'We don't know she's headed to the U,' Shoswitz objected over the radio.

Boldt took the microphone from Gaynes, and said, 'Yes, we do, Captain. I'm getting there ahead of time to put Gaynes on foot.'

'You'll stay in formation,' Shoswitz ordered.

'We're crossing University Bridge. I'll report when we have Gaynes deployed.' He put his foot to the gas, in part to cover the sound of Shoswitz screaming.

By the time the 43 pulled to a stop and Samway disembarked, clutching the box given her by Manny Wong, Boldt was parked across the street from the University's transit hub while Gaynes watched from inside a nearby KFC. For all his efforts, Shoswitz had outsmarted himself. With two cars stuck in traffic he'd been reduced to Boldt's van and a couple of cruisers. With the cruisers unable to show themselves for fear of scaring off Samway, Boldt and Gaynes led the surveillance. Samway headed out on foot into the crowds of college kids. 'She keeps checking her watch,' Gaynes reported, now following on foot. Ten minutes passed, by which time Shoswitz had reassembled his crew. The Ford, driven by Lee and now once again with Jilly Hu as passenger, parked on 45th Avenue. Danny Lincoln amazed everyone by arriving on his bike, his messenger's backpack strapped on tightly.

'We're coming back toward you,' Gaynes reported. 'I smell another bus. This guy is careful.'

Boldt relayed the information to his team, believing Flek may have used the stop as part of his plan: while Samway walked around the U, Flek could buy himself time to move to the next location and set himself up with a viewpoint. Thankfully, no one from Boldt's team had followed her off the bus – something Flek may have been watching for. Boldt reported his theory to Shoswitz, warning that Flek might be a step ahead at each phase of Samway's progress, suggesting the cruisers be pushed out well away from the center of the action. Shoswitz concurred. The team now came down to Boldt's van and the Ford.

Samway led Gaynes right past Boldt's van, reentered the transit hub, and boarded the 67, whose electronic display carried the words 'Northgate P & R.'

Gaynes slipped in beside Boldt. 'Now he wants to lose her in the mall,' she said.

'He's watching,' Boldt warned. 'It gets tricky now.'

Boldt drove on. The bus exchanged passengers at 11th Street and 45th Avenue and headed north on Roosevelt Way NE. Again, traffic became the nemesis. To part the traffic with a light or siren was unthinkable, and yet both Boldt's van and Lee's Ford fell farther and farther back as traffic worsened.

'This keeps up,' Gaynes warned, 'and we lose her.'

'Suggestions?'

'We slip over to Eighth or Fifth, running parallel, and use our stuff if we have to.'

'I like it,' Boldt said. He nudged his way left, his blinker flashing. A Navigator let him through with a polite flash of its headlights. The Ford remained behind the bus. Gaynes called in the change of plans.

'Was about to suggest that,' Shoswitz said. It was the only time Boldt had smiled in the last two hours.

Boldt ran red lights on Eighth Avenue and quickly passed the bus's reported parallel position.

Gaynes suggested she leave the van upon their arrival at the mall. 'I can be in that parking lot ahead of her.'

The 67 made one stop after the mall. 'We don't know the mall is her destination,' Boldt said.

Gaynes pushed. 'Is he going to have her ride the bus

all the way out here, and then skip the mall? He can get her lost in there, L.T. It has to be the mall.' She hesitated. 'This is one time you're going to have to gamble.'

Boldt pulled to the curb. To his right, he spotted the bus two blocks away, also slowing. 'Go!' he shouted.

Gaynes popped the passenger door open. Boldt watched as she entered the mall's vast parking lot. A moment later she looked like just another person walking from a parked car toward the mall. To his right, Boldt saw passengers disembark the 67. He studied body types, tortured by the agonizingly long stream of people – until finally he spotted Samway among them. To his relief she still carried the package. They had guessed right. Gaynes would call it gambling – he might never live this down.

He looked on as Gaynes made visual contact with the mark from a hundred yards away and quickened her pace accordingly. Keeping an eye on Samway, Gaynes made it into the mall *ahead* of the young woman, a position where marks seldom thought to look. Russ Lee and Jilly Hu pulled up on the far side of the mall, announcing their position to Boldt over the radio.

Boldt felt his stomach knot. A mall. The crush of a thousand shoppers. The perfect place to either disappear, make a drop, or spot a tail. All Flek had to do was watch from an upper balcony to see if anyone was following Samway.

Jilly Hu had been used in the coffee shop. Shoswitz sent Lee into the mall as backup for Gaynes, on strict instructions to keep use of his cell phone to a minimum, and then only in believable situations, fearing the phone might catch Flek's eye.

Five minutes passed in relative silence. Agony. Six. Boldt's throat stung of heartburn. Ten. Shoswitz wondered aloud over the radio if they should risk sending Hu in to assist. Boldt suggested not. 'It's Gaynes, Captain.' His only explanation of his confidence. Twelve minutes. He felt ready to go in there himself.

Fourteen minutes. Boldt's cell phone rang. He let out a long breath. It was Bobbie Gaynes.

'She's moving again, L.T.'

'Where?'

'West side. You should have her . . . right . . . now.'

'Got her.' Boldt saw Samway push through the wall of doors. She seemed struck by the warm air.

'Get this, she bought herself a thong swimsuit. You suppose she deducts those things off her taxes?' She added, 'What now? I don't want to stick out.'

'We see who picks her up,' he answered.

The area surrounding the mall was not a place for pedestrians; cars were the preferred mode of transport. Samway wasn't headed for a car, as it turned out, but the sidewalk beyond. If Gaynes followed she would be easily spotted. The same applied to Danny Lincoln, who had arrived on the scene, riding his bike, only moments before. The unmarked cars were a possibility, but not a good one.

Gaynes made for Boldt's van. Lee reported in, having returned to the Ford. Boldt's team collectively held their breath.

Samway walked behind the mall and north on Fifth Avenue NE, where Lee and Hu made visual contact. She crossed Northgate Way with the light and walked due west over the interstate bridge. Boldt and Gaynes sat in the front seat listening as Lee reported the woman's progress. Gaynes caught sight of her briefly and pointed far off into the distance.

Boldt looked across the interstate, worried there might be a car waiting, worried it was about to get ugly. 'The motel,' he said to Gaynes, as he noticed the tower and sign placed to advertise on the highway.

'You think?'

'Flek takes a room near the mall. It gives him access to public transportation, a lot of cover if he needs it – the mall being so close, the interstate in his front yard. Flek is inside that motel watching her approach from a window.'

Shoswitz barked an order for Lee to follow. Boldt cut in and suspended the order – overriding a captain. 'Send Lincoln on the bike,' he said. 'Flek is watching. She's heading to that motel.'

THIRTY NINE

She was inside the motel.

Following the resolution of the sickout, Special Operations – Special Ops – continued under the command of Patrick Mulwright, a forty-something binge drinker, part Irish, part Native American, who looked about sixty. The man's two different colored eyes – one green, one almost brown – lent him a crazed, mongrel look that forewarned of his disposition. Boldt and Mulwright's histories went back too far, overlapped too much, which happened in any organization, but was particularly difficult in a police department where lives depended on reaction and response time.

Special Ops gained access to leading-edge technology far in advance of any other unit, the way the FBI always had the cool toys ahead of any city law enforcement. Mulwright passed out digital cellular phones with walkie-talkie capability to each of the operatives involved, although the method of their distribution – having an undercover 'street person' drunkenly wander the area surrounding the motel pushing a grocery cart (in which were hidden the communications devices) – took an inordinate amount of time. The digital devices could not be scanned, nor the conversations overheard, meaning that all parties surrounding the motel could monitor and communicate via the same walkie-talkie channel without concern that Flek would hear them. At the same time, the secure police frequencies remained available for communication back and forth between the field and headquarters at Public Safety.

Mulwright brought with him long-distance video and audio surveillance, high-powered binoculars and monoculars, which included night vision capability if needed, and four Emergency Response Team officers prepared to put their lives on the line and kick Flek's room if and when required to do so.

The slightly chaotic and scattered attempt to keep Samway under surveillance quickly streamlined and took on the feel of a well-run operation. Mulwright swallowed his dislike of Boldt, not allowing it to interfere with operations.

The police net was carefully structured in concentric circles. Well out of sight, positioned at key intersections several blocks away in every direction, four police cruisers – radio cars – occupied the four corner posts of a 'contained perimeter.' Included within this perimeter were Boldt and the Ford, with the wild card, Danny Lincoln, still pedaling, but now with a police vest hidden beneath his Nike windbreaker. Everyone involved kept a weather eye on the sidewalks, in case Flek approached on foot. The good money had Flek already inside.

Mulwright and his Special Ops Command Center personnel occupied an Ore-Ida panel truck, its painted sides and roller door advertising a NEW! thick-slice potato chip with thirty percent less fat. It was parked on the curb immediately in front of the motel, offering the ERT team quick access to the motel, if needed. A lone police sniper, under Mulwright's authority, was positioned on a rooftop west of the motel, covering the building's back side. Seventy minutes after Samway headed inside, operation 'Baywatch' was in place – so named by Mulwright because the motel's small indoor pool happened to be peopled to overflowing with bikini-clad women who, according to a welcome marquee, were attending a press-on nail and cosmetics conference. Judging by the pool, not many were attending the seminars.

When Courtney Samway was spotted inside the pool area, slipping into the hot pool in the recently purchased lime green thong and matching top, it was Boldt, not Mulwright, who formulated a plan to discover which room she was in, and thereby concentrate Special Ops' considerable assets.

'You feel like a swim?' he asked Bobbie Gaynes.

Although Boldt and Gaynes had both been at the stripper club the night they had brought Samway in for questioning, Gaynes and the girl had not met face to face. Gaynes had gone backstage to the dressing rooms, but Samway had come out into the club offstage, leaving Boldt to detain her and get her into one of the cruisers. He needed someone in that pool area, and he wanted it not only a woman, but a woman he trusted.

'In front of all these guys? With twenty-power monoculars?' she returned. 'My thighs? Forget it. Try Jilly. She'll knock their socks off.'

Boldt disagreed. 'We used Jilly out front of Wong's store, and again in the coffee shop. She's used up. I could probably pull a woman from one of the radio cars, but the inexperience could burn us.'

'L.T.!' she objected. 'Use a guy. Use Milner. I've got a feeling he has a great bod under there.'

'There must be a dozen women in there, Bobbie. No men. I send a guy in and nobody – nobody – is going to miss it. Another woman wanders in, nobody may notice.'

'I'm supposed to buy a suit in the gift shop, I suppose.'

'If they sell them,' Boldt said. 'Over at the mall, if they don't.'

'I'm sure they do,' she sighed. 'And real beauties at that. I don't want to do this, L.T.'

'If she came down for a dip, she brought a room key with her, and it's probably lying on a towel.'

'And if it's one of those electronic card keys?' she asked.

'Then you follow her to her floor and do a little police work.'

'In a gift shop bathing suit,' she groaned.

'In a gift shop bathing suit,' he confirmed.

'And you're going to order me to do this,' she tested.

'We can go to the front desk and ask about Flek, flash badges and mug shots. But if he's bought off the front desk clerk, then we lose. Lose big-time, if that seven-rounds-a-second bullet hose comes into play.'

'And I gotta do this now because she won't stay long.'

'Might not. That's true.'

'And then we got nothing.'

'Nothing.'

'I'll be laughed off the fifth floor. You know that, L.T.'

'Not by me,' he said, lifting the binoculars and sighting in through the semi-fogged windows of the indoor pool area. 'She's still there.'

'I'll have to take a room in order to use the pool.'

'We'll expense it,' he said.

'And I leave my piece here, I suppose, on account I gotta change in some ladies' locker room or something. So you send me in naked,' she said, referring not to the bathing suit but to the fact she would have to leave her weapon behind.

'You go in naked,' he suggested, spinning her meaning, 'and I'm pretty sure they'll notice you.'

'Ha, ha,' she returned.

'Try not to get noticed, okay, Bobbie? And no heroics! Get inside, pull the room number, dip your toe and change your mind. Use your cellular the minute you can, but watch who's overhearing. I've got two in the hospital already. Okay, Bobbie?'

'You owe me.'

'You watch,' Boldt said, 'you'll probably get asked out on dates as a result of this.'

'Yeah, to a spa! I can't believe you're serious. I can't believe you're making me do this!' She unclipped her belt holster and left her weapon behind with Boldt. They both knew he couldn't order her to do this; by unclipping her weapon, she had just volunteered. She pocketed her cellular.

'Carry the phone with you. If it rings once and stops, we've made Flek, and I want you the hell out of there.'

'Got it.'

'And I mean it about no heroics.'

'No heroics,' she repeated. Pausing with her hand gripping the door handle, she said, 'Hey, L.T. It's heroic of me to just get into one of those gift shop suits. I'm telling you: you owe me.'

It took Gaynes longer than Boldt had hoped. Registration, shopping for the suit, changing into it – Boldt kept checking his watch. By the time Gaynes came through a sky blue door wearing a yellow skin-tight Speedo a size or more too small, a rainbow set of Olympic rings running diagonally up her middle, Samway had come up the steps of the hot pool and stood there dripping wet. Boldt thought it was all for nothing. But then the teenager walked the short distance to the real pool and slipped down inside for the cooling effect, momentarily blocked from view by another woman drying herself off.

As wolf-whistles carried loudly across the Special Ops walkie-talkies, causing Boldt to grin, Bobbie Gaynes walked casually relaxed toward the smaller hot pool and stood for a moment before setting down a pink towel. Boldt could tell from her numb hesitation, from his own familiarity with her, that something was wrong: too many towels; too many keys; no keys at all. Something wrong. He called over to Mulwright to see if the man had picked up similar feelings.

'Who would'a thought she'd have a set of lungs like that?' Mulwright asked, exposing himself to the possibility of a future lawsuit. 'Get a load of that! Who would'a thought?'

For his own reasons, Boldt thought of Daphne at that moment – of waking up in her houseboat to find her there in her running clothes. He worried the kiss in Denver had ruined things between them. She seemed to be avoiding him. Had the kiss been his fault – not something they both wanted?

He strained to locate Gaynes through the binoculars.

Some of the women clearly knew each other or were at least comfortable chatting as they sat waist deep on the pool steps. Conversations carried on, in and out of the water. Most of the women were a little paunchy. Two of the thinner girls wore butt floss and postage stamps though even one of these showed cottage cheese in her hind cheeks. There wasn't much tan in the room, but there was plenty of cleavage. A room service waiter delivered what looked like iced teas.

He watched as Gaynes seemed to study the towels and keys by the hot tub. He caught himself grinding his teeth: 'Not too obvious,' he wanted to call out across the distance that separated them. If he got another officer injured he would turn in his badge. He worried for her – wondering if there was any chance Samway had caught a glimpse of her during her interrogation at Public Safety.

A creepy feeling wormed inside him. Perhaps he had taken too big a chance. If Samway recognized her – for whatever reasons – then all bets were off. He had stranded Gaynes there without her weapon – a fact of which he was painfully reminded by the gun on the passenger seat. He checked the binoculars in time to see Samway climb out of the lap pool. She tugged once on the thong, and crossed back over to the hot tub. A few older, envious eyes followed her as well as those of Special Ops.

She swayed without trying, conditioned by all those hours on the stripper stage, provocative and sensual. She lowered herself into the hot water. Boldt watched as Gaynes turned to speak. 'Be careful,' he spoke quietly into the vehicle with only his ears to hear.

Bobbie said, 'I moved the towels getting in,' pointing behind Samway. 'Sorry about that.'

Samway glanced back at the row of the towels and keys. 'No problem.'

'Here for the seminars?' Bobbie asked her innocently.

'No.'

'That's a great suit.'

'Thanks.' Bored. Or maybe the hot water was getting to her.

Samway looked Bobbie over, trying to see into the water. Bobbie felt uncomfortable. Pulling on her own suit she said, 'Borrowed it. It's so small, it hurts.'

Samway chuckled. 'You ever tried one of these?'

'No.'

'You should. All the comments about butt floss? I'm telling you, it feels fine. And it's killer for the tan line.'

'I'm not exactly the right shape,' Bobbie said. 'What, are you twenty or something?'

'Close.'

'Yeah, well I'm not. Not even close,' she added, again making the girl smile.

One of the women kicked on the jets, and Bobbie kept quiet while Samway floated in a boiling bubble stream. Gaynes had heard Matthews talk about wanting access to suspects – especially violent suspects – ahead of police intervention, ahead of the emotional barriers, attorneys and defensive postures. Now, she finally understood that urge – she wanted desperately to get Samway talking and to pick her brain for all the juicy details she could extract. But she held her tongue . . . briefly. A few women climbed out; a few more climbed in. There was a lot of flesh and not much fabric in the room. The talk she overheard centered on the looks of the male presenters at the seminar.

Bobbie tried, 'Highway noise bad on your floor?'

Samway, her eyes closed, said, 'Didn't really notice.'

'You must not be on the second floor,' Bobbie said.

'Third,' Samway said.

'I'm on the highway side,' Bobbie told her, scoring one for herself. *Third floor.* 'It's pretty bad over there.'

'We've got a view of the Space Needle from ours,' Samway said.

Gaynes could take that pronoun – 'we' – to the bank. Despite the hot water, she felt a chill: Flek was here, on the third floor. Things were going to get ugly.

'It's a small room,' Samway conceded, 'but it's still a pretty view.'

'First time to the city?' Gaynes asked, just to sound conversational.

Samway turned toward Gaynes and offered a penetrating, suspicious look that made Gaynes feel queasy.

One too many questions, perhaps. Or maybe there had been something in her tone. Or maybe the cop in her just leaked out now and then. Whatever the case, Samway recoiled from the conversation, like a snake. She crossed her arms nervously, glanced around the room as if expecting others to be watching her, mumbled something about having to go, and climbed out of the pool.

Bobbie spun around, knowing that this was her moment. She had pushed it too far. She could no longer wind up in the elevator alongside the girl without it seeming forced. She had to get a look at that key, that room number. But Samway cupped the key as she checked to make sure she had the right towel, and Bobbie didn't get even a glimpse.

Samway glanced back. Bobbie's position in the tub left her looking right up at the girl's ass. It was then that an overlooked opportunity occurred to her. She quickly pulled herself out of the pool and grabbed for her own towel. Samway wrapped the large towel around her, tucked it into her top, and slipped her feet into some Dutchboy shoes.

Bobbie toweled off and wrapped up. As Samway made for the door, Bobbie caught up. She had never done anything like this – had no idea how to approach it, but felt convinced it was just the trick she needed.

As they pushed through the door nearly side by side, Samway, clearly uncomfortable, said, 'Nice meeting you,' trying to be rid of Gaynes.

'I, ah—' Bobbie wanted to stall until onto the elevator. 'Nice meeting you too,' she said. 'Same here.' She was more uncomfortable to the point of nausea. 'Do you think—' she said, hurrying to keep up with the nervous Samway. 'Do you really think I'd look okay in one of those suits?'

They stepped into the elevator. Samway clearly felt trapped. Bobbie had mentioned the second floor – she had to push 2. Samway pushed 3, and it lit behind her touch.

The doors shut. The elevator rattled as it lifted.

Bobbie pulled off the towel to display herself to the other woman. She turned once as if on a runway, intentionally awkward. She blushed. She knew if ever there was a body not to wear a thong, it was hers. But she wanted to convey more as well. When she came fully around and faced Samway again, she spoke before the other could. 'I think you're beautiful,' she said in a creamy voice. She took a slight step forward, just enough to invade Samway's space. She whispered hoarsely, 'I realize this is a little sudden—' purposely nervous, 'I mean I don't even know your name. But if you're not doing anything tonight . . . I mean . . . you want to hit some clubs or something?'

'Listen, you're sweet,' Samway said warmly, calming considerably, 'and if you want to try the suit, I think you should. But I'm a dancer. Men's clubs? And a lot of my girlfriends are into other girls, you know? That's fine. But not me. And besides, I gotta work tonight anyway.'

'Where?' Bobbie said, trying to look crushed.

'Pleasure Palace.'

'I mean the suit,' Bobbie said.

Samway parted the blanket and pointed to the logo sewn into the waistband. She couldn't resist showing her tiny waist and perfect legs one last time. As she did so, the key dangled in her left hand, the room number facing Bobbie. 312.

Bobbie felt her heart skip a beat.

'Nike,' Samway said. 'Got it over in the mall. A sports shop.'

The elevator stopped.

'Thanks,' Bobbie said. 'And sorry if I made you uncomfortable.' She said privately, 'You're *very* beautiful. Your body too.' She felt herself blush again, and figured that was okay. She stepped off the elevator, her knees like water.

'No problem,' Samway called after her. 'Have a good one.' The elevator doors slid shut.

Bobbie pulled the cellular phone out of her rolled-up towel and made the call. 'Room 312.' She felt ready to faint. What if Samway had accepted her proposition?

When the sniper on the back side of the motel confirmed the presence of two adults in room 312, he erroneously mistook Samway and her own reflection in a mirror as the movement of two adults. It was this officer's confirmation that Patrick Mulwright used to make a raid, and therefore, ultimately, the chaos that ensued.

Moving Special Ops or ERT officers through any public area presented great risk to civilians and enhanced the possibility of operational compromise. People tended to either panic or follow when they spotted black-clad figures bearing assault rifles.

Boldt could have assigned any of the detectives to talk to reception, but reserved the job for himself, his weapon double-checked beforehand. He approached the registration desk and asked to see the manager, revealing his identity only by passing a business card, never showing his shield or speaking his rank. He wore a radio earpiece in his left ear, familiar with the floor plan supplied by Gaynes. The existence of that earpiece bothered him, no matter how subtle its look, but he saw no way around being connected to Mulwright's communication network. He simply had to monitor radio traffic in case of developments. Because of this, he kept one hand up to his ear, scratching, shielding the earpiece from view as best as possible.

The woman behind the desk looked up. Boldt repeated softly, 'The manager. You're coming with me.' There was no telling who Flek might have bribed.

The receptionist nodded nervously and indicated a door to the right. Boldt stepped through a moment later. The manager, a woman in her mid-forties, had reddish hair and carried a slightly frightened and disapproving look once Boldt was introduced. He waited for the receptionist to sit down.

'We have a situation,' he said to the manager. 'Room 312 may be harboring a fugitive. We'd like to empty several surrounding rooms as quickly as possible before conducting our raid.'

'I'll have to contact the owners.'

Boldt said, 'I'm not here to win your approval. I don't need your approval, only your cooperation. My counterpart simply wanted to kick the room, and we already would have if I had not intervened. But since we believe the individual in question may be in possession of tactical weapons, I prevailed. I want to empty those neighboring rooms, now. Right now!'

'How?'

'Telephone,' Boldt answered. 'You call up to each of the rooms and tell them that the smoke alarm system is malfunctioning and that the city safety code requires you to empty everyone from the room. They're to come down the stairs, not the elevator, quietly and orderly. You say you don't expect it will take more than ten minutes or so to clear up.'

'All of the rooms on the third floor?'

Boldt spotted a diagram on the wall and approached it. 'These four rooms on the third,' he said, drawing the area surrounding 312. 'These above and below.' He added, 'First, I need to confirm the registration on 312.'

The manager typed furiously, her troubled eyes more on Boldt than the screen. 'Robert Grek.'

Boldt nodded as if this made sense. 'And Mr Grek has no other rooms in the motel?'

The manager checked the computer. 'Only the one. King bed. Smoking.'

'Very well.' Boldt picked up the phone receiver from the cradle and handed it to the manager. 'Sound as natural as possible. Calm. Confident. The problem's going to be resolved shortly. You're not at all concerned by this.'

She nodded.

The receptionist stood.

'Sit down,' Boldt said, distrusting her, not wanting her out of his sight.

'We have a customer.' She pointed through a rectangle of one-way glass that looked out on the desk.

'The customer will wait,' Boldt announced. To the manager he said, 'Can you put anyone else on the front desk?'

She nodded, her fear more apparent.

'Do it.'

The manager summoned an employee named Doug to the front desk using the public address system. A moment later, the man stepped in behind the reception desk.

'Call,' Boldt said sternly, indicating the phone. 'Please,' he added, somewhat sarcastically. Mulwright was out there preparing his team. He didn't trust him to wait. 'We need to do this quickly.'

Two heavily armed ERT operatives entered the motel's north fire stairs exactly five minutes after the last of the manager's phone calls. Two others ascended the building's south stairs at the exact same moment. Wearing protective vests, Boldt, Lee, Hu, and Bobbie Gaynes entered the lobby, passing the gathering of evacuated families who, until that moment, had believed their rooms' smoke detectors were malfunctioning. With the stairwells covered, the Boldt team split up, Lee guarding the lobby, Boldt, Gaynes, and Hu dividing up to ride the two elevators so that Flek could not slip past.

Boldt had in his possession a master key. One of the ERT guys carried the steel ram, to be used to take out the door jamb's interior security hoop. Boldt's pulse hovered around a hundred and twenty.

Mulwright, acting as CO – command officer – choreographed each team's movements to coordinate perfectly, so that as Boldt stepped off the elevator on the third floor, one member of each stairwell team was already silently running toward him and room 312.

In a flurry of hand signals, Boldt indicated he would clear 312's lock, to be followed by the ram. The order of entry was the two ERT men, then Hu and Gaynes, and finally Boldt.

The door's lock mechanism made a noise as Boldt turned the key, any element of surprise lost. The second or two that it took the ram to explode the interior hardware felt fatally long to Boldt.

The two black-clad ERT men lobbed both a stun grenade – 'a dumb bomb' – and a phosphorus charge – 'white lightning' – a fraction of a second before rushing the room, weapons ready in the familiar leapfrog dance of advance and cover. They arrived to find Courtney Samway lying on the bed in underwear and bra, her nose and ears both bleeding from the dumb bomb, her hands frantically waving behind her blindness due to the white lightning, her screams penetrating even the cement block wall so that they echoed not only down the stairs, but out onto the street. The TV was tuned to a pay-per-view movie where a police gunfight raged. Within seconds, the room was crowded with all but Boldt, as the team searched under both beds, through the room's only closet, and its small bathroom.

Boldt was first to notice the communicating door that connected with the adjacent room. He pointed it out, picked up the ram from the hallway floor and signaled for his team to divide, all the while his mind grinding through the reality of the situation: if Flek had taken the adjacent room, then the manager, on Boldt's orders, had just asked him to come down to the lobby because of a smoke alarm problem. Flek would have fled the room immediately, either remaining inside the motel, or disguising himself and slipping out unseen.

The team raided the communicating door from both sides simultaneously. They found an oily pizza box and the recently opened package that Samway had delivered. Empty. SID would later find the fingerprints to confirm it. Bryce Abbott Flek had escaped. And Boldt had helped him to do so.

FORTY

'The minute he got the phone call from the manager, he pulled on a pair of boxer shorts, threw a towel over his arm, and headed down to the pool,' Samway said from the other side of the cigarette-scarred interrogation table in the box. Mulwright, Boldt and Gaynes occupied the other side of the table.

Samway wore an extra-large black police wind-breaker to cover herself. The effects of the stun grenade had required a visit to the emergency room, costing Boldt precious time. She had punctured an eardrum and wore some foam padding over her left ear, but other than that was medically sound.

'The rifle?' Boldt asked.

'I ain't saying nothing about no rifle,' she replied. 'Not until I see me a lawyer.'

'Young lady,' Boldt addressed her, 'you are in legal quicksand. The more you move, the deeper you sink. Do you understand? We've been through this attorney thing before. One has been assigned to you and is on the way, just like last time. But just like last time, you are far better off to cooperate now and save yourself some heartache.'

'In a backpack. He carried it with him.'

Samway continually glared angrily at Gaynes, recognizing her from their pool encounter. After a long stare she complained, 'Dyke bitch.' She told Boldt, 'She hit on me!'

Boldt wondered if Flek had walked right past the front desk, right past that one-way glass in the office. It seemed unlikely. He said, 'I would have seen him in the lobby.'

'There's an entrance to the pool from the weight room on the second floor,' Jilly Hu informed Boldt.

'And we didn't hear about it?' Boldt thundered.

'We knew about it,' Mulwright countered. 'It's on the floor plans of the building,' he said, referring to the city fire department's data. 'We re-deployed assets to cover the various exits. Higher priority.'

Boldt complained, 'You did this *after* the suspect had already fled the building.'

'Hey,' Mulwright countered. 'Don't lay that shit on me! You were the one wanted to wait. I was the go-guy. If we'd have gone, like I said we should'a, then it wouldn't be this bimbo in the chair, it would be our boy.'

'Who you calling a bimbo, Moon Face?' Samway countered, shouting because her voice could not adjust to the temporary loss of hearing in the one ear.

'You, Lap Dancer. I'm calling you a bimbo, and you know what? I'm wrong. Bimbo's a compliment to a slut like you. You're street trash, whoring for some asshole who goes around beating on people and heisting VCRs. You think that's a man you been spreading 'em for? You think he didn't know what was coming, leaving you behind in the room like that? He could'a got you killed! You know that? You understand that? You think he cared? He tell you the police were coming? Did he? No. He didn't, did he? I can see it on your face. He burned you. He *sacrificed* you, Sweet Tits. And you know what? He's laughing over some beer somewhere. He skates while you get the dumb bomb. And here you are *defending* him, *protecting* him. Give me a fucking break!'

'What do you mean, beating on people?' Of everything Mulwright had said to her, this is what stuck.

Boldt said, 'We mentioned the assaults the last time we talked to you.'

She squirmed. Maybe she'd been high the last time. Maybe she didn't remember.

Boldt explained, 'We think he broke the neck of a woman police officer.'

'He'll break your neck someday when he's tired of what's between your legs,' Mulwright added.

'Dream on, Pizza Face. He don't get tired of it. You ever seen me dance?'

'The only dancing you'll be doing where you're going will be for some bull dyke who's got you in her love pack.'

For the first time, Samway's composure cracked. The men missed it, but Bobbie Gaynes recognized the woman's vulnerability from their conversation in the elevator.

'You realize that, don't you?' Gaynes said, cutting off Boldt before he could speak. 'Sergeant Mulwright is right about that. You play dumb with us and you'll be locked up. You go to trial. With what we've got, you're an accessory to first-degree assault. With your record, you're screwed. You'll be sentenced to an adult women's correction facility – medium security, most likely – six to a cell, thirty in the showers at the same time. And the hell of it is, not only will the dykes make claim to you, make you do things you've never dreamed could be done by two women, but the screws – the guards, men mostly – will make you go down on them for a pack of cigarettes, a pack of gum, anything and everything you want. And you'll want it all – but they're the ones who get it.' She waited a moment and informed the others, 'We try to fix the system. Reform it. We really do. But I'm not so sure it's even possible anymore. You know? No matter how hard we try, the bigger women are going to take lovers, and a bad screw is going to slip through every now and then.'

'We can keep you away from all that,' Boldt said, picking up on the angle.

'They got the virus in those places,' Mulwright said, his eyes wet and unflinching. 'Your tongue's going to be tasting some virus, sweetheart.'

'That's enough!' Boldt barked sharply. 'Jesus . . .' he moaned.

A knock came on the door. Sheila Hill leaned her head inside and summoned Mulwright, a look of complete disgust on her face. As he reached the door, she grabbed onto his shirt and hauled him out of the interrogation room, her anger carrying through the door as she closed it again.

Gaynes apologized to the suspect. 'That was uncalled for. Sorry about that.'

Samway looked paralyzed. She muttered, 'I want me a lawyer.'

'One's coming,' Boldt said.

'Would you like us to leave the room?' Gaynes offered, for the sake of the cassette player running.

'No . . .' a confused Samway said. 'What do I have to do?'

'Some place we could find him,' Boldt said.

'Tinker's.' She came back quickly with it, and Boldt trusted it for this reason.

'Tinker Bell?' Gaynes asked the suspect. To Boldt she

285

said, 'A fence down in Kent.' She added, 'I forget his real name: Billy, Teddy? Burglary'll know.'

Samway nodded and whispered, 'He does business with Tinker. But if you raid Tinker's, Abby'll know it was me. And if he knows it was me who talked . . .'

'Not necessarily,' Boldt said. 'We can get around that.'

'I've heard him speak to Tinker on the phone.'

'The phone,' Boldt mumbled. 'He clones phones. We know that. We need the number of the phone he's currently using.' He was thinking back to his own idea of triangulation – maybe Flek would lead them right to himself. The number called from the Etheredge facility had not been used since his brother's death. Boldt needed the current number.

'Billy Bell is his real name, I think,' Gaynes interrupted, still stuck on remembering the name of the fence. She repeated, 'Burglary'll know.'

'You keep me out of jail,' Samway demanded, though weakly. 'You get me into one of them places where they play volleyball and stuff like that. Minimum. Work release. Something like that.'

'We need the cellular phone numbers he's using,' Boldt repeated. 'If you supply us with those phone numbers, then maybe Tinker never connects our visit to Flek.'

Meeting eyes with Boldt, she studied him. This offer clearly appealed to her. 'Phone numbers?' she asked, emphasizing the plural. 'He's only got the one cell phone anymore.' She waited, expecting Boldt to chime in, but he simply maintained the eye contact and waited her out. 'You guys got the others when you raided his pad.'

Boldt waited her out. 'Tell me what I want to hear,' he said.

'I've got the number,' she assured him.

Boldt pulled out his pen and started writing.

FORTY ONE

'I wanted you to hear this,' Boldt told Daphne, who occupied one of the two chairs on the other side of his desk, 'in part because Sanchez is still *your* investigation,' he reminded. He could tell she had gone for a morning run because it flushed her cheeks with color throughout the day. She wore a pink button-down Oxford, a small gray skirt and black leggings. She smelled sweet but not overpowering. Typical of her. He motioned to Bobbie Gaynes. 'She gave me a partial report over the phone.'

'Let's hear,' Daphne said.

Gaynes said, 'Burglary raided three fences, including Billy Bell, in order to pull the attention off the Flek case and lessen Samway's exposure. All three were caught with hot merchandise in their possession, and all three shown photo arrays that included Flek. Bell ID'ed Flek as part of an agreement for a 'walk.' Burglary ran descriptions of the electronic gear Flek had stolen from the various houses – the makes, models, and some serial numbers – and Bell was good for most all of it – he not only remembered it coming through his shop, but had computer records of actual serial numbers in a bunch of cases.'

'Modern criminals,' Boldt mumbled. 'They never cease to amaze me.'

'Most all of it,' Daphne quoted, repeating what Gaynes had said. 'Why "most" and not "all"?'

'Because none of the Sanchez gear could be accounted for by Bell.'

With the fifth floor busy once again, there was never silence in Boldt's office. But no one spoke for several long seconds and it felt like silence to him. He said, 'We can invent explanations for that.'

'Right as rain,' Gaynes agreed.

Boldt suggested, 'Flek tossed the gear because it was tainted by the assault.'

'Entirely possible,' Gaynes agreed.

'This guy?' Daphne asked. 'Not this guy, no. You invited me in on this for my professional opinion?' This seemed aimed at Boldt. 'He does a job, he wants some reward. He's a hardened criminal,' she reminded him. 'Is he going to scare off because he threw some woman down the stairs?'

'Or snapped her neck from behind,' Boldt amended. 'Dixie can't rule out that possibility.'

Daphne asked Gaynes, 'How much can we trust what Bell says?'

'Not much,' she conceded. 'But I happen to trust it in this case. He knows about LaMoia and Sanchez, along with the rest of the city. He knows we mean business.'

Daphne said, 'So when the Sanchez assault is reported by the papers to be an officer, Flek tells Bell to ditch the gear.'

Gaynes replied, 'Possibly. But then Billy Bell would remember that gear all the more.'

'So . . .' Daphne complained, confused.

Gaynes said, 'I think Bell is right with this. He has a lot to lose. Burglary can put him down for the stash they found. Why toy with us? I just don't see it.'

'Because he's afraid of Flek,' Daphne answered, 'just

289

as everyone else seems to be.' She glanced at Boldt, trying to judge his reaction, but he wouldn't give her that.

'Could be,' Bobbie allowed.

Boldt interrupted, 'The point being that if Bell is right with this, then he fenced most of the gear Flek lifted *except* the Sanchez electronics. If true, that needs explaining. We have to listen to that. We assume Flek did John, and as such remains at the top of the department's Most Wanted.'

'Meaning what?' Gaynes inquired.

'Sanchez failed to pick him out of the photo array,' Daphne reminded them both. 'And at least once, she did not discount the possible involvement of more than one person.'

'So where are we going with this?' Gaynes repeated impatiently.

'We look the Sanchez assault over real carefully,' Boldt said. 'Start again. Build the case from the ground up and try to fit Flek into it. She worked one of the cases – that ties her to Flek's world. Let's know everything there is to know. We work Samway again. But we let nothing inhibit the manhunt. That remains our top priority.' He added, 'Flek is going to have answers for us.'

'But if Flek didn't do Sanchez,' Gaynes persisted, still annoyed by her own confusion, 'then where are we going with this?'

Boldt looked over at Daphne, and meeting eyes, saw her concern for him. For a woman typically capable of containing her emotions, this spoke volumes. She knew exactly where they were going with this. But it was Boldt who voiced it.

'To the devil,' he answered.

Daphne nodded in agreement.

'In house,' Gaynes gasped. Then she added, 'Oh, my God!'

FORTY TWO

'It was a difficult meeting,' he told Liz.

Boldt presented the contradictory evidence surrounding Flek's possible involvement with the Sanchez assault at a divisional meeting attended by captains Hill and Shoswitz as well as the captain of detectives and a deputy chief to whom all the captains reported. The meeting became heated as Boldt suggested that though they suspected Flek for the LaMoia assault and intended to pursue him to the very edges of the earth, questions persisted about the Sanchez assault and that he could not rule out the possibility of 'the involvement of internal personnel.' Deputy Chief McAffrey stated that he would reluctantly assign it to Internal Investigations for review. Boldt asked that I.I.'s involvement be curtailed until he and Matthews had reviewed all the evidence, circumstantial and otherwise. McAffrey agreed to give Boldt forty-eight hours. Sheila Hill skillfully negotiated Boldt's cushion to seventy-two. Boldt left the meeting with a clock ticking in his head. In the middle of an active fugitive pursuit as well as at the start of a total case review on Sanchez, his plate was full.

He ate a gyro while Liz tried the Greek salad. Their relationship sat between them on the table like a tall vase of flowers or a lit candle one can't see past. Boldt had never felt so awkward in her presence.

'Mud up to the axles,' Boldt said after an uncomfortable silence. 'That's how this feels. Work. You and I. Everything.'

'What I feel is a need – a real need – to get things right. And they aren't right now. We imposed on John and Kristin for *weeks*, and that wasn't right. We need to have them over to dinner, buy them a real special thank-you gift. But you're barely home, and when you are, you don't even talk to me.' She poked at the salad. Boldt felt it in the center of his chest.

'I kissed a woman,' he announced apologetically. It tumbled out of him and he felt a flood of relief with the confession. It would be work, but now they could make real progress.

She stabbed again and missed. She knocked over the bowl spilling oily cucumbers onto the table. They slid around like transparent hockey pucks. She wouldn't look up at him. Her lower lip trembled. He felt like dying.

He said, 'It was only the one kiss. It stopped at that. Not that that makes it any better.' He paused. 'But it was enough to tell me something is very wrong. I've let this separation drift us apart. I couldn't face you without telling you about it, and I couldn't tell you about it without facing you.'

Her mouth hung open. She had some pepper stuck between her teeth. Any other day he would have told her about the pepper. The fork fell into the bowl. She didn't notice. 'Who?' she asked.

'Does it matter?' he scoffed. 'It's not who, it's why.'

'Then why do I feel jealous?' she asked. 'Why do I feel this is somehow my fault?'

'It's both our faults,' Boldt said. 'But it doesn't feel that way.'

'Good,' she said. 'That somehow makes me feel better.' She asked, 'Emotionally? Are you emotionally attached?'

'It was a single kiss. It's not an affair.'

'But of the heart?' she asked with difficulty. 'Where's your heart in all this?'

'Broken at the moment, as I imagine yours is. But the pieces are all with you, Elizabeth, with *us*, every last piece.'

'I need air. I need time to think!'

'I . . .' Boldt began.

But she stood and made for the door, her purse trailing by its strap. She held herself high – ever Liz. Boldt felt as if he were swimming underwater. Consumed in darkness.

He pushed the food aside, his appetite gone, wondering what came next. He felt sick. Sick, and incredibly cold.

FORTY THREE

Boldt wished that Liz had blown up at him in anger, because as it was, her level-headed wait-and-see approach only served to increase his sense of guilt.

Boldt wasn't a drinker. The only outlet for his frustration was work. Work consumed him, took his mind off nearly anything. And he wanted that.

Boldt contacted one Frederick Osbourne at AirTyme Cellular and provided him with Flek's cell phone number, which Samway had supplied in the course of her second interrogation. Osbourne explained that the technology and methodology existed to locate analog cellular phones, but that it was not a real-time process. He, Osbourne, would begin tracking Flek's cellular calls and report back to Boldt. Of all their current efforts to locate Flek, Boldt held to the hope that Osbourne's radio triangulation would come through.

Sinking back into despair, Boldt blocked calls, prevented visitors, and spent nearly four hours in his office reviewing the Sanchez jacket, which had swollen to a thick file, though under Daphne's care remained properly organized and easily navigated.

There Daphne was, right there in his hands. He couldn't seem to escape her. He focused his attention on the Brooks-Gilman case – the investigation that Sanchez had taken over in the wake of the Blue Flu reassignments. Prior to her assault, she had identified that Flek used garage door openers to break and enter.

Boldt understood that he had allowed her work on the case to mislead him. It was the I.I. case that seemed more likely to have gotten her beat up, the I.I. case that interested him. Yet without I.I.'s cooperation, he didn't know how he might break that case. Flek's testimony still seemed the most important first step. If Flek had an alibi for the night of Sanchez's assault, then Boldt had the necessary ammunition to pressure I.I. into including him in on what they knew about whatever had led to Sanchez, Schock and Phillipp all ending up in the hospital.

He called down to the lab and reached Bernie Lofgrin. He asked about the boots recovered from Flek's closet in the first raid.

'What about them?' Lofgrin asked.

'Guy I spoke to said they were Converse, but have you compared the tread pattern to that Nike pattern you found on Sanchez's leather jacket?'

'I have, and I sent them to Property. That's where her jacket is as well.'

Mention of Property reminded Boldt of Ron Chapman and his visit to the Cock & Bull the night Schock and Phillipp had been 'mugged.'

'Property,' Boldt repeated.

'That's right,' Lofgrin said. 'Do you ever read your E-mails?'

'I was out of town,' Boldt said, spinning around to check his computer. Seventeen messages. In the chaos of LaMoia's injuries and Samway's surveillance, he'd fallen behind. He began to scroll through them, pulling up the one from Lofgrin as the man said into his ear, 'Tread pattern lifted from the jacket came back as Air Nike. Flek's closet contained two pair of Converse All Stars. Both are ubiquitous, but they're not interchangeable. Not even close.'

'Same size?' Boldt asked, reading from his screen that the impression from Sanchez's jacket had been a size 12.

'Flek wears a fourteen,' Lofgrin answered. 'Again, no match to what we lifted from that jacket.' He waited. 'Lou? You there?'

'Thinking.'

'Not what you wanted to hear,' Lofgrin stated, 'or you would have hung up on me, as you always do.'

'Do I?' Boldt asked, astonished to learn this about himself.

'Every time,' Lofgrin confirmed.

'The Nike . . .' Boldt said. 'Is it a distinct print?'

'You bring me the shoe and chances are I can tie it to Sanchez's jacket. A little visit to Property is all it would take.'

There it was again: Property. He made sure to thank Lofgrin before hanging up. Who said you couldn't teach an old dog new tricks?

He called down to Property. Riorden answered. Riorden ran with Pendegrass, both of them on Krishevski's squad. Krishevski and Pendegrass had both been discharged in the chief's health service sweep. Riorden had somehow survived. Boldt elected to skip the small talk. By now, news of Boldt and LaMoia's late-night visit to Pendegrass would have reached Riorden – he could do business with the man, but he wasn't going to win any friends.

'I need you to check your logbook for me,' Boldt informed him.

'For?'

'Schock or Phillipp,' Boldt said. 'Any visits in the last ten days?'

Silence on the line. 'Let me check,' Riorden replied. Boldt waited to hear the pages of the logbook turning –

he had the ears of a bat – but heard nothing, not even the clicking of computer keys. 'Nothing I see, Lieutenant. You might want to check yourself.'

This time it was Boldt who left the silence on the line. 'Yeah . . . okay . . . thanks . . .' he said, knowing his ears had not failed him. Why hadn't Riorden even bothered to check the log? Out of obstinacy? Pissed off over Boldt's questioning of Pendegrass? Did the Flu still continue *inside* these walls?

The thought that a handful of officers might yet still be sabotaging the efforts of those officers who had remained on their job during the Flu stayed with Boldt on his extended ride home.

He stopped at The Joke's On You and played six ballads during a break in the comedy routine. Bear Berenson finally interrupted him, saying, 'That's some really dark shit you're playing, man.'

He drove next to Carkeek Park and walked the water's edge, wondering what to think about Riorden's apparent refusal to assist him. As dusk fell and the Sound washed gray from green, as radio towers winked and jets flew almost silently overhead, Boldt felt overwhelmed. His personal life was in tatters. Fellow officers were backstabbing his efforts to set the record straight on Sanchez and perhaps Schock and Phillipp in the process. His knee-jerk reaction was to call Daphne, but he wisely ruled that out. Instead, he made the drive home. Home, where he belonged.

He climbed out of the car, accidentally kicking an empty Starbucks cup into the driveway. As he bent to retrieve it, the driver's door window blew out above his head cascading down as a thousand cubes of tempered glass.

His detective's mind immediately registered that he'd

been shot at – an intended chest shot. A kill shot. His next coherent thought was *Flek!*

He edged beneath the car instinctively, defenseless but partially protected and less vulnerable. He waited for the second shot, hoping there wasn't enough of him exposed to take a bullet. His heart raced out of control and he wondered if a heart attack might kill him instead. Ten seconds passed. Twenty . . .

The shot had not made any noise. Even the window shattering had sounded like little more than a hand clap and pebbles spilling onto pavement. He didn't want Liz alerted, didn't want to bring her to the door for any reason. One Boldt as a target was enough. A *long shot*, Boldt thought, recalling the rifle Manny Wong had sold Flek. Probably from on a roof or up in a tree, and at a long distance, which might explain why he had not heard any report from the weapon. Not even a trailing echo. Maybe Wong had saved his life by resighting that scope.

He stayed there under the car, collecting himself, wondering if a German sniper sight was searching the edge of the car, looking for enough flesh to sink a bullet into.

He heard tapping on a window. He couldn't see, but he knew it was Liz, inside the house, wondering where he was. She'd seen his car. Perhaps she had heard the dull pop of the driver's door glass. His kids would be getting ready for bed. Maybe already in bed. The rest of the world was going about its business.

It took him a moment to extricate his right arm and ease himself out from under the car. He didn't want Liz to come looking for him. She'd come home without consulting him. For a moment a husband's anger boiled inside him. Maybe his sniper was doing him a favor. Could he tell his wife he'd just been shot at? In his own driveway?

Did he have any choice?

He squeezed himself out from under the car and ran, crouched low, to the back of the house. He entered through the kitchen door, sat Liz down and explained that he'd just been shot at. He wasn't going to tell her to take the kids and leave. That would be left for her to decide. They embraced. Boldt felt himself swell with tears – the fear of the last few minutes wanting an outlet.

Boldt groaned.

'Who?' she asked.

'Daphne,' he answered, believing her still questioning the kiss.

'The gun shot,' she corrected, tension steeling. 'Who shot at you, and what are you going to do about it?'

He leaned back, drew his weapon from its holster, and checked it as he spoke to her. She didn't like that. A tension settled between them. 'I'm going to check the park. I think the shot came from there. If I'm lucky, I find a shell casing. Doubtful, but worth a try.' He hurried so that she wouldn't interrupt. 'After that, I'm going to go out there and look for the bullet, which is probably the only chance we have for evidence.'

'You're going to report it,' she stated with no uncertainty.

'All they'd do is look for a slug and a shell casing. Believe me, I know how this works. And when we find the slug or the shell casing, it'll be from a Chinese manufacture long-barrel assault rifle.'

'You *do* know who it is,' she said.

'A pretty good idea is all,' he admitted. 'But that doesn't win convictions.'

They met eyes – hers filled with concern. Then she softened and said, 'Lou, if you'd kissed some waitress at a bachelor party . . .' surprising him. 'But this isn't the same thing. Not even close. I've changed over these last couple of years, I know that. I'm not so sure you have. Which is fine. Let me just say this: if you don't want me, I don't want you. But for the sake of the kids, I'd do anything not to break us up. Not now. Not so young anyway. I'm angry with you. Not so much for what you did, but for allowing it to happen. I've got my faith to keep me strong. What do you have?' She stepped back and crossed her arms defiantly. 'Go find your slug. Tonight, I'll sleep with Miles. For their sake, we're loving and cheerful in the morning.'

'Maybe I'll wait 'til morning to look,' he suggested, hoping they might still talk it through.

'You?' she asked. 'Do you know yourself at all?'

'Maybe not,' he answered.

'Maybe not,' she agreed. 'You're a cop. Once and forever.' Her eyes sparked, a thought clearly filling her head. That look on her face grew with intensity. 'You're a *cop*! Meaning our phone is unpublished, and always has been. Your name – our address – is not in any phone book, any listing, anywhere. So how did this guy know which house to watch? Right? I mean, that's the point of the privacy, of all the secrecy. Right?'

'The Internet?' he wondered aloud. 'I don't know,' he answered, somewhat lifelessly. Her reasoning bored into him deeper the more he thought about it. Who was the cop in the family now?

How, indeed, he wondered, looking at that assassin's bullet in a whole new light.

FORTY FOUR

He spent an hour in the park, and found no evidence of
his would-be assassin. He searched his driveway in the
dark. Again, nothing.

In the dim light of dawn, Boldt methodically searched
his driveway a second time. Flat-bottomed wisps, like
micro-clouds, hovered in the air twenty feet off the
ground. Birds awakened with their percussive morning
calls and crackles, not yet song. Someone across the
street had NPR playing too loudly. Boldt could almost
make out the news stories himself. There would be
nothing there about the attempted assassination of a
cop; nothing there about a police manhunt for Bryce
Abbott Flek that grew in scale each day. Presently, that
manhunt included not only SPD, but King County
Police, the state sheriff's office and the Washington
State Transportation Department; nothing on the news
about Boldt's attempt to locate Flek's cellular phone
while in use.

When he discovered a small hole in the garage's gray
clapboard siding, the only convincing evidence that
drew him to it was the fresh splinters of wood showing.
Seattle's dampness aged any exposed wood quickly – a
week or two and a broken branch or a recently sawed
two by four might be mistaken for a year old. But these
tiny slivers of missing wood surrounding the oddly
shaped hole were a golden blond. The hole's location
at knee height puzzled him, and it took a moment to

convince himself the slug could have ricocheted off the blacktop and landed so high up on the wall, but as an investigator he knew better than to doubt the obvious – *anything* could happen. He had not thought to look at this height. He had cost himself time.

He dug the slug from the garage wall with a hammer and flat blade screwdriver, taking more of the clapboard than necessary to ensure he didn't further damage the slug. He wanted it as intact as possible for SID's ballistics analysis.

Like an expectant father, Boldt waited in a formed fiberglass chair inside Bernie Lofgrin's office. Lofgrin joined his friend at the first opportunity.

'I'd really appreciate a case number to assign that slug,' Lofgrin said.

'Later.'

'Suit yourself, but the work goes down in my log and it's easier for all if that number's attached. The computer won't accept it without a number, which means it will stand out. Get noticed. Be brought to my attention during some forensics audit, and therefore to your attention.'

'I'll call down a number,' Boldt told him.

'Oh, goodie,' Lofgrin said. 'Because by that look on your face, I was afraid it was personal. And you know the new lab policy about doing personal work for officers.'

'No, it's not personal.'

'Not that I wouldn't make exceptions for my closest friends,' Lofgrin said, still prying, 'but I'd have to know to make those exceptions well before the computers became involved. You can see my point.'

'I see your point.'

Lofgrin added, 'How's Floorshow doing anyway?'

Boldt felt a hole in the center of his chest. He hadn't checked up on LaMoia in days. He felt awful about it. 'Better, I think,' he said.

'Give him my best.'

'Right.'

'Here we go,' Lofgrin said, indicating a lab woman approaching Lofgrin's office. 'Your ballistics report.'

She knocked on the open door and Lofgrin admitted her, introducing her to Boldt, who missed her name. She looked first to her boss, then to Boldt. 'Is this some kind of test or something?' she asked them both, clearly irritated. To Lofgrin she complained, 'Does the upstairs brass know that we didn't lose anyone to the Flu? That we don't need this kind of thing to prove our competency? Our loyalty.' To Boldt she said, 'Are you the messenger here, Lieutenant? I've got better things to do than be tested like this.' Addressing Lofgrin she said, 'Maybe we should remind the brass that we're *civilian* employees, that we have actual, active cases to work – pressing cases – and that school got out for most of us ten years ago.' Throwing the file onto Lofgrin's desk, she said meanly, 'Someone tell the person who did this to stop blowing smoke up my ass.' Meeting eyes with Boldt, she said, 'I *quit* smoking.' She stormed off.

Lofgrin grinned. 'I just love a passionate employee,' he said.

'What the hell's going on?' Boldt asked.

Lofgrin opened the manila folder and read from the single page it contained. He nodded to himself and smiled. 'Oh, I get it,' he mumbled.

'I don't,' Boldt said.

'Somebody's pulling your chain on this slug, Lou. No wonder you didn't want to give me a case number – you sly dog! Are you in on this?'

'In on *what*?' Boldt said, raising his voice.

'Someone *is* apparently testing us.'

Boldt said, guessing, 'Fired from a Chinese manufacture assault rifle? Can you determine that?'

'You're not serious? Come on! This slug? This baby was fired from a rifle that's down in Property. Confiscated in that gang raid where Williamson and Hobner were both shot. This is the rifle that winged Williamson. She's right: I mean why waste our time with something like this? And you, Lou, a part of it? You ought to be ashamed.'

Boldt repeated for his own sake, 'This gun is supposed to be locked up in Property?'

'Supposed to be?' a confused Lofgrin replied. 'This is some kind of joke, right?'

Boldt didn't think so. He'd been on the receiving end.

FORTY FIVE

Addressing Sergeant Ron Chapman from outside SPD's Property room, Boldt said, 'Ronnie, we've got some confusion about a confiscated weapon.' He handed the man some paperwork from SID. It bore a reference number for the rifle that had fired on Boldt.

'Is that right?' Chapman replied. 'What kind of confusion?'

'Just need a look at it, is all,' Boldt informed him.

'That, I can do.'

While Chapman consulted the computer, Boldt flipped pages in the log book – accomplishing what Riorden had refused to do for him.

'Help you there?' Chapman inquired.

'Looking for visits by Schock and Phillipp.' Boldt added, 'I asked Riorden. I'm not sure he had time to check for me.'

'They're in there somewhere,' Chapman answered dryly. 'They've been down here.'

'Since the Sanchez assault, or before?' Boldt asked, flipping more pages, looking for the right date.

'Couldn't say.'

Boldt found the records of Sanchez's four visits and worked forward. On the next page he found Schock's and Phillipp's signatures. Again, as with Sanchez, there were no case numbers listed. 'No case numbers,' he mumbled. Looking up, he caught Chapman staring at him – something was wrong in those eyes, though the man volunteered nothing. 'Ronnie?'

'It's down in the warehouse,' he said. 'The rifle. You want a look?'

Technically, the Property room consisted of two different secure storage facilities, both located in Public Safety's sub-basements. 'The boneyard,' located on Public Safety's ground floor, held any physical evidence involved in an active case or any case pending trial within the next calendar year. Caged and managed by an armed uniform officer of at least the rank of sergeant, along with a staff of two or three plainclothes officers per shift, the boneyard remained open twenty-four hours a day. Several years earlier, Narcotics – Drugs, as the officers called it – had managed to administratively separate the chemical evidence confiscated in arrests from the guns, knives, magnets, and bell bars that typically populated Property. The Drugs evidence was kept locked in a vault inside its offices on the fourth floor, just down the hall from Burglary.

Property's second facility – 'the warehouse' – occupied half of the building's lowest floor, on the same grade as the lower level of SPD's sub-level parking garage. The warehouse was located behind a double-wide four-inch solid steel vault door with a combination tumbler and two-key perimeter locking system and a security alarm that had to be turned off from inside the boneyard – a floor above – no more than five minutes prior to entry. All this because the warehouse not only accepted all the overflow weapons and munitions from the boneyard, but also the heavier artillery that occasionally surfaced in raids.

Entering the warehouse always gave Boldt a chill because of its size and contents. The Public Safety Building occupied most of an entire city block, and half its basement was one enormous room. Boldt's first reaction – no matter how many times he came here – was awe. The room was crowded with row after row of floor-to-ceiling freestanding steel shelving, and was dimly lit by bare bulbs in the ceiling.

Chapman read from the clipboard, dragging himself down aisles of shelves stacked high and deep with tagged items of every description, though predominantly weapons – from Swiss Army knives to machetes; zip guns to flame throwers. House lamps. Garden hoses. Gloves of every make and description. The space smelled musty despite the constant hum of overworked dehumidifiers.

Chapman said something about Ken Griffey Jr.'s homerun count. Boldt barely heard it, his gut churning, his mind racing. Sanchez had visited Property and had ended up in hospital; Schock and Phillipp, the same. Boldt had called down to Riorden the night before and had nearly been shot. He had thought Flek had thrown that shot, but he had not. And where did Chapman fit in?

The Property sergeant dragged a rolling ladder down the aisle and climbed high up to the sixth shelf. He banged around up there for several seconds, descended the ladder and returned to the end of the stack, where he verified the row number and letter.

Chapman's movements were lazy – too many years on the job to get worked up over another man's worries. That, or he was trying to cover for his own nervousness.

Chapman climbed the rolling ladder for a second time. He dug around on a shelf and handed down a tagged rifle.

For a moment, Boldt felt a sense of relief, for his fear had been that the rifle wouldn't be there at all – that it had been removed from Property and used in an attempt to assassinate him. He sniffed the barrel – not used recently. Then he held the rifle at arm's length as Chapman climbed back down to his level. And his chest tightened. He fumbled for the label. The numbers were right. He double-checked them.

'Something the matter?' Chapman inquired, sensing Boldt's disposition.

'It's the wrong rifle,' Boldt replied. 'It's not even the right make!'

His words echoed in the space. His stomach knotted.

Ron Chapman looked at him and said, 'Oh shit! We got problems!'

Boldt instructed Daphne and Bobbie Gaynes to meet him in the Garden Terrace of the Four Seasons Olympic Hotel, where he had tea for three and a plate of currant scones waiting. Although not a regular, Boldt took afternoon tea at the Four Seasons whenever he felt he could afford it, about once a paycheck.

Neither Gaynes nor Matthews was fooled by his choice of location. They arrived together, having walked from the office. 'So, L.T.,' Gaynes said, sitting in a chair facing the man and leaving the other half of the love seat he occupied for Daphne, 'what's so important that we can't talk about it at the house?'

'Am I so transparent?'

'Not wearing that vest you're not,' Daphne said. Boldt was a big man. He carried the protective vest better than most. He'd bought a shirt two sizes bigger than what he typically wore to accommodate the vest. All this at Liz's insistence. His concession to their negotiation for his return to the job.

He explained, 'I promised Liz I'd wear it.'

Daphne Matthews looked pale. 'I think you owe us an explanation.'

He took them through his last eighteen hours – the attempt on his life, the visit to Lofgrin, the wrong rifle in storage.

Daphne reached out to grab his hand, but caught herself and dragged the butter to her plate. Daphne and butter did not go together, so Gaynes looked on in amazement.

'Someone threw shots at you?' Gaynes gasped.

'One shot,' Boldt answered clinically. 'And it wasn't a warning shot.'

Gaynes stared down at the scone on the plate before her. 'Well, there goes my appetite.'

'I have a theory I'd like to share with you,' he told them.

Gaynes interrupted. Daphne seemed frozen in the love seat. 'Flek found your crib?'

Boldt addressed her and said, 'Liz caught that too. Flek has no way of knowing where we live. I'd have to put him low on the list.' He let them think a moment and said, 'Someone switched out the rifle.'

'You're giving me the weebies here, L.T.'

'Someone switched out the rifle. It is *not* the weapon confiscated in the Williamson shooting. Sanchez paid four visits to Property, just before her assault. Schock and Phillip paid two. What if that's the I.I. case no one will talk about?'

'Sweet Jesus!' Gaynes blurted out.

'The Flu,' Daphne whispered, knowing him better than others did.

He found room to smile. He appreciated the connection the three of them had. 'Let's say that word got out to a select few that the walkout was inevitable, that negotiations had broken down. Let's say that all this happened well ahead of the rest of us ever hearing even a rumor of cancelled overtime. The rank and file,' he said.

'Paychecks stop. People borrow. Then the borrowing stops, and families suffer. So what if a couple of our boys decided they needed underwriting? An insurance policy?'

'Heist some weapons from Property and sell them into the market,' Gaynes suggested.

Daphne objected, 'But a weapon was there. Just the wrong one. Property can't make a mistake? With *that* inventory?'

'Exactly,' Boldt said. 'Exactly what we're supposed to think: human error. And that's probably what I.I. was checking up on.'

Gaynes disagreed. 'Ron Chapman would not condone this. Not ever.'

'Maybe not,' Boldt agreed, 'but he suspected something, or discovered something that put him onto it. I've got to tell you: he looked as surprised as I was to see the wrong weapon attached to the label.'

'Then who?' Gaynes asked.

'Remember what Wong said?' he asked Gaynes. 'Remember what he mumbled a couple of times? "Cops and guns," he said. Said it at least twice. It bothered me at the time, not for the words themselves – I mean the guy's a gun dealer – but for the *way* he said it: like he was disgusted or something. "Cops and guns." One day they're selling them to him. The next we come along, and we want them back.'

Daphne followed his logic. She said ominously, 'Someone tried to kill you with one of those guns. Are you saying Manny Wong sold Flek an assault rifle that had been black-marketed by one of us?'

'Might be Flek,' Boldt said. 'Might not. The sooner we catch him, the better.'

Gaynes said, 'You have other enemies?'

'Earlier in the day I'd been arguing in a closed meeting

that maybe Flek had not done Sanchez, that maybe we had to look inside our own ranks.'

Daphne said, 'It's all circumstantial.'

'Extremely,' Boldt agreed, 'but it starts to add up.'

Gaynes said, 'Wong sold one of the Property Room weapons back to Flek? Isn't that a bit of a coincidence?'

'Agreed,' Boldt said. 'When we find Flek, it won't be his rifle that threw the shot. We need him in custody. We need that rifle for comparison. Flek's a screw-up. He's a burglar with a temper. He hurt John, and we're bringing him in for that. But it's not the only reason he's our top priority. Flek can help fill in some of the answers, whether he knows it or not.' He added, 'My guess is that at this point – once my discovery in Property gets out – there are people or persons who won't want us to bring him in. Won't want certain questions answered.' He added, 'Bryce Abbott Flek has become their scape-goat.'

Gaynes reminded them, 'Whoever stole those weapons has to have someone from Property in their camp.'

Boldt suggested, 'Who in Property would have had inside information that a walkout was imminent?'

'Krishevski?' Gaynes asked timidly. 'Sweet Jesus,' she repeated, reaching for a scone to quell her nervous stomach.

FORTY SIX

When Boldt entered through the back door, he knew that something was amiss, not only from Liz's perplexed expression, but from the faint strains of Oscar Peterson coming from the study – his music room. Why would Liz play an LP but leave the living-room speakers off?

She motioned toward that music, 'Mac Krishevski's here.'

Boldt's chest tightened as he stripped off his sport jacket, the new shirt, and tugged at the Velcro strips that secured the vest over his undershirt. 'Too hot in this thing,' he mumbled. As he slipped back into his shirt, he asked, 'Did he call first?'

She shook her head. 'Just showed up. We talked a few minutes, but he insisted I go about my regular stuff and that he'd enjoy himself with your collection.'

'How long?' Boldt inquired.

'Nearly an hour ago. I figured you'd want to see him.'

'Thanks.'

The kids were in the living room, Sarah in front of a video, Miles building a Lego fort. They didn't seem to notice him at all.

Krishevski looked older than when they last had met. Tension filled his eyes, the skin surrounding them stained blue with fatigue. This was not a pleasure visit.

'Mac?' Boldt asked from the doorway of the small room. He rolled up his shirt sleeves.

His study, a ten-by-twelve-foot dead space partially beneath the stairs, was occupied by nearly two thousand vinyl LP jazz albums filed floor to ceiling, a 200-watt vacuum-tube stereo, a speaker system with hand-wrapped copper coils, and a single leather recliner within an arm's reach of the controls.

'We got business to discuss,' Krishevski said. He climbed out of the recliner and offered it to Boldt. To be polite, Boldt declined and moved a ladder-back chair in from the living room. Boldt could see Liz trying to figure out what was going on. He told her, 'No calls, please, sweetheart. I'm going to speak to Mac in private for a few minutes.' She nodded back. He closed the door. Krishevski turned down the music and returned the recliner to a sitting position.

'Not the best news, I'm afraid,' Krishevski said.

'We might have a beer,' Boldt offered.

'Thanks anyway.'

Civility between two men who were borderline enemies.

Boldt placed his chair and sat down. 'So?'

'Whole fucking world's a mess. You ever notice that?'

'What's on your mind?'

'Don't shoot the messenger,' Krishevski requested.

'I'm the one being shot at, not doing the shooting.'

Krishevski's apparent surprise confused Boldt. Was he that good an actor, he wondered.

Boldt continued, 'So if you've come to warn me, you're about a day late, and at least one slug short.'

'I *am* here to warn you. But no matter what you believe, I'm only the messenger. And the message is pretty damn simple: you get your hands on the video, and the video they got never gets shown.'

'And what video would that be?'

Krishevski reached over and turned up the volume. 'We gotta talk.'

'I've got something for you.' The man making the phone call identified himself to Daphne as Frederick Osbourne of AirTyme Cellular. He continued, 'A lieutenant named Boldt left both his and your names in case I had anything, and I'm only getting Boldt's voice mail.'

Information concerning Flek's cellular phone, she realized, her heart leaping in her chest. She and Boldt had discussed Osbourne. 'Yes,' was all she could think to say.

'It's not real-time. He and I went over that. I'm sorry about that. We're working on it; we have some good ideas, actually, how we might improve that. I explained the various technologies and their limits to the lieutenant when we spoke. But I think you'll find it interesting. Would you like to come over to the offices?'

'It's seven o'clock,' Daphne pointed out. 'If you have a location for the suspect, perhaps you could just give it to me over the phone,' she suggested.

'Not exactly a location,' he answered. 'More like a theory. I think it better explained in person. Can you get hold of Lieutenant Boldt?'

'I can try. Yes.'

'You'll want to see this before eight o'clock . . . at least before eight-thirty. Sorry I've called so late, but I only put it all together just now. By eight-thirty you'll have lost him.'

'Lost him,' Daphne repeated, her mind whirring as she realized Osbourne believed he had *found* him. 'I'll be right there.'

Liz knocked on the door to her husband's study, waited a moment and then let herself inside. Krishevski occupied the throne of the recliner while her husband sat in a chair facing him like a child in the principal's office. She paused, looked her husband in the eye, and said, 'Phone call for you.'

'No calls right now,' he reminded her politely.

'It's *her*,' she said. 'Says it "important."' She drew the quotation marks in the air.

'I'll have to call her back.'

'I'll tell her,' Liz said. She seemed to take pleasure in it. She pulled the door shut, wondering why the music was playing so loudly and what it was meant to cover.

The AirTyme Cellular Regional Control Center – 'RC-squared,' Osbourne called it – occupied portions of the twenty-first and twenty-second floors of the Columbia Center skyscraper. Normally such real estate would have commanded quite the water view, but RC-squared was a blacked-out control room that stepped down in tiers to a curving wall of projection screens mapping cellular phone traffic over a seven-state area that included portions of Utah, Nevada, and northern California. It looked like something from Mission Control. Daphne counted seventeen people at computers, all wearing telephone headsets. The room was alive with hushed, indistinguishable voices.

'Wow,' Daphne said, sensing that Osbourne expected some kind of reaction.

He checked his wristwatch. 'We're pressed for time. I wanted to show you what I've come up with. So, if you'd direct your attention to the last screen on the right, Lieutenant Matthews.'

'As I'm sure you're aware,' he continued, 'the U.S. Congress passed a bill requiring us to geographically locate nine-one-one calls placed from cellular telephones, which presented us with a serious task in terms of the older generation analog phones. The new generation digital phones have GPS chips – Global Positioning Systems – inherent in their technology. But the older analog models without the chips have only their signal.

'There are several ways to attempt to locate an analog cellular phone that's in use, and probably a half dozen companies competing for the best methodology,' he continued. 'All of these methods were derived from the military. The two most common are DF, direction finding, and TDOA, time difference of arrival. Both are variations on something called triangulation. We use a company out of Canada that has taken TDOA one step further into something called hyperbolic trilateralization. Triangulation and trilateralization work off the same principle: if you have three antennas, all receiving a radio signal from the same source, and you can measure and record the time that a source radio signal arrives at each of those antennas, then you can plot the location of that original source signal. A cell phone signal lights up several towers at a time, sometimes as many as a half dozen or more. These towers pass reception and transmission one to the other in what's called a hand-off, as they determine which is the closer or more optimal tower. Because trilateralization works at very high speeds, constantly measuring the time to base, as we call it, its method of triangulation is far more accurate than many of its competitors. You with me so far?'

'I think so.'

'The long and the short of it is, the older method of triangulation could take several minutes or even hours to process accurately. This newer method I'm talking about is a real-time system with pinpoint accuracy because it's measuring a cell phone transmission in nanoseconds and plotting the location accordingly. Your problem is this,' he stated. 'Full government compliance is not mandated for another eighteen months. AirTyme has the hyperbolic trilateralization software and, of course, our firmware network of towers and transmission centers, but the two are not yet fully married. Adding to our difficulty – two of the three towers we may be using to measure time to base may belong to one or more competitors. They will gladly provide us the TDOA data, but it takes time to arrange. We estimate full network compatibility in ten months.'

'You're losing me,' she admitted. 'You do, or do not have a way to locate that cell phone number Lieutenant Boldt gave you?'

'With the help of our competitors, we can run the software on data previously gathered. In terms of your needs that means we can . . . if you envision it as laying the TDOA software on top of information we've already collected . . . the software then analyzes that data and spits out a location for us, though that data is typically hours old because we've had to gather it elsewhere.' He saw her disappointment register. 'The only other technology available to us – log-on signals – *is* real-time, but allow no location accuracy whatsoever. To my knowledge no one's come up with anything for log-ons. But that's one of the areas we're looking into for you.'

'You said I might miss him,' Daphne reminded, looking at her own watch, 'which implied you had *found* him, or did I misinterpret?'

Osbourne reached forward and tapped the man in front of him on the shoulder. The computer technician danced his fingers across the keyboard. Until that moment, Daphne had not realized this person was a part of their discussion. Osbourne said, 'Eyes on the screen to the right.'

The screen was enormous, perhaps a hundred square feet, half the size of a small movie theater screen. On it appeared a color map of the city that Daphne clearly recognized. The dark green to the left she took to be Puget Sound.

Osbourne said, 'If the person you're interested in had been calling on a newer phone, our GPS technology would have done the work for us. The only short-coming of GPS is line-of-sight interference, which TDOA gets around, and therefore ends up comple-menting the technology perfectly. But your suspect is calling out on an older model analog, I'm afraid. Each time he placed a call in the last eighteen hours, our network, and our competitors' networks, recorded those signal transmissions, for his and hundreds of thousands of other phones, all concurrently, twenty-four/seven. A tower receives his signal, and the com-puters time-stamp that arrival for the sake of billing records. Downtown, his transmission signal might light up six or eight towers, all at fractions-of-a-second differences. We have a record of all of that.' He tapped the man's shoulder again. 'What you see next are the various transmission locations of calls he has made. A red dot means he was standing still. A red line means he was moving. We shade that line pink to burgundy, to indicate direction – pink being the area of origin, burgundy, termination.'

Daphne then saw the screen fill randomly with a half dozen red dots and another dozen lines. Some of the lines were as short as half a block, others as long as a mile or more, turning corners repeatedly.

Fascinated, Daphne studied the graphic. She could quickly identify the areas of town where Flek spent the most time. He seemed to avoid the downtown area near Public Safety altogether. *No surprise there*, she thought.

To the left of the screen she noticed three long pink-to-burgundy lines in the middle of Puget Sound. She turned her head slightly toward these.

'Time of transmission and termination are in parentheses alongside the respective dot or line.'

'So we know exactly when he was in each of these locations.'

Osbourne glanced over at her. 'And I can see your interest lies properly in the lines to the left, those over the Sound.'

'What exactly are we looking at there?'

Again, Osbourne tapped the man on the shoulder. He leaned forward and said softly, 'Enlargement, please.' A flashing box of dashes surrounded the lines in question and then that area of the Sound filled the screen entirely, so that the three colorful lines were between two and six feet long. The respective transmission times could be clearly read: 10:17.47; 20:36.16; 10:19.38. Osbourne explained, 'I thought to understand the technology, to understand the situation and make an objective decision on how you wanted to evaluate the data, you needed to see this, Lieutenant, or I wouldn't have asked you to come over. But these three transmissions include the only two that occur at like times, offering the only overlap, the only possible site where you might locate the individual in question.'

Daphne shook her head, still not fully seeing what this offered her.

'It so happens,' Osbourne said, 'that our digital mapping service uses Alpha Maps, with research by Cape Flattery Map Company, the same maps at the front of the phone books. Small wonder, since we're a phone company. The point being that the Alpha Maps include all the ferry routes.' Another of those instructive taps on the shoulder. The full screen included the city once again, this time with dashed lines leading from the piers out across the Sound. The dashed lines on the map ran incredibly close to the color transmission lines drawn by the software. Osbourne pointed. 'That's the Bainbridge Island ferry route. The Winslow route. He traveled into the city on the ten-fifteen ferry yesterday morning, back out to the island on the eight-thirty – back in on the ten-fifteen this morning.' He tapped his wrist. 'The eight-thirty ferry leaves in twenty minutes. If you hurry, you can make it.'

Daphne shook the man's hand and took off for the door at a dead run.

Krishevski said to Boldt, 'You learn to cut your losses in this job. And that's what I recommend. Someone taking pot shots at you – I hear this guy you're after bought a rifle.'

'It's not him.'

'I don't want to hear that.'

'It disturbs you?' Boldt asked. 'What? That they missed?'

'It isn't like that.'

'Isn't it?' Boldt asked.

'Hey, this isn't my *affair*.' Krishevski leaned on the word. 'You know that.'

The emphasis destroyed Boldt. He understood immediately where the conversation was headed.

Krishevski glanced hotly toward the door and lowered his voice, and now Boldt could barely hear him. 'They have video, Lou. A security camera from a Denver hotel.' He added, 'I'm not party to this.' He didn't convince Boldt. 'I'm here strictly out of a desire to keep your personal life from being dragged through the press. Once this surfaces, not only do the wife and kids suffer but one of you is going to leave CAPers, and

321

it ain't going to be the psychologist, on account she's the only one they got. So where's that leave you? Vice? Traffic?'

His ears whined. He needed names. He needed some chance to stop this from happening. 'You'll go down with them, Krishevski,' he warned.

'Me? Who do you think called you the other night and put you onto Schock and Phillipp's assault?'

Boldt sat there stunned.

'See? That's the whole point of my visit. To cut the losses. They're ready to fry your ass. Don't let them do this. For once, just walk away. Do everyone a favor. Leave it be.'

Boldt tried to respond in a voice that said he had no intention of bending, that he knew what he was talking about, 'You, Chapman, Pendegrass—'

'It's not what you think.'

'Then someone had better enlighten me.'

Krishevski couldn't make the recliner sit up. He struggled like a child wanting to be free of a high chair, and finally got it. 'Okay, I lied,' he said.

Boldt felt a bubble lodge in his throat.

'No one sent me. I'm here to head off our both being dragged through the mud.' He met eyes with Boldt and said, 'I think I can do that. But I'm in as deep as you are, believe me.'

'I don't.'

Krishevski smiled nervously. 'Chapman had a video. These guys will trade you straight across – that video of Chapman's for the one from the Denver hotel.'

Boldt's pager and cell phone rang nearly simultaneously. He shut them both off without paying the slightest attention to them, never breaking eye contact with Krishevski.

'I'm to get this video and deliver it to you,' Boldt said

calmly. He added sarcastically, 'And you're not connected to this.'

'Don't go there,' Krishevski said emphatically.

'I'm not left a lot of choice,' Boldt pointed out. 'If you came here on your own – if you're so squeaky clean – then what's to prevent you from talking?'

'I'm not so squeaky clean,' he admitted. 'I've been fired. I don't want to face jail time as well.'

'Uh-huh,' Boldt said knowingly.

'My crime – if you're going to call it that – is trying to correct stupidity. Other people's stupidity. Ron Chapman has a video that is trouble for some of my guys. And now I'm jammed because I tried to help. We're all jammed. That's as far as I'll go, as much as I'll say. Deliver Chapman's video, it all goes away.'

'And Sanchez? Does she stand up and walk?'

'I'll go out the front,' Krishevski said. 'Tell Liz and the kids good-bye for me.'

FORTY SEVEN

By the time Daphne reached the State Ferry Terminal, the vessel destined for Winslow on Bainbridge Island was booked full for vehicles, though was still boarding passengers. She parked her red Honda in the lot and walked briskly toward the ferry. Her purse thumped at her side. A warning light flickered at the back of her brain – the neck scar she carried was a wound inflicted on a ferry while in the line of duty. Boldt had been with her then; she wished he was there now.

All the state ferries were behemoths of welded steel and layer upon layer of white and gray deck paint, weary water buses transporting hundreds of thousands of passengers annually. The ship seemed about as wide as it was long, a mirror image of itself, with two pilot towers bow and stern. It amazed her that something made of hundreds of tons of steel, and carrying in its hold hundreds of tons of vehicles, and on its various decks several hundred passengers, could nonetheless somehow manage to float, to navigate open water. She never felt perfectly safe on one.

Mixed into her thoughts, as she moved up the outer stairs to the vessel's spacious deck lounges in search of Bryce Abbott Flek, was the portrait of the man she created from her own psychological evaluation based on his criminal history. Short-tempered, randomly violent, prone to excessive drug use in times of acute stress, he was to be avoided. And she was pursuing him. Alone.

On a ship. She would maintain surveillance but not make contact. Eventually Boldt would take her calls, return her messages – she was outraged that he had apparently either turned off his pager and phone or left them behind somewhere. In her mind her job was to identify and locate Flek, report his location to Boldt and consult on what to do from there. Meeting the ferry with an army of Bainbridge Island police was out; she knew that much. Flek was not the type to pressure with hundreds of potential hostages available to him. Like a wild horse, he was better observed than handled. If a lasso was to be thrown, then timing was everything. Mixed in with this rational thought was a burning desire to speak with him *before* he knew who she was. Before contact with police. Before his arrest. Rarely did such opportunities present themselves.

As it happened, he saw her first. She felt a burning sensation from behind her, and turned, only to meet eyes with him way across the stern deck area. She didn't want to turn away too obviously, but she didn't want to stare either. Flek apparently took the prolonged eye contact as female interest on her part, or at least as a green light to pursue her. Whatever the case, he started across the cabin toward her. It was only as she turned and walked away from him that it occurred to her he might have seen a photo of her – a press conference? One of the pieces on Boldt's closing of the prison? Courtney Samway had identified Boldt, but not Daphne. But what if Flek had seen her in the press coverage of that Denver hotel? What if Abby Flek was hunting her, not the other way around?

Her nerves unwound, and for a moment she felt desperate, losing her professional composure and wanting to scream for help. Then she reconsidered. He's a wolf, she told herself, a man who preys on women. Courtney Samway had been plucked from a stripper stage in Denver – Flek was a conqueror. It was nothing more than her looks, and their exaggerated eye contact that now caused Flek to pursue her. She refused to hurry, refused to fuel any suspicion in him. Her cell phone, still switched on, remained in her purse along with her gun. She felt tempted to reach for one or the other. Instead, she stopped alongside a group of tourists who were admiring the city's night skyline. She gripped the ship's metal rail with both hands to steady herself, prepared for a confrontation.

She stood there, head bent, hair tossed in the ferry's breeze, the sound of a foaming wake boiling below her, catching sight of seagulls flashing in the ship's outboard lights, the city's stunning night skyline receding in the distance. She stood there, all of her muscles taut and tense, her senses heightened, her skin prickling, expecting to hear a stranger's low voice from over her shoulder. Expecting to shudder from head to toe. He wouldn't dare harm her so close to others who could later identify him. In fact, she realized – fighting off her experience of several years earlier – a ship was no place to make trouble, for there was no escape except to jump overboard, and in the Sound's lethally frigid waters, that was no option at all. She looked up, turning her face into the wind.

Flek was now gone, nowhere to be seen. She controlled herself and turned slowly as if savoring the breeze, and looked to the stern. Gone.

A flutter of panic in her chest. Had she lost him? Had she lost her opportunity? Was he testing her, watching her right now to see if she followed, if she sought him out? Maybe it wasn't even him. They had been separated by a good distance inside that cabin. She supposed it could have been another man, someone else, her mind devilishly playing tricks on her.

She was damned if she did, damned if she didn't. To go after him could tip her hand. It all had to do with appearances and intention, she convinced herself. People strolled the ferries constantly, checking out all the various decks and cabins. All she had to do was put one foot in front of the other and take her time. *Stroll*, don't walk, don't hurry. Use peripheral vision. Don't inspect the ship, enjoy it. She would *stroll* in the opposite direction from him – toward the stern. The crossing was thirty-five minutes. Ten of those had passed. It was a large, crowded ship, with hundreds of passengers, but a ship, a finite space, nonetheless. She would methodically work this deck stern to bow, then the next deck bow to stern. She would cover every inch of the ferry, top to bottom. Her police training kicked in: flush him out. Patience, she reminded herself, glancing at her watch.

She had about twenty minutes in which to find him.

The size of the vessel only became apparent when one started searching it. The hundreds upon hundreds of faces blended one to the next, like sampling perfumes, to where she could not distinguish one from the other without staring intently, and she did not want to stare. Worse, the ferry's population moved continuously, scores of passengers moving constantly from deck to cabin and deck to deck, to the cafeteria and the toilets. Men, women and children, though more men on this commuter leg. And whereas some wore suits, most did not, and these others wore jeans and a brown jacket, the ubiquitous recreational dress code of the Pacific Northwest.

Daphne moved through this shifting sea like the ferry through the dark waters, hellbent and determined, but all the while attempting to give off an air of restless boredom. More than a dozen times she believed she'd spotted him, only to realize it was not Flek at all, disappointment and self-doubt stinging her. The more she searched, the more she convinced herself she had never seen him. An apparition. A wish, unfulfilled.

She spent the majority of her time on the main level – a huge, open deck broken in the middle by stairs and the cafeteria. Cell phone records suggested that Flek used the crossing to make cellular calls. Her own stubborn belief demanded that if he made such calls they would be placed as far away from others as physically possible. After a thorough search, she shifted her attention to the outside decks.

The minutes dragged on, Daphne's discouragement flaring toward impatience. Her strides increased in tempo and length. Those men facing the water with their backs to the ship hid their faces in partial shadow, requiring her to slow and pay special attention. She was amused by how many men spent the crossing on their cell phones.

Minutes ticked past.

Only as the ferry turned past Wing Point and angled up Eagle Harbor toward a shimmering Winslow did she move her search to the parking decks. Everyone on the ferry had to get off.

She descended through the smell of oil and the sea. There were two levels of parked cars on either side of a single open hold for vehicles. She checked the two upper side wings first, walking the long rows of parked vehicles, amazed at how many drivers chose to ride out the thirty-five minutes dozing behind the wheel or listening to NPR. The hold was dull paint and dim lighting, vehicles bumper to bumper, all aimed toward the bow. Vehicle after vehicle. Face after face. No Flek.

She reached the lower center hold, facing well over a hundred vehicles. Time running out. The water churned violently at the bow, noisy in her ears and tangy in her throat. She approached one of the ferry personnel and took full advantage of his interest in her. 'Listen,' she said, raising her voice above the engine noise, 'is there any law preventing a woman from asking a few of these good people for a lift?'

'Not as far as I'm concerned,' the man replied. 'When we dock, these cars roll. Don't be standing out there then, I'll be yelling at ya.'

'Thanks,' she said.

'There's a couple taxis,' he told her.

'Thanks,' she said again.

The information about the taxi caused her to reconsider her plan. If she spotted him, then maybe the taxi would do. She could follow. Then again, maybe someone else would beat her to those taxis. Or maybe Abby Flek wasn't in a car, despite her conviction at this point that he had to be. He was in possession of a fairly large rifle, perhaps stolen goods as well. It seemed unlikely he would travel on foot.

A thought occurred. Boldt had been shot at the night before, sometime around 11 P.M. Bryce Abby Flek had taken the 8:30 ferry to Winslow – Osbourne had evidence supporting this. The next day, this same morning, Flek had ridden a ferry back from Winslow to the city. Granted, there were numerous return ferries, but what were the odds that Flek had returned that same night to take a pot shot at Boldt? It seemed unlikely, if not impossible, to her. She reached into her purse and grabbed her phone – she wanted to tell Boldt immediately. But as she prepared to dial, she looked up to see that most, if not all, of the vehicles were now occupied. Out the bow, the well-lit dock at Winslow quickly approached. If she were to do this, it had to be immediately. She had only the one chance.

She returned the phone to her purse, rehearsed a few opening lines, walked to the center of the four rows of vehicles and started down the aisle in front of her. She looked left to right, catching sight of every driver. She approached only men, and did not confine herself solely to this center aisle.

She tapped on a window and waited for the driver to roll it down.

'Excuse me,' she said, 'do you happen to know who won the Mariners' game?'

The stranger's hopeful expression faded from his face and he answered, 'They aren't playing today.'

'Oh,' she said. 'Well, thanks anyway.'

She moved on, crossing past the front bumper of a minivan and settling on a black BMW. Knock, knock. 'Excuse me,' she said, 'do you know if there's a Costco in Poulsbo?'

'I doubt it,' he answered.

'Thanks anyway,' she said, and continued on.

The ship smoothly slowed. She wanted to be seen making as many appeals as possible. For this reason, she moved laterally, port to starboard as well as working her way back toward the stern. She was midships when she spotted Flek. He sat behind the wheel of an old model Cadillac or Plymouth. A gas hog.

She approached the passenger side and knocked. The thing had a Landau roof that looked like burned coffee grounds – too many years in the elements.

He turned the key and put down the window electronically. 'Hey there,' he said.

'Excuse me,' Daphne said, a little flirtatious, a little hopeful, a tiny bit cautious, 'you wouldn't be heading north by any chance, would you?' The island's only major road ran north toward the bridge at Agate Passage.

'Suquamish,' he answered. 'You need a ride?'

'Poulsbo,' she replied, affecting disappointment. She had a destination now – the Port Madison Indian reservation town of Suquamish. He'd been smart enough to leave the city each night, smart enough to hide in a place that neither Boldt nor anyone else ever would have thought to look for him – past the affluent enclave of Bainbridge into the isolation of a reservation town.

'There's a casino the other side of the bridge. Pretty well traveled. I could leave you there,' he offered. 'Or I'll tell you what,' he said before she could respond. 'It's nothing to run you into town. A couple miles is all. Hop in.'

'You sure?' Her heart fluttered in her chest. No matter what the police side of her believed about seizing such an opportunity – and it warned to err on the side of caution – the psychologist hungered for a chance at conversation with this man 'in the raw' – unaware of who she was, his guard down, his true personality exposed. Her own ambitions had threatened her before, but as a scientist she could justify this in any number of ways, none of them very reasonable if she'd been forced to listen to herself. At that moment, she knew she could refuse him and walk away – she could lift the car's registration as she passed to the rear. She could call Boldt and organize a manhunt. But conversely, it might prove tricky every finding him again. Perhaps it was a friend's car, perhaps a joy ride he would ditch within the next few hours.

Boldt could still be notified. The manhunt could still take place. Suquamish was tiny. It wouldn't be too difficult to find this old car. Or perhaps they could lay a trap for him back at the ferry landing. Perhaps she would pull her weapon and walk him into the Poulsbo Police Department and claim the collar herself. Sanchez was her case, after all. But none of that mattered right now. First she had a decision to make.

She opened the door and climbed in. 'Thanks,' she said, laying her purse on the seat next to her. Then reconsidering, she set it on the floor. 'It's awfully nice of you.'

'How could I say no?' he asked.

A flicker of fear. Did he know her? Something in the way he had said it. The ferry arrived at the pier with barely a nudge, and the deckhands busied themselves. The psychologist sensed the danger. Who had trapped whom, she wondered. The door handle cried out for her to grab hold and get out of the car while she still could. It grew in size, begging for her to use it.

'None of those others would help you out?' he said. Had he sensed her reluctance and constructed a good line to ask?

'They all live on-island,' she replied, that door handle still calling to her.

The cars up ahead started their engines, and the foul smell of exhaust filled the old car nearly instantly. Eldorado – the glove box read. He pulled the transmission into gear. As he did, she heard the familiar click of all the doors locking at once. She didn't look. She didn't want to make a point of it, but she knew he'd locked the car, or the vehicle itself had done so automatically upon leaving PARK – but it seemed to her it was too old a car for that safety feature.

Very subtly, she adjusted her arm on the door's armrest and fingered the window's toggle. The window didn't open – whereas it had moved for him only a moment earlier. Flek had disabled the windows with the child lock from the driver's door controls. How much was paranoia, how much reality? She felt an icy line of sweat trickle down her ribs.

The cars and trucks began to roll. She understood perfectly well that this was her last chance to attempt to flee. To do so would alert Flek and cause him to break any patterns he had established. The psychologist battled the cop, and the cop battled back, and the psychologist argued again, and Flek took his foot off the brake.

In the end, the decision was made for her. He drove off the ferry and into traffic.

FORTY EIGHT

Mac Krishevski's offer of a trade left Boldt's head spinning. He didn't know how much the hotel video might have caught, but it didn't matter – it would look worse than it had been. Liz and the kids would suffer, and so would Daphne. SPD's brass would require one of them to transfer departments, and Krishevski was right that it would be him. He'd never work Homicide again.

He took a long walk up the hill and into Woodland Park, all the while mulling over the possibility of trying to steal or leverage possession of the damning video. It wasn't his style: he'd need LaMoia if he were to try such a thing.

He wasn't thinking about returning any phone calls. He intentionally left his cellular and pager turned off to give him the peace and quiet necessary for the decision he had to make now. He knew that when faced with a difficult tangle, if you pulled one way the mess miraculously came undone, if you pulled the other it ended up an unforgiving knot. He couldn't remember ever being cornered like this. He rebelled against it, but recognized too that he couldn't let his own rebellion get in the way of clear thinking. He knew the wrong decision would have horrible consequences.

From somewhere up on this same park his would-be assassin had thrown a bullet at him. He realized a little too late that he wasn't wearing the vest. A part of him would have welcomed a sniper's bullet at that particular moment. But he knew one wasn't coming. He wouldn't be that lucky tonight.

FORTY NINE

'You don't look like a hitchhiker.'

'No,' Daphne agreed. The trick was to control her nerves, to not let her concern show. As a professional, she knew all the tricks, though as a possible victim, many of these now eluded her. She explained, 'I'm meeting a friend in Poulsbo. One of the deckhands told me there's only a couple taxis here at the dock, and I'm late as it is, and if I missed that taxi—'

'From the city?'

'Yes.'

'I thought so.'

'And you?'

'Here and there,' he answered.

'As in here and there?' she asked. 'Or as in anywhere? You mentioned Suquamish.'

'Friends there.'

'Are you Native American?' He looked more Polish, with a hint of Mediterranean in the skin color and around the eyes.

'No way. Just friends up there. You know. Some business acquaintances.'

'What do you do?' she asked.

He glanced over and grinned, though not playfully. It was an asocial grin, a grin that said to leave well enough alone, a grin she had seen worn on the faces of child killers and rapists and multiple murderers. Too many to count – but only the one mattered at the moment. She experienced that glance as voltage deep within her. It disemboweled her. Disturbed her. It dawned on her then. *He knows who I am!*

'Electronics,' he answered. 'I'm kind of like a sales rep. I handle a lot of lines.' But there was that look again that said he could tell her anything he wanted because she'd never have the chance to repeat it. She saw Maria Sanchez lying in that hospital bed as still as a corpse except for the lonely eyes. Was he the man who had done that to her?

'Like electric company stuff?' she asked. 'Or more like my VCR? You can't program my VCR, can you?'

He laughed at that, and pulled a cigarette pack from his pocket and offered her one. When she declined, he cracked his window and lit up.

'Can't get my window to work,' she said, as innocently as possible, her finger showing off the problem.

'Oh, here,' he said. And her window operated again. They were traveling a busy roadway at forty-five miles an hour. 'Thing is constantly on the fritz,' he offered.

'Electronics. Maybe you could fix it.'

He laughed again, enjoyed a pull on the cigarette and made a spitting noise with his lips as he exhaled. He said, 'Let me guess: you're a model.'

Her turn to laugh. She threw her head back and chortled to the faded ceiling fabric. 'I'm flattered! Thank you.'

'I've seen you someplace,' he said, his inquiring expression making her uncomfortable. She felt him undress her with his eyes. Men did this all the time with her, but this one actually penetrated beyond the clothing to where her skin burned hot, and she felt repulsed by him. She imagined him with Samway: abusive, sexually dominant, taking what he wanted when he wanted it. The woman in her wished the car could drive faster, that Poulsbo would arrive sooner. She could see him dragging her by the hair into the woods, tying her up to some tree and having his pleasure with her. Leaving her there, half naked, gagged, to starve to death or be consumed by the elements. Such things happened more frequently than the civilian population knew – women of all ages disappeared at an alarming rate. The Bryce Abbott Fleks were responsible – the professional in her knew this as well.

'I'm a psychologist,' she said, hoping it would put him off as it did so many people.

'A shrink?'

'Not exactly. A counselor is more like it. People come to me with their problems.' She debated going for the heart, or sitting back to see where he took this, but the desire to dominate won out. She didn't want him controlling; she wanted him back on his heels. 'Relationship problems, grieving the death of a loved one, control issues. You'd be surprised how many people can't control themselves.'

'The TV?' he asked. 'You on a show or somethin'? Is that where I seen you? *Sally Jessy?* Somethin' like that?'

'I've been interviewed by local news a few times, but nothing recently.'

'Maybe that's it,' he said.

She couldn't tell if he was teasing or not. It felt a little to her like the cat batting the mouse in the face with the claws retracted, playing soft because there was plenty of time and both the mouse and the cat knew who was running the show. It was this control issue that she seized upon. She needed him off balance, or she needed to just shut up and get through the ride, but the psychologist in her wanted to get inside him in a much different way than he wanted to get inside her.

'You still look like a model to me,' he said, working on the cigarette. 'You should have waited for the taxi,' he suggested.

A stabbing pain at the V of her rib cage. 'How's that?' she asked, doing a decent job of concealing her sense of terror that resulted from the comment.

'You took a chance thumbing for a ride like that. There are a lot of creeps out here, you know? These islands? A woman as fine as you . . . You understand what I'm saying?'

'Well then, I'm glad it was you who picked me up,' she said. She waited a moment and told him, 'At least you don't strike me as a creep.'

They both laughed. Flek first, from the gut and honestly. Daphne followed with the best she could manage – laughter was not an easy concept for her.

The gun was in her purse at her feet. So was the cell phone.

He said, 'You can put it up on the seat if you want.' He'd caught her staring. 'I won't steal nothing from it.'

She covered quickly, 'Just trying to remember if I left something back at the office or not.'

'So take a look,' he suggested.

'It's only lipstick,' she vamped. 'A different color.'

'I like the one you got on.'

'Thank you.'

'Not that you care.' He sounded suddenly bitter.

'Sure I do.'

'That's bullshit, and we both know it. Pardon the French.'

'I care what I look like,' she told him. 'That's all I meant.'

'Priorities,' he said in a dreamy voice. 'So you being a psychologist and all. My brother got smoked last week. Dead. What do you think of that?'

'I'm sorry for your loss. But what do *you* think of that?' she asked. 'That's the more important question.'

He glanced over at her. 'I miss him.' A whisper that ran chills down her spine.

'That's only natural. Grief is expected at such times. As painful as it is, grief is a healing force. A cleansing force. It's good to just let it happen. Men, more so than women, can have a problem with that. They bottle up their grief. It comes out as anger or violence or both.' She hesitated. 'Are you experiencing any of that?'

'I didn't ask for a free session or nothing.'

'Pardon me. Professional liability, I guess. I was only trying to help.'

'You can't help. Nothing's going to bring him back. Nothing helps.'

'I didn't mean any offense,' she said.

Flek reached down, hooked the strap of her purse and yanked it up to the seat alongside of her. He had the reaction time of a lizard. She had barely seen his arm move.

'Jeez,' he said, landing it next to her. 'Thing weighs a ton! You oughta have wheels for that thing!'

The gun and two spare magazines made it very heavy. She panicked, her brain locking as she stared at her purse. She froze a moment too long and they both knew it.

'The lipstick,' he said brightly, the grieving brother suddenly gone.

She didn't like the fact that he could throw the switch so quickly. Another in a long series of red flags alerting her to his instability. Boldt had plenty to fear from this man – Flek was capable of pulling the trigger.

He said, 'Try the other color. I'll tell you which is best, which I like. It's a date, right? Poulsbo? A dinner date. Right? I'll tell you which one is better.' He switched on the ceiling light.

340

'I ah—' They approached the Agate Passage bridge. 'Listen,' she said, 'I don't want to put you out. If the casino is easier for you, let's do that. I can call a cab from Poulsbo and he'll be there in a matter of minutes.'

'Don't try to change the subject!' he objected. 'I'm telling you: I think you look great. But try the other color and I'll tell you what I think.'

'But I left it . . . I think. The lipstick . . . I'm sure I did.'

'Look,' he said, nudging the purse closer to her with his open palm. As he touched the purse his head snapped up, his eyes intense and dangerous. Had he felt the gun barrel? *He knows!* she thought, this time with more certainty. 'See if you've got it . . . if you brought it with you . . . I'd like to see it on you.' He couldn't take his eyes off her purse. She thought he might wreck the car.

She couldn't open the purse. Her gun was near the top – she'd made sure of that on the ferry – right where she could reach it in a hurry. 'I don't think so,' she said. 'You said you like this color. That's good enough for me.'

'Come on,' he pleaded.

She dragged the purse to her lap as they drove onto the bridge. She was thinking that if there was a place to pull the weapon and force him over it was there, where the car was restricted. She hadn't thought any of this out clearly enough. Improvisation was fine, but did not come naturally to a mind preoccupied with considera-tion, even fear. She angled the purse toward her and slipped her hand inside. The cool metal of the weapon washed a sense of relief through her. The rose lipstick had settled on the bottom amid Tampax, a Flair pen, and loose quarters. Her fingers danced between the two: the handgun and the lipstick.

Flek watched all this with one eye while driving with the other, unable to see into the purse. 'Well?' he asked, as if knowing the dilemma she faced.

She pulled her hand from the purse ever so slowly and produced the lipstick and a crumpled tissue. 'Found it!' she crowed.

'I knew it!' He pounded the steering wheel, suddenly a little boy. 'Lemme see. Lemme see.'

She snapped the purse shut, wondering if that was a mistake. 'You mind?' she said, taking hold of the car's rear view mirror.

'Go 'head.'

She smudged her lips onto the tissue, removing the sand colored lipstick and then carefully applied the rose, her attention on the mirror. She could feel him staring.

He said, 'Both lips. You do both lips. My mother . . . she used to wear this really red lipstick. Would do just the top lip, the upper lip, you know, and then kiss her lips together to get it onto her lower.'

'Bright colors, you can do that,' Daphne said. She kissed her lips together a few times and presented herself to him. 'Duh-duh,' she trumpeted like a fanfare. 'What do you think?'

He stared a little too long. She caught herself checking the road. 'She wore bright lipstick all the time, your mother?'

'I got it,' he said confidently, meaning she could take her eyes off the road. 'I'm not gonna hit no one.'

In control, she thought. 'What about the rose?'

'It's sexier,' he said.

He successfully turned the attention away from himself, and she felt resentful of this. She wanted to get back to discussion of his mother. 'My mother—' she said, 'I'm probably older than you . . . but she wore this fire-engine red lipstick, and I mean really big on her mouth.'

342

'My mother was a waitress,' he said. 'And she sold clothes too for a while. And bartended and stuff. Changed jobs all the time, but I don't think she *ever* changed that lipstick.'

'Is she still alive?'

'Booze got her. It was a long time ago.'

'Do you drink?'

He glanced over at her again. 'That one's way sexier than the other one.'

'You think?' She tried to sound flattered.

The road, state highway 305, swung left past the casino toward Poulsbo. Suquamish – Indianola was to the right. Flek followed traffic.

'You want to get a beer?' she asked, as they neared the casino. Her thought process was quick and therefore flawed, though she tried to work all angles before speaking, her mind a flurry of thoughts and considerations. She wanted a chance to telephone Boldt, to tell him where she was and what she had in mind. He could then call ahead to Poulsbo and arrange for the local police to pick up Flek moments after dropping her off. He would never be out of her sight. She might even be able to start an interrogation immediately after his booking. It felt like a plan to her, but she needed this chance to call Boldt *ahead* of her being dropped off. A bar seemed the perfect place – her cell phone from a toilet stall, well away from the ears of Abby Flek.

'Right now?' he asked.

'One beer would help relax me – before this dinner,' she said.

He jerked the wheel hard, throwing Daphne against the door. The tires cried and the huge car fishtailed slightly. An oncoming car sounded its horn as Flek shot the Eldorado across to the far side and bounced it into a gas station next to the casino. He hit the brakes hard and threw her forward against the dash. 'Sit tight,' he said, leaving the car running. 'Couple beers coming up.' He jumped from the car and hurried inside.

FIFTY

Daphne sat back in the front seat of the 1978 Eldorado, the wind knocked out of her – more from nerves than Flek's bad driving. This was not the pit stop for beer she'd had in mind. She caught a glimpse of their suspect through the crowded shelves of the gas station's mini-market as he grabbed a cold six-pack from a wall cooler. Within seconds she had her purse open and the cellular phone out, though her eyes remained on Flek who was already at the cash register under the sterile bluish glare of tube lighting.

She had to look down to dial. She nervously punched in Boldt's cellular, and got the number wrong. She cleared the last three digits and reentered them correctly. She hit SND.

The phone signaled a busy cellular circuit. She ended the call, pushed RCL and hit SND again.

Flek had a wad of bills in hand. He leafed through them, and pulled one out, and handed it to the clerk.

She heard the ringing tone bleeping in her ear. *Answer the phone!* she willed. Or would Boldt's cellular be turned off this time of night and her only way to reach him be the home number? Liz had sounded so hostile when she had taken the call earlier. What was that about? Did she even want to know? *Answer the damn call!*

'Boldt,' came his voice, small and thin over the bad connection, cellular to cellular.

345

Flek had a couple of dollars and change in hand as he pushed out the swinging glass door and into a light drizzle that started that exact same instant.

Boldt had roughly explained the predicament over the Denver video to Liz before bidding her goodnight and heading back into town.

'I've thought about it,' he had said, 'and I don't see how I can just walk away.'

'It's not the principled thing to do,' she agreed. He loved her for this ability of hers to disconnect and walk the moral walk, talk the moral talk. Her religious faith, rekindled during her struggle with lymphoma, burned brightly. When tested, she fell on the side of right, of good, even if it meant ostensibly insurmountable personal challenges. Her earlier anger at him was 'surface anger' – as she called it. When faced with this kind of challenge, they were a team again. She loaned him her own personal courage, and at no cost, no spousal bargaining. 'You're known for your integrity, love. You can't escape it, even if you so desire – and I don't think you do. Do you?'

'If they're good for this – whoever they are – then they've got to stand up for it. And they're not going to. Not on their own.'

'If it's time for you to leave this job, then it's time,' she said.

'What they intend to do – it will hurt. Hurt badly. Our friends. Your church. You want to look at that carefully before we decide this.'

'Listen, I'm not saying I fully forgive you for all that has happened, but I'll survive it . . . *we* will survive it.' She added faintly, 'We're survivors.'

'It's no easy decision. It can't be made lightly,' he

cautioned, although more for himself than for her to hear.

'We don't decide these things. They're not ours to decide. We choose to listen or not.'

'You're saying the decision is already made,' he suggested.

'I'm saying there never was a decision. There was only a question of whether we'd listen or not. And you always listen. You're a good man, Lou. I love you for these moments.' Again, she added an afterthought. 'I dislike you for certain others.'

'We've never been quite at a moment like this, Elizabeth. It's going to rain hard on this house.'

'We can take it. Or not.' She added, 'When you listen, when you do what's right, things have a way of working out. Maybe not this week or next, maybe not this year or next. We could be in for some challenges, individually or together. Who knows? But there comes a time when you look back and say: "So that's why that happened like that." I'm telling you – it happens every time.'

In-bound traffic had improved in the past few hours. He wasn't going to sleep; he knew that much. It seemed right to get into the office and continue probing the Sanchez case before his time was occupied with defending himself.

His cell phone rang and he answered, 'Boldt.'

It wasn't until he heard her voice that he remembered he owed Daphne a return call.

'Lou . . . Thank God,' she said breathlessly.

Flek crossed through the drizzle at a run, the six pack of beer held steady in his hands so he didn't shake the cans.

She whispered frantically, 'I'm with *him*, Lou: Flek!

347

They traced his cell phone! Hang on! Don't hang up, even if you think I have.'

He popped open the car door and hurried behind the wheel, setting the six-pack of beer down between them. 'Damn rain!' he said.

'Daffy?!' Boldt called out, hearing a man's voice in the background. A car sounded its horn from behind him – he had unintentionally slowed to forty miles an hour. He sped back up.

She said calmly, 'So, I've caught a ride with a really nice guy, and he's taking me clear in to Poulsbo to meet you, even though it's out of his way.'

'Poulsbo? You're with him!?' an incredulous Boldt asked her defiantly. Anger rose in him.

Only then did he recall the message Liz had delivered – the phone call he had turned down. It seemed every time he turned around, he was to blame for something.

'I know,' she answered, reading from her own script, ignoring his. 'It's really nice of him, isn't it?'

'Poulsbo,' Boldt whispered again into the phone. 'It'll take me an hour or two to get there unless I can get one of the news choppers. Jesus, Daffy!' SPD no longer owned its own helicopter, but leased time from one of three news stations that ran traffic choppers.

'Friends?' she said, still on her own script. 'I thought it was just going to be the two of us. No . . . no . . . *you can bring your friends* if you want . . . I'd love to see them. No, it's fine. It'll be a great dinner. Bring them! I'm sure . . . Really . . . Okay . . . See you in a few minutes . . .'

The call did not go dead; Boldt could hear the two voices, but at a distance. Daphne had apparently pretended to end the call, but had left the line open. Boldt drove with the phone pressed to his ear.

Friends? Boldt thought. She wanted backup. She intended to collar Flek herself. Sanchez was her case, and she intended to clear it. Perhaps this was more about her being a police officer than a psychologist. But where in Poulsbo? When? How was Boldt supposed to orchestrate this from miles across the Sound without putting her at risk?

He left the cellular phone line open still held to his ear and simultaneously used his car's police radio to ask Dispatch to place an emergency land line call to LaMoia's hospital room. He quickly explained Daphne's situation to the man, leaving out his own troubles. 'I figured you, of all people,' Boldt told him, 'would know the best bar and restaurant in a place like Poulsbo. 'Cause I haven't got a clue where she's headed.'

'Give me five,' LaMoia requested through a jaw wired shut.

When the radio called his name a moment later, and Boldt acknowledged, LaMoia said, 'The Liberty Bay Grill. It's the only game in town.'

Flek popped two beers and handed Daphne hers. 'Quicker than stopping,' he said. 'We're both in a hurry.'

'Yeah, thanks,' she said, accepting the beer. She didn't like the taste of beer; if they had stopped for a drink it would have been red wine, a Pine Ridge Merlot or Archery Summit Pinot Noir, something above this dime store drool. She gagged some of it down for the sake of appearances.

'Tell me about your brother,' she said. 'What was he like?'

The wide car cut through the night following the road to Lemolo and Poulsbo. Flek downed half the beer before the first minute was up.

The whirring of the tires was the only sound for the next few miles. The longer the silence, the more difficult. She sipped some beer.

'He was the best,' he said, as if the minutes had not passed.

'The Black Hole,' she said. 'There are times you can't think. You can't sleep. You're not hungry.'

He looked a little surprised. He downed more of the beer.

'Have you experienced that?' she asked. 'Insomnia. Loss of appetite.'

'No appetite for *food*,' he said, his eyes sparkling. '*Other things . . . sure.*' He killed the beer and reached for another. Daphne had barely taken an inch out of her own can. She did the honors, popping the next for him.

'You're not a cop, are you?'

There were few questions that could freeze her solid, but this one managed. In all, perhaps a second or two lapsed, but to Daphne it felt like minutes. She coughed out a guttural laugh, at which point Flek joined her. A pair of nervous people chortling contagious laughter at a silver windshield. Oncoming cars and trucks passing with that familiar, if not disturbing, *whoosh*, that rocked the car side to side. Flek steered with one hand lightly on the wheel. Daphne kept one eye on the road, ready to grab that wheel.

'Well, good,' he said, when she didn't answer. 'Pass me the Gold. It's in the box.' He pointed to the glove box.

Cuervo Gold Tequila. Half empty. Or was it half full on this night – she couldn't be sure about that. He downed two large gulps from the bottle and offered her some. She declined as politely as possible. He wrestled with his left pocket, lifting his butt off the car seat to get a hand down deep, and came out with a plastic aspirin container, meant to carry ten for the road. It carried small capsules instead – she couldn't identify the drugs in the limited dash light.

'I won't bother to offer,' he said, dropping two down his throat and chasing them with the beer. He clicked the aspirin traveler shut with the one hand, in a move that was far too familiar to him. He slipped the container back into his pocket.

Possession, she thought, knowing they now had charges that would support his arrest.

He said, 'Does it bother you?'

'Only that you're driving,' she answered.

He laughed. 'I think I can handle it.'

'Does it make it any better?' she asked pointedly.

'Let's not go there, okay, *Mom*? Session's over, Doctor. Ten, fifteen minutes, the patient won't care.' He added. 'The patient won't be here.'

'Then we've got ten minutes,' she suggested.

'Five is more like it. Let's not for now.' He pulled on the beer, then stuffed it between his legs. 'Remember, I'm doing you a favor here, going all the way to Poulsbo. Don't push it.'

'I was offering to help, is all.'

'Yeah? Well, save it.' He drummed restless fingers on the top of the beer can in his crotch. 'I've got all the help I need.'

'That's temporary help,' she said, not giving ground.

'Depends how regular you are in administering the dosage, Doc! Ritalin. Prozac. They've tried it all on me, Doc. Started on me when I was eleven years old. You lift a couple toasters, they give you a pill. Wasn't me who started this,' he said. Looking over at her, he added, 'Oh . . . gee . . . am I scaring you? It's you who wants to talk, not me.'

'It's called a glow plug, isn't it?' she asked. He looked

351

a little surprised by her knowledge, but recovered quickly.

He sang, badly out of tune, 'You . . . light up my life . . .' and laughed hotly, before putting out the fire with more beer.

'It won't bring him back.'

'Shut up!' he roared. The car swerved, and Daphne felt weightlessness in the center of her stomach and a flutter in her heart. He shoved on the brakes and the car skidded to a stop on the side of the road. A pickup truck zoomed past, its horn cascading down the Doppler scale. 'What the fuck business is it of yours?' he hollered, his eyes wild, spittle raining across the seat. 'Jesus!' He drew on the beer again, leering. 'Why can't you just shut up about it!'

She glanced down at her purse. The gun, she thought. But suddenly all felt calm within her. This was her domain: the wild frenzy of minds losing grip. This was the moment she had hoped for: the anger breaking loose and opening up a hole through which she might travel. In a perfectly calm voice she said, 'You're experiencing guilt over your brother's death. You blame yourself. You're torturing yourself.' She pointed to the beer. 'You're medicating yourself.' She hesitated. He was actually listening to her, though through elevated respiration, dilated eyes, and an increased heart rate, judging by the pulse in his neck. 'You can do damage, you know, assuming that kind of responsibility for another. Don't beat yourself up over this.'

He coughed out a sputter of disgust, turned his attention back to the road and floored the accelerator, fishtailing back out onto the pavement.

Daphne felt a penetrating calm. She was inside him now. They both knew it.

'What do you know about it?' he said.

'Do you think you're the only person to experience grief and guilt? What you're going through is a process. But you're handling it wrong. Tell me about the guilt you feel.'

He waited a moment and said, 'Pass the Gold.'

'No, I'm not going to. I don't feel comfortable with that.' She wanted control. If he accepted her refusal then she had him right where she needed him.

'Yeah?' he said a little tentatively, 'well, this is my car. Fuck you!' He stretched for the glove box, and Daphne blocked his effort. She could sense his fence-sitting; he was debating opening up to her.

'No,' she said. 'It's not the answer.'

They wrestled, though she didn't put up much resistance. She wasn't about to control him physically and didn't want to start down that road. If he turned to physical violence, she had only the weapon to stop him.

He tripped the glove box and grabbed for the bottle.

She said, 'Talk to me, Abby. Tell me what you're feeling.'

Force of habit: bring the subject closer by establishing rapport. Seek permission to use the subject's first name. Befriend, don't belittle. But she had slipped – there had been no introduction, no reason for her to know his name. She had trapped herself in an amateurish mistake, and she reeled with self-loathing.

On hearing his nickname, his head turned mechanically toward her, the road and the traffic there a distant thought. Daphne kept one eye trained out the windshield, her attention divided between her purse at her feet and the murderous rage in the driver's eyes.

He looked her over through dazed eyes, a mind stunned by what he heard. She thought that perhaps there were gears spinning in there, perhaps only the violently loud rush of blood pulsing past his ears. He looked numb. Bewildered.

It all happened at once. His words disconnected as his mind sought to fill in the blanks. 'Who . . . the fuck . . . are you?' His right hand dropped the bottle, his left took the wheel, and with one lunge, his fingers were locked around her throat and pressing her head against the door's window. He was halfway across the seat, fingers twisting painfully in her hair and turning her head toward the dash, the car losing its track, the rear wheels yipping.

She saw her salvation lying in the bottom of the glove box. But she could not reach it, could not speak.

His strength consumed her. She reached forward, fingers wavering for purchase, but he'd stuffed her into the seat against the door and she couldn't make it. Suddenly his knee was bracing the wheel, his left hand gone from it, and her window came down electronically, and her head thrust through the opening until fully out in the stinging dark rain. He let go her hair, grabbed hold of her left breast, squeezed and twisted until she screamed, turning with the pain. Just as he wanted.

The window moved up electronically, now choking her throat.

'Who the fuck are you?' he screamed. The window nudged up another fraction of an inch. Her windpipe would be crushed. She couldn't manage more than a grunt. Her fingers danced closer to the glove box.

He must have been halfway across the seat and steering with his left hand, but he'd lost the accelerator in order to hold her there. The car slowed noticeably, and he headed for the side of the road.

Finally, she felt the soft plastic between her fingers. She hoisted the cool cup that she'd seen inside the glove box. It was blue. It was used to keep single cans of beer cold. She turned it, because she didn't know if she had the lettering facing him.

She spun it, and shook it, and tried to grab his attention.

The window came down and he pulled her inside. She sucked for air, grabbed for her neck and massaged her throat.

On the cup was printed in white a single word:

ABBY

The car was pulled off the road, engine running. It smelled of exhaust and human sweat and tequila. Flek panted, glancing over at her and wondering what came next. Daphne's face and hair were soaking wet, her neck a scarlet bruise. The windshield fogged as they sat there. Flek reached out and gently picked up the cool cup.

He said dreamily, as if nothing had happened between them. 'He bought it for me at a truck stop. This trip we took once. David. My brother—'

She said nothing, knowing it best to allow him to calm. Her breast burned. Her weapon beckoned, but she dared not move. She glanced down quickly only to see her purse had fallen on its side, the knurled handle of the handgun showing. She extended her knee and placed her foot over the weapon, covering it. She knew now what he would do to her if he found out who she was. All she wanted was out of that car – but she also knew he could not feel threatened by her departure, could not feel she would go running to police, or he would never let her go. One slip of the tongue had brought her here to this moment; she guarded her words carefully. She had a role to play.

Her voice rasped dryly as she spoke, requiring deep

breaths to get any sound out at all. 'You could have killed me,' she said.

Flek had left. The adrenaline had kicked the drugs in ahead of schedule. He ground his teeth so hard she could hear them – like a rock scratching slate. 'Out there in eastern Colorado. Might as well be Kansas, it's so damn flat. There was a "T" on the cup when Davie bought it – TABBY – but he scratched it off with his penknife and handed it to me, saying it was my birthday present.'

'I'm going to get out of the car now,' she announced, having no trouble playing the terrified and wounded stranger. 'You're going to drive off and leave me.' With her foot, she tried to stuff the handle of the gun back inside, but it wouldn't go, so she covered it again.

'No, no, no . . .' he said, suddenly aware of his predicament.

The car idled on the side of the road.

'This was a mistake on my part,' she said. 'I should have taken the taxi.'

'A little late for that.'

'You're upset over the loss of your brother. You're lucky I'm a professional, because I understand that. I've seen men in your condition before. Another woman would report you to the police—'

He said sarcastically, 'And you're not going to!'

'No, I'm not. That would hardly be fair. It would only further aggravate your mental condition.'

'I do *not* have no "mental condition"!' he objected. 'I am not no mental case!'

'Your grief,' she said calmly. 'I'm referring to your grief over your brother's loss.' She would have to turn her back on him to try manually for the door lock, and the car was one of those where the nub of the lock barely protruded when in the locked position, so it was not going to be an easy feat. There wasn't a master-control-lock in her door panel – there was only the one window toggle and it was once again child-locked and inoperable.

'We've got ourselves a situation here,' he said, rubbing his sweaty face with an open hand.

'I'm going to unlock the door,' she informed him, 'and I'm going to get out of the car. All you have to do is drive away and there is no situation.'

He seemed to be talking to himself more than her. 'The thing is, you look so familiar to me, and I been trying to sort that out. And then you go and speak my name like that, and I'm thinking you *are* a cop, and that's where I seen you. Something to do with Davie. And now you say you won't tell no one, but that's bullshit and we both know it.' He hit the accelerator. The rear wheels shot out plumes of mud and the car slowly squirreled back out into the lane nearly hitting a passing car that swerved to avoid them.

Daphne turned and went for the lock, deciding she could jump at this slow speed. It accelerated quickly. She only had a moment . . .

She heard the breaking glass and felt the blow simultaneously. The nauseating smell of cheap tequila engulfed her. One moment she was struggling with that damn door lock. The next, there was only pain, and the dark, blue, penetrating swirl of unconsciousness.

FIFTY ONE

Waiting for the 9:10 ferry to Bainbridge in the enormous State Ferry parking lot, his cellular voyeuristically held to his ear, Boldt agonized as he overheard the events that led up to the struggle between Daphne and Flek, Daphne's calm pleading that followed and the final crashing of glass that had silenced all discussion. Only the faint groan of the car engine told him the line was still active. He couldn't be sure if the car had been wrecked or if Flek was still driving.

Movement in his rearview mirror attracted him, or perhaps it was the magnetism of the man he saw there, walking with a limp through the light rain. The passenger door came open and a bruised and battered John LaMoia climbed into the car painfully. He glanced over at his lieutenant – everything below his eyebrows and above his chin a mass of swollen black and purple and yellow-orange skin – and said through a wired-shut jaw, 'Couldn't let you have all the fun.'

'Now you've screwed up everything,' Boldt said, 'because now I've got to drive you back to the hospital instead of boarding this ferry.'

'No way,' the man mumbled, his words barely discernable. 'Haven't been on a ferry in years.' He added, 'Don't worry – I'm not feeling *any* pain, Sarge. Matter of fact, I feel pretty great.'

Boldt's ear adapted to the odd speech impediment brought on by the man's wired jaw. He sounded half southern, half drunk. Medicated to the hilt.

Boldt handed him the phone and said, 'No talking into it, but what do you hear?'

LaMoia pressed his other ear shut, though the move was clearly painful. 'Eight cylinder. Twin barrel maybe. Bad pipes.'

Boldt was not thinking in terms of a gear head. He had wanted a straight answer. 'But it's a car. Right?'

'You tell me.'

'A car engine. Idling or running?'

'This baby's on the road, Sarge. Three thousand RPM and cruising.' LaMoia added, 'What channel is this anyway? Sport-Trax?'

'She left her cell phone on.'

'You told me,' LaMoia reminded him.

'But it's *still* on. There was a struggle, and no one's doing any talking.' Boldt spoke frantically. 'I made the call to Poulsbo PD from a pay phone. Told them they couldn't use any radios because this guy's a scanner. They have one plainclothes detective over there. He was going to sit on the Liberty Bay Grill with some radio cars nearby as backup. Maybe we've still got a shot at him.'

The ferry lights approached.

'Finally,' Boldt said.

'No chopper, I take it,' LaMoia surmised.

'All tied down for the night. One pilot was available, and he said with drive time and prep it would be an hour and a half before he'd be off the ground. Ferry's thirty-five minutes. I opted to have the car once I'm over there.'

'Hang on a second, Sarge. We got some action here. This guy's pulling off the road – some place bumpy.' LaMoia handed the cell phone back to Boldt who listened intently.

'He's pulling over,' Boldt told his sergeant. 'Stopping . . . Oh, thank God!' he said with a little too much emotion.

'What?' LaMoia begged.

'She's groaning. It's her! She's alive!' A loud scratching. The line went dead. Boldt knew it was not just silence on the other end, but a full disconnect. 'Oh, no . . .' he moaned. He passed the phone to LaMoia, who jerked it to his ear.

'She may be alive,' LaMoia said, 'but this baby's dead.'

'He disconnected the call.'

'Or the battery went dead,' LaMoia suggested. 'How long has that thing been on anyway?' He added angrily, 'And how the fuck did she find this skel ahead of you anyway, Sarge? What the hell's that about?'

'I found him,' Boldt answered. 'She just took the call. Flek's cell phone records,' he said, the words catching in his throat like chicken bones. 'I . . . had . . . them . . . work . . . their . . . call . . . logs.'

'Sarge?' LaMoia knew that tone of voice in his boss.

'That's why she left the call open, John. It wasn't so I could listen in, it was so I could *find her*.'

'Sarge?' LaMoia repeated.

'Get Gaynes over to AirTyme Cellular in the Columbia Building. A guy named Osbourne. Wake him up if we have to. Escort him, I don't care. Just get him downtown. Now!' He added in a dry whisper, 'Now before her battery dies . . . and she along with it.'

FIFTY TWO

She awakened in a dark, confined space, foul smelling and warm. It took her a moment to identify it as the Eldorado's trunk. By now Flek had found her weapon and her ID wallet. By now he understood that to kill her – a cop – meant the death penalty, if caught. By now he was plotting what to do, this man wired on a glow plug cocktail. Whatever the stakes previously, for Bryce Abbott Flek they had just escalated.

Her wrists were handcuffed, her ankles tied together with white plastic ties. Sight of the ties stirred memories of Sanchez and Kawamoto, and stole her breath. Her mouth was gagged with an oily rag. Pulled tightly around her sore head, it was knotted in the back. She felt a strange sensation on her neck and decided it was damp blood: whatever injury she had sustained, it was not life threatening. The man behind the wheel was another story.

The car rattled and bounced and she blamed the pounding headache as much on the seeping fumes as the blow to her head. A pinkish-red light from the taillights seeped through the car fixtures. Her blouse, soaked in tequila, radiated a sickening smell of her own fear, perfume, and the alcohol. She had no idea where they were, no idea where they were headed, though by the sound of oncoming traffic passing quickly, she knew they were traveling fast, and with so few roads in this area, it meant either toward or away from Poulsbo. If headed away, then her message to Boldt had failed. Only the open phone line presented any ray of hope – however faint – and only then, if Boldt figured it out.

She credited her training – her ability to transcend the moment, to rise above a patient's despair and think clearly – for the steadiness of thought she experienced. She did not wallow in self-pity or succumb to fear. Instead, after a quick flirtation with the latter, she began to reposition herself in the trunk, knowing what had to be done.

She had been inside a trunk once before in her life. A different life, it felt like. A different woman. She had no intention of this experience resulting in the same outcome. This time someone would die. And she wasn't going to allow that person to be her.

FIFTY THREE

The ferry steamed on through the dark, churning waters interminably. Wind and rain frothed the waters into sharp, angular chop, unique to the Sound, but the ferry plowed down the peaks and beat them out its wake as a subdued, white, rolling foam.

Boldt and LaMoia sat off by themselves on a mostly empty deck. A few tired businessmen occupied the other seats, and a couple of kids with backpacks. On these milk-run legs, the ferry definitely lost money.

'You shouldn't have come along,' Boldt said.

'True story,' LaMoia answered through his clenched jaw.

'What do we feed you?'

'Ensure, through a straw. If I puke, I die. Nice thought, isn't it?'

'Then why?'

'The last time this happened, she got cut bad, and you . . . you beat yourself up pretty hard over that. I hear you been beating yourself up over my little accident. It ain't worth it, Sarge. My gig. My choice. My bad,' he said. 'I'm slow, but I'm not useless. Besides, I knew you could use the company.'

Boldt's cellular rang. It was Gaynes. She said, 'Osbourne provided Daphne with a location for Flek that probably pretty well matches where you are right now – in the middle of the Sound.'

'And she went off of that?' Boldt asked,

'She had a time to work with: the eight-thirty ferry to Bainbridge.'

'So we're at least an hour behind her.'

'You're right about Osbourne. He has the capability of pretty much pinpointing a call's location, the only bummer being that none of it is real-time. It's taking him about fifteen minutes per transmission signal, which ain't bad, but ain't great.'

'Transmission signal?' he asked.

'The phone, being on an open circuit, was constantly transmitting. So he asked me to pick various times of the call for him to reference. I chose three different times, each several minutes apart. Her call originated less than a mile from Sandy Hook – west, northwest of there. When you get near the Agate Passage Bridge, you should call me. I'll help direct you.'

'And a few minutes later?' Boldt asked. 'Where was she then?'

'He's still processing. Says it's west of there, probably near Lemolo. He'll have an exact in a few more minutes. Maybe five more minutes, he says.'

'Let's plot the last known reference,' he advised.

'But unless we know where he was ahead of that,' she suggested, 'we won't know in what direction he was headed. You want the direction, don't you, L.T.?'

'We'll be off this ferry in fifteen minutes,' Boldt said. 'I want answers by then. What if Flek's headed back for this ferry? I need to know that! I could drive right past the guy.'

'Understood.'

'So have Osbourne pull some help. An officer's life is at stake here.'

'I'll suggest that.'

'Don't suggest it, order it!'

'Right,' Gaynes said, though she didn't sound convinced.

'Whatever you can do, Bobbie,' Boldt said. It was as close as he could get to an apology.

'He has a couple guys working on another technology. We could pull them, but I don't advise it, L.T. What they're working on is some kind of real-time technology. It could be the ticket.'

'She disconnected the call!' Boldt objected. 'That's not real-time, that's waste-of-time.'

'These guys are cell phone nerds, L.T. They think they've got something going. I'm reluctant to butt in on that. I will if you want, but I think we cut them some slack here and see what they can do for us. They're pretty excited about this other possibility. Your call,' she said.

Boldt said to LaMoia, 'Osbourne's using manpower on a long shot, and Gaynes wants me to go along with that.' Boldt never consulted LaMoia on such decisions, and the sergeant's obvious surprise reflected that.

LaMoia said, 'A wise old cop once told me that the dick in the field's in a better position to make the judgment call than the suit back in the office.' He was quoting Boldt back to himself, though not verbatim.

'I'm not in the office!' Boldt protested. 'And I'm not a suit.' It was the ultimate slur, and Boldt wanted nothing of it.

LaMoia's words garbled. 'You're on a boat in the middle of nowhere, Sarge. That's even worse.' LaMoia was looking a little green. 'I think maybe I need some air.'

Middle of nowhere, Boldt thought. To him, it summed up both his professional and private lives. It had started with the Flu, this feeling; he had no idea where or when it would end.

Into the phone, Boldt said, 'It's up to you and Osbourne. Just get me something by the time we're back in the car.'

'Thanks, L.T. Back at you.' She disconnected the call.

FIFTY FOUR

'You know what a talented person can do with a color scanner and a paint program these days? And I'm talented. Yessiree. Courtesy of our corrections programs, which taught me damn near everything I know. Maybe not hundred dollar bills, but you, Lieutenant Daphne Matthews, just gave me my passport outta here. You and your ID and your badge. Before that, what choice did I have? Hide out, jumping islands for six months, lift a driver's license and give it a run at the border before it's reported. That's shaving it a little close for this boy. But a cop's badge? Are you kidding me? I surrender your weapon at the border and drive right across, all official-like. Slam dunk. Gone and lost forever. The way it should be.'

They were parked in dark woods, the air laden with the pungent smell of pine sap. Flek had propped her up to sitting in the trunk, the rain falling down on both of them. Her clotted blood began to melt and paint her blouse that eerie but familiar rose. He held a cellular in his hand, switched on. Hers or his? She wondered if he had disconnected her original call to Boldt, or if it had been transmitting all this time. She held to that hope.

What Bryce Abbott Flek did not know was that she had spent the last ten to fifteen minutes scrunched down into one corner of the locked trunk, the right taillight's plastic housing pulled away, shorting out its connection in an endlessly repeating stream of three short, three long, and three short bursts. They had traveled good road for most of that ride, and she had to think that some car or truck had been back there, some Boy Scout or former Marine alert to a taillight blinking Morse code. She counted on someone having taken down the plate number, of calling it into authorities on a hunch that the SOS meant something. This, along with Boldt's earlier call into Poulsbo for backup, a call she was also counting on having been made, seemed certain to alert authorities to her general vicinity. The psychologist in her wouldn't succumb to the evidence at hand – the fact that Flek looked and sounded unstable, apparently the victim of another glow plug or two, that he held her weapon in the waist of his pants and had a glassy look in his eyes that forewarned her of that instability. That he was capable of violence against her, she had no doubt. She had already witnessed this firsthand. But a larger agenda loomed behind those eyes, and she wanted her chance to redirect its course. The first step was the gag. She needed the gag removed to have any chance whatsoever. She made noise for the first time, sounding like a person with no tongue.

She had no idea of their location. She guessed they were somewhere on or near the Port Madison Indian Reservation because it was dark as pitch out, only a faint amber glow to the bottoms of clouds many, many miles away. The road was gravel and mud. Though in a partial clearing, they were surrounded by tall giant cedars, ferns, and thick vegetation. She heard a stream or river nearby. If she could run to that water, she could swim it, or float it, and he'd have a hell of a time finding her. She could climb a tree and hide. Wait out the sunrise. She clung to these positive thoughts in the face of her impending execution. Did he know enough to blame her for his brother's murder as well? On the surface, Flek seemed to be explaining why he was now going to kill her, though the psychologist knew that if that had been his intention he'd have already carried through with it. Either he was plagued by doubt, or he had something else in mind. She tried to talk at him, the rag tasting like gasoline on her tongue.

'When *you* talk,' he said, 'you'll tell me his phone number – I don't want to hear nothing else from you, not another word. Just the phone number. This Lieutenant Louis Boldt. This one did this to Davie. A pager's fine. His cell phone. But nothing in no office. No land lines. I call once. One call. You understand? You screw this up, and it's on you what happens next. Maybe I fuck you. Maybe I just snuff you sitting right there like that – all wet and disgusting. Maybe you go out ugly, lady. Ugly and unlaid and dead. Not much worse than that.'

She tried again. Grunts and groans lost on him. Swallowed by the relentless rain.

'This is very important what I'm telling you,' he said. 'Just the man's phone number. That's all. Then the rag goes back on. You can nod now and let me know you understand. Anything more than the phone number right now, and I'll knock your teeth out with the butt of the gun, and then you will pay. God Almighty, how you will pay. So how 'bout it? Do I get a nod?'

FIFTY FIVE

'Listen up,' a stranger's voice demanded over Boldt's cellular phone. He had been expecting the report from Gaynes. The ferry had slowed and was nudging toward the small but well-lit dock at Winslow. 'Badge number six five six four. Your partner, Matthews. Right?'

'I'm a lieutenant. I don't have a partner. Who is this?' Boldt said. He already had LaMoia's attention. He gestured toward the phone and pointed back into the dark of the Sound, toward the city, and LaMoia got the idea; the sergeant pulled out his own phone and made the call to Gaynes. Boldt placed his thumb over the phone's talk hole and whispered, 'It could be Daffy's, it could be his.'

'Got it!' LaMoia said.

Flek announced into Boldt's ear, 'I've got her badge in my hand or I wouldn't know the number. Right? Even a dumb cop can figure that out. You want her alive, you come get her alone. That's the deal. And believe me, I'll know if you're alone or not. And if not, then not. No second chances. A hunter'll find her in a couple of years.'

Boldt pushed the phone's antenna down, held the device away from his mouth and said, 'You're breaking up . . . I can't hear you. Hang on—' He disconnected the call.

While Boldt was still staring at the phone, second-guessing himself, LaMoia, with Gaynes on the line, said 'What's up?'

'I hung up on him before he could give me the drop point.'

'You what!?' LaMoia hissed through his teeth loudly enough to attract attention.

The ferry gently bumped the dock and weary passengers headed toward the exits.

'Osbourne requires fifteen minutes to triangulate the call. I'm trying to buy Daphne some time.'

'Or get her killed.'

'I'm aware of the stakes, John.'

'Jesus, Sarge, I don't know.'

'Tell Gaynes that Osbourne has to kill all the towers over here, or at least effect a circuit busy on my line.' He repeated strongly, '*Circuit* busy – not line busy. I don't want Flek thinking it's me. I want him blaming the system.' As Boldt's phone rang again, he glared at his sergeant. 'Now, John! Now!'

LaMoia relayed the message into his phone.

His ringing phone in hand, Boldt, already moving toward an exit, shouted back, 'I'm going below decks for the interference. Handle that and hurry it up. We're out of here!'

'And make it *fast*!' LaMoia said into his phone. 'I don't care what he says – he's got to do it. The guy is threatening to kill Matthews. No, you heard right!' He added harshly, 'Now, Bobbie. Now! And if there's any way to keep *my* phone working, do it!'

FIFTY SIX

'Shit!' Flek shouted, holding the phone at bay, his whole body shaking. For a moment he seemed ready to throw the thing, or to bust it up against the car, but some tiny string of reason fought off the agitating effects of the glow plug, and he restrained himself. 'Lost him,' he announced. 'Second fucking time.'

Daphne tried to speak, this time with far more purpose. She leaned forward to kneeling and pleaded with him to remove the gag again.

'No shouting!' he cautioned.

She shook her head. Prayers were not a part of her psychologist's tools, but she prayed silently nonetheless. As long as that gag remained on, she had no way to effect change.

Her prayers were answered. Flek stepped forward and unknotted the rag.

For a moment she said nothing, savoring the fresh air, and not wanting to rush him. When she did speak it was gentle and soothing, almost a whisper, devoid of fear or the trembling rage that she felt inside. She said, 'We may be too far away from a cell tower. Maybe if we got closer to town . . . maybe then the reception would improve.'

Flek surveyed the area. Looked at her. Looked back at the sky.

There were so many places to start with a personality like his – drug-induced and filled with bloodthirsty rage and revenge. But it was a bit like those action films where the hero has to cut the right wire or the bomb explodes – to come after him from the wrong angle was to incite that rage, not defuse it. It was not something one jumped into lightly. She tried to strip away her own emotions, to work past her own agenda, and see this patient clearly. Right now, clarity of thought was everything.

He looked back at her.

She said, 'Fresh batteries help. I have a spare battery in the bottom of my purse.'

Perhaps he had overdone the glow plugs. Or perhaps on some level he knew the kind of trouble he had just brought onto himself by making contact with Boldt, by announcing his kidnapping of a police officer. Whatever the case, the man didn't seem to hear her, his own internal voices too loud for her to overcome.

'We could try to get closer to town,' she said. 'You could cuff me to the door. I don't need to ride in the trunk.' If the Morse Code had been seen, then police were looking for this car. The closer to town, the better.

If he brought her inside the car with him, then she had a real chance at freedom, cuffed to the door or not. At the right moment she might deliver a properly placed kick to the head and end this.

'I could look for the towers while you drive.' She didn't want to mention the phone's signal meter, because for all she knew the signal was perfectly fine out here. She wanted his attention on solving the problem, not assessing it.

She opted for silence, allowing his fuzzy logic to sort out her suggestions. To push too hard was to push him away.

'I'm going to put the gag back on, and you're going to lie back down. We'll drive closer to town.'

To beg or plead was to admit subservience, and her job was to convince him of their partnership, to make herself needed and wanted. She fought off the temptation to whine and grovel. She took a breath and said calmly, 'But when you reach him, he's going to want to hear my voice. Count on that! You know he will, Abby. And what then? Stop by the side of the road and pop the trunk? What if someone drives by? But a man and a woman in the front seat of a car – what's so suspicious about that? I'm trying to help you, Abby. Obviously, I want to live. I think he'll do what you want. I really do. But he's going to want to hear my voice.' She added, 'You could make him release Courtney. Have her delivered somewhere. It might take a little time—'

'Shut up!' he roared, his eyes floating in their sockets. Dizzy. Dazed. He shook the phone again, pulled it close to his face and pressed a couple buttons. He held it to his ear, yanked it away in frustration and ended the attempted call with a final stab of a finger.

'You fuck this up,' he warned her, 'and you will know so much pain you will wish you were dead. You will *beg* me to kill you.' He grinned wickedly. 'And I won't. Not until I'm good and ready. Not until I've had every inch of you.' He added, 'You ask Courtney about that. She knows.'

He stepped forward. Daphne could taste her impending freedom.

FIFTY SEVEN

'Osbourne can't kill the system, Sarge,' LaMoia reported from the passenger seat, 'but they can lock a phone out from the entire network – all the carriers – and that's what he's done: he's locked out both Matthews' and the number we have for Flek. Both phones will get a circuit-busy signal.'

'Flek is known to carry more than one cloned phone,' Boldt reminded. 'He's *got* to kill the system.' Samway had said he had only the one, but Boldt wasn't convinced.

LaMoia repeated the request into his phone and then listened. 'Don't work that way,' LaMoia said. 'Air-Tyme's one of three carriers. Only some of the towers are theirs. They attempt an AirTyme handshake first, but if that fails, it's rerouted, first come, first serve – the call's going to go out.'

'What about the location?'

'A couple minutes more to pinpoint it exactly, but we know it came from off-island.'

'My phone's good to go?' Boldt asked.

LaMoia checked and awaited an answer. 'That's affirm, Sarge.'

Boldt flipped open his phone, pulled his notepad from his jacket and dialed a number, all with one hand. LaMoia maintained the open line to Gaynes. They crossed the bridge at Agate Passage. Still on the phone, Boldt pulled the car over in a park and ride just ahead of the signage for the turn to Suquamish – Indianola.

He listened more than he talked, and then hung up the call. 'You know how I feel about coincidence,' he told LaMoia.

'What's up?'

'Poulsbo PD never made contact at the restaurant, but they have this nine-eleven call reporting a taillight of an old Eldorado sending SOS out its right blinker.'

'Son of a bitch.'

'They observed our request for radio silence, but still alerted their cars via their MDTs,' mobile data terminals. 'Nobody caught sight of the Eldorado. But the caller reported that it turned off three-of-five here,' he said, pointing to the intersection not a hundred yards down the road. 'North, toward Suquamish.' Boldt added, 'I say we trust this one. If it's right, it buys us a hell of a lot of time over running out to Poulsbo and back.' Boldt looked out at the dark road. 'If it's wrong information, or if it's Flek trying to mislead us, then we lose any possibility of a jump on him.'

'Old Indian saying,' LaMoia replied, his jaw wired, his words sounding drunken. 'When you come to a fork in the road, take it.'

'That certainly helps a lot,' Boldt said sarcastically. But it did help; it briefly lightened the moment.

'I can see her doing that, Sarge. The SOS. You know? Who else but Matthews? You know her better than anyone. What do you think?'

Boldt pushed down the accelerator and turned right at the intersection. North, toward Suquamish.

FIFTY EIGHT

'This thing is out of hand. Does it feel that way to you?' Daphne asked. He didn't know handcuffs. He'd clamped the left cuff way too tightly to her wrist so that her hand felt cold and her wrist felt broken. She winced with pain every time the car bumped, which on the dirt road was every few yards.

'No talking.' He said this, but lacked the authority of his earlier insistence. She knew he wanted to talk, needed to talk. It was the only way for him to build his confidence.

'Have you thought about why we've pursued you?' she asked.

'To fry my ass,' the driver answered.

'You see? It is out of hand. That's not it at all.'

'Right,' he snapped. He reached for a beer. It was his fourth.

'Have you thought about how Davie would play this?'

'Don't you talk about him!'

'He wouldn't know how to play it, would he, Abby? Because Davie wasn't like you. Davie took the straight road. Davie was doing fine until you talked him into letting you hit that delivery.'

'Shut up!'

'There's a tower,' she said, pointing through the windshield. Sweet and sour – she needed to be both for him, play both roles herself, one moment the accuser, one moment the accomplice.

Flek slowed, but kept driving. He tried the phone and once again nearly lost his patience. He reached over the backseat and fished in her purse and came out with her phone. Same reaction to his attempt with it.

Daphne didn't believe in coincidence – Boldt had trained her not to, along with every other detective with whom he'd worked over the years. If the circuit was busy, then that was Boldt's doing. And if that was Boldt's doing, then she still had hope.

'What the fuck am I thinking?' Flek said. He sped up the car. It had finally occurred to him, she realized, to use a pay phone. She had wondered how long it might take him to see this. Get him into town – Boldt was on the same page as she.

The clock continued running in her head. Osbourne had said triangulation took time. Did they have a location on her? Was there a radio car waiting around the next corner, and three more coming up their tailpipe?

'My guess is Davie would encourage you to work it out, not get yourself killed.'

'I told you to shut up!' He shoved the beer can onto the dash so that it wedged tightly between glass and vinyl. He tugged the gun from his waist and extended his trembling arm toward the floor of the car.

'No!' she hollered.

But Flek pulled the trigger, shooting her left foot. The bullet traveled through her and out the floor of the car. 'That's one!' he shouted madly, saliva spraying from his wet lips. 'I got eight more in here, and I'll use every damn one before I bother to finish you. NOW YOU SHUT UP!'

For a moment she felt no pain whatsoever, her brain frozen with shock. But then the burning began. It raced up her leg, through her gut, and she vomited.

'You disgusting bitch!' he screamed at close range, beating her with the butt of the gun, directly on the wound he'd caused with the bottle.

Her head swooned, but she struggled for consciousness and managed to sit herself upright and turn her head slowly to face him. The burning in her left foot was now an inferno. She could barely hear her own voice as she spoke. 'What now, Abby?'

'Shut the fuck up!'

'You're going to have to bandage that, or pull a tourniquet, or I'm going to bleed out on you. And then what? Then I'm a dead cop, and Boldt isn't going to deal with you. You're damned if I die, Abby.' She needed to speak but could barely find the strength. 'You . . . know . . . that, don't you?' Her words were long strings of stretched taffy, her mouth disconnected from her brain. The purple goo loomed at the edges of her eyes, pulsing with each tick of her heart. She pushed it back, but it consumed her, determined to shield her from this pain. For a moment she maintained consciousness. She thought she saw a phone booth up ahead. A streetlight in the rain. But then the black hood of unconsciousness slipped over her head, and all hope was lost.

FIFTY NINE

The fix on the transmission point for Flek's first call came only moments after Boldt turned right off 305 and onto Suquamish Way NE, a minute or two after Daphne had been shot.

Reading from the back of his hand where he'd scribbled notes, LaMoia said, 'The exact fix is North 47 degrees 45.45 minutes, West 122, 36.2 minutes. Give or take forty feet.'

'In English,' Boldt requested.

'A couple hundred yards east of something called Stottlemeyer Road NE. It's in the north end of the Indian Reservation.' LaMoia fished the official SPD road atlas from the glove box where it was required to reside, and leafed through the nearly three inches of pages at a blistering speed. 'You know what, Sarge?'

'It isn't in there.'

'Correctomundo,' LaMoia answered.

'Dispatch!' they said, nearly in unison.

'What do you want to bet they can track us from there?' Each and every SPD vehicle now carried a GPS location transmitter, enabling Dispatch computers to monitor location. On radio cars that carried MDT terminals, this same technology allowed patrol officers to monitor their GPS position on a moving map, and follow computer-generated directions for the fastest possible route, taking into account reported traffic delays. Boldt's unmarked car lacked the MDT, but still possessed a GPS transmitter in the trunk.

'The system goes out wireless,' Boldt instructed his sergeant. LaMoia never paid any attention to in-house memos. 'As long as our phones are working, so's the GPS.'

'It's ringing,' LaMoia said. Less than a minute later Boldt turned left on Totten Road, following LaMoia's instruction. Precise directions followed, as a woman twenty-three miles away, on the other side of Puget Sound, stared at a computer screen tracking Boldt's car to within a margin of error of forty feet.

Right on Widme Road, and straight through the dark woods, Boldt driving twenty miles an hour over the posted limit and nearly rolling the car on a sharp right that appeared out of nowhere. The road bent immediately left and continued to its conclusion at Lincoln, where LaMoia pointed left and the driver followed.

The darkness combined with the rain to lower visibility to a matter of yards, not miles. Two cars passed them on Lincoln, both Boldt and LaMoia straining and turning to get the best possible look.

'I don't think so,' LaMoia said after the first. 'That ain't no Eldorado,' he declared of the second.

'You're the gear head,' Boldt said, his driving strained by the divided attention. 'Tell Dispatch we want a "Lights Out" a quarter mile from our last turn. We'll leave the car there and go on foot.'

'Affirm,' LaMoia answered.

Stottlemeyer was the fourth right.

'Three tenths of a mile, Sarge,' LaMoia announced.

Boldt pulled the car over into muddy gravel, less than two hundred yards from where Flek had phoned him. The moment his hands left the wheel, they grabbed for the vest in the backseat. He announced, 'One vest, one field operative.' LaMoia looked ready to object. 'You'll stay here, monitor the Poulsbo channel, and keep with Gaynes at AirTyme.' He fiddled with his own phone. 'Mine is set to vibrate. You call if anything breaks. I call if I spot them.'

'And when you do?' LaMoia said optimistically.

'I'll try to direct you in around back. Then we ad lib. If I can't get close, then I'll make myself a target and lure him to where you get a shot.'

'Oh, yeah. There's a brilliant plan. There's a good match: my nine-millimeter on him; his German scope on you.'

'We ad lib,' Boldt repeated. 'We're not going to know 'til we see the situation. Maybe there's an old farmhouse or something. Maybe we wait for backup.'

'You'll pardon my rank, Lieutenant, but you're full of shit at the moment. You're not making any sense.'

'My orders are for you to stay in the car,' Boldt said.

LaMoia objected, 'Why? So you go get yourself killed by some worthless skel?'

'Those are your orders.'

'Bullshit!' LaMoia fired back.

Boldt doubled-checked that all the phones came with similar services. 'You've got call-waiting, don't you?'

'Yeah,' a disgruntled LaMoia answered.

'So stay on the line with Gaynes and listen up for my incoming call.'

'As ordered, *sir*!'

Boldt said calmly, 'You're injured, John. You're slow. And doubling up out there only doubles the noise we make. This is not heroics; it's what makes sense.'

'To you.'

'To me,' Boldt said.

Boldt checked the car's interior light before opening the door, making sure it would not light up as the door came open. He adjusted the vest as he stepped out into the rain – its woven plastic exterior would act as something of raincoat. There would be no flashlight. He would allow his eyes to adjust and do his best in the dark. He walked slowly at first, unable to see more than a few feet in front of himself, his pace and stride increasing the longer he stayed out in the rain. He reached a muddy track to his right not far down the road, and stayed to the edge, where his sinking into the sloppy turf wouldn't show up in headlights, in case Flek was suddenly on his way out. He stooped low and felt the mud. The tire tracks seemed recent to him. Given the rain, they would have been beaten down in a matter of hours.

He was less than a hundred yards down that track when he heard a car roar to life. With the sound bouncing in the trees, it seemed to come from *behind* him, not from in front as expected. He crouched and reached for his weapon, only to realize that in his haste he'd strapped the vest in the way of his gun – an amateurish mistake that made him realize he had too much emotion working against him.

When the car horn sounded out on the road, he realized it was his own car that he'd heard start, LaMoia behind the wheel. He ran for the open road.

'What the hell?' Boldt said, as he jumped into the passenger seat, dripping wet. LaMoia was just shy of being a qualified stock car racer. He was the best and fastest driver of all the detectives. Boldt's car took off like someone had switched engines in the past few minutes.

'Turns out Osbourne had a couple guys working on a hunch—'

'Gaynes told me as much,' Boldt recalled.

'The hunch had to do with a part of the reserved bandwidth that isn't used for the calls themselves, but, as I understand it, has to do with tower handshakes.'

'What's it mean, John?' Boldt asked impatiently, strapping himself in.

LaMoia glided the car on all four tires through a left turn that had Boldt clutching to the dash. Both hands on the wheel, the driver said, 'It means that the reason we see those little bars on our cell phones for signal strength is because the phone and the towers are constantly talking to each other – and here's the catch: *whether or not* we're currently making a call. As long as the phone is on, it's looking for the nearest tower and reporting to its own processor what kind of signal strength is available, which comes back out of the phone as those little bars. To do so, it sends its own ID every time – like a few thousand times a second!'

'And Osbourne can see it's his phone,' Boldt mumbled.

'*Both* their phones, but, yes, that's right. He can see them real-time – no more fifteen-minute delays. They can't triangulate. They can't pinpoint them unless he makes a call – and we're back to a delay at that point. But *they can watch movement*, tower to tower, as the phones continue checking for the best handshake. And both those phones are currently moving, Sarge.' He didn't take his grip from the wheel, but his index finger pointed straight ahead. 'East. They've been moving east for the last ten minutes or so. The phones appear to be at rest at the moment.'

'Which means we're gaining on them,' Boldt said.

'Bingo!' said the driver, as he pushed the car past ninety on a two-lane road swollen with rainwater.

SIXTY

Daphne awakened to Bryce Abbott Flek pouring luke-warm beer down her face. It spilled down her chest and into her blouse, and she pushed him away as she came to. The first thing she did was look down at her foot because it felt different. He had removed her boot and sock and used the bootlaces to tie two cotton ends of the Tampax she carried as plugs on the entrance and exit wounds. One of the shoelaces was tied tightly around her left ankle, reducing blood flow. It hurt, but surprisingly held short of screaming pain.

'Key to the cuffs,' he said, sipping from the beer he'd just used to shower her awake.

'Zippered pocket of my purse.' He went after them. 'How long was I out?'

'Five minutes. Maybe less.'

It had felt like hours to her. But she doubted she had hours now, and that thought electrified her. If Flek had his way, this was meant to be the last night of her life, she realized. She would bleed out if she didn't receive medical attention. Regrets and fear piled up inside her, and she struggled to be rid of them. Eventually, they won out. She said, 'What you wouldn't let me tell you – we only want you as a *witness*. We have nothing but circumstantial evidence against you. But there was an assault that we don't think you're good for, and we wanted you in to clear that up.'

'Sure you did,' he said. 'Here's how it's going to be.'

He glanced outside nervously. The sidewalks were empty due to the hour and the rain. 'I'm going to take those off,' he said, meaning the cuffs, 'and help you over to the pay phone. And we're going to call your friend and you're going to say hello. And if anyone sees us, you're going to hold onto me tight like you've been loving me a hundred years. And if you don't, the next shot goes through the other foot, and then up the legs, and so on. Clear?'

'I got it.'

'Fast and easy,' he said. Then he added, 'You got any change in here?' and dug deeper into her purse.

SIXTY ONE

'Hang on!' Boldt hollered into his cellular. 'Let me write this down. I'm not thinking too clearly right now.' It was no exaggeration. When his phone had rung he had not expected Flek, believing the man's cellular phone was jammed. He scribbled into his notebook. 'Miller Bay North . . . directly across from Quail. The street's name is Sid Price?'

LaMoia, overhearing his lieutenant, said, 'Sounds like a game-show host.'

'Okay . . . okay . . .' Boldt said into the phone.

LaMoia tapped his watch frantically.

Boldt acknowledged the signal with a nod and spoke into his phone. LaMoia wanted time. Boldt had to remember that Flek considered him still on the mainland, not a few precious miles away.

'I can catch the nine-fifty ferry if I hurry,' he said into the phone. 'No . . . we don't have a helicopter . . . No, we don't! And that means an hour or so at the earliest. I understand that, but there's nothing I can do . . . It's the best I can do . . . Exactly . . . Yes, alone. But I want to talk to her. If I don't hear her voice, the meet's off.' He waited. 'Okay.'

Boldt felt his heart pounding in his chest.

'Lieutenant?' her weakened voice inquired. She avoided use of his first name; she didn't want to give Flek any hint of their friendship, not so much as an ounce of added leverage. 'I'm wounded—' Boldt heard a

387

struggle as the phone was ripped from Daphne's hand – he could visualize this clearly as if he were standing by whatever pay phone they occupied. *Wounded!* His stomach knotted.

'One hour,' the man said. The line went dead.

'She's wounded,' Boldt reported in a whisper.

'Wounded, how?'

'He hung up.'

LaMoia one-handed the wheel. 'Yeah? Well, the only reason he wants a meeting is to take you out.' With the call to Bobbie Gaynes pressed to his ear, LaMoia warned his passenger. 'My batteries are going to go, Sarge.' Boldt's had already failed, though a cigarette lighter cable now powered his phone. They'd be down to that one phone in a matter of minutes. 'Get back to Dispatch,' LaMoia instructed his lieutenant, slamming on the brakes and skidding the car thirty yards to within a few feet of a stop sign and a T intersection that offered either a right turn to the south, or a left to the north. The quick braking pasted Boldt to the dash. Concentrating on the phone, LaMoia reported, 'They're rolling again – east, northeast. South end of Suquamish.' He pointed out the windshield to the right. 'A mile or two that way.' Osbourne's tower-tracking technology was working.

Boldt called Dispatch and reported the proposed location for the meet. The car idled smoothly at the intersection. Both men held tightly to their phones, their faces screwed down in impatience. LaMoia said something about them being 'men of the millennium.'

Boldt shushed him with a raised finger and explained to the dispatcher, 'I need a look at three hundreds yards in any direction. Elevations. Obstructions. Get a detective in there and pick a spot that has the best long-range rifle shot at the location I just gave you. A long-range rifle shot,' he repeated. 'Right . . . Right . . .' Boldt began to sketch a slightly crooked finger onto a blank page of his notebook. It angled thinly to the right. He marked an X to the left of the middle knuckle. 'Fastest route from here?' he asked. A fraction of a second later he pointed north, and LaMoia left two plumes of steam and black-rubber smoke behind the vehicle as it jumped through the turn. 'I'll hold,' Boldt said. He didn't mean the dash, but he held to that too.

He cautioned LaMoia, 'You've got to keep them reporting their movement. If you step on it,' he said, indicating his crudely drawn map, 'we beat them to the drop an hour before he expects to see us.'

'And *we* get the jump on *him*,' LaMoia said gleefully.

'Maybe,' Boldt said, grabbing for the dash as they skidded through the next turn, the burning rubber crying out its complaint.

SIXTY TWO

'You need to focus on what Davie would think of all this,' Daphne advised.

'I warned you to shut up!' he reminded angrily.

'Yes, you did. It's true. And maybe I'm just delirious from blood loss,' she suggested, 'but I want to help you if I can.'

'Fuck you.'

She said, 'Does the name Maria Sanchez mean anything to you?'

'I seen the news,' he said.

'Was that you? The Sanchez place?'

He scoffed. 'Cops are all the same. If it's easy, then that's your man.'

'What if they'd put this on Davie?'

'Davie didn't have nothing to do with it!'

'But you did?'

'According to the news.'

'I'm asking you,' she said. 'I'm trying to tell you that that's the primary reason we wanted to collar you: Sanchez. We need answers. I've gotta believe,' she said, trying her best to keep her brain functioning, to use vernacular capable of establishing a rapport, 'that Davie wouldn't want you going down for something you didn't do.'

'You don't know nothing about Davie. What he did for me.'

He didn't complete the thought, but Daphne's mind

raced ahead looking for answers. '*What he did for me . . .*' Suddenly she saw it, she understood what he was talking about. Psychologically, it changed everything. Davie was a martyr. She said to Flek, 'The robbery he went down for, he confessed to . . . It was *yours*. He let slip about a delivery coming into the store, and you pounced. But you were about to get caught. Sitting on two convictions, with a third looming, you're fifteen to twenty without parole. Three strikes. And so Davie takes the fall for you, and big brother picks up bags and splits for Seattle.' It was Flek who suddenly looked wounded. 'But big brother can't leave well enough alone. He hears about little brother's work in the private commerce program – a program his brother has qualified for because he's such a model prisoner – and here comes another scam, and little brother can't say no.'

Flek glanced over at her with a look of crestfallen failure. The truth could soothe, or the truth could aggravate, and Daphne had taken a huge chance trying it out on him, but for the first time since climbing into this car in the belly of the ferry, she felt progress. She just wasn't sure she could retain consciousness long enough to take advantage of it.

'We couldn't find any record of Davie having worked the phone solicitation on Sanchez. All your other burglaries were on his list. *That* is why we wanted to question you, Abby. Granted, our Burglary division would have heralded the arrest. You'd have gone away for five to twelve. But we're overcrowded, and with the crime being nonviolent, you'd be out in two. But breaking the neck of a policewoman and kidnapping another? You want to think about that for a minute?'

'That's a bullshit charge, and you know it.'

'The kidnapping?' asked the hostage.

'Sanchez,' he said.

'Do you have an alibi?'

'What if I do?'

'Then I shot myself in the foot. It's my gun – it'll fit. It happens more often than you think.' She added, 'Besides, I'm a woman. None of these guys think a woman can handle a sidearm.'

'You'd lie through your teeth to save yourself right now.'

'You're missing the point, Abby. What would Davie want you to do? That's got to be your focus. You want his name linked to this assault? Does he deserve that? He was a good kid, Davie was. He stepped up when others would have walked away. But now you're dragging him through it, and there's nothing *he* can do about it. But you—'

'Shut up!'

'He's dead,' she said bluntly, knowing this was the button that had set him off. 'He's dead and gone, all through a string of mistakes. *Your* mistakes, Abby. And if he's looking down right now, then his soul is tortured. Is that what you want? Did he take the fall for you to have it end up like this? Him dead. You a cop killer?' She let this sink in. 'That's what you have in mind, isn't it? Kill Boldt. Or me? Or both of us? Put the blame onto Boldt instead of yourself? Do you see that's all you're doing? Do you realize it won't do anything to take away the voices?'

He snapped his head toward her as if she'd poured salt on a wound.

'You hear voices. They started right after your brother's death.' She said, 'You think they're bad now? You've never killed a man, have you, Abby? It's not something you forget. It's not something you walk away from and all is forgiven. You blame Boldt for Ansel – but you've got that wrong.'

His eyes burned into her as he turned the car right onto a street marked Sid Price. A damp and dark narrow lane. Enormous trees. Close quarters. She couldn't be sure he'd even heard her.

He drove down a small dirt track, a dead-end driveway that led down to a muddy patch of lawn and a boat launch into Miller Bay. The narrow waterway was only fifty yards wide at this point. Flek parked the car up from the boat ramp. He lowered both windows, shut off the car and turned off the lights. Daphne could smell the low tide and mud flats. It smelled like death.

'Don't do this,' she pleaded. 'I can still get you out of most of this. But if you go through with it . . .'

Paying little attention to her, he leaned over awkwardly and reached under the seat and worked to untwist some hidden wire. If she was to have a chance to fight back, it was then, with his head lowered. But she couldn't summon the strength, nor the courage. She could barely keep herself conscious. She had lost great quantities of blood. Perhaps she was dying. She had heard Flek mention one hour and she no longer believed she could or would make it that long, certainly not conscious.

'Please,' she said.

He sat up, the Chinese assault rifle in hand. The German scope. He had wired it high under the seat, so that even a thorough check beneath the seat by a traffic cop might not have revealed it. He said, 'Cops lie, lady. They lie about me doing that other woman, and now you lie to save your ass. They'll lie about anything, if it makes their job easier.'

He sought out the oily rag and gagged her again, a man going about his business. He turned on the car's interior light and met eyes with Daphne. 'If I get Boldt, I'll spare you. If I don't, it's you who's gonna pay. Say your prayers.' Then he was gone, down toward the water, the rain and the darkness absorbing him.

SIXTY THREE

'Gaynes says the signals have stopped moving,' LaMoia reported.

'Then that was them,' Boldt said, his attention fixed on the entrance to the street marked Sid Price. The Crown Vic was parked down a muddy lane, called Quail, from which they had an unobstructed view across Miller Bay Road. A big monster of a car had turned through the rain only a few minutes before, its taillights receding. LaMoia had guessed it was an Eldorado.

'Shit, Sarge,' LaMoia complained. 'He could lay in wait for you anywhere down there. We gotta rethink this.'

'We're at least a half hour ahead of when he expects us,' Boldt reminded. 'That's in our favor. We need to move while it still means something.'

'We may have the jump on him, but he's got the sniper's rifle. Our peashooters are good at ten or thirty feet, Sarge. He's dead on the money at two hundred yards.'

'We had his sight recalibrated,' Boldt informed the man, who knew so little of the investigation to this point. 'He wanted a hundred and fifty yards. Manny Wong gave him seventy-five.'

'No shit? And you're counting on that? What are you smoking? If he's tried the thing out on a range – which you can bet your ass he has – then everything's back on target. I wouldn't put a hell of a lot of faith in this guy missing, Sarge. I'd be thinking about shooting him first. That usually has the more desired effect.'

'His first shot will miss,' Boldt said confidently. 'You have to hit him before he throws that second shot.'

'Me and who else?' LaMoia complained. 'I got me a peashooter here. I got to know where he is if I'm to be useful. And I won't know until *after* that first shot.'

Boldt cupped his penlight so the light barely shone down onto his open notebook, but it was enough to see by. He had sketched in the information provided by Dispatch and analyzed by Patrick Mulwright, head of Special Ops, who volunteered to help out. Intelligence, a division where Boldt had been lieutenant for a year, provided high-resolution military satellite images of Miller Bay. Within fifteen minutes of Boldt's request, Mulwright had come back to him with three likely sniper points: rooftops; either of two high-tension electric towers that strung four hundred thousand volts suspended across Miller Bay; and a marina, directly across the water.

Boldt and LaMoia ruled out the nearby rooftops. Shooting a cop from the roof of a neighborhood house left too great a possibility of witnesses.

'It's one of the two towers,' LaMoia said confidently.

'Across the water,' Boldt added. 'It gives him the distance for the scope, and the water gives a natural break to slow down or prevent any pursuit on our part. He escapes while we're attempting to catch up.'

'And what,' LaMoia asked skeptically, 'he goes on foot from there?'

'Osbourne confirmed he'd been over here at least twice. He could have anything planned. He could have friends on the reservation. He could have left a car or a bike for himself.'

LaMoia agreed. 'That tower over there makes sense.'

'So you take the car,' Boldt said. 'I'm on foot.' He had rearranged the vest to sit beneath his sport coat, his weapon at the ready.

'The advantage of the towers,' LaMoia said, pointing out through the windshield, 'is that he can see over the houses. He can see *us* if he's looking.' Boldt quit the flashlight. 'Not that he's up there yet. But he could be any minute now.'

'He can see you coming,' Boldt warned. 'And if he does, he'll take out Daffy. If he can't get me, he'll take her.'

'Now you're getting the point,' LaMoia fired back. 'And he wants you coming alone. He'll want to see a car drive up with one person inside. If there's backup, he'll see it.'

'But I've still got that half hour.'

Faint light from cars passing out on the main road cast enough light for LaMoia to trace a finger across Boldt's notepad. Boldt could now clearly understand the man's awkward speech patterns caused by his wired jaw. 'You drop me over here. Right now. Believing he'll be facing this direction, I come up from behind. You drive back and park someplace with no view of either tower. You give me a good ten minutes because you're right: I'm a little slow. You can't scout it, Sarge, as much as you want to. He could see you. Even now, he could see you, and that blows it for Matthews. Who knows what he has planned for her? Maybe the car's rigged. Maybe the first bullet is meant for her if he smells a double-cross. At the appointed time, you drive in and see what you see. If my phone worked, I could call you, but it doesn't, so we do this blind.' He added, 'You hear a couple guys throwing shots, you'll know I'm onto something.'

Boldt wouldn't give up. He didn't want to drive into the drop blind. Protecting Daphne meant knowing the layout. He wanted a first look. Pointing to his crude map, he said, 'I could make for this tower now, after I drop you off, and at least provide cover if he spots you—'

'As if you could hit him at that distance.'

'He doesn't know what I'm shooting,' Boldt protested. 'Providing there aren't any shots thrown, then there'd be plenty of time for me to still arrive by car. If Mulwright described this right, this closer tower is far enough above the drop site that it wouldn't really be in the direction he's facing.'

LaMoia didn't like it, but he said, 'Okay, so I agree. Is that what you want to hear?'

'That's what I wanted to hear,' Boldt agreed.

Boldt dropped LaMoia on a dead-end lane on the opposite side of Miller Bay, about a half mile from the high-voltage tower and the flashing red light that topped it. He crossed back to the west side and parked the car well off Miller Bay Road where it could not be seen by passing traffic.

He crouched as he walked through the tall grasses and marsh plants, the high-voltage tower dominating his view. It rose a hundred feet or more on four interlaced steel legs, looking like an incomplete version of the Eiffel Tower, its four outreaching struts supporting six high-voltage lines, each the thickness of a man's forearm, that drooped lazily before rising again to the tower on the opposite shore. The sign hung on the chain link fence surrounding its base warned of the lethal electricity, punctuating its message with yellow lightning bolts. Boldt climbed over the fence and dropped to the other side, arching his back to look up and take in the enormity of the tower and the gray night sky that cried down its rain.

The metal was wet and slick, and just the thought of water and electricity turned his stomach as he made a strong jump to reach the first of the steel ladder rungs welded to the western-most corner. He pulled himself up, slipped, dangled, and tried again, his rubber-soled shoes finally finding purchase. A moment later he started to climb.

The Eldorado had been parked on a muddy patch of grass facing the water, its dim interior light revealing what appeared to be a single figure on the passenger side of the car. It was too far for him to see if it was her, but he sensed it was. His chest knotted. His eyes stung. The car was perhaps a hundred yards south of the tower, the nearest home up a rise forty or fifty yards west. A concrete boat ramp led down to the water immediately in front of the Eldorado. The inlet was narrow at this point – no more than twenty or thirty yards across – shaped like a crooked finger, with Boldt at the knuckle as it gently pointed east.

He looked for LaMoia across the narrow body of water, but did not see him. He studied the opposing tower, silvery black in the night rain, knowing now how a person would ascend and looking there, on any of the rising legs, for a human silhouette or similar pattern that did not belong.

He felt Daphne in Flek's crosshairs, if for no other reason than the man would be using the rifle's scope to sight the opposing shore as he anticipated Boldt's arrival. He hoped that scope might also commit Flek to tunnel vision, focused so intently on the car and his hostage that he might fail to fully take in the surroundings.

Boldt climbed higher, and higher yet.

*

Ten minutes passed, the weather vacillating between a light drizzle and a moderate downpour. Boldt, chilled and soaking wet, imagined LaMoia and Flek as equally miserable. A half moon briefly appeared, turning the unseen, invisible night rain into a shimmering curtain of silver wire, extinguished a moment later by a low rushing cloud and more drizzle. Perched as he was, remaining quite still, Boldt finally discerned movement to the left of the opposing tower as LaMoia emerged from marshland and waited, stone still.

After several agonizing minutes, LaMoia moved again, keeping toward water's edge. He reached the base of the tower, hesitating only briefly before moving on, and thereby signaling his lieutenant that the tower was empty. He approached the boatyard on the opposite shore.

Boldt took his eye off the man long enough to sweep his surroundings – the rooftops, the main road, and some of the houses beyond. His next thought sent a shudder of panic through him: what if Flek was hiding in the trunk, waiting for Boldt to step up to the car? What if he didn't trust himself at two hundred yards, and wanted only a few feet instead? What if the person in the passenger seat was Flek himself and Daphne had been left in some situation where she would perish if not saved, and would not be saved unless Flek was successful?

His panic mounting, Boldt began to descend the tower's treacherous steel ladder. He wanted to get closer to that car.

The first reports of gunfire – a series of quick, dull pops – barely reached across the water, muted by the wind and falling rain. Boldt lifted his head and concentration away from the next descending ladder rung to see several more soft yellow flashes followed a moment later by the echo of the more slowly traveling report. The shots briefly illuminated the boatyard as a mosaic of geometric shapes, silhouettes of masts and daggerlike keels. Some of the shots had come from Boldt's left – LaMoia, he figured – the rest, quite a volley of shots, from high up on the deck of one of the dry-docked boats: Flek.

By the time Boldt had his weapon in hand, there was near total silence. He knew there was no point in making any attempt at cover shots, no point in revealing his position. He hurried down the ladder at a brisker pace.

To Boldt's right came the clunking, soft metallic sound of shots landing in the body of the car. Flek was shooting for Daphne. The shots had fallen low. The next shot took out the windshield of the Eldorado. Boldt hurried his descent, now taking two rungs at a time. He squeezed off three quick shots out over the water, hoping to distract Flek.

He saw the white of a muzzle flash and knew from the color that the barrel was now trained on him. He *heard* the shot whiz by, ripping its way through the falling rain. Flek's scope was giving him trouble.

Two more dull pops from the left. LaMoia had sneaked closer to his target.

Flek returned a volley of high-powered rifle shots at LaMoia, the bullets chewing into boats. And then all at once, the tiny figure of a man jumped from a boat and ran for water's edge, carelessly spraying a few bullets behind him in hopes of keeping LaMoia low. Flek splashed into the water, keeping his weapon held high, and walked the mud bottom, making straight for the opposite shore. The Eldorado.

Daphne.

The cornered animal, pressured by LaMoia's deadly

proximity, had reacted and was heading to the nest to finish the job. Heading away, making his opponent's handguns even less effective.

Feeling the heat of LaMoia's firepower, Flek had fled to the cover of water, offering only the smallest of targets as he swam.

Boldt missed a rung and fell.

It happened so quickly: one moment descending; the next, free-falling. He dropped his gun, lunging to grab hold of absolutely anything he could, but hit the tower's cement pad on his left foot, twisting his ankle and buckling his knee. White pain blinded him. He forced himself to breathe in order to avoid passing out. He could see past his fallen gun, down to the water, Flek's arms sticking up and holding the rifle as he quickly negotiated the narrow passage, swimming and walking through the chest-deep water. Flek and that weapon would reach shore within the minute. Boldt tried to stand, but cried out and fell with the pain – fell to within an arm's length of his handgun.

Across the narrow bay, LaMoia appeared at water's edge. But Flek spun around and managed several shots in that direction, and Boldt saw LaMoia dive for cover.

No contest. Flek would reach the Eldorado – and Daphne – unchallenged. He intended for Daphne to pay for his brother's death.

Boldt again tried to stand. Again he fell, this time onto his back, writhing in pain.

He looked up into the sky, and there was the answer.

Boldt rolled. LaMoia crawled toward the water's edge. Boldt cupped his lips and shouted, 'No, John! Get back!' knowing full well that LaMoia would make the swim in an effort to save Daphne. 'Back! Back!' Boldt shouted, pleased to see his normally disobedient sergeant retreat toward the boatyard.

Lou Boldt was no crack shot. He regularly visited the firing range and put in the time required of him to place four out of eight shots somewhere on the body. Given a brace on which to rest his hands, he could manage a head shot on a lighted target thirty feet away. But something the size of a forearm, in the dark, at a hundred feet . . . he wasn't convinced he could hit it once, much less accomplish the repeated hits he believed required of him. Nonetheless, he dragged himself to the base pod of the nearest leg and braced for the shot. He steadied his two-fisted grip, checked once over his shoulder at Flek, now only a matter of yards from shore, returned his rain-blurred vision down the barrel, stretching it long and dark to the bead that he aimed onto the glistening, silver, high-voltage cable well over-head. He had six shots available.

The first missed entirely, racing up into the night sky. Rain stung his eyes. He cleared his vision with the swipe of a hand, held his breath, took steady aim and squeezed. A blinding shower of sparks – he had nicked the line, or perhaps the insulated support binding it to the tower. His third shot missed. The fourth rained more sparks, this time like fireworks. The fifth severed the line. Boldt pulled his hands from the steel and rolled.

It fell like a dragon's neck spitting fire, a blinding, lightning arc as it grounded first to one of the tower's legs, and then, whistling and veering through the black sky and grounding to another, dancing like a fire hose that has broken loose. It fell directly for Boldt with alarming speed, several tons of high-voltage cable without a home, all the while spitting sparks into the rain-laced air. Boldt could smell the burning ozone as the dragon's head free-fell for him, curving away only at the last instant, and winding itself up again, lighting higher and higher, that static-charged roar chasing its every move.

It whispered and whipped through the wet air, suddenly like a broken rubber band, rebounding toward the distant tower across Miller Bay, taking its hissing sound and metal smell with it. The air became a flurry of white lightning and small explosions. It raised its head one final time – higher, higher, higher – stretching for the heavens, before turning and diving like a Kamikaze, the buzzing of electrically charged energy, rich and ripe and destined for the ultimate ground of all: water.

It struck Miller Bay with a small explosion, a huge, white, pulsing light ripping through the water in waves that reminded Boldt of dropping a pebble in a still pond.

Flek, no doubt, saw it approaching, this white apron of raw voltage. Saw it like a tsunami ripping through the water toward him. When it hit, it lit his body unnaturally – a glowing white stick in a black pond. The weapon he held above his head exploded as its ammunition combusted. For a brief few seconds, Bryce Abbott Flek was his own fireworks display, culminated by the detonation of what sounded like a small bomb, which experts later said had probably been his head.

The houses north of Miller Bay were black and without power. Boldt dragged himself to the chain-link fence, a section of which had been melted by that tongue of fire, and crawled out and onto the wet ground, half-walking, falling, stumbling, rolling his way toward that Eldorado. LaMoia would later say that he looked like a man who'd spent weeks in the desert.

LaMoia came the long way around, over a mile of roadway, the last half of which he hitched a ride with a volunteer fireman; he wasn't going anywhere near that water, littered as it was with the carcasses of dead fish and the gruesome remains of one human being. Despite the time it took him to reach the Eldorado, LaMoia arrived to find Boldt still crawling, twenty yards out. He briefly kept the fireman at bay, helped the lieutenant to his feet, and together they approached the Eldorado, from which there was no movement, no sound.

'Please, God,' Boldt whispered under his breath.

'Matthews?' a tight-jawed LaMoia called out, his crippled body attempting to support Boldt. The blind leading the blind.

'Daffy!' Boldt hollered.

The exploding windshield had rained cubes of tempered glass into the vehicle so that she seemed covered in huge, sparkling diamonds. For a moment the scene looked almost beautiful. But her body was slumped against the car door, perfectly still, her face scratched, her chin bleeding.

'She's bleeding!' Boldt chortled excitedly. 'She's bleeding!' he said, gripping LaMoia's shoulder with enthusiastic force.

A heart had to be beating for a body to bleed. Homicide cops rarely saw bleeders.

'I believe she is!' LaMoia said, tears choking him as he leaned Boldt against the car and he and the fireman hurried to the passenger door to try for a pulse.

SIXTY FOUR

'My last conscious thought was that we needed him alive.' Two days after her ordeal, Daphne's voice remained weak and trembling.

They sat in the front seat of Boldt's Crown Vic, outside the home of Ron Chapman, awaiting LaMoia. Boldt wore a walking cast on his left leg. Daphne wore a cast on the same foot. Ever the pair.

'He didn't feel the same way about you,' Boldt reminded her.

'He assumed he'd be blamed for Sanchez, but he didn't do her. He claimed to have an alibi. The AirTyme cellular records put him on the Bainbridge ferry for the night you were shot at. Flek did the burglaries, no question about it. He pushed Kawamoto down some stairs. But not Sanchez. Not you. Certainly not Schock and Phillipp. He's not good for any of that.'

'Which is why we're here – to get to the bottom of it.'

'Despite the obvious risks to our careers that video represents,' Daphne reminded him.

'Leave well enough alone?' he asked. 'Is that what I'm hearing? We put Flek down in the books for the Sanchez assault, and we walk away from it?'

'There are those who wouldn't give that a second thought, given the stakes.'

'And are we them?' he asked. 'Daffy, I'm not going to force this on you. It's both of our careers. We either do this unanimously, or not at all.' He added, 'I thought we'd—'

'Been over it?' she interrupted. 'So did I. But sitting here now, ready to dig back into it, it feels a lot different. It would be *so easy* to cover it up.'

'Say the word,' Boldt advised her, glancing up at the dashboard clock.

LaMoia parked across the street. He crossed, and slipped into the backseat. He carried a file under his arm that Boldt had been expecting. 'It arrived a few minutes ago,' he informed his lieutenant. 'Typical I.I. – they hand-delivered it, and made me sign off on it twice.' Speaking to Daphne, LaMoia said through his wired jaw, 'If it's any consolation, Matthews, I've been jammed in a lot worse ways than this – the video, I'm talking about – and I know the value of a person keeping his mouth shut, if it comes to that. No pun intended.'

Daphne thanked him.

Boldt flipped open the folder LaMoia had delivered and angled it to catch the street light. He read the contents, flipped pages and read some more. 'Ronnie wasn't cut out for this.'

'He denied any involvement when Sanchez interviewed him,' LaMoia pointed out.

'Hopefully, we can change that,' Daphne said.

'I feel like I'm visiting a convalescent home,' Ron Chapman said, sitting across from Boldt at his own kitchen table. He'd been reluctant to speak with them, but Boldt had flashed him a look at the I.I. folder, and Chapman had acquiesced. The story of Bryce Abbott Flek's fiery death had already come and gone from the papers and newscasts. Public interest in the case had faded as quickly as the fish had washed out to sea from

Miller Bay, as quickly as it had taken work crews to restore power to eleven hundred households. In the world of local TV, two days proved to be an eternity.

Boldt, Daphne and LaMoia sat side by side across the table from Chapman.

'Between us we've got over forty years, Ronnie,' Boldt reminded the man.

'Some good, some bad,' Chapman said. 'I've never had a beef with you, Lou.'

'The three of us over here have an ongoing investigation into that assault of the female officer.'

'Sanchez,' Daphne said.

LaMoia told the uniform, 'Mine is more of a personal interest. Sanchez and I were . . . friends.'

'I'm with you,' Chapman told the three.

'You've always been straight with me, Ron.'

'Same here, Lou.'

'And I need you to be so now.' He repeated, 'Straight.'

'I've spoken to I.I. already, if that's what this is about.'

'That's part of what it's about,' Boldt acknowledged. 'Krishevski paid me a visit. Told me about a video you have. Wouldn't tell me what's on it.'

'So maybe you're wasting your time.'

'You want to go down with them?' Boldt asked, having a vague idea of who 'them' was. 'I.I.'ll get you for hindering prosecution – you understand that, don't you?'

'I got no comment, Lou.'

Boldt said, 'I was with you when you discovered that rifle being switched. I think it surprised you.'

He waited a moment. ''Course it surprised me,' Chapman said.

'This is about the Flu, Ronnie. That's what I think.

408

It's about some of the guys buying themselves a little extra insurance that the cash flow would be there when the guild funds started running dry. It's about inside information, which is where Krishevski fits in: he talked when he shouldn't have. The best pressure we have is that a missing assault rifle took a shot at me.'

Chapman's eyes went wide.

LaMoia suggested, 'You'll be hooked up to that if you keep playing it the way you are.'

Daphne explained, 'The shooting offers us the best leverage in terms of getting one of them to talk.' She had no idea what she was talking about, but she hoped Chapman didn't know that.

'And I fit in, how?' Chapman asked, vamping.

Boldt said, 'Property has always been a clean department, Ronnie.'

'Damn right.'

'And now this,' LaMoia said. 'Gotta break your heart.'

'It does,' the man insisted.

'And us too,' LaMoia said.

Daphne added, 'We hate to see anyone look bad.'

Boldt said, 'And we understand that when a guy is dealing with I.I. he's not about to so much as whisper a fellow officer's name without damn good proof, because no matter what anyone says, any kind of I.I. association hurts an officer, jams him up. Even ruins him, sometimes. And for no good reason.'

'Agreed.'

'It was Krishevski's shift,' Boldt stated, as if certain. 'How long do you cover, Ronnie?' Boldt readjusted his cast. 'Krishevski has three officers under him: Pendegrass, Riorden, and Smythe.'

Chapman was feeling uncomfortable. 'I'm aware of that, Lou.'

'Who was it? What was it?' Boldt tried to sound convincing. 'One of them stole some assault rifles. Probably more like two of them, given the way the mechanics work – one guy having to trip a button upstairs in order for the vault to come open downstairs. They sold them into the marketplace for some spending money.'

'Is that what's on this missing video?' LaMoia asked. 'Or was it you who threw the switch to open the warehouse?'

'I didn't throw no switch. I didn't have nothing to do with that.'

Daphne speculated, 'You saw something.'

Chapman answered, 'I caught one of Sergeant K's guys in house on my shift, and he hadn't signed in. You gotta sign in, Lou – that's on penalty of death in our unit. There were threats exchanged. Obviously, I realized something wrong was going down. Something had come out of the warehouse, and it came out on my shift – that was on purpose. And if it came out, then it had to go somewhere. Had to leave the building. And fast.'

'The garage,' Boldt nodded, understanding the logic. The warehouse and the lower deck of the parking garage were on the same level.

'I don't know if these guys planned on covering their backsides later or not. Maybe they're just plain stupid.' He looked at LaMoia. 'Maybe they planned to give me what someone gave you, what someone gave Sanchez. Schock, Phillipp. You gotta be some kind of stupid to try any of this. But I got the leg up on 'em. If I hadn't, maybe somebody would have clubbed me in an alley or on the way out of a bar or something.'

'Leg up, Ronnie?' Boldt asked.

'You remember that vandalism in the garage . . . must be two years ago now?'

'Vaguely,' Boldt answered.

'I.I. had a pair of cameras installed.' He recognized Boldt's blank expression.

LaMoia said, 'The video.'

'No one knows about those cameras,' Chapman said. 'The brass wanted it that way. They didn't want anyone knowing. They knew the vandalism had to be internal, cop to cop, and they wanted to put somebody right for it. The wiring for the closed-circuit stuff runs into the boneyard. They installed it saying they were doing maintenance. Thought they'd hidden the VCRs where we'd never see them – way up on a shelf in the back. But I knew. I *had* to know. I've been in that room going on twenty-one years. I know every creak, every sound. I've been fighting rats and spiders so long that I've given them names. I know every inch of those shelves. But no one knew I knew.'

'The videotape,' LaMoia repeated.

The ruddy-cheeked man grinned. 'I grabbed it that night, knowing it was my insurance package. Locked it away good and tight. And if anything happens to me, it goes directly to KSTV's News Four at Five.'

'Oh . . . my . . . God,' Boldt gasped, realizing Chapman had images that could ID the cops responsible for the theft. 'I.I. caught on, how?'

Chapman explained, 'I loosened a wire, put a blank tape into the VCR, hoping to satisfy I.I. But it didn't, of course. The Flu hit. I.I. sent Sanchez to talk to me.'

LaMoia guessed. 'You reported that visit to Krishevski.'

Daphne read the man's face. 'Not Krishevski. Then to whom?'

'I need that tape,' Boldt said.

'It's hidden. They watch me. Probably you too, now. They want that tape. They get hold of it, and a week from now you'll find me face down in my shower, or lying up next to Sanchez with my neck broke.'

'Where does Krishevski fit in?' Boldt inquired, recalling the man's visit to his home two days before.

'Don't look at him for this.'

'He knows about your videotape.'

'I imagine that's right.'

Daphne said, 'Having part of the story isn't going to help.'

Chapman agreed, but couldn't quite bring himself to talk.

Boldt reminded Chapman, 'When we looked in the warehouse for the rifle, there *was* a rifle. Your doing?'

'I've *never* tampered with evidence. Never will.'

'Those videotapes,' Daphne said. 'You tampered with those.'

'Hey!' he complained. 'Those weren't part of Property. You show me one piece of paper saying those were part of Property.'

LaMoia tipped back in his kitchen chair. 'Okay.' He sighed. 'I say we leave this for I.I. to mop up. He's not going to help us.'

Chapman looked over at Boldt, the first real sign of fear on his face.

Boldt looked the man in the eye. 'You don't want to go down on the record as having told anyone anything.'

Daphne added, 'Because you've seen what they did to Sanchez.'

Chapman told her, 'I got a family. I got kids.'

Boldt suggested, 'So I'll tell *you* what's right, and you'll stop me where I'm wrong.'

Chapman nodded his okay.

Boldt closed his eyes and assembled the pieces. When he reopened them, he looked straight at Chapman. The two pairs of eyes locked together. 'You figured out these guns were stolen and you accused Krishevski because his guys were on that tape.' He paused. Chapman made no corrections. 'Either he told you, or you figured out he wasn't directly involved. So when Sanchez shows up four different times, asking questions, Pendegrass gets worried. The next day Sanchez is in the hospital.' Another pause. Chapman's eyes were glassy. 'Your loyalty is to the room itself, not to any officer. Krishevski feels pretty much the same as you do. Knowing you possess this incriminating tape, Krishevski suggests his boys will return the stolen weapons. They'll make it right, if you keep quiet. And until you and I pulled that gun off the shelf, you thought they *had* returned them.' He added, 'How am I doing?'

Chapman said, 'Krishevski couldn't believe his guys could do such a stupid thing. Blamed himself for leaking news of the sick-out. Practically begged me to let him set it right. He's not the one you're after.'

'Schock and Phillipp take over the I.I. case for Sanchez and pay a couple visits to Property. You're thinking Pendegrass is checking the log, and you're worried for them. You go to the Cock and Bull looking for Pendegrass, to tell him to lay off Schock and Phillipp, but they're right behind you, and Pendegrass and company take a baseball bat to their heads as well – in part to scare you, to let you know who's boss.'

Again, Chapman made no corrections.

'Krishevski calls me anonymously because he suspects his boys did Schock and Phillipp. He won't condone that. He knows they need to be stopped. He plays it cool when I show up at the bar, putting on a good act.' Boldt paused. No comments from Chapman. 'I call down to Property and get Riorden. I start asking about visits by Schock and Phillipp, and suddenly I'm on the list.' He paused. 'I've got to have that tape, Ronnie.'

'No chance! But you don't need me!'

'Help me out here, Ronnie.'

'I.I. installed *two* cameras, one upstairs at the street entrance, one downstairs on level two.' He hesitated. 'They switch tapes once a day. Fresh ones in place of the ones for the day before. So I knew my switch had to be done that night, before they arrived to put in the fresh tapes. I replaced the tape in the camera on sub-level two with a copy, and took the real tape for myself. Figured it might take them a while to realize. My guess was they marked and stored the tapes and kept them around in case any more vandalism was reported. Maybe erased them after a while, for all I know.'

'It leaves me the tape for camera one,' Boldt said, finally understanding.

'I don't know if it will do you any good, just seeing a car pull into the garage. I've got the one with the actual business going down, and it stays with me. I don't think they're too worried about that other one. A couple cops coming and going. Where's the foul? But you, Lou. Maybe you can make something out of it.'

'Maybe so,' Boldt said, glancing at LaMoia, who was already wearing a grin.

SIXTY FIVE

Boldt climbed the steps of the Pendegrass home with difficulty, due to the walking cast. In his hand, he nervously wormed the keys to the Crown Vic and the black remote that opened the doors or trunk. In his left hand he carried a videotape.

In a quick shuffle, he had sent Liz and the kids across town to stay at the Four Seasons for the night, promising his wife it was only as a precaution. Liz loved the Four Seasons. She had accepted the request surprisingly calmly, despite the late hour. Boldt took this as a sign they were on the mend. He climbed the steps hoping that he and LaMoia and Daphne had prepared for any and every eventuality, knowing full well that one never could. There were always holes in any plan, especially those made hastily.

He drew in a deep breath and knocked sharply on the door.

Pendegrass answered. He wore those same Air Nikes that Boldt remembered only too well. The two men stared at each other.

'So?' Pendegrass finally said.

Boldt held up the videotape for the man to see. 'I couldn't talk Chapman out of his, and I never will. So I guess if you're set on that tape, then whatever you've got of my Denver trip goes out to whoever you plan on seeing it.'

'And this?' Pendegrass asked, eyeing the tape in Boldt's hand.

'This is the one you overlooked. Even I.I. overlooked its importance. This is the one that's going to hang you once I get it to SID for analysis. This is what you want to trade for, whether you know it or not. It's the original. If you had me followed from Chapman's then you know I went back downtown. This is why. This tape. I substituted a *Mister Rogers* for it. You think anyone will ever notice? Not a chance. Because I.I. doesn't understand the importance of the second tape.'

'As if I know what you're talking about.'

'You think I'm wearing a wire? Is that it?' He raised his arms, still sore all over. 'Search me. Go ahead.'

'I'll pass. Whatever it is you're trying to do, nice try, Boldt.'

'You've got a VCR,' Boldt stated. 'Five minutes. Give me five minutes.' He waved the tape. 'It's a real eye-opener.'

An impatient Pendegrass considered this and finally stepped back from the door, admitting Boldt, who inside was a nervous wreck. If Pendegrass had slammed the door in his face, it might never have worked.

The TV occupied a tabletop in a cluttered living room that smelled of cigarettes. Pendegrass's wife looked in on them, but the man waved her away and she closed the door tightly, a concerned look overtaking her tired face.

Boldt handed the man the tape and remained standing. He identified the VCR's remote, and pocketing his own keys, took control. This had been Daphne's suggestion: maintain control over the physical environment.

416

'The way I figure it,' Boldt explained, 'you and the others didn't think there was much to fear from the second security video – the one set up to record the entrance.' Boldt pressed a button on the remote. The television showed a grainy black-and-white security video of SPD's parking garage. 'But I'm telling you, you underestimate Bernie Lofgrin.'

Pendegrass maintained a look of confidence, though Boldt had to believe there were cracks.

'There are three men visible in that car. You in the passenger seat, Riorden driving, and Smythe in the back,' Boldt said, advancing the tape to the place where Detective Andrew Smythe's face showed clearly through the vehicle's backseat window. 'You want me to keep going?'

'We come and go at all hours. All of us do. Yourself included. This proves what?'

'Your car went down to level two . . .' he advanced to tape, 'as can be clearly seen.'

'I don't know where you're going with this, Boldt, but this proves absolutely nothing. Zero.'

'I'm not going anywhere with this,' Boldt corrected. 'It's Bernie Lofgrin you should be worried about. The guy's a wizard. You see this post right here?' Boldt pointed to the freeze frame of the car on the screen. 'It's been scratched a dozen times by cars clipping it too close. For Lofgrin, it's going to be all about those scratches. They ended up like marks on a measuring stick running up the wall.'

Now Pendegrass looked concerned. Any cop knew well enough to fear the things the lab could do.

'Lofgrin will measure the height of the rear bumper against those scratches as you fellows arrived, and then he'll compare that to the height of the same bumper upon your departure less than ten minutes later.' He stopped to win Pendegrass's attention. 'What you should have done . . .' Boldt advised the man, '. . . was take the assault rifles, but *leave* the military shipping cases. But that would have taken more time, right? That's what I'm thinking: you were in a hurry. The guns don't weigh much at all. But those military shipping cases add up. Lofgrin can measure the height of that bumper going in and coming out. He will prove that when you left that garage ten minutes later, you were carrying over two hundred extra pounds in the trunk. A dead body? I don't think so. Given the missing video-tape recorded on that same night, and at least one missing weapon, what do you think I.I. is going to make of your visit?'

'Circumstantial bullshit. You won't get to square one with this.'

This was the sticking point of Boldt's argument. The evidence on the tape *was* circumstantial – and *only* circumstantial – but Boldt needed Pendegrass to believe otherwise. 'Might be,' Boldt agreed. 'How do you think I.I. will look at it? About all they ever deal with is circumstantial evidence. People are going to get questioned about this. People working in the boneyard. You. The others. Deals will be offered to one of you. Chapman will be subpoenaed to turn over that other tape. The best laid plans . . . A cop was shot at with one of those stolen weapons. This cop!' Boldt said defiantly. He walked over to the VCR and took the tape back. 'You guys talk it over. My offer's on the table for tonight and tonight only.'

Pendegrass stood there like a statue.

Boldt said, 'Once Bernie Lofgrin gets this, it's out of my hands.'

Pendegrass tried to sound convincing. 'It don't mean nothing.'

Boldt stopped at the front door. 'Then you've got nothing to worry about.'

SIXTY SIX

Boldt's plan came down to the next few hours. If he was to turn circumstantial evidence into incriminating evidence, he believed it would happen before morning.

He lived twenty minutes from Pendegrass, and he spent much of the time with his eyes trained on his rearview mirror and his right hand gently touching the videotape in the seat beside him. He couldn't be sure, but he believed the same car that had been following him all night – to Chapman's, downtown, and to Pendegrass's – was still back there: a narrow set of headlights with a blue cast to the light itself.

Riorden and Smythe lived the closest to him, and he assumed one of them would be awaiting his return home. Either there would be an offer to trade tapes, or violence. He doubted any call would be placed to his home with an offer – even Property cops knew better than to leave a paper trail.

As he pulled into his driveway, a Seattle mist filled the air, fog passing so low to the earth that it gently rinsed everything, everyone, in its path. He ran his wipers even though it wasn't completely necessary. He didn't want any surprises.

He turned off the car, that dreaded sense of foreboding enveloping him, as well as a deepening sadness that cops were involved. He loved the uniform. He loved the department and what it stood for. It was as simple as that.

He picked up the video and slid it beneath the seat as he and LaMoia had planned. Once outside the car, he used the remote to lock all doors at once. He slipped the bulky keys into his pocket, wondering what felt so wrong. After three or four thoughtful steps he realized what it was.

The silence.

The neighbor's dog did not bark at him, did not scratch at the fence. If Pendegrass, Riorden and Smythe had been the three men who had assaulted him a week earlier – which he now believed – then they knew well enough about that dog. Its silence became all the more frightening.

Pendegrass had taken the bait.

'Hello?' Boldt called, lugging that walking cast along with him. His hand sought out his weapon. The back door to his house suddenly seemed extremely far away.

He reached the bottom of the back steps. It was dark up there on the porch. There wasn't a light on in the kitchen or the back of the house, which was not the way Liz would have left it. Someone had shorted the circuit, blown a fuse. He didn't want to go up there, but didn't want to drag the cast around to the front door, even though there would be a street light there, and neighbors who might see him or hear him if he called out.

He heard a car door thump shut *behind* him. One street away. Connected, or coincidence, he asked himself. Adrenaline filled him, for he'd been here before in nearly this exact situation. Only now there was no dog to come to his rescue. Now he carried this cast on his leg.

He glanced back toward the car, wondering if he could beat the arrival of whoever was coming through the woods toward him – whoever had parked a street away and was now breaking twigs and brushing past bushes to reach him. With a good leg he might have made it. But as it was, he simply stood and listened.

He had believed that Pendegrass would demand an exchange of tapes. He'd made contingency plans, but he didn't want to exercise them.

The sounds from the woods stopped. Whoever was there was quite close now. Boldt switched the weapon to his left hand, grabbed the wooden rail with his right, and started the climb up the back porch stairs, one clumsy step at a time. He slipped, let go the rail and fished his keys out of his pocket. Only a few feet more to reach the back door. He wanted to get the key in the lock and the door open as quickly as possible.

This is how Sanchez felt, he decided. Someone had cut the lights, the walk from the garage to the house impossibly far.

He fingered his keys.

Again, noise came from behind him in the woods.

Boldt turned at the top of the stairs. 'I thought you were going to call,' he shouted, eyes straining to see in the dark.

'I thought you would have headed straight downtown,' the muffled voice of Pendegrass said. He stepped out from the thick shrubbery that separated Boldt from his backyard neighbors. 'That would have been the right card to play. Coming home. That was a stupid move.'

He heard someone immediately behind him, in the dark of the porch. 'Riorden?' he asked.

Whoever was back there didn't answer. That troubled him. If it was negotiation they were after, why remain silent?

Pendegrass stepped closer, barely visible in the dark. He wore a balaclava over his head. 'You think too much,' he said, adding, 'Sometimes a person is better off just accepting the way things are.'

'You haven't seen Sanchez,' Boldt reminded him. 'To me, that's the way things are.'

'She's getting better, I hear,' Pendegrass said. 'Movement in both legs. She'll pull through this, you watch, and then what'll be the point of all the fuss?' He repeated, 'What'll be the point of all these heroics on your part? Who'll care? Flek did Sanchez, and Flek's dead. Case closed.'

'If only it were true,' Boldt lamented.

'And that's worth getting the shit beat out of you?'

'Already had the shit beat out of me,' Boldt reminded him. 'Is that all? And here I was thinking you're going to kill me.'

'Giving up the tape buys you a simple beating. Call me generous.' He had reached close enough for Boldt to make out the dark clothing and the ugliness of the faceless balaclava.

'I thought we were going to trade.'

'That's what I mean: you think too much,' Pendegrass said. 'And don't be thinking about that gun. You're outgunned here, old man. Drop the gun. Keep it at a simple beating.' He waited only a moment before ordering Boldt for a second time to drop his weapon. But Boldt held onto his gun, albeit with his left hand.

'Is that Riorden or Smythe behind me?' Boldt asked the night air. 'Because whoever it is . . . he gets my first shots.'

'Drop the gun. You think that vest is going to save you?' Pendegrass asked.

'It forces you to aim,' Boldt replied, disappointed that Pendegrass had spotted the bulk of the vest.

'I'm aiming right at your head,' came a deep voice from behind Boldt. Smythe.

Chills ran down his spine. Boldt didn't know the man well, but he knew him to be a crack shot. He tossed his weapon into the grass at the base of the steps, mentally marking its exact location. 'You missed the first time you tried,' Boldt said, assuming the attempt on his life had come from Smythe, not Pendegrass, who drank too much to be a good shot.

Pendegrass said, 'I thought that was your friend from Colorado. Your dead friend.'

'Have you informed Smythe here, that if he hadn't been so greedy and had returned the rifle as Krishevski ordered you to do with all the other rifles . . . if he hadn't been so stupid as to use it on me . . . maybe I'd never have been the wiser about any of this?' Boldt saw Pendegrass's hand twitch – the one holding the sidearm. *Body language*, Daphne would have told Boldt. The bulge at the man's ankle filled in the blanks. It was a drop gun – a second gun. And its purpose became clear.

Boldt had half expected a confrontation like this. But only then did he understand Pendegrass inviting Smythe along. It wasn't for the man's marksmanship. Boldt sensed a hesitation in Pendegrass that he blamed on how dark it was up on the porch. The man's handgun carried a barrel-mounted silencer. He'd come prepared.

Turning his head slowly, Boldt asked the shadows, 'Why'd he ask you along, do you think?'

'Shut up,' Pendegrass called out, a little loudly for a residential neighborhood. If Boldt could keep him at that volume, maybe someone else would notice the dog had been silenced.

Boldt answered his own question. 'One guy against a guy in a cast? How hard can that be? I'll tell you why he invited you—'

'Shut up!'

'He needs it nice and clean. Needs it to look like I shot you after you shot me. Only it's Pendegrass who shoots us both.' He looked back to Pendegrass. 'Isn't that right,

Chuck?' He spoke again to the dark porch. 'You sure you want to be aiming at me? I'm not armed. But he is. And look at his ankle. He's carrying a drop as well. What's with that?'

'Shut up!'

'Because otherwise . . . if I get shot, if there's an officer down with no one to blame – there's gonna be one hell of a manhunt. If you'd hit me the other night . . . it might have been blamed on Flek. But Matthews interviewed him before he died. Did you know that? Now you boys have made a mess of it. And Chuck here intends to clean it up and keep himself in the clear.'

'That's bullshit, Rod,' Pendegrass called out.

Boldt reminded him, 'He had me *inside* his house, tape in hand. Why'd he let me go? Why'd he let me come back here?'

'My wife!' Pendegrass answered quickly. He ordered, 'The tape, Boldt. Now! No more of this! I want that tape.'

'It's in the car,' Boldt said.

'No fucking way,' Pendegrass barked.

'Search me. Ask him,' he said motioning to the porch. 'He was here waiting for me. He saw me get out of the car.' He turned slightly. 'Did I have a videotape on me?'

For a moment there was only the drone of an airplane far off, and the low constant hum of traffic.

'I didn't see it on him,' Smythe confirmed.

'Untuck your shirt,' Pendegrass ordered.

Boldt did as he was told. No tape fell out. 'I'm telling you, it's in the car.' He added, 'But then again, I wouldn't shoot me just yet, if I were you. What if I dropped it off at a friend's on the way over?'

From Boldt's right, a third voice. 'Then I'd have seen

you,' Riorden said. Also wearing a balaclava, he stepped around the corner of the house, there to block any attempt at an exit to the street. To Pendegrass he said, 'He didn't stop anywhere.'

The third part of the puzzle. No more surprises.

'No one's going to shoot you, Boldt,' Pendegrass stated. 'All we want is that videotape.'

'We were going to trade,' Boldt reminded.

'Change of plans. You ever get any idea to breathe a word of any of this, and Matthews ends up like Sanchez or worse. That's my leverage on you. That, and the tape. That's my promise.'

Boldt felt another chill race down his spine. Pendegrass had made the wrong threat. He had also just made an admission of guilt by mentioning Sanchez. Boldt had much of what he wanted. 'Front seat of the car,' Boldt said. 'Take the tape and get out of here before I lose my temper.'

Pendegrass chuckled, amused. 'I'm quaking all over.' He moved toward the Crown Vic, though never taking his eyes off Boldt. He tried the passenger door, but found it locked. 'Keys,' he called out to Boldt.

Boldt let the keys dangle from his right hand, thinking that if Pendegrass or the others had half a brain they would wonder why he'd opted to have his keys out and ready in his right hand. Smythe might think he'd intended to open the back door of the house, but then why not switch hands with the gun when Pendegrass had walked out of the shrubs? But they weren't thinking: that was just the point. They hadn't been thinking when they'd stolen the guns off Krishevski's tip about the strike; they hadn't been thinking when they'd broken Sanchez's neck in an attempt to rough her up and get her off the I.I. investigation; they hadn't been thinking when they'd tried to cover it up by making it look like Flek. Guys like this didn't think – they reacted. It was all they were capable of. 'Thing's got a remote,' Boldt informed him, letting the keys hang from his hand. 'I'll do it for you.'

He lifted his right hand, pointing the small remote device toward the car the way people aim clickers at their televisions. Straight-armed and determined. Again that eerie silence, punctuated only by the keys ringing together like tiny bells. Boldt pushed the button. The doors to the car clicked open. Pendegrass pulled on the door handle and opened the passenger door. He leaned inside.

Boldt pushed the remote's other button. As the car's trunk popped open, Boldt shut his eyes, collapsed to the steps and rolled down them.

LaMoia came up out of the car's trunk lobbing a phosphorus grenade, a police issue semi-automatic clutched tightly and ready to fire. Boldt heard one shot; he wasn't sure from where. He caught hold of his fallen handgun on the roll, and opened his eyes to the devastating pure white glare of Pendegrass coming out the passenger door, burning brightly in that light like an angel. He had let go of the videotape, and it floated through the air in an eerie slow-motion arc. One hand shielding his eyes, casting a triangle of black across his brow, he raised the tip of that silencer toward Boldt, who saw no choice but to fire. He aimed low, tracking his shots as two holes appeared in the side of the Crown Vic, and a third found the man's knee, bludgeoning it into a bloody pulp.

The force of a ton of bricks hit Boldt's chest, knocking the wind out of him. He'd been shot.

'Drop the weapons!' he heard LaMoia order through his wired teeth. A siren cried in the distance. 'On the ground! Now! No one gets hurt!' his sergeant shouted.

They had two witnesses to Pendegrass's mention of Sanchez: Boldt and LaMoia. Even if other charges failed, they had all three on assaulting police officers, attempted murder and deadly force.

Boldt felt down and determined he'd been hit in the vest, not flesh. It didn't feel that way. His breathing was labored, he couldn't speak.

The phosphorus died down, hissing like a winded runner, and Boldt could see again.

Smythe was down, fatally wounded – Riorden's doing, not LaMoia's. In testimony it would come out from Riorden that he and Pendegrass had in fact intended to kill both Boldt and Smythe, just as Boldt had guessed. Boldt for obvious reasons; Smythe for his stupidity and greed.

Pendegrass lay bleeding, passed out against the car, the fallen videotape just out of his reach, his fingers still stretching for it.

LaMoia, soaked through with sweat, kept his weapon aimed at Riorden's back. The man was leaning spread out flat against the wall of the house, bleeding from his left arm. 'You got him?' LaMoia inquired, indicating Pendegrass.

'I've got him.'

'It's a mess.'

'Yes, it is,' Boldt agreed.

LaMoia hopped out of the trunk, walked over to Riorden and placed the barrel of the weapon against the base of the man's skull. 'The location of the Denver video,' he said ominously.

'John,' Boldt complained, 'that's not how to do it.'

'We did this your way, Sarge. We do this other thing my way.' He jabbed the gun. 'You give up the video and your shooting of Smythe goes down as a stray bullet. With all this other shit, you'll still get life, but you won't get lethal injection.' He added, 'You've got three seconds to decide. One . . . two . . .'

'Chuck has it!' the man spit out onto the wall. 'Locked up, I think. I don't know.'

LaMoia backed off, pulled his cell phone from his pocket and hit a button. 'You there?' he asked, when a voice answered. 'It's Pendegrass. And you've got all the probable cause you need.'

SIXTY SEVEN

Boldt stepped out of interrogation room A, 'the box,' at 4 A.M., an empty mug that had held tea in his hand. LaMoia was still in the next room over, getting interviewed by his fellow Homicide officers just as Boldt had. Any officer-involved shooting required the surrender of one's weapon, a half dozen interviews and a mile of paperwork. It wouldn't all sort itself out for another week.

She sat in one of the gray office chairs, the kind with four spread feet on black rollers. Her left ankle, encased in a removable cast, looked more like a ski boot. Only Daphne Matthews could look so beautiful at four in the morning.

'Hey,' he said.

'Went a little differently than you thought,' she told him, barely able to conceal her anger. She didn't like him taking chances like that.

'He took the bait,' Boldt said. 'That's what we needed.'

'At what cost?'

'I'm not saying it wasn't messy. I'm not saying I might not do it differently, given hindsight. I considered involving the department for backup. But these guys were too well connected. They would have heard we were out to sting them, and we would have either come up empty or dead. So John took the trunk, and we went for it.'

'You sent me to Pendegrass's house without telling me. Why? Too big a risk?'

'No. Because you might have talked me out of it.' He paused. 'You're mad.'

'Damn right.'

'So are they,' he said, indicating the interrogation room.

'Every right to be.'

He sighed. 'Yeah. Well I'm whipped. Give an "old man" a ride home? They confiscated the Crown Vic. I'm without wheels.'

He won a partial smile from her. 'Old man?' she quoted.

'Pendegrass called me that.'

'So blowing out his knee was generous of you.'

'Damn right.' He added, 'More like lucky, I suppose. I'm not very good prone like that.'

'You're pretty good prone,' she said, pursing her lips and letting him know that they could still tease. The kiss had been forgotten. Or at least wiped away.

She tapped her purse.

Boldt missed the message. He said, 'Are we going?'

She clicked the purse open. Inside was a black plastic rectangle. A videotape. She explained, 'I kicked the Pendegrass home, ahead of SID, as soon as I got John's call. I looked everywhere. Turned the place upside down. Couldn't find it.'

'Then what's that?' he asked.

'Bernie Lofgrin says that you owe him your original Chet Baker, the one's that's autographed.' It was a 1957, original vinyl in perfect condition, one of the prizes of Boldt's jazz collection. Small change, Boldt thought. 'He says that he doesn't want to know what's on the tape, and that as far as he's concerned there never was a tape.'

'His guys found it.'

'They make these books with fake leather bindings that aren't books at all, but hold videotapes in your bookshelf. His guys found it in the bedroom while I was out searching the garage. Lofgrin brought it to me, as lead on the search and seizure, and I had to tell him . . . tell him what I thought it was . . . before he put it onto the inventory. Lou, I've never done anything like this.' She passed it to Boldt.

He held the tape in his hand. His reputation. Possibly the end of his career on Homicide. He couldn't be sure. And then he handed it back to her. 'We return it to Bernie right now while there's still time, and he puts it into the inventory,' he told her. 'I'll give him that album anyway . . . just because he was willing to go that far.'

Tears formed in her eyes as she looked up at him. She nodded. This was what she wanted to hear.

He said, 'It isn't us . . . doing something like this. And besides, Pendegrass will mention the tape . . . it's going to come out. The best thing we can do is stand up to it. Sheila Hill is ultimately the one to decide if our relationship compromises her department, and she's been in a few compromising positions herself. You don't need to know about that. She'll go light on us, believe me.'

The tears spilled down her cheek. Tears of joy, he hoped.

'Am I allowed to say I love you?' she whispered.

'Hell, no,' he said, offering her his hand and extricating her from the chair, 'but that kind of thing goes both ways, so you be careful.'

'Yes, sir.'

'That's better,' he said, touching her in the small of the back and aiming her toward the elevator. He couldn't do the stairs in the cast. It would be a while until he could do the stairs again. 'Look at us. A pair of gimps.'

'Yes,' she said, laughing through her tears, 'a pair of gimps.'